CARA HUNTER

D0177441

Cara Hunter is the author of the *Sunday Times'* bestselling crime novels *Close to Home*, *In the Dark*, *No Way Out*, *All the Rage* and *The Whole Truth*, all featuring DI Adam Fawley and his Oxford-based police team. *Close to Home* was a Richard and Judy Book Club pick and was shortlisted for Crime Book of the Year at the British Book Awards 2019. *No Way Out* was selected by the *Sunday Times* as one of the 100 best crime novels since 1945. *The Whole Truth* was also a Richard and Judy Book Club pick in 2021. Cara's novels have sold more than a million copies in twenty-nine territories worldwide, and the TV rights to the series have now been acquired by the Fremantle group, who are in script development with a network. She lives in Oxford, on a street not unlike those featured in her books. *Hope to Die* is her sixth novel.

Hope to Die

CARA HUNTER

PENGUIN BOOKS

PENGUIN BOOKS

UK | USA | Canada | Ireland | Australia
India | New Zealand | South Africa

Penguin Books is part of the Penguin Random House group of companies
whose addresses can be found at global.penguinrandomhouse.com.

First published 2022

002

Copyright © Shinleopard Ltd, 2022

The moral right of the author has been asserted

'Karma Chameleon' words and music by George O'Dowd, Jonathan Moss,
Michael Craig, Roy Hay and Phil Pickett. Copyright © 1983 BMG VM Music Ltd.
and Concord Entertainment Ltd. All Rights for BMG VM Music Ltd. Administered by
BMG Rights Management (US) LLC. All Rights Reserved Used by Permission.
Reprinted by Permission of Hal Leonard Europe Ltd.

Set in 12.5/14.75pt Garamond MT Std
Typeset by Jouve (UK), Milton Keynes
Printed and bound in Great Britain by Clays Ltd, Elcograf S.p.A.

The authorized representative in the EEA is Penguin Random House Ireland,
Morrison Chambers, 32 Nassau Street, Dublin D02 YH68

A CIP catalogue record for this book is available from the British Library

ISBN: 978-0-241-99016-2

www.greenpenguin.co.uk

For the Oxford pride
I couldn't have got through it without you

And for the real Chloe Sargent
A very special person

Previously . . . in the Fawley files

In *The Whole Truth* I included a summary of the police characters at the beginning, to help people coming to the series for the first time. So many people got in touch to say they loved it that I'm including one again here. There are a few updates to the old hands, and the first chance to meet the new members of the team.

Name	**DI Adam Fawley**
Age	46
Married?	Yes, to Alex, 45. She's a lawyer working in Oxford.
Children?	The Fawleys' ten-year-old son, Jake, took his own life two years ago. They were devastated, and thought they'd never be able to have another child. But against the odds, Alex fell pregnant again, and they now have a precious three-month-old daughter, Lily Rose.
Personality	Introspective, observant and intelligent, outwardly resilient, inwardly less so. He doesn't care that Alex earns more than he does, or that she's taller than him in high heels. He's good at lateral thinking and bad at office politics. He's compassionate and fair-minded, but it's not all positives: he can be impatient, and he has a short temper. He was brought up in a dreary north London suburb, and he's adopted, though he only discovered that by accident – to this day his parents have never discussed it.
	He doesn't watch crime on TV (he has enough of it during the day); he listens to Oasis and Bach and Roxy Music (Alex once told him he looks like Bryan Ferry, to which he replied 'I wish'); if he had a pet it would be a cat (but he's never owned one); his favourite wine is Merlot, and his favourite food is Spanish (though he eats far too much pizza); and surprise, surprise, his favourite colour is blue.

Name	**DS Chris Gislingham**
Age	43
Married?	Yes, to Janet
Children?	Billy, 2
Personality	Chirpy, good-humoured, hard-working, decent. And a serious Chelsea fan.
	'Always described as "sturdy" and "solid", and not just because he's getting a bit chunky round the middle. Every CID team needs a Gislingham, and if you were drowning, he's the one you'd want on the other end of the rope.'

Name	**DS Gareth Quinn** (recently reinstated)
Age	36
Married?	A long-standing Lothario, Quinn is now in his first serious relationship.
Personality	Cocky, ambitious, good-looking. Fawley describes him as *'sharp suit and blunt razor'*.
	'Quinn took to DS like a dog to water – zero hesitation, maximum splash.'

Name	**DC Verity Everett**
Age	34
Married?	No. But has a cat (Hector).
Personality	Easy-going personally, ruthless professionally. Lacks the confidence she should have in her own abilities (as Fawley is well aware).
	'She may look like Miss Marple must have done at thirty-five, but she's every bit as relentless. Or as Gis always puts it, Ev was definitely a bloodhound in a previous life.'

Name	**DC Andrew Baxter**
Age	39
Married?	Yes, but no children.
Personality	Stolid but dependable. Good with computers so often gets lumbered with that sort of stuff.
	'A solid man in a suit that's a bit too small for him. The buttons on his shirt gape slightly. Balding, a little out of breath. Halfway to high blood pressure.'

Name	**DC Erica Somer**
Age	29
Married?	In a relationship with a DI in Hampshire Police, Giles Saumarez.
Personality	Her surname is an anagram of 'Morse' – my nod to Oxford's greatest detective. In the last book, Erica discovered she had cysts on her ovaries and was sent for an MRI. She also had an argument with another Thames Valley officer which has resulted in a disciplinary process.

Name	**DC Thomas Hansen**
Age	25
Personality	Just transferred into Fawley's team, after DC Asante moved sideways into Major Crimes. Previously at Cowley. Shrewd, understated and effective.

Name	**DC Chloe Sargent**
Age	24
Personality	On secondment with Fawley's team. She was previously in the PVP (Protecting Vulnerable People) unit. Tough but kind, hard-working and insightful.

Name	**DC Bradley Carter**
Age	23
Personality	Temporarily covering for DC Somer and determined to make the most of it. Ambitious and out to impress.

The other members of the team are **Alan Challow**, **Nina Mukerjee** and **Clive Conway**, in the CSI department, **Colin Boddie**, the pathologist, and **Bryan Gow**, the profiler.

It's a perfect night for it. No cloud, and barely any moon-light. Though cold comes with clear skies – they said on the radio it could hit freezing tonight. But he's done this before and he's come prepared. The backpack is digging into one shoulder and he hoists it a little higher, then starts off again. His stride is sure, despite the dark: he knows where he's going – he did the full recce a couple of days ago. All the same, it's hard slow-going at night, especially with all this kit. But he made allowances for that, and in any case, this game is all about patience. The right time, the right place, the right conditions.

The path is winding up through the woods now, and he feels the earth give like mattress beneath his feet; gen-erations of leaf litter compressed to sponge. There are owls calling to each other, invisible in the thickets above his head, and small animals moving in the undergrowth, and – louder than any of them – the thud of his own heart. When he breaks through the treeline at last he stops on the ridge and inhales deeply on the cold damp air, peppered with woodsmoke from the house in the valley below. There's nowhere else for miles – the only sign of habitation is a scattering of lights on distant hills, mirroring the constellations. It's completely silent now, out in the open. Not a wisp of wind, just the earth breathing.

He scans the sky for a moment, then swings down the backpack and crouches next to it, flicking on his torch. He pulls out his mount and night-sight and, his excitement growing, starts to snap them together.

'So what do you think? I know Ben's really young to be a godparent, but if it hadn't been for him –'

I load the last of the supper plates and straighten up. Alex is watching me from the other side of the kitchen. She looks a little apprehensive, though I don't know why: she can't really think I'd say no.

'Of course – I think it's a great idea.'

There's a photo of Ben and Lily stuck to the fridge behind me; his small face managing to look thrilled and nervous all at once, because he's never held a baby before and is clearly terrified he's doing it all wrong. It was Ben – our eleven-year-old nephew – who phoned the ambulance when Alex went into premature labour and there was no one else in the house. Certainly not me. I didn't even know it was happening. Because I was in the cells at Newbury nick, twelve hours and counting from a rape and murder charge. I'm not about to go into all that again – I'm guessing you know already, and if not, I'm sorry, but I've tried damned hard, these last few weeks, to stop obsessing about it. Let's just say that I have two people to thank for being here right now, stacking my dishwasher rather than slopping out a cell. One of them is my wife; the other is

3

Chris Gislingham. Gis who's in the dictionary under 'dependable'; Gis who doesn't know it yet but will be needing to get his wedding suit cleaned, because when Lily is christened in a few weeks' time, he'll be standing up next to Ben as her other godfather.

And right on cue there's a crackle on the baby monitor and I can hear the little breathy snuffling noises of my daughter waking up. She's a miraculously sunny child – hardly ever cries, even when she needs changing. She just gets this bemused look on her little face, as if surely the world isn't supposed to work that way. The rest of the time she lies there in her cot, smiling up at me and kicking her tiny feet and breaking my heart. She has her mother's blue-lilac eyes and a soft down of her mother's dark auburn hair, and even though I'm as biased as the next new dad, when people tell us how beautiful she is I just think, *Hell, you're right, she bloody is*. Beautiful, healthy and, more than anything, *here*. Against all the odds, after losing Jake, when we thought our last chance was gone –

'I'll go,' says Alex. 'She's probably just hungry.'

Which is mother code for 'so you wouldn't be much use anyway'. She touches my arm gently as she goes past and I catch a drift of her scent. Shampoo and baby milk and the butter-biscuit smell of her skin. In the last few months of her pregnancy Alex looked haunted, like someone locked on the brink of terror. But that last day, the day Lily was born, something changed. She found herself again. Perhaps it was the hormones, perhaps it was the adrenaline; who knows. Alex has never been able to explain it. But it was the old Alex who worked out where the evidence against me had come from, and made sure,

4

even as they were lifting her into the ambulance, that a message got through to Gis. The old Alex I have always loved, the old Alex who laughed and was spontaneous and stood up to people and could out-think pretty much everyone I know, including me. I didn't realize it until much, much later, but a daughter wasn't the only gift I was given that day; I got my wife back too.

* * *

Transcript 999 emergency call
21.10.2018 21:52:08

Operator 1:   Emergency, which service do you require?

Caller: Police, please.

Operator 1:   Connecting you.

    [*Ringing tone*]

Operator 2:   Go ahead, caller.

Caller: I'm at Wytham [INAUDIBLE 00.09] may be in trouble.

Operator 2:   I'm sorry, I didn't catch all of that – can you repeat?

Caller: It's that big house on Ock Lane [INAUDIBLE 00.12] heard something.

Operator 2:   You're at Ock Lane, Wytham?

Caller: Well, not exactly – the thing is [INAUDIBLE 00.15] definitely sounded like it.

Operator 2:   You're breaking up, sir –

Caller: My phone's about to die [INAUDIBLE 00.17]

Operator 2:   You want the police to attend – Ock Lane, Wytham?

Caller: Yes, yes –

[*Dial tone*]

Operator 2:   Hello? Hello?

* * *

'According to Google, this is the place.'

PC Puttergill pulls on the handbrake and the two of them peer out of the window. It may have 'Manor' in its name but it's actually just a farmhouse, though to be fair, a pretty hefty one – a gravel drive, a five-bar gate and an old mud-spattered SUV parked outside an open barn. It looks quiet, private and a little run-down, as a certain type of old-money home so often does. What it certainly doesn't look like is a place where bad things happen.

'What did the control room say again?'

Puttergill makes a face. 'Not much, Sarge. The line was bad and they couldn't hear half what he was saying. When they tried to call back it just went to voicemail.'

'And who lives here, do we know?'

'Couple called Swann. Pensioners. They aren't answering the phone either. Though they should be expecting us – the station left a message.'

Sergeant Barnetson gives a heavy sigh, then reaches into the back seat for his cap.

'OK,' he says, his hand on the door handle, 'let's get on with it.'

They trudge up the drive, the gravel crunching beneath

6

their feet, puffing white in the cold air. They can almost feel the temperature dropping; there'll be ice on that SUV by morning.

The front door has a wrought-iron carriage lamp and a fake-old bell you pull like a lavatory chain. Barnetson makes a face; it'll be bloody horse brasses next.

They hear the bell ringing deep in the house, but despite the light in one of the upstairs windows there are no signs of life. Puttergill starts stamping to keep warm. Barnetson rings again, waits; still nothing. He takes a couple of steps back and looks up at the first floor, then gestures to Puttergill.

'Can you try round the back? I'll wait here.'

It's so quiet he can hear Puttergill's feet all the way along the side of the house. A distant knock, a 'Hello, anyone in?', a pause. And then, suddenly, the sound of running and Puttergill appearing round the corner and slithering to a halt in a spatter of gravel.

'I think there's someone in there, Sarge – on the floor – it's too dark to see much but I reckon they could be injured –'

Barnetson strides up to the door but even as he stretches out to knock there's a crunch of bolts being drawn back and the door swings open. The man on the step is late sixties or early seventies, slightly stooped, an angular and bony face. He's wearing the sort of threadbare cardigan that keeps for thirty years if you look after it, as he evidently has. He doesn't look like someone bad things happen to, either. In fact, as Barnetson is already concluding, Puttergill must have got the wrong end of the stick: no one with a casualty in their kitchen could possibly look as composed as this.

'Yes?'

His vowels are more clipped than his hedge.

'Mr Swann, is it?'

The man frowns. 'Yes?'

'Sergeant Barnetson, PC Puttergill, Thames Valley Police. We had a call from a member of the public. They thought you might be in need of assistance.'

There's something on the man's face now. Irritation? Surprise? His glance flickers away. He doesn't, Barnetson notes, ask them what the caller said or why they thought something was wrong. 'I think,' he says heavily, 'you'd better come in.'

He heads off into the house and the two officers exchange a glance. There's something, obviously, but clearly nothing that drastic, and certainly not a corpse. So, what? Break-in? Some sort of minor domestic?

The hall is paved with quarry tiles. There's a rack of wellington boots, hooks with waxed jackets and tweed caps, a line of musty watercolours running along the wall, most of them hanging skew. Somewhere upstairs a loo is flushing. Barnetson glances back at Puttergill, who shrugs and makes a mental note to suggest a tea-stop at the garage on the bypass on the way back: it's not much warmer inside than it was out.

'It's in here,' says Swann, gesturing forward. They round the corner after him, two steps down and into the kitchen.

Thirty seconds later Puttergill is stumbling blindly out of the back door and throwing up what remains of his lunch over the crazy paving.

* * *

8

'So they think it went well?'

Everett tries to catch Somer's eye, but she's just staring at her hands.

The ward around them whirrs with hospital white noise. Bright nurse voices, rattling trolleys, the swish of curtains on metal rails.

'Erica?'

Somer looks up and takes a heavy breath. 'As far as I know.'

'But they caught it really early, right? That's what they said – before – when –'

Before, when Somer was told she had a malignant tumour on one of her ovaries. She makes no answer to Ev's question, leaving all the others festering in the air, unasked.

Somer starts to fiddle distractedly with the plastic bracelet round her wrist. Her mouth is trembling with the effort not to cry.

Ev reaches for her hand. 'What about your mum and dad? Have they been in?'

Somer bites her lip and shakes her head. 'I can't face seeing them. It's bad enough –'

The sentence dies. Ev suspected as much. And she gets it – the last thing Somer needs right now is a deluge of parental sympathy, however kindly meant. But Somer has a sister too – and a boyfriend. Where are they?

Somer glances up, reading her mind.

'Kath's in Washington.'

There's a silence. A silence filled with Giles.

Giles who loves Somer; Giles who for some reason was being shut out, even before Somer's diagnosis. Ev doesn't understand it. She didn't then and she doesn't now.

She sighs. 'I'm sorry, but I have to ask. Why don't you call Giles? He doesn't even know you're here, does he?'

The tears spill over now, but Somer makes no move to brush them away.

Ev feels bad even sparing a thought for him – Somer's situation is so much worse. And it's not just this – there's a looming disciplinary process at work that's been put on hold for the time being but isn't going to go away. Giles deserves some pity all the same, though: the poor bastard must be wondering what he did wrong.

She gathers her courage and opens her mouth to say something.

But at that exact moment there's a ping from her phone.

* * *

The kitchen is filling up with people now as the CSI team start to arrive, led by Alan Challow, dragged from his Sunday-night TV supper and evidently none too pleased about it.

'*Mindhunter*,' he says, though no one actually asked. 'Funnily enough, it's the first time I've ever seen a fatality like this one done properly,' he says, nodding towards the corpse. 'Most of those TV people just don't have the balls.'

Nina Mukerjee glances across from the other side of the kitchen table, where she's unpacking her forensic kit. 'Well, can you blame them? I mean – look at him.'

Because it's not balls this victim is missing. He's on his back, legs twisted, the wall behind a detonation of blood and bone and brain matter, and a dark stain spreading from his flung arms like some sort of macabre snow angel.

There's the sound of voices at the front door. Barnetson makes a face. 'The suits,' he says. 'Right on cue.'

The sergeant may be irritated at having to hand off to CID but Puttergill only looks relieved. He's spent the last half-hour hugging the open window, taking deep breaths and answering in monosyllables.

'What have we got here, then?' It's Gareth Quinn, filling the low doorway. Barnetson gives a non-committal grunt. Quinn isn't just a suit, he's a Hugo Boss bloody suit. Too flash, too smart-alecky, too prone to cut corners. And no one has any right to look that chipper at this time of the night, not at a scene like this. But as Barnetson well knows, it was only a couple of weeks ago that Quinn got his stripes back: this will be his first murder as a re-minted DS, so small wonder he's so keen. The DC following a few steps behind looks a good deal more apprehensive. Barnetson hasn't come across him before, so he must be a transfer in. Probably his first job in plain clothes. *Green as grass*, he thinks. Though not as green as Puttergill, who looks ready to throw again.

'This is DC Hansen,' says Quinn to anyone who's interested. 'Asante's replacement.'

Barnetson remembers now – there was talk about it at the station in the summer, back when Fawley was arrested. Something about Asante coming up with evidence against him and Gislingham not wanting to work with him after that. Seems Gis got his way, though given that Asante's ended up in Major Crimes he's hardly likely to be complaining. And from what Barnetson's seen, Fawley's been bending over backwards to make it clear that, as far as he's concerned, he has no quarrel with Asante. So as at now Fawley has two DSs on the same team, which is a challenge at the best of times, never mind when one of those is Gareth Quinn with a point to prove.

Hansen looks round the room, making discreet eye contact with anyone who looks up. Barnetson gestures towards the corpse. 'Hope you didn't get takeout on the way here,' he says drily.

Hansen flashes him a wry grin. 'No such luck.'

'So what have we got?' asks Quinn, moving across to the corpse.

Challow looks him up and down. 'As any competent detective would know, *DS* Quinn, there's no bloody point wearing protective clothing unless you put the hood up.'

Quinn flushes a little, then runs his hand back through his hair so it lies flat before yanking up the hood. Barnetson sees Hansen suppress a smile. He's a quick study, that one.

'And in answer to your question, what we have is a shotgun to the face at close range. Though a smart chap like you has probably deduced that already from the rather telltale absence of a head.'

'Any ID?'

'Nothing in his pockets. No wallet. No phone. On the other hand, you can at least tick the box on the murder weapon.'

There's a gun on the kitchen table, an old-fashioned one with a polished wooden handle. But there's something else as well. Mukerjee hasn't started numbering the evidence yet, but Quinn doesn't need a plastic marker to know this is important. A knife, still clutched in the dead man's hand. A knife with blood along the blade.

* * *

'Apparently the old man admitted it straight up.'

I can hear voices in the background, which accounts for Quinn's super-competent 'I've got this' voice. I could have gone to the scene myself but decided to let him run with it. Only I'm wondering now if that was a mistake. For a start, I can't remember the last time we had a shooting in Oxford. But it's not just that: Quinn's sent me the photos. Something about this isn't sitting right.

I glance up at Alex and give her that look she knows so well. The 'shit I've got to go in and it's bound to take all night' look. But she just smiles.

'It's fine, don't worry. It's part of the deal.'

Part of the deal if I'm going for Chief Inspector this year. We've talked about it, on and off, for ages. But then there was Jake, and then there was the baby and the Gavin Parrie case coming back to haunt us, and it was never the right time. Until – perhaps – now. But it'd be a big change. Maybe even back to Uniform for a bit. Not much more money, and much less hands-on too, even if I do stay in CID. But after twenty-mumble years in the force, and at my age, I need to decide pretty damn soon if I'm happy staying put, and if not, if I've got enough ambition – and, frankly, energy – to try to move up. Though as Harrison has already told me, in that ponderous 'I'm giving you great advice here, lad' tone of his, 'Chief Inspector is a stepping stone, Adam, not a place to get stuck.' So if I go for it, I'm going for Superintendent. And trust me, that is a Big Deal.

Alex touches me lightly on the arm; she knows what I'm thinking. Always. 'Like I said, it's OK. Just try not to wake me up when you get back.'

I pull her close and kiss her hair, feeling her body soften against me. 'Don't hold me to it.'

'Promises, promises,' she murmurs, her lips on mine.

* * *

They told Ev that Gantry Manor would be hard to find, but that was before half Thames Valley turned up and parked out front. The house is lit up like a filmset by the time she gets there, the air throbbing with blue light. The neighbours would be having a field day. If there were any.

Quinn's at her car door before she even opens it.

'Evening, Sarge,' she says with a smile.

Quinn's eyes narrow; he's pretty sure she's taking the piss (which she is), but if he wants the rest of the world to acknowledge his rank he can hardly call her out on it.

'You're just in time – I'm about to take the suspect down to the station to be processed. Fawley's meeting me there.'

She glances across to where two uniformed officers are helping a tall elderly man into the back of a squad car. He has plastic bags taped around his hands.

'What have we got?'

'Fatal shooting.'

She nods; hence the bags.

'Householder told Uniform it was self-defence.' Quinn cocks his head towards the man. 'He claims the vic broke in and threatened them.'

Ev frowns. 'But you don't believe him?'

Quinn raises an eyebrow. 'Let's just say he has a few questions to answer. Starting with why the hell they didn't call 999.'

*　*　*

Somer turns over and pulls the blanket closer around her. She's never had a talent for sleeping, and this is the perfect storm. The scratchy bed, the incessant just-too-loud-to-ignore noise and, even more raucous, the drone inside her own head. The questions she knows Ev wanted to ask – the questions she'd have been asking herself if their positions were reversed. Will she need chemo? Has the cancer spread? Can she still have children? Probably, probably not, and unclear, in that order. But there's little comfort in any of it. The prospect of chemotherapy ter-rifies her, and the idea that in some notional happy future world she might actually have a baby is a bad joke.

She curls up tighter, pushing away the pain. The real pain and the Giles pain. She's written to him, torn it up, written again, and even six or seven versions later she still hasn't sent the poor, scaled-down, barely comprehensible message she ended up with. She was going to ask Ev to post it – she swore to herself she would – but somehow that never happened either. It was all too hurried at the end – Ev rushing off to her busy police life. She'd looked embarrassed, as she left, as if she was worried Somer might envy her. But she didn't. She doesn't know what exactly she felt, but she knows it wasn't that. The job and all it used to mean seem very long ago and very far away.

A long-dead life where she was sharp and ambitious and incisive and professional, and perhaps, in some parallel world, still is. She's oppressed, suddenly, by the thought of that light-hearted, uncancered Erica stalking her for the rest of her life, doing all the things she would have, could have, should have done. Though her new numbness does have at least one advantage: the disciplinary procedure still hanging over her has lost all power to panic. A shit treated her like shit and she gave as good as she got. If Thames Valley want to fire her for that, then fuck it, she'll do something else. Though what, and how, and when, are yet more questions she has neither the energy nor interest to address.

* * *

Margaret Swann is in what she's referred to as the 'drawing room', with a uniformed female officer for company. This part of Gantry Manor must be older than the rest – the ceilings are lower, the windows smaller. There's an inglenook fireplace, a piano draped with a tablecloth, dried-flower arrangements, too much furniture. It all adds up to a distinct run-down country pub feel, which isn't helped by the string of horse brasses over the hearth. It must be ten years since Ev saw any of those.

Swann is sitting in the corner, a tiny thin woman, all bones and sharp edges. Her hair is an unnatural orange-brown, with a hairslide to one side which makes her look like a withered eight-year-old. She has her arms wrapped around herself as if she's frozen with cold, though the log burner's been restoked and the room is warm. *It's probably shock*, thinks Ev. Even if she didn't see the body, having something like that happening in your own kitchen – Jesus. They're going to have to replace the lino for a start; that stain is never going to come out.

'Can I get you something?' Ev says. 'Tea?'

The old woman huffs a little and shakes her head. She doesn't look up. The officer exchanges a glance with Ev. A glance that says, 'I didn't get very far either.'

Ev moves over and takes a seat on the sofa. 'Do you mind if I ask you some questions, Mrs Swann? I know you've been through a terrible experience, but it's really important for us to take statements from witnesses as soon as possible.'

The woman looks up. 'Where's your senior officer? I'm not wasting my time with some WPC.'

'I'm a Detective Constable, Mrs Swann. We don't have WPCs any more. And DS Quinn is busy with your husband.'

'Where is he? What have you done with him?'

Ev sits forward. 'He's been taken to St Aldate's.'

Her eyes widen. 'The police station? What on earth for? He hasn't done anything – that man – that *person* – he *attacked* Richard – in our *own home* –'

Whoa, thinks Ev. *One step at a time.*

'There's no need to be alarmed, Mrs Swann. It's just that in circumstances like these there's a procedure we have to follow.'

She lifts her chin, defiant. '*We're* the victims here, young lady.'

It's a good ten years since anyone called Ev that, either. She takes a deep breath. 'I understand how you feel, really I do, but until we've questioned your husband –'

17

'*He* broke in here, *he* broke the law –'

'Mrs Swann, a man is dead.'

There's a silence. Ev holds the woman's gaze until she looks away, then clears her throat. 'So, perhaps we could start by you telling me exactly what happened here tonight.'

*   *   *

Adam Fawley
22 October
00.16

Quinn's waiting outside when I pull into the St Aldate's car park, shifting from one foot to the other. He manages to stop himself looking at his watch, but it must have taken a supreme effort.

'Sorry, I got held up.'

He gives a non-committal nod. 'He's been processed. For murder. So ready when you are.'

'Lawyer?'

'No. He was offered one but turned it down. We're good to go.'

'OK, Sergeant, let's get him brought up, shall we.'

The lighting in Interview One is unforgiving at the best of times, but at this time of night it's positively funereal. Perhaps that's why, when they bring Swann in, the first word that comes to mind is Death. He's not quite the Grim Reaper, but only just this side of cadaverous all the same. I'm guessing he was at least six-four as a young man – he's taller than me even now, despite the stoop.

He has a stark hooked nose, piercing eyes and an uncertain stride, though the custody-issue overalls could well be responsible for that. He also has a cut to his right palm.

He takes his seat, sits back slowly, then raises his gaze and gives me a long, cold look.

'So who would you be, then?'

*　*　*

Margaret Swann takes a deep breath. 'We heard a noise downstairs. Someone moving about.'

'Did the alarm not go off? You have one, don't you?' Ev remembers seeing the box on the front of the house, its red bulb flashing.

Margaret Swann sniffs a little. 'We don't set it. Not unless we go away. It's too fiddly – always going off by mistake and making that dreadful blaring noise. Richard said the security light would be enough to put people off.'

Not this time, evidently. Though Ev makes a note, because the old man's right – house thieves are almost always opportunistic and surprisingly easily deterred; in all her time on the Burglary team she never saw a break-in at a house with a closed gate or a functioning alarm.

'And what time was this?'

A shrug. 'Nine thirty. Around then anyway. I like to read in bed in the winter.'

So there would have been a light in an upstairs window, at least. And in any case, how many burglars would risk breaking in that early in the evening? Ev frowns; Quinn was right. This isn't adding up.

'And your husband? He was in bed too?'

'Yes. He was watching the television.'

'So you hear a noise, then what?'

* * *

Interview with Richard Swann, conducted at
St Aldate's Police Station, Oxford
22 October 2018, 12.37 a.m.
In attendance, DI A. Fawley, DS G. Quinn

GQ: For the purposes of the recording, Mr Swann
    has been arrested on suspicion of murder after
    a fatal shooting at his home, Gantry Manor,
    Ock Lane, Wytham, on the evening of October
    21st 2018. Mr Swann has been apprised of his
    rights, and has declined a solicitor at this
    stage. He is aware he can ask for legal
    representation at any time.
    OK, Mr Swann, let's start by hearing your
    version of events.

RS: My wife and I were in bed and heard a noise
    downstairs. I remember it was just after 9.30
    because my television programme had just
    started.

GQ: What sort of noise did you hear? Breaking
    glass? Something like that?

RS: No. It was more like someone moving about.
    When you've lived in a house for a long time

20

you get to know the noises. It was obvious there was someone downstairs.

GQ: Why didn't you call 999? That would have been safer, surely?

RS: In case you haven't noticed, we're some way from the nearest police station. By the time anyone got there the culprit would have been long gone. Assuming, of course, that you people bothered coming out at all. And for the record, since you're bound to ask, I *was* going to call you. I was on the point of doing so when those two uniformed chappies turned up.

GQ: Right. So to return to the sequence of events, you heard an intruder, and you decided not to call the police but go down and confront him yourself, even though you're - what? - in your seventies?

RS: Seventy-four. And I'm fully entitled to defend both myself and my property. I know my rights -

AF: What you're entitled to, Mr Swann, is the use of 'reasonable force'. What is, and is not, 'reasonable' is determined by the level of threat confronting you at the time. That's what we're trying to establish. Especially given the fact that the man you shot was found not only dead but - quite literally - with his back to the wall. That doesn't strike me as the stance of an aggressor.

RS: [*silence*]
Like I said, I heard the noise and went downstairs. I told Margaret to stay where she was.

GQ: I assume there were no lights on downstairs at this point?

RS: No, none. But I could hear him – he was in the kitchen.

GQ: He was in the *kitchen*, even though he must have known there was next to no chance there was anything valuable in there?

RS: We keep cash in a tea caddy. People our age often do. I assume that was what he was after.

GQ: OK, fair enough. So you go through to the kitchen, and – what? – confront him?

RS: Right.

AF: What did you say?

RS: [*turning to DI Fawley*]
I told him to eff off. To get the hell out of my property and not come back. Pointed the gun at him.

GQ: And what happened then?

RS: He laughed – called me 'Grandad'. Said I didn't scare him and it was probably just an effing air gun. Then he came at me with that knife. That's when I shot him.

AF: And he ended up by the wall?

RS: Evidently. I can't tell you any more than that. It all happened very fast.

AF: But you still maintain you were in fear of your life?

RS: He was three feet away from me, and at least forty years younger, and he had a weapon. Of course I was in fear of my life.

AF: You could tell his age? You just said the
    ground floor was in darkness.

RS: There's a security light at the back of the
    house, and the kitchen blinds weren't drawn.
    There was easily enough light to see it was a
    young man.

AF: Did you recognize him?

RS: Never seen him before in my life.

AF: There hadn't been any strangers hanging round
    the house lately – people who might have been
    checking out the property?

RS: Of course not – we'd have phoned the
    police. That's what you're supposed to do,
    isn't it?

GQ: So according to you, the shooting was an act
    of self-defence?

RS: Not 'according to me', it's what happened.
    [*holds up his hand*]
    You can see that with your own eyes. And you
    have the knife. What more do you need?

AF: Thank you, Mr Swann. You've been very clear.
    [*silence*]

RS: So is that it? I can go?

AF: Where's the gun kept?

RS: What?

AF: It's a simple enough question, Mr Swann.

* * *

'So, your husband goes downstairs, leaving you in the
bedroom. Can I ask why you didn't call the police? Or if

not the police, someone else who might have helped – a family member, a neighbour?'

An arch look. 'There's no telephone in our bedroom. And I don't have one of those mobile things. I don't want brain cancer, thank you very much.'

'And you stayed upstairs? You didn't see anything?'

Margaret Swann shakes her head. 'No. Nothing at all.'

'What did you hear?'

She frowns. 'I'm sorry?'

'You've clearly had no problem hearing me so far, Mrs Swann. I can't believe you didn't notice a shotgun going off in a silent house.'

*　*　*

RS: I keep my gun in an appropriately secured safe. And before you ask, I have a permit, and it's fully up to date.

GQ: Yes, we've already checked that.
[*passes across a sheet of paper*]
This is a plan of the ground floor of your house, yes?

RS: [*hesitates*]
Yes – though I don't know where you got that from –

GQ: I asked one of our forensics team to do it for me. Could you show me, on this diagram, exactly where the gun safe you mentioned is located?

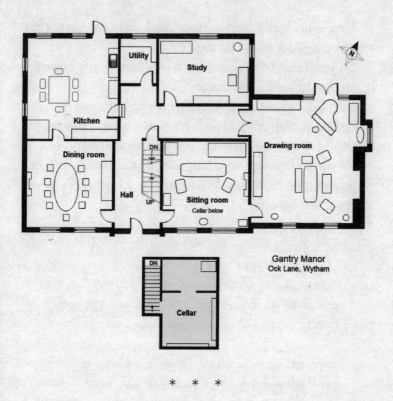

Gantry Manor
Ock Lane, Wytham

* * *

Margaret Swann looks irritated, as if she's dealing with a halfwit. '*Of course* I heard the gun go off.'

'And did you hear anything else? Voices?'

A pause. 'I think I heard Richard shouting something before the shot. But I couldn't hear what it was.'

'And then what happened?'

'I went out on to the landing and called down to Richard – I was frightened – I thought he'd been shot. But he came out of the kitchen straight away and told me to stay upstairs. I didn't come down until you people came.'

'How did he look – your husband?'

That was clearly unexpected. 'Shocked,' she says, after a moment. 'As you would expect.'

'So you must have been able to see him pretty clearly – if you could see his expression?'

She shifts in her seat. 'Clearly enough, obviously.'

But no mention of blood. Not on his face, not on his clothes, even though the kitchen was an abattoir.

Ev allows the silence to lengthen a little, makes another note, and then looks up. 'Where are your husband's night-clothes, Mrs Swann?'

* * *

GQ: Thank you for confirming that, Mr Swann. The gun safe is indeed in the cellar. You see, that's what we're struggling with.

RS: [*silence*]

GQ: Because we tried it. There's no way you could have gone down there without putting on the light. Not to mention the fact that the cellar door makes quite a racket.

RS: [*silence*]

GQ: So you're asking us to believe that you managed to open that door, put on the light, go down and retrieve the gun and come back up, all without the intruder noticing what you were up to?

RS: [*silence*]

AF: You can see why we find that troubling.

RS: I think I'd like to speak to my lawyer now.

GQ: You will now be returned to the cells. You should also be aware that, given the nature

```
of the possible charge, we will be seeking
authorization from a magistrate to hold you
for up to 96 hours, pending further enquiries.
Interview concluded at 12.57.
```

* * *

Margaret Swann is not blinking. 'I don't know what you mean.'

'When our uniformed colleagues arrived, Mr Swann answered the door in a shirt and cardigan, and a pair of slacks. But you said he was watching television in bed. So where are his nightclothes?'

'What difference does it make?'

Oh FFS, thinks Ev. *I don't believe you're that stupid. But if you want me to spell it out, I'll spell it out.*

'If someone's shot at that close a range, it causes a huge amount of damage. Explosive damage. Body matter is flung in all directions.'

Swann looks revolted.

'So you can appreciate why I'm asking about your husband's clothes. His dressing gown, pyjamas, whatever it was he was wearing. Because one thing's for sure – it wasn't that cardigan and slacks.' She stops and leans forward, stressing the point. 'They'd have been literally drenched in blood spatter, brain tissue –'

Swann turns away, squares her shoulders a little. 'I put them in the wash.'

Ev can hear the gasp from the officer behind her, and she's a hair's breadth from doing the same herself.

'You *washed* them? Even though you must have known it would be crucial evidence in the police inquiry?'

Swann makes a non-committal noise that manages to convey an equal measure of indifference and disdain.

Ev glances back at the officer. 'Can you check the washing machine, please, and get everything in there bagged up? Assuming CSI haven't done so already.'

The officer nods and heads for the door. Ev returns to Swann. 'Is there anything else you haven't told me, Mrs Swann?'

Swann has her hand to her chest now, her breath rasping. She makes no move to reply.

'So let's get this straight. Your husband shot and killed someone, you didn't call the police to report it, either before *or after* it happened, and in the meantime did everything you could to eliminate the evidence. You do realize that alone is a criminal offence?'

Swann turns to face her. There's a flush to her cheeks. 'I'd like you to call my doctor, please. I'm beginning to feel unwell.'

*   *   *

Oxford Mail online

Monday 22 October 2018 Last updated at 07:24

BREAKING:
Fatality after 'serious incident' at Wytham

Thames Valley Police have confirmed that an unnamed person lost their life as a result of a 'serious incident' at Wytham last night, after residents reported a significant police presence in the area around 10.30 p.m. Officers and vehicles remain on-site at an isolated property on Ock Lane, on the outskirts of the village.

The precise nature of the incident has not been made public, with the Thames Valley Police statement confirming only that 'Officers attended a property in Wytham on the evening of October 21st, after a serious incident which regrettably resulted in a fatality. Anyone with information about this incident should contact Thames Valley CID on 01865 0966552, or call Crimestoppers in confidence on 0800 555 111.'

More news on this as we hear it.

* * *

Adam Fawley
22 October
08.15

'OK, settle down, everyone. There's a lot to get through.'

I guess it's no surprise there's a buzz in here this morning. Like I said, people don't get shot in this town. And certainly not by septuagenarians.

Quinn's on whiteboard drill. He was hyper enough last night, and he's giving off so much energy now he looks like a Ready Brek kid. Sorry, showing my age on that one. Google it – you'll see what I mean. Gis is here now, too, so we're going to get our first real-life run-up at that division of responsibilities we talked about back when Quinn was first reinstated. It was all very sensible and grown-up, and Quinn was bending over backwards to be positive and reasonable. Only that was then, when all we were dealing with was a couple of muggings and some petty drug-dealing. But now there's a body, and a possible murder charge, and Quinn's going to grab all he can get. I know that, and Gis knows that, and right now Gis is the one I owe.

I look round the room again and wait for the noise to settle. There are three new faces here: one replacing Asante, one covering for Somer and one more who's just arrived today on secondment from PVP (and before you think I've gone all *Line of Duty* acronyms on you, that stands for Protecting Vulnerable People. From domestic violence and child abuse to modern slavery. It can be a brutal brief and you have to be tough to hack it). We've been a pretty tight-knit team these last few years so this is a lot of new blood in one hit. But hey, maybe that's a good thing.

'Right, before we start, for those of you who haven't worked with me before, we have two DSs on this team, DS Quinn and DS Gislingham. On a big investigation like this we'll work to the standard model of a Receiving DS, who collects and reviews evidence, and a Resourcing DS, who allocates tasks based on what we find. In this case it makes sense for DS Quinn, who was on-scene last night, to take on the former, while DS Gislingham will do the latter. Is that clear? Speak now or forever hold your peace.'

A couple of nervous laughs (the newbies) and some intrigued side glances at Quinn (old hands, like Ev).

'OK,' says Quinn, as I sit back down, 'this is where we are right now. The incident took place at approximately 9.45 last night, at Gantry Manor, Wytham, home of Richard and Margaret Swann. There was a 999 call from a member of the public at 9.52 but there were problems with the phone line so at that stage the operator wasn't clear exactly what we were dealing with. Turns out it was *that*.'

He gestures at the photos pinned to the board. They're not for the faint-hearted. I, for one, am very glad I don't do cooked breakfasts.

'As you can see, the vic had been shot in the face at close range, and as at now we have no idea who he is. There was nothing on the body and – to state the bleeding obvious – no chance of any sort of visual ID either. Both the Swanns are claiming he broke into the house and Richard Swann says he threatened him with a knife when he went downstairs to confront him. There's some damage to the back door and Swann has quite a deep cut on his right hand. A blood-stained knife was also recovered at the scene, still in the dead man's hand.'

He pauses, looks about. 'So, on the face of it, their story makes sense. Only it doesn't end there. Not by a long way. Because we had a rush job done on those prints and they are not, repeat *not*, in the system.'

A ripple round the room now.

'As we all know, it's *extremely* unlikely that a habitual housebreaker wouldn't already be in the system. So either we're looking at a complete rookie who got unlucky, or –'

'– he's bloody good and has never been caught,' finishes Baxter grimly.

Quinn looks across at him. 'Which I don't buy. Not for a nanosecond. He wasn't even wearing gloves, for Christ's sake. And there's no evidence he went looking for stuff to nick – there are no prints anywhere else downstairs. Even if we believe Swann's cock-and-bull story about him being after the money in the tea caddy it makes no odds – there were no prints on it.'

'More to the point,' says Gis, 'there are none on the back door either, even though, as DS Quinn just said, the so-called intruder wasn't wearing gloves. And yes, I suppose he *could* have wiped the door down as soon as he got inside – hands up anyone who reckons that's a runner?'

No one moves.

'Which leaves us,' says Quinn, 'with rather a lot of questions.'

He takes two strides to the flip chart and flicks over the top sheet. He was clearly in the office even earlier than I thought. I spot a smile curl Ev's lips and see her nudge Baxter and mouth, 'Here's one I prepared earlier.'

QUESTIONS

1 WHY DIDN'T THE SWANNS CALL 999, IF NOT BEFORE THE SHOOTING, THEN AFTER?
> NB 35 MIN DELAY BETWEEN WITNESS 999 CALL AND UNIFORM ATTENDING – PLENTY OF TIME FOR THEM TO CALL 999 THEMSELVES

2 WHY DID RS CHANGE HIS CLOTHES? (FOUND IN WASHING MACHINE)

3 HOW DID RS GET THE GUN FROM THE SAFE IN THE CELLAR WITHOUT INTRUDER NOTICING? (SEE FLOOR PLAN)
> WAS THE GUN NOT IN THE SAFE? ← WHY NOT SAY THAT UPFRONT?

4 IF THE INTRUDER WAS THREATENING SWANN HOW DID HE END UP WITH HIS <u>BACK TO THE WALL</u>?

Quinn turns and looks round the room. 'Me and the boss interviewed Swann last night, but we didn't get a satisfactory answer to *any* of these questions. As soon as we pressed him on the gun he clammed up and asked for a lawyer.'

Quinn's clearly getting a head of steam on this, and he has a point – more than a point. But we can't afford tunnel vision. But before I can say anything, Chloe Sargent pre-empts me. She's the one on secondment from PVP. Petite and blonde and soft-spoken, but bright too, and a lot tougher than she looks. She'd have to be, not just in PVP, but working this job at all, with a surname like that.

'I know it looks bad,' she says. 'I mean, none of us would act the way the Swanns did. But they aren't police officers. They're an old couple, in the dark, with a stranger in the house.'

'They're a bit odd too, if you ask me,' says Ev, backing her up. 'At least, based on what I saw last night. And *very* private. I bet they don't get many visitors.'

'Right,' says Sargent. 'I can easily see someone like Mr Swann panicking in those circumstances, but then it all goes wrong – the gun goes off and he panics again and makes things worse by trying to cover it up.'

I like the way she thinks. It's almost like having Somer here. Almost.

'There's no way of knowing, DC Sargent,' I say, seeing her blush slightly that I know her name. 'And I have to say I'm as sceptical as DS Quinn right now. *But* – and this is important, people – even if the Swanns are their own worst enemy, it's still quite possible they're telling the truth, even if not the whole of it. As DC Sargent said, they're elderly people in an isolated house with someone they don't know – possibly armed – in their kitchen.'

'You sound like a defence barrister,' says Ev drily.

I turn to her. 'Exactly. And that's how we need to think. Unless and until.'

OK, I know, I do say that quite a lot. Ev's not the only one trying not to smile.

I nod to Quinn. 'Sorry, Sergeant. I interrupted.'

He looks up, checks his tablet. 'Right, yeah, so, next up, *Mrs* Swann. She was interviewed at the scene by DC Everett, and basically claimed she was upstairs the whole time. But when Ev asked her why she'd stuck the old boy's jim-jams in the wash she pulled a sicky, so we had her taken to the JR. Better safe than sorry blah blah blah.'

He turns to Ev. 'Anything to add on that score?'

'I rang the ward just now and they kept her in for observation,' says Ev. 'Not for the first time, by all accounts – apparently she's been in there at least four times in the last eighteen months, though they were a bit cagey about telling me why without authorization. But I'll check in again later and see if she's up to talking. Though given the way she reacted last night, it might be best to send someone other than me. As in, a man with a badge. The bigger the better.' She stops, smiles. 'I mean the badge, obvs.'

There's a flurry of laughter and Gis is grinning, but Quinn's still playing it absolutely straight.

'Right,' he says. 'So in terms of next steps, the PM is this morning, and we're hoping for initial results on the forensics early this afternoon, and we also need to talk to the –'

OK, I think, *time for me to intervene.* To Gis's immense credit, his face is completely impassive, but he knows as well as I do that we're now straying well on to his turf.

'Thank you, DS Quinn,' I say, getting to my feet. 'That was an excellent summary. DS Gislingham will now allocate tasks for today.'

I don't wait around to referee the next bit. I have things to do, and Gis has been managing Quinn for months; it's down to him now.

*　*　*

'Ah, Ichabod Crane, I presume,' says Colin Boddie, surveying the corpse. The body has been stripped and laid out on the table, but there's only a scatter of teeth and skull fragments where his head should be. The recovered brain matter is on the trolley, a gravelly bright-red sludge in a gleaming stainless-steel basin.

The CSI technician glances up from the other end of the table. 'You do know Ichabod Crane and the Headless Horseman are two different people, right?'

'Yes, yes, I know,' says Boddie tetchily, flushing a little under his mask. 'Don't be so literal, Giddings. It's just a little light humour to start the day.' He pulls on his gloves and gives the technician a heavy look. 'One for that Instagram account of yours.'

Now it's the CSI's turn to flush – they've been posting Boddie's special brand of mortuary humour on @overheardinthemorgue for months, but they didn't realize Boddie knew.

'So,' says Boddie briskly, logging that as a win, 'shall we get started?'

* * *

When Gis divvies up the tasks, Ev gets Gantry Manor. She gets Hansen too, who immediately offers to drive – an offer she politely but firmly refuses. She made the mistake of going to Eynsham with Baxter once and it was Country & Western all the way. Hansen looks more like an R & B man to her, but you can't be too careful, not in such a confined space.

It's a fine, clear morning, and with the trees on the turn it should be a pretty drive, as well as a useful chance to get to know Hansen a bit better. He was at Cowley for a couple of years before transferring to CID, but their paths never crossed and she knows nothing about him beyond that. She spent the odd idle moment trying to work out what his backstory might be, given neither his accent nor surname gave much of a clue, then overheard someone in the canteen one day mention that though he was born and brought up in Bristol, his father is Swedish and his mother Vietnamese. Which explains the glossy black hair, the blue eyes and the amazing bone structure. Ev's also pretty sure he's gay, but until he mentions it, she won't be.

He certainly doesn't mention it in the car, but in the half-hour they spend together she finds him funny, thoughtful and – praise the Lord – a cat-lover (which has never yet failed her as an indicator of decency in the male half of the human race). He obviously knows what he's doing professionally too, judging by the one or two questions he asks about Gis's briefing. So far, so good. It's not that she had a problem with Asante, but one thing you could never accuse him of was being a team player.

When they pull up outside Gantry Manor there's crime-scene tape across the gate and a young PC fending off a couple of journalists. But that's all: both the weather and the location are on their side – it's too far and too chilly for casual nosey parkers.

They leave the car on the side of the lane and make their way up to the house. Three uniformed officers in high-vis jackets are doing a fingertip search of the garden, supervised by a visibly tetchy Barnetson, his nose red with the cold, who tells them in terse tones that it has been, thus far, 'a complete waste of bloody time'.

Their own mission, thankfully, is not only indoors but rather more likely to yield results. 'Fawley wants us to get a feel for the Swanns,' Gis had said as they left. 'What sort of people they are. Neither of them will be there so take the opportunity to have a poke about in their dirty washing. And I do mean literally.'

'But be careful,' says Ev, as she sends Hansen off to the sitting room. 'Make sure you leave everything exactly as you found it. I don't reckon much gets past Margaret Swann.'

There are four bedrooms upstairs, two of them under dust sheets, and one little more than a box room, with a single bed and a faded candlewick counterpane. Though the stack of John le Carré paperbacks and half-empty packet of Rennie suggest it's rather more than just a guest room.

There's a lot more clutter in the master bedroom – more dried flowers, china ornaments of milkmaids and chubby Victorian urchins, an ancient TV and an old free-standing wardrobe rammed tight with flannel shirts, A-line skirts, sensible shoes and, at the far end, a dinner jacket and a dark-coloured evening dress in dry-cleaner bags that don't look like they get out much.

There's nothing on Richard's side of the bed but Margaret's more than makes up for it. A white plastic jewellery box, full water glass, wind-up alarm clock and a framed photograph of what must be the Swanns on their wedding day. Ev picks it up; Richard has slicked-back hair and a vague resemblance to the young Prince Philip, though that might just be the height; Margaret's in a shiny high-necked ruffled dress that doesn't look very comfortable.

Ev puts the picture frame back down but manages to jolt the table in the process, spilling some of the water. She reaches into her pocket for something to mop it up, hearing her mother's voice berating her for her clumsiness. But something about the spill makes her pause, then raise the tissue slowly to her face. *Well, well, well,* she thinks. *Who'd have thought.*

When she goes back down she finds Hansen working his way methodically round the sitting room, taking notes and photos.

'Anything?' asks Ev, glancing round herself. She was in here last night, but it was too rushed and too gloomy for a proper look.

Hansen makes a face. 'Not much, to be honest. They read the *Telegraph* and the *Mail*, they don't have anything other than terrestrial TV and as far as I can tell they don't have any kids, either. Though they did once own a brown cocker spaniel.' He nods across at a now-yellowing photo in a pale-green papier-mâché frame. *Benjy* it says, in ornate, sentimental lettering.

Ev shivers a little. Even in her coat, it's cold in here. The log burner has long since gone out and there's evidently no central heating.

'Just storage heaters,' says Hansen, reading her mind. 'I didn't think you could still get those.'

'They've probably been here since the 1970s,' says Ev grimly. 'Rather like the Swanns.'

Hansen smiles briefly. 'Actually, according to one of those property market sites, the house last changed hands in 2005.'

Well, thinks Ev, *they didn't buy it as a do-over, that's for sure*. She doubts it's even been redecorated; surely no one in their right mind would have actually gone out and bought this carpet.

'Do we know where the Swanns were before?'

'No. Sorry. I can try and find out?'

Ev shakes her head. 'It's not a high priority. That far back, it's hardly going to make a difference.'

* * *

There's nothing Somer likes about hospital, but visiting times are definitely the worst. She doesn't actually *want* people coming and seeing her in this state, but everyone else assumes there's no one here because she's Billy No-Mates. She's had enough surreptitious and/or kindly looks to last her a lifetime.

So when the pretty, sympathetic nurse comes over with

a smile and announces she has a visitor, her heart sinks. She wasn't expecting anyone, and poor Ev isn't likely to be rushing back after the welcome she got last time –

'Hello, Erica.'

Seeing him for the first time in all these weeks, and her breath catches painfully in her chest. She'd started to forget what a beautiful man he was. Is. The blue of his eyes. The smile that would catch her unawares and flip her heart. But he's not smiling now.

'Why didn't you tell me?' Not said in anger. In sadness. Incomprehension.

She looks away, her eyes filling with tears.

'I didn't tell anyone.'

But Giles knows that's a lie. He must do – otherwise how is he even here? Someone must have told him. Ev? Kath?

'Your sister rang me. She's worried about you. Especially with her being stuck in the US.'

So it was Kath. Kath who will be even more worried now she's found out that Giles knew nothing about any of it. Giles – who Kath would have assumed was being the most tremendous support, because that's the sort of man he is.

'Can I sit down?'

And that's the sort of man he is too. A man who doesn't presume. Who doesn't turn up with grapes because that's just such a cliché. Who doesn't bring flowers either because he knows that might be overwhelming.

She nods. They sit in silence. She can feel the eyes on them. That kind nurse who's just glad someone's come to see her; the women visitors who are envying her having a man like that; the other patients wondering why this bloke

40

hasn't turned up before. Or perhaps she's imagining it. Perhaps no one else has even noticed.

'Do you want to tell me about it?'

She can feel her lips trembling. 'Not really.'

'When are they letting you home?'

She shrugs. Easier than talking.

She's trying to avoid looking at him. At the hurt in those sad blue eyes.

'Look, I understand now. Why you were – well, you know. I get it. I just want to help. If you want me to.'

He reaches a hand across the bed, tentative, towards hers.

* * *

At the back of Gantry Manor, Clive Conway is on his hands and knees on the step, examining the door.

'Mind yourself,' says Conway distractedly as they approach, his voice muffled by his mask. 'There's still puke on those slabs.'

Hansen makes a face and looks down at his feet; he's wearing rather nice shoes.

'What have you got?' asks Ev.

Conway straightens up. 'Well, someone definitely jemmied this door. Pretty cack-handedly, in my opinion, but it did the job.'

Ev looks up at the security light on the wall a few feet away. 'They wouldn't have been put off by that? It was pretty bright last night when I was here.'

Conway shrugs. 'Evidently not.'

Ev turns back to the door, her face thoughtful. 'But it

41

would be easy to stage this, wouldn't it? If that's what you wanted to do?'

Conway clearly hadn't anticipated that, but takes it in his stride. 'Yes,' he says, after a moment. 'Like I said, I'd hardly call this a professional job. Pretty much anyone could have done it. Probably not the old dear, admittedly, but the husband, definitely.'

Ev is silent, staring at the door.

Hansen frowns. 'You think that's what they did? Faked it?'

Ev's turn to shrug. 'I don't know. I just think we need to keep an open mind. At least until we get the results back from the lab.'

Conway nods slowly. 'Well, it would explain one thing, that's for sure.'

Ev looks up at him. 'As in?'

'As in, if it really was your vic who did this door, what sort of tool did he do it with? And, rather more to the point, where the hell is it now?'

* * *

Swann's lawyer is old school. A heavy Harris tweed jacket, well-worn tie, well-shined shoes. He looks like he's just walked straight out of a gracious Georgian office on Woodstock High Street, which perhaps he has.

Gis shows him into Interview Two, where Richard Swann is waiting, babysat by Chloe Sargent.

'Good morning, Mr Swann,' says Gis briskly, taking his seat and gesturing to the lawyer to do the same. 'I won't bother asking how you slept.'

'I assume this won't take long?' interjects the solicitor. 'I have another meeting I need to get back to.'

'It'll take as long as it takes,' says Gis genially. 'The sooner we get a full account of what happened last night, the better it will be for all of us. Including your client.'

Swann looks up, his eyes beady under his heavy brows. 'I've already told you. What part of "he broke in" do you not understand?'

Gis grins. 'No, the big picture is pretty clear. It's the little picture I'm a bit hazy on.'

Chloe Sargent suppresses a smile.

'But before we begin,' he continues, 'I need to remind Mr Swann that he remains under caution, and that this interview is being recorded. As he was advised last night, he does not have to say anything, but anything he does say may be used in evidence, and it may harm his defence if he does not mention when questioned something which he later relies on in court. We're all clear on that?'

He looks at the two men opposite: Swann hesitates then nods; the lawyer checks his watch and opens his notebook with a sigh.

Gis reaches for the recording machine. 'Interview commenced at 11.35, those present, DS Chris Gislingham, DC Chloe Sargent, Mr Richard Swann and Mr Timothy Unwin, Mr Swann's lawyer.'

He turns to Swann. 'So, let's start at the beginning, shall we?'

* * *

Telephone interview with Jonathan Martin
22 October 2018, 11.39 a.m.
On the call, DS G. Quinn

GQ: Ah, Mr Martin, Detective Sergeant Quinn,
Thames Valley. Glad I finally got through –
we've been struggling to reach you.

JM: Sorry about that – I've been on the motorway –
the phone was off. What's up?

GQ: I believe you made a call to the emergency
services at 9.52 last night, is that right?

JM: Yup, I was up near Wytham Hill.

GQ: And what were you doing there? It's a pretty
odd place to be at that time of night.

JM: Not if you're a photographer it's not. I was
hoping to get some shots of the Orionid meteor
shower. The weather conditions were damn-near
perfect, and I needed somewhere elevated
without much light pollution. Hence, Wytham.

GQ: Right, OK, so can you talk me through what
happened? The 999 operator didn't get much by
way of detail.

JM: Yeah, sorry about that, my battery gave out.
I'd been listening to a podcast on it and
didn't realize. Bloody thing. Why can't you
carry a spare like you used to? They just want
you to keep on buying new models –

GQ: Mr Martin?

JM: Sorry – right – I was just putting my kit
together when I heard it. A bang, like a
gunshot.

GQ: You're sure – you recognized it?

JM: Well, I don't own a gun, but I've watched enough crime stuff on telly. And whatever it was, it had to come from that house – it's the only one for miles.

GQ: And you called 999 immediately? I'm just trying to get a fix on the timings.

JM: Yes, pretty much straight away.

GQ: You didn't go down to the house? Didn't you think they might need help?

JM: I couldn't – there was a bloody great electric fence in the way. I did hang about for a bit, you know, to make sure the police did actually turn up, but then I saw the old boy come outside and he looked fine, so I realized they must be OK –

GQ: You *saw* him?

JM: Yeah. Sorry, I should have said.

GQ: And you could tell how old he was?

JM: Well, I had my telescopic with me, and the night-sight, so yeah, it was pretty easy to see.

GQ: What was he doing?

JM: I think he was taking out some rubbish – he was holding a plastic bag.

GQ: What sort of bag?

JM: You know – one of those black refuse ones.

GQ: Did it look full? Heavy?

JM: Hard to tell, but he definitely wasn't struggling with it. I remember thinking that he must've shot a rat or something, and he was getting rid of it.

GQ: So he comes outside – what happened then?

JM: He went down the garden with the bag.

GQ: You're absolutely sure about that?

JM: Oh yeah. He went across the lawn and disappeared into the trees.

GQ: And did he have the bag with him when he came back?

JM: No idea, I'm afraid. I stopped watching after that. I mean, it was obvious there was no harm done. I was a bit embarrassed, actually – if the phone hadn't died I'd have called you back and told you not to bother –

GQ: Have you not seen the news this morning?

JM: No – like I said, I've been on the road –

GQ: That shot you heard – it wasn't just a rat that got killed.

JM: [*pause*]

Someone *died*?

GQ: Afraid so. You didn't see anyone arrive at the house by any chance? Before the shot, I mean. You were probably in the vicinity at the time.

JM: No, like I said, I was there for the Orionids – it was only after the shot that I focused on the house. Shit –

GQ: We'll need you to come in and make a formal statement.

JM: Sure, of course. But hang on a minute, this whole thing – it makes no sense – if someone had just been shot, what was the old boy doing pissing about in the garden?

GQ: Right now, Mr Martin, that is the million-
    dollar question.

* * *

Safe to say, Ian Barnetson has had more enjoyable days. It's the worst kind of weather for this sort of palaver. Heavy with damp and a vicious chill that grits your bones, no matter how many layers you put on. As his team assemble on the gravel outside Gantry Manor for the second time in a few hours, they look as demoralized as he feels, stamping their feet and breathing gusts of painful cold air.

'OK,' he says, trying to get some authority, if not enthusiasm, into his voice. 'Let's just get this over with as quickly and efficiently as we can, shall we?'

One of the PCs mutters something under his breath, but not quite quietly enough.

'And yes, Grover, you're right,' says Barnetson, fixing him with a stare. 'I don't see how we could have missed it the first time either. But what we know now, and didn't know then, is that "it" actually exists. Richard Swann was seen out here with a black plastic bag *after* the shooting took place. A black plastic bag that isn't in the bins, hasn't been burned and wasn't put out for recycling, which by a process of elimination means it must be up here some-where. So we're looking for any areas where the soil looks like it might have been disturbed. And if we don't find anything in the garden, we're going to widen the search to the woods at the back and the paddock down this side, that all right with everyone?'

Murmurs of 'Yes, Sarge.'

'Right. Simmons and Anjali, you start at the back; Grover, you're with me.'

*   *   *

Adam Fawley
22 October
13.45

'How are you feeling now, Mrs Swann?'

She's staring resolutely out of the window, even though the only thing visible is grey sky. And I know she saw us arrive. There's just the one chair by the bed, and Baxter gets the short straw.

She still hasn't acknowledged my presence, so I pull my warrant card from my jacket. I don't usually bother doing routine interviews like this, but after what Ev said at the meeting I decided pulling rank may actually haul something out of this woman. And then Quinn called when I was on the way here and told me we have a witness. A witness who actually saw Richard Swann after the shooting. That's a line of questioning his lady wife won't be expecting.

'I'm Detective Inspector Adam Fawley,' I say. 'I'm the Senior Investigating Officer on this case. This is my colleague DC Andrew Baxter.'

She looks across, sniffs, and turns away again. Baxter didn't even merit a glance.

I drag the chair out, making as much noise as possible and earning myself a disapproving tut from one of the nurses.

'Your doctor said you were well enough to speak to me, so I'm hoping you'll be able to give us some more details about what happened last night.'

'Where's my husband?'

'He's being interviewed by my colleague. He has a lawyer with him.'

She lifts her chin and looks away. 'He's done nothing wrong.'

I nod to Baxter, who gets out his notebook.

'So perhaps you could tell me your version of what happened?'

Maybe I put a little too much emphasis on 'version' because she gives me a sour look.

'We were upstairs. I was reading and Richard was watching television. We heard a noise downstairs, and Richard went down.'

'Do you know where the gun was at that time?'

'I have no idea. Presumably in the safe. He is always extremely careful about that.'

'I see. So he goes downstairs, then what?'

'I heard him shout something, and then a shot. I've already told that woman all of this.'

I try my most charming smile, the one that gets Alex giving me side-eye. 'I really do appreciate your help.'

Another sigh. 'Yes, I heard the shot.'

A silence. A silence I'm perfectly comfortable with. I'm not so sure about her.

She stares at me now. 'Well?'

'What did you do then?'

She frowns. 'What do you mean?'

I shrug. 'Did you go downstairs? Call the police, what?'

She gives me a withering look. 'You know perfectly well that I didn't call the police.'

'But you did go downstairs.'

'No, I went to the *head* of the stairs. I was concerned about Richard.'

'But you told my officer that you put your husband's pyjamas in the wash – you must have gone downstairs at some stage.'

'That was later.'

'So you went into the kitchen at that point – you saw the man?'

'No,' she says firmly, 'I did *not*. For your information, the washing machine is in the scullery.'

I do my best not to smile. The rest of the world has a utility room; Margaret Swann has a scullery. It's like something out of *Downton Abbey*.

'So you never saw the man – you have no idea who it might have been?'

'As I told that woman, we don't make a habit of fraternizing with that sort of person.'

'And while you were doing the washing, what was your husband doing?'

She frowns again. 'What do you mean?'

'Was he with you, in the sitting room, upstairs?'

'Oh, I see. He got changed upstairs and came back down.'

'And then?'

'And then what?'

'Did he stay in the house?'

She reaches for the water jug beside her bed and pours herself a glass. Her hand is shaking slightly. I sense Baxter stir behind me, but he says nothing.

'Mrs Swann? I'm asking if your husband went outside at all before the police officers arrived. It's a straightforward question.'

But I don't get an answer. In fact, I don't get anything at all. She calls to the nurse, says she's feeling 'unwell', and we're summarily ejected.

I turn to Baxter as we make our way down the corridor. 'What was that all about – with the water?'

He gives a wry smile. 'I was just wondering what was really in the jug.'

I glance across. 'Meaning?'

'Meaning I just got a text from Ev. Apparently the old buzzard has a jug like that by her bed at home, only that one's neat gin.'

I nod slowly, wondering whether it's significant or just a red herring. Though it might, at least, account for all those hospital admissions. I make a mental note to chase up on Margaret Swann's medical records.

I leave Baxter in the lobby, telling him I'm going to visit Somer, and though he offers to come with me he looks relieved when I say it's best I do this alone.

It takes me ten minutes to find the right ward, time I don't really have, but I'd feel bad coming here and not seeing her. And it's not just that: Gis took me aside as I was leaving the station.

'Can you look in on Somer while you're at the JR, boss? Ev's worried about her. I don't think she's doing so well.'

I doubt I would be either, in her position. She hasn't told me what's wrong with her – not officially – but she's in an Oncology ward. Enough said.

I give my name at the nurses' station, and they point me

in the right direction, but when I round the corner I see there's someone with her. I've only met him once but I recognize him. Giles something. A DI with Hants.

I check my pace and turn. I don't want to intrude, and I can't see my presence adding anything useful. Not now.

The last thing I see as I turn the corner is Somer's face. She's smiling. Not the broad smile of real joy, but a smile all the same.

*   *   *

Margaret Swann does her best to conceal her irritation with the nurse. She was useful enough when it came to repelling those tiresome police officers but now it's all fuss, fuss, fuss. No, she doesn't have the pain any more; no, she doesn't need a drink of water; no, she doesn't want the nurse to 'pop across' and get the doctor. This place, it's all 'popping' this and 'slipping' that. As if the patients are all halfwits. It drives her mad.

She flaps her hand at the nurse, who finally gets the message and goes away. Margaret turns over and puts her back to the rest of the ward. Those stupid policemen with their supercilious smiles and ponderous heavy hints, they clearly think she really is a halfwit. But that sort of nonsense she can handle. Richard – now that's another matter. She's still worried about what he might say. Not deliberately, no, he wouldn't do that: he's good at keeping secrets. They both are; they've had a lot of practice. But there are things he doesn't know, things he might hint at without even realizing. She purses her lips. She'd been in two minds whether to tell him all those weeks ago, but she told herself it was nothing: they'd been so careful, no one could possibly have found them. It was just a mistake – a random coincidence. She wishes now that she'd checked, that she'd made sure, but in the moment she'd acted without thinking, out of instinct and from bitter lessons learned too well: the only way to survive this is to turn your back. Walk away. And she'd been vindicated – or so she thought – because there'd been nothing after that. No follow-up. No repetition.

Until last night. Until this.

And now the police will be going around lifting up old stones just to see what's underneath them, and it's absolutely imperative that Richard doesn't say anything that might give them away. They've spent too long – and too much – covering their tracks for all that to come out now.

She pulls the thin blankets up around her shoulders.

She isn't cold. But she is trembling.

* * *

'Did you see the email?'

Nina Mukerjee is standing at Alan Challow's door. He looks up and then turns to his laptop and opens his inbox. It's a blizzard of technical language, like all reports from the lab, but he knows his stuff.

He takes a breath. 'Well, well, well,' he says, half to himself. 'Who'd have thought.'

* * *

I'm with Gis and Quinn when Boddie's call comes through.

'Hold on, Colin, I'll put you on speaker.'

He's obviously still in the mortuary; there's a tinny echo and I can hear the sound of water sluicing in the background.

'So what have you got?'

'Well,' he says. 'It had a certain lurid Grand Guignol appeal, I'll give you that.'

Quinn rolls his eyes and I know what he means; this is classic Boddie.

'Go on.'

'But the bad news is that there's absolutely nothing either on or *in* the body that'll help you ID him. No tattoos, scars, birth- or otherwise distinguishing marks; no helpful metal plates or healed breaks. No obvious indication of drug use either, though I'll need to wait for the tox screen for confirmation. Other than that, no sign of disease, excellent muscle tone, and all major organs in good working order. He'd be a remarkably healthy specimen – if he still had a head. And he was clean and well nourished too – he wasn't living on the streets, that's for sure.'

'Age?'

'Late teens, early twenties. Certainly no older.'

'So that's it?'

There's a pause. I can almost hear that 'I know something you don't know' smile of his. Quinn mouths 'prick-tease' at the phone.

'Come on, Colin,' says Gis cajolingly. 'Don't keep us on tenterhooks.'

'There may not be anything to ID him, but there was something, all the same.' He laughs. 'Must be your lucky day, Fawley. Someone up there likes you.'

'Care to elaborate on my good fortune, Colin?'

'It was when I was doing the skeletal dissection. I noticed it at once, of course.'

He stops. Waits.

'Go on,' I say heavily.

'The left humerus is slightly wider than the right.'

Another pause. But this time I know what he's getting at.

'He was left-handed.'

Boddie gives another brisk laugh. 'Wonders will never cease – you've been listening to me all these years, after all. But yes, you're right. Now take a look at your crime scene photos.'

Quinn reaches for his tablet, pulls up an image of the victim, then twists it to face us.

'The knife,' says Gis, pointing, 'it's in his right hand.'

* * *

Sent: Mon 22/10/2018, 15.05   **Importance: High**
From: AlanChallowCSI@ThamesValley.police.uk
To: DIAdamFawley@ThamesValley.police.uk

Subject: Case no EG2508/19J Gantry Manor – urgent

Quick heads-up pending the full report. We just got preliminary results back from the lab re the knife recovered at the scene. The blood on it derived from two different sources. Most of it was Swann's but there were other traces on the inner side of the handle that were clearly transferred from the victim's palm. I take it you've done this enough times to know what that means, but call me if you need a refresher.

AC

*　*　*

Barnetson looks down at the sorry pile at his feet. It's not much to show for three hours' work. A lager can that was almost certainly tossed in from a passing car, a trowel with a bent blade, an old gardening glove with holes in the fingers and a furred-up tennis ball that's probably been here since the dog died. But no screwdriver, no mobile phone, no wallet and no rogue black plastic bag. There's no sign that anything's been buried recently either – in fact, there's not much sign of anything at all having been done in this garden for a good long while. The lawn is ankle-high in leaves and ivy is crawling through the broken greenhouse glass. Plants, shed, fence: everything is brown and rotting and slowly coming to pieces in the damp.

Grover is still poking listlessly at the borders with a stick. 'I just don't reckon that bag's out here, Sarge. We've been through the whole place twice now.'

'It has to be somewhere,' counters Barnetson. 'It didn't just vanish into thin air.'

*　*　*

Sometimes evidence is like buses: it all comes at once.

Quinn picks up a stack of photocopies and hands them to Chloe Sargent, indicating to her to pass them out.

'OK, people,' he says now, raising his voice above the chatter. 'Let's get started.'

He looks round. 'Things are moving pretty fast, so this is just a quick update on where we are. First, DS Gislingham has interviewed Swann again, this time in the presence of his lawyer.'

Gis turns to face the room. 'Let's just say he wasn't in a very talkative mood – it was basically "No comment" all the way. He did give us a prepared statement, but that just repeated everything he said the first time. Including, for the record, absolutely no mention of the fact that – as we now know – he went walkies down the garden straight after the shooting.'

'Did you ask him about that?' asks the DC who's covering for Somer while she's off. Bradley something. Carter. Bradley Carter. He has one of those perky-at-the-front haircuts and a chubby, schoolboyish look, but he's ambitious, as I can tell by the glance he slides in my direction.

'No,' says Gis, 'we didn't. For the very good reason that we only found out about it afterwards.'

Carter's frowning. 'So we'll talk to him again?'

'Not yet,' replies Gis. 'The boss –' a nod to me – 'wants to hold off on that.'

I look up. 'That's because we have a hell of a lot of

blanks to fill in first. The next time we sit down with Richard Swann I want us to know as much about this crime as he does.'

'So as at now,' says Gis, 'Swann's been sent back to the cells while we try to work out what the heck we're dealing with here.'

'Speaking of which,' says Quinn, holding up the hand-out, 'everyone's favourite subject: forensics.'

There's a rustle of activity as people turn to the right page.

'We knew Swann must have washed and changed his clothes before Uniform got there, so surprise, surprise, there was no gunshot residue on his hands. The PJs we dug out of the washing machine didn't yield anything either. Not even any residual blood.'

Gis gives a wry grin. 'Guess those stain-remover things actually do what they say on the tin. Who knew, eh?'

Subdued laughter. I don't think Gis is actively trying to piss Quinn off, but he seems to be managing it all the same.

'Far more significant,' says Quinn, raising his voice a little, 'the knife. The blood on the blade was Swann's, but there was also blood on the handle – blood that came from two, repeat *two*, different sources – both Richard Swann *and* the victim. And given the vic still had his hand round the knife when we found it, there's only one way that could have got there –'

'They faked it,' says Hansen, almost too quickly. 'To make us think Swann had been attacked.' And now he's looking awkward, either because he doesn't want to look like a swot, or didn't mean to cut across a DS. And especially not this DS.

'Right,' says Quinn, staring at him.

'But what about a previous injury?' Carter again. Who clearly has no problem looking like a swot. I'm guessing this must happen around him a lot because a couple of people are suppressing smiles. 'Before the gunshot?'

Quinn frowns. 'Like what, exactly?'

Gis is shaking his head. 'There was nothing on the body, according to the PM. No injuries at all, not even bruising. And no defensive or other injuries on the hands that could have caused any sort of bleeding.'

Carter frowns. 'But it could have been a head wound – before the shot, I mean. We can't exactly check for *that* now, can we.'

Quinn snorts. 'What sort of head wound? You think Swann gave him a clip round the ear and then asked him to hang on a minute while he got his gun? "Hold my beer while I nip down to the cellar?"'

Gis cuts across him because Carter's gone very red. 'OK, Carter, it was a good point and you're right that we need to be careful not to get blinkered in a situation like this, but I tend to agree with DS Quinn: it's pretty unlikely. Especially given what else Boddie found.' He nods again to Quinn, who holds up the next sheet of paper.

'The PM report,' he says. 'Most important thing to note here is that the vic was left-handed. And as you can see,' he says, gesturing back at the photos on the whiteboard, 'the knife was found in his *right* hand. Proof, if anyone still needs it,' a pointed glance at Carter, 'that the Swanns staged that scene. Swann cut him*self*, then put that knife in the vic's hand after he was dead so we'd find his prints on it. Unfortunately for him, that wasn't all we found.'

'So,' says Gis. 'To sum up – right now everything is pointing to the victim never having broken into that house at all. That whatever this was, it wasn't a burglary.'

Chloe Sargent is clearly still processing all this. 'So the Swanns faked the break-in as well?'

Ev turns to her. 'Clive Conway said the damage to the back door was pretty basic. Anyone could have done it. And there was no screwdriver or anything like that in the victim's pockets. In fact, there was nothing in his pockets, period.'

'It's probably all in that black placky bag,' says another DC, to murmurs of agreement.

Gis smiles. 'Yeah, well, Barnetson is on the case on that, so watch this space.'

Baxter now. 'So the knife wasn't the vic's either – is that what we're saying?'

Ev gestures at the picture on the whiteboard. 'That looks more like something from a kitchen drawer.'

The implication is clear.

Hansen looks up. 'I checked that, actually. The Swanns have only one set of matching knives – some heavy old-fashioned things in the dining room, obviously kept for "best". The cutlery in the kitchen was just a mishmash of different stuff. That knife could easily have been one of theirs – trouble is, we'll never be able to prove it.'

But Baxter isn't convinced, not yet. 'We're getting a bit ahead of ourselves, though, aren't we? Even if he wasn't a burglar, doesn't mean it wasn't self-defence. There could have been an argument – Swann's a stroppy old git – he loses his rag, next thing you know – bam –'

'So why not admit straight up that that's what happened?' says Hansen. 'Did he think we wouldn't believe him?'

'What I think we can all agree,' I say carefully, 'is that right now we have a lot of theories and very few facts. We don't know what this man was doing there, we don't know if they were expecting him and we don't know how or why he ended up dead. They could even have lured him there with the express *intention* of killing him.'

General murmurs of demurral here, and I get it – I find that hard to believe too – but we can't afford to close down any possibilities. Not yet.

I wait for the noise to settle. 'But whatever the answers to those questions, in my opinion they all point to the same conclusion: they knew him. Even though they've flatly denied it, they knew who he was.'

I look round, drilling down the point. 'There's a connection between these people – there has to be. If we can establish what that is, we'll find out why he's dead. And that means finding out who the hell he is.'

Gis makes a face. 'Easier said than done, though, boss. We can hardly put his picture in the paper.'

'So let's find some other way,' I reply, over a couple of ghoulish wisecracks. 'Starting with how he got to Gantry Manor in the first place. It's miles from anywhere and he had no car.'

'Unless the Swanns moved it?' asks Sargent.

Baxter's shaking his head. 'There wouldn't have been time – not with all that laundry they were doing.'

I nod towards him. 'Right. So no car and I doubt very much he was on foot. Not at that time of night, down an unlit lane. So what does that leave us with? A cab?'

Quinn nods. 'That'd be my bet.'

Gis turns to him. 'I guess I could get the *Oxford Mail* to run a follow-up based on that.'

Ten minutes later Gis has nearly finished doling out tomorrow's tasks and the room is starting to clear, but I'm still at the whiteboard.

'What is it?' says Quinn, appearing at my shoulder. My first assumption is that he just wants to get an inside track Gis doesn't have, but I check myself. It's all too easy to treat Quinn like a cliché, largely because he spends so much time acting like one. But there's more to him than that, all the same.

I gesture towards the pictures of Swann and his wife. 'Make sure someone's doing some digging on these two as well, will you?'

He nods. 'OK, I can do that.' He hesitates. 'Any particular reason?'

I shake my head. 'Nothing specific. I just can't shake the feeling I've seen them somewhere before.'

* * *

Oxford Mail online

Monday 22 October 2018 Last updated at 16:44

Police appeal for witnesses in
relation to fatal Wytham shooting

Thames Valley Police have issued an appeal to anyone who might be able to help them identify a man who was shot dead at Wytham last night. Officers were called to an isolated property on Ock Lane, on the outskirts of the village, after a member of the public reportedly heard gunfire emanating from the property.

Detective Sergeant Chris Gislingham told us: 'We do not know who this man was, or how he travelled to Wytham last night. He was a young man, probably in his early twenties, and he must have friends and family who are concerned about his whereabouts. That's why it's important we identify him as soon as possible. We're particularly interested in hearing from any taxi or minicab drivers who might have dropped off a male passenger in Ock Lane yesterday evening. You can contact us in confidence on 01865 0966552, or at the TVP social media feeds.'

DS Gislingham declined to comment on the circumstances that led to the victim's death, or on reports that the shooting was the result of a burglary gone wrong. The identity of the householders has not been made public, but neighbours have said they are an elderly couple who have lived at the property for at least ten years. 'They seem like very respectable people,' said one neighbour, who asked not to be named. 'They keep themselves very much to themselves. They must have been terrified, at their age, finding an intruder in the house at that time of night. I mean, it's everyone's worst nightmare, isn't it?'

DS Gislingham advised anyone with concerns about their home security to download the Thames Valley Home Security Guide at https://www.thamesvalley.police.uk/police-forces/thames-valley-police/areas/advice/home-security-guide/.

*   *   *

63

Telephone interview with Suresh Gupta
22 October 2018, 6.15 p.m.
On the call, DC T. Hansen

TH: CID, DC Hansen speaking.

SG: I'm ringing about that bloke – the one at the station, yeah?

TH: I'm sorry – I'm not sure –

SG: That story on the *Oxford Mail* website? My brother-in-law saw it and showed it me. It said to ring if you'd picked him up.

TH: Oh, I see, hold on a moment, let me get a pen. What's your name, sir?

SG: Suresh Gupta – I'm on the cab rank at the station.

TH: And the number you're calling from is the best one to contact you on?

SG: What? OK, right, yeah, it's my mobile.

TH: Thank you. Now, perhaps you can explain exactly what happened?

SG: Right, OK. I picked him up, like I said, and took him out to that place. Gantry Manor or whatever it's called. Out by Wytham. Twenty quid it was.

TH: And this was Sunday night?

SG: Yeah.

TH: What time?

SG: I reckon I picked him up around 9. But he'd have been there a bit before that. There was a bloody enormous queue.

TH: OK. So you wouldn't know which train he'd been on?

SG: Nah. No way.

TH: Did he say anything in the cab? About where he'd come from - where he was going?

SG: Nah, barely said a word the whole time. Just stared out of the window and did stuff on his phone. Though he gave me the address on a piece of paper so I got the impression he hadn't been there before.

TH: And what happened when you got to Gantry Manor?

SG: He got out and paid. Didn't say anything - just paid.

TH: From a wallet? Or just loose cash?

SG: A wallet.

TH: How did he seem?

SG: How d'ya mean?

TH: Did he look apprehensive? Excited?

SG: Perhaps a bit pissed off? But I wasn't really looking, to be honest.

TH: And what happened then? Did you see him approach the house?

SG: I had to turn the cab round so, like I said, I wasn't really looking, but I deffo remember him walking up the drive.

TH: You're sure - he went right up to the front door?

SG: Last I saw - but he'd stopped to get something out of his backpack, so I can't be sure -

TH: He had a *backpack*?

SG: Yeah, didn't I say? Sorry, mate –

TH: Can you describe it?

SG: Just a dark-coloured thing. Black, maybe. Not that big.

TH: You didn't see any logos – anything like that?

SG: Nah. Those things all look the same. And in any case, I wasn't really looking.

TH: Thank you, Mr Gupta. That's incredibly helpful –

SG: So can I go now, only my shift's starting in half an hour –

TH: I won't keep you much longer, I promise. Just a couple more questions. Can I ask if you recognized him – had you ever seen him before?

SG: [*laughs*]

You're joking, right? I see hundreds of blokes look just like him.

TH: How would you describe him?

SG: Well, it were dark and, like I said, I weren't really looking. Just an ordin'ry bloke, yeah?

TH: So if we asked you to come in and help us with an e-fit –

SG: Well, I'm not sure – like I said, I've got work –

TH: We can sort out a time that suits you. It would be really helpful.

SG: [*pause*]

Yeah, OK. I suppose so.

TH: Excellent, I'll check when the e-fit artist is available and call you back.

* * *

Hansen puts the phone down and looks across the office. He was hoping DC Everett was around – she'd be a useful sounding board. Because he's still getting the hang of the whole Receiving/Resourcing DS thing, and something like this seems to land smack in the grey area right in the middle. Probably more 'receiving' than 'resourcing' but as it happens DS Quinn isn't here. Unlike DS Gislingham, who's at DC Baxter's desk, looking over his shoulder at something on the screen. Hansen gets to his feet and goes over.

'Sarge?'

Gis looks up and smiles. Hansen likes Gis – he gets the impression most people do. He doesn't *dis*like DS Quinn, but he's definitely trickier. Brighter, but trickier.

'We just had a call passed through from the switchboard. A cab driver from the station rank. He picked up our dead guy on Sunday night.'

Gis frowns a little. 'He's sure?'

'Oh yes, he dropped him at Gantry Manor.'

Gis exchanges a glance with Baxter; this sounds promising.

'Can he describe him?'

Hansen makes a face. 'Not well. But he's agreed to come in and talk to an e-fit operator.'

Baxter shrugs. 'Better than nothing.'

'And it's not just that,' says Hansen, aware he sounds a bit too much like an over-eager rookie. 'He saw the vic walk up the drive. Hardly your standard housebreaker MO –'

Gis gives a grim smile. 'Er, no –'

'– *and* he had a backpack with him. A backpack that seems to have disappeared off the face of the earth.'

Baxter raises an eyebrow sardonically. 'Maybe that's where all that stuff is that we didn't find in his pockets.'

Gis taps the young DC lightly on the arm. 'Good stuff, Hansen. Give Barnetson a call, will you? Get him to add the backpack to the MIA list. And in the meantime, we'll get hold of the station CCTV.'

He turns to Baxter and flashes his widest smile. 'Or rather, DC Baxter will. Given how much he loves that sort of thing.'

Baxter gives him a look, but it's obviously an old joke. 'Yeah, right.'

Hansen makes to go, but Gis stops him. 'Not so fast, young Hansen, I've got a job with your name on it too.'

* * *

Barnetson ends the call and sticks his phone in his pocket. They'd all but finished, and still have nothing to show for it. Not a screwdriver, not a phone or wallet, and definitely not a bloody backpack.

He turns to Grover. 'Apparently the dead man turned up with some sort of rucksack.'

Grover frowns. 'Is that what they think was in the plastic bag?'

Barnetson looks round. 'Maybe,' he says distractedly. 'It's probably about the right size.'

Grover sighs. 'Any suggestions where we look, Sarge, cos I'm all out of ideas.'

Barnetson stares at him, then looks away. He's all out of ideas too.

* * *

First thing the following morning, Gis and Quinn are standing by Baxter's desk, staring at printouts. It's the Swanns' phone records since the start of the year.

Gis shakes his head. 'This is really all there is? In over nine months?'

Baxter nods. 'That's what I thought too. So I double-checked with BT that the line was working. Which it is. Though judging by that list, I don't reckon the Swanns would even have noticed if it wasn't.'

'Three calls from the Swanns' GP,' says Quinn thoughtfully. 'Most of them recent. Do we know why?'

Baxter shakes his head. 'It's a fair guess it's about Margaret given how many times she's been in the JR, but we're still waiting on authorization for her medical records and, frankly, I can't see her agreeing. Though it could be completely irrelevant to the case, of course.'

Quinn sighs. 'I hope you have some good news, Baxter, because this isn't doing it for me.'

Baxter gives a dry smile, turns to his screen and opens up a file. 'How about this?'

It's CCTV. From the station, by the looks of it. At the bottom of the screen it says *21/10/2018 20:41:06*.

'The cab driver says our vic could have been in the cab queue for anything up to half an hour,' says Baxter. 'So I went back to eight thirty and worked forward from there.'

He presses Play and the two sergeants lean forward, one over each shoulder like good and bad angels, a thought which may also have occurred to Baxter, judging by the small smile he now has.

The camera is trained on the ticket barriers, and the three of them watch as people come along the platform and through the doors. It's obviously cold – everyone's wearing scarves and gloves, quilted jackets and heavy coats. Groups of boisterous blokes wearing football scarves who've clearly had a few, one or two elderly ladies, a couple of priests in cassocks. Well, this is Oxford. But it's mainly students. Alone, in groups, in pairs.

It's Quinn who spots him first.

'There,' he says, pointing. 'That's him.'

He's about the right height. Not tall – no more than the five foot seven which Boddie estimated in the PM. Dirty blond hair, dark trousers and jacket, and – there – a small backpack slung over one shoulder. He sticks his ticket in the barrier and collects it the other side.

'He has a return,' says Gis softly. 'He was planning on going back.'

On the screen the man stops, looks round the concourse, then makes for the main doors. A few moments later he disappears out of sight.

Baxter winds back the footage a little way and presses Pause, then sits back. 'I checked the cameras on the platforms and he got off a Chiltern train from Marylebone, so in theory there's half a dozen places he could have got on between here and there –'

'Nah,' says Gis. 'Most likely he came from London. At

least let's rule that out first. Have you contacted Chiltern for the on-train footage?'

Baxter nods. 'On its way.'

'Right,' says Gis, 'looks like we're cooking with gas. Finally.' He points at the screen; the man's by the barrier, frozen in mid-gesture, one arm outstretched. 'Get a still of that out to the press office pronto, will you?'

'It's not the best angle,' says Quinn. 'You can't really see his face – it's always the bloody same with these things.'

'Doesn't matter,' replies Gis. 'It'll be enough. If you know him, it'll be enough.'

* * *

Thames Valley Police @ThamesValleyPolice   9.29
🚨🚨**APPEAL**🚨🚨
Do you know the man in this picture? He arrived at
Oxford station at approx 8.45pm on Sunday, possibly
travelling from London. We need to identify him in
relation to a serious incident at Wytham later that
evening.
Contact the force with info/footage – reference
7713954632

* * *

By mid-morning, Thomas Hansen has been on the task Gislingham gave him for nearly three hours and is actually rather enjoying himself. He read *I'll Be Gone in the Dark* when it came out and was absolutely engrossed – the idea that familial DNA could catch a killer who'd evaded capture for nearly fifty years had him deciding there and then to retrain as a forensic scientist. Though it only took a couple of days of cooler reflection to realize that the idea was, in purely practical terms, a complete no-no. He'd never be able to fund himself through a course like that, for a start. But all the same, his interest hasn't waned, and in the last six months he's done a lot of reading, and listened to a few podcasts, and ended up a bit of a self-confessed wonk on the subject. And even though what he's doing now isn't, strictly speaking, the same thing, the pleasure it offers has to be darn close. The kick of the hunt, the tracking down, the elimination of false positives, the final, conclusive identification. Because he's worked it out. He knows. More than that, he knows he's right.

He gets up and wanders round to Gislingham's desk. Only he's not there.

'In with the boss,' says Ev as she passes him on her way back from the coffee machine. 'I just saw him go in.'

'Ah, right,' says Hansen, already in retreat. 'I'll see if I can find DS Quinn.'

Everett eyes him. 'Is it important?'

Hansen nods. 'Yes, I think so.'

'Then DS Gislingham will want to know. And Fawley will want to know.' She smiles. 'And in any case, why shouldn't you get the credit? You've got to learn to blow your own trumpet a bit more, young Hansen.'

She smiles again, then goes on her way. Hansen, left to himself, takes a breath, squares his shoulders a little, then forces himself the few last yards to Fawley's door.

* * *

72

Thomas Hansen looks like he's been sent to the headmaster for talking in class. I'm all for having an air of authority, but I'd like to think I'm a bit more approachable than that.

'Sorry to bother you, sir.'

'That's fine, Hansen. What is it?'

'DS Gislingham said you wanted more info on the Swanns. I've been doing some digging.'

Gis and I exchange a glance. Promising? He wouldn't be here otherwise.

'What've you got?' says Gis.

Hansen looks down at his notebook. 'Gantry Manor isn't actually owned by the Swanns – not directly. It belongs to a company called Alder Properties Ltd. Richard Swann is the main shareholder.'

'OK. So where were the Swanns before?'

'Ah, that's where it got interesting. I couldn't find them.'

Gis frowns. 'What the hell does that mean?'

'I couldn't find any record of them living anywhere else. In fact, I couldn't find any record of them at all.'

That bell that's been ringing ever since I saw the Swanns? It's clanging even louder now.

Thomas looks at Gis and then at me. 'So I checked with DVLA. I mean, I knew he must have a licence, with that SUV out the front. And that's when I realized what must have happened – I was staggered there's no sort of central record of this stuff, but I've checked and I'm definitely right –'

73

'Spit it out, Hansen,' says Gis. 'We haven't got all day.'

Hansen swallows. 'They changed their name. The Swanns. By deed poll. I mean, who does that, apart from Mafia?'

Gis gapes at him. 'They *changed their name*? When?'

'Just before they moved here, 2004. Their real name is –'

'Rowan,' I say, as it all finally falls into place. 'Their name is Rowan. Dick and Peggy Rowan. At least, that's who they used to be.'

Gis is staring at me. 'Holy fuck,' he says.

Hansen clearly has no idea what we're talking about. Then again, the trial was fifteen years ago. He was probably still in short trousers.

Gis glances at him, not unkindly. 'Google "Camilla Rowan",' he says.

Hansen scrabbles for his mobile. A moment later he's raised his eyes to look at me. He's gone rather pale.

'They're *her* parents?'

I nod. 'You wanted to know why they changed their name? Well, there's your answer. And frankly, who can blame them.'

* * *

Camilla Rowan

From Wikipedia, the free encyclopedia

Camilla Rowan (born 30 September 1980), a former physiotherapist from Gloucestershire, England, is serving a life sentence for the 1997 murder of her newborn baby. She served the first years of her sentence

74

in HMP Holloway, London, but when that prison closed in 2016 she was transferred to HMP Heathside, an adult female/closed category prison in Esher, Surrey. She was born in Gloucester, England, to Richard ('Dick') Rowan, a property developer (born 1944), and his wife, Margaret (known as Peggy), *née* Cummings (born 1950). The family lived in Shiphampton, and Rowan attended Burghley Abbey, a prestigious private girls' school. Rowan vehemently denied killing her child at her 2003 Old Bailey murder trial, but the jury returned a unanimous verdict of guilty, and Justice Sir Jacob Gordon sentenced her to life, with a recommended minimum term of seventeen years.[1] Rowan's legal team have lodged various appeals against her conviction, and the Criminal Cases Review Commission reassessed the case in 2016,[2] after the journalist John Penrose conducted a re-examination of the evidence as part of the documentary series Infamous, which aired on Netflix in March 2016.[3]

Contents [hide]

'There was a Netflix show about the case, wasn't there?' says Gis. 'Couple of years ago?'

I nod. Alex watched it, but I tuned out most of the time. Too much like hard work. Or actual work. But there are some things I remember, things I hadn't taken much notice of at the time. Like how mercilessly the Rowans were pursued after the verdict, and not just by the press. The abuse they suffered, the vandalism, and – far more important, given where we are now – the lengths all that finally pushed them to.

I glance up at Gis, and it's obvious from his face he's remembering the same thing.

'So what do you think – could the vic be another journo?'

And he's right to ask: it's by far the simplest explanation. The Rowans manhandled mountains to stay under the radar: they moved house, they changed their name, they obliterated their old lives. And now suddenly, all these years later, without warning, there's a ring on the bell one dark night and the whole ordeal starts up again. The idea that they'd take a gun to a random housebreaker strained everyone's credulity, including mine; taking a gun to someone who brought that nightmare back to their door? That's a theory that makes sense.

But it needs stress-testing, all the same.

I take a deep breath. 'Wouldn't a newspaper have reported one of their reporters missing by now?'

Hansen looks at Gis, and then at me. 'Could be a free-lance, looking to make a name for himself?'

'Well, let's just hope he's not about to manage it. For all the wrong reasons.'

Gis nods grimly. 'Careful what you wish for, eh?'

* * *

```
Channel:            Netflix
Programme:          Infamous, season 4
Number of episodes: 4
First shown:        09/03/2016
```

[THEME SONG - 'KARMA CHAMELEON' [CULTURE CLUB]]
TITLE OVER:
INFAMOUS

FADE IN

THE CHAMELEON GIRL

MONTAGE: shots of Camilla Rowan - as a baby, as a toddler, on a swing, with her parents in the garden, building a sandcastle, with her pet dog, on her pony, etc.

<u>VOICEOVER</u>

She was a little princess. An only child from a wealthy and high-profile family, and the apple of her father's eye. Smart, pretty, and popular, and so good at sport she played at county level. A responsible, kind-hearted girl who raised money for charity, and was trusted to babysit her neighbours' children. Everyone agreed: Camilla Rowan had a bright future ahead of her.

So what went wrong?

How did Camilla the beloved daughter, happy student, and school captain - a girl who, by all accounts, had never put a foot wrong - turn, seemingly overnight, into Milly Liar the murderer? Reviled in the press, screamed at in the street, and charged with killing her own child.

MONTAGE: clips relating to the trial - newspaper headlines, people holding banners and shouting outside the court, Camilla trying to escape the cameras, her hand in front of her face, her parents trying to fight their way through journalists outside their house, the words 'baby killer' daubed in red paint across a garage door, interspersed with vox pops/news broadcasts/clips from later interviews:

She deserved everything she got - anyone who
could do that to an innocent child. If you ask
me, in cases like that, life should mean life.

NEWS ITEM 1

There were dramatic scenes outside the Old Bailey
today, as Camilla Rowan appeared in the dock for
the first time. Protesters hurled abuse at the
23-year-old, who had arrived at court flanked by
her parents and defence barrister.

VOICE 2

Rowan was given a full psychiatric assessment
before her trial, and was deemed fit to plead. But
the full results of that assessment have never
been made public. Is she a sociopath? Is she a
narcissist? Or is she just a pathological liar?

VOICE 3

The Camilla I knew - she just couldn't have done
anything like that. Not her own baby. Not *any*
baby. I didn't believe it then and I don't
believe it now.

NEWS ITEM 2

After six sensational weeks the trial of Camilla
Rowan came to a shocking conclusion today, with
the former head girl being sentenced to life for
the murder of her newborn child.

VOICE 4

The reason why we're still so obsessed with this
case, even all these years later, is that it
challenges so many of our basic human beliefs -
about trust and truth, about our capacity for
cruelty, and the sanctity of maternal love. I
think we're all terrified that if we dared look
into the darkest corners of our own hearts we'd
find Camilla Rowan staring straight back at us.

*Cut to: John's office. Files, desk, photos and docs from the
case pinned on a board behind.*

JOHN PENROSE

I covered the Camilla Rowan case for the *Guardian*
back in 2003. I sat through every day of the

trial, and I watched her that whole time. And I had no more idea of who she was at the end than I did at the beginning. The verdict didn't come as a surprise, and at the time I definitely didn't think there'd been any great miscarriage of justice. But there were still things that bugged me. Questions that neither the prosecution nor defence had managed to answer. So after I filed my last report I thought I'd spend a few days seeing what I could find. Thirteen years later, I'm still doing it.

Because this is the sort of case that, as a journalist, you only encounter once in a lifetime. It raises question after question after question, and yet the one person who could give us some answers still steadfastly refuses to do so. We all know she lied, but that doesn't mean she lied about everything. Are there scraps of truth hidden in the bizarre and deeply disturbing story she told the police, and has never since deviated from? If there are, she's not telling. But the truth, as they say, is out there. And to find it, I needed to understand not just the woman she became, but the girl she was before.

TITLE APPEARS OVER, TYPEWRITER STYLE:

Part one

"And you used to be so sweet"

Panoramic drone shot over Gloucestershire countryside. Summer sunlight. A village with a church, stone houses, a river winding through.

VOICEOVER - JOHN PENROSE

It all started here, in the small country town of Shiphampton, deep in the heart of the Cotswolds, one of the most beautiful and prosperous areas of the UK. Camilla was born in nearby Princess Alice Hospital, Gloucester, in 1980, by which time her parents, Dick and Peggy, had been married for seven years and almost given up having a child. Right from the start, she was their miracle baby, indulged and doted on, and given every advantage money could buy, including a pony, music lessons, and a private ballet teacher.

RECONSTRUCTION of little girl doing ballet movements.

When she was six, the Rowans entered a nationwide competition to find a little girl to front a new TV advertising campaign for My Little Pony. There were over 5,000 entries, and Camilla made it through to a shortlist of six. This is her screentest.

CLIP of Camilla Rowan in close-up, sitting at a table stroking a My Little Pony toy and smiling. She has her hair in bunches and is wearing a pink dress with a lace bodice and puff sleeves. She has a gap in her front teeth.

CAMILLA

I just *love* My Little Pony, and your little girl will too.

VOICEOVER – JOHN PENROSE

She didn't get the gig.

Various shots of John on the phone, putting it down, leaving messages asking for a call back.

VOICEOVER – JOHN PENROSE

I contacted the Rowans a number of times through their lawyers while we were making this documentary, hoping they'd agree to take part, but they've refused to speak to anyone from the press ever since an incident a few weeks after the trial, when a journalist claimed Dick Rowan threatened him with a gun. The allegation was never substantiated and no charges were ever brought, but the extensive coverage of the incident provoked a fresh backlash against the family, along with threats of violence from certain quarters. So it's perhaps understandable that the Rowans have tried to keep a low profile ever since. None of their other family members were willing to speak on camera either, probably for the same reason, but there was one person we were able to talk to: Sheila Ward, who worked for Dick Rowan for more than 20 years, and had a lot of contact with the family when Camilla was growing up.

Cut to: sitting room, gas fire, Border terrier on sofa, potted plants, etc.

TITLE OVER: Sheila Ward, Dick Rowan's secretary, 1971–1996

SHEILA WARD

I knew Dick back when he was still just a builder. In the early days, when he'd just started out on his own and they were living in a semi in Gloucester. Back then he'd roll his sleeves up and plumb in a bathroom himself if he had to. But then he started to make money, and went into 'property' and they bought the house in Shiphampton. By the time Camilla came along they were moving in very different circles. I didn't see them socially much after that. I'd babysit, but I didn't get invited to many of their parties. Dick was a local councillor by then, and

treasurer of the Shiphampton Rotary Club, and
Peggy was doing a lot of charity work, and things
for the school. She was always very much the
power behind the throne.

JOHN'S VOICE (off)

Were they good parents?

SHEILA WARD

Depends what you mean by good. They were quite
strict. Peggy kept a big chart in the kitchen,
showing what chores Camilla had done, and
whether she'd got good marks at school or kept
her room tidy. It had gold stars stuck to it and
if she didn't get enough stars by Friday her
pocket money would be docked or she wouldn't be
able to have ice cream. And there was another
big chart with her schedule. Brownies, ballet,
swimming, piano. There were set times for
everything. Of course when she was little
Camilla didn't mind – she just wanted to please
them. She always wanted to please them.
Especially her mother.

JOHN'S VOICE (off)

What about as she got older?

SHEILA WARD

Oh, she still wanted to please them, so she kept
to the rules. She just got cleverer about how she
did it.

JOHN'S VOICE (off)

And boyfriends – did the Rowans have rules about
that?

SHEILA WARD

(*laughs*)

Oh yes – there were a *lot* of rules about that. Who
she saw, where they went, what time they got back.
But like I said, by that time Camilla had got a
lot cleverer at bending them. And of course, they
had no idea what she got up to at that school.

*RECONSTRUCTION, soft-focus: girls playing hockey on sunlit
playing field with Victorian buildings behind, girls walking*

*in a crocodile wearing uniforms and straw hats, girls singing
in a chapel choir, etc.*

VOICEOVER

Burghley Abbey in Warwickshire is one of the most
prestigious girls' schools in England. Founded in
the 19th century, it boasts celebrities and minor
royals among its old girls. It's very sporty,
very musical, and very, very expensive.

*Cut to: sitting room, evening. Lamps lit, fire in background,
bookcases, oil painting on wall.*

*TITLE OVER: Marion Teesdale, Housemistress, Burghley Abbey
School, 1986-2014*

MARION TEESDALE

I sat in on Camilla's admissions interview before
she came to Burghley and I remember how confident
she was, even at that age. She'd only have been
around seven at the time, but she was very
articulate, and very comfortable talking to
adults. It was obvious that her parents had
coached her – every time she answered a question
she looked across at her mother for approval. Her
father didn't say a great deal – I got the
impression he was quite reserved. Camilla started
the following September as a day girl. It was a
thirty-mile round trip to drop her off and collect
her every day, and there was Saturday-morning
school as well, but her mother insisted that she
was too young to be living away from home.

JOHN'S VOICE (off)

Aren't the fees cheaper for day pupils as well?

MARION TEESDALE

Yes, of course, but Mrs Rowan made a point of
saying that that wasn't the reason.

*MONTAGE: sequence of images taking Camilla from junior to
senior school, her face being circled each time in red pen.
School photographs, sports team photos, on field trips, on a
French exchange, etc. Last photo, of a hockey team, shows
Camilla with her friends Melissa Rutherford and Leonora
Staniforth.*

*Cut to: kitchen. Aga, hanging rack of copper pans, kids'
drawings stuck on the fridge, view of countryside from the
window.*

*TITLE OVER: Leonora Neville, née Staniforth, Camilla's school
friend*

Cam, Melissa and me were best friends right from
our first or second week at school. They sat us
alphabetically in the first year so we were all in
a line together and that's pretty much how it
stayed. Then Cam said we should call ourselves
the chameleon girls, you know, from Cam-Mel-
Leon – she was always really clever about things
like that – and the name just stuck, especially
with that Culture Club song.

*Intercut: footage of the three girls wearing T-shirts with
chameleons on, and their names printed below. They're
singing, rather raucously, lines from 'Karma Chameleon':
"Didn't hear your wicked words every day / And you used to
be so sweet I heard you say".*

And it was sort of fitting that Cam's name came
first – she was always the leader, always out in
front. She just had that sort of personality.
Everyone wanted to be in her gang. Not that we
had gangs at Burghley Abbey – way too common –
but you know what I mean. And Cam was the only
one in our year who had a swimming pool. Mel
lived in Shiphampton too and I was only three or
four miles away so I'd bike over and we'd spend
hours round the pool in the summer, just hanging
out. And her parents were always very welcoming.
I think they were concerned about her having lots
of friends because she was an only child.

JOHN'S VOICE (off)

You called her Cam just then. Did you always call
her that?

LEONORA STANIFORTH

Oh yes – that's what everyone called her, except
her mother. That whole 'Milly' thing – the papers
completely made it up. We kept telling them no
one ever used that name, but they didn't take any
notice. They were just desperate to write a
headline saying 'Milly Liar'.

*Cut to: office. A big sleek desk, shelves of legal books and
framed certificates on the walls, views of the City skyline
outside.*

TITLE OVER: Melissa Rutherford, Camilla's school friend

MELISSA RUTHERFORD

It was only after I left that I realised what an
inward-looking place Shiphampton was. It was a
real goldfish bowl – everyone knew everyone else's

business. I suppose that's one reason why the whole Cam thing was such a bombshell. No one saw it coming, and they couldn't believe something like that had been going on right under their noses and no one knew. And then there was the trial, and there were journalists crawling all over the place and people just closed ranks. They always call places 'close-knit' after something terrible happens, don't they? I guess that's why. I never thought of that before.

JOHN'S VOICE (off)

So it was the sort of place where appearances mattered?

MELISSA RUTHERFORD

God, yes. All those twitching curtains and bitchy gossip dressed up as concern. There was a hell of a lot of keeping up with the Joneses. The Rowans really felt that, you could tell. I mean, there was no question that they were wealthy, but Dick Rowan was a self-made man, and some people were a bit sniffy about that, even in the 1990s. That's why they had such high expectations for Cam – not so much academically but socially. It sounds like something out of Jane Austen, I know, but I got the impression there was definitely pressure for her to 'marry well'.

(*pause*)

She had a lot to live up to. Seriously. I didn't envy her.

JOHN'S VOICE (off)

Did you know? About the pregnancies?

MELISSA RUTHERFORD

She never told me. She never said a word about any of it.

Cut to: Leonora

JOHN'S VOICE (off)

Did you know?

LEONORA STANIFORTH

No, I didn't know.

Cut to: Marion Teesdale

JOHN'S VOICE (off)

Did you know?

MARION TEESDALE

No. No one at the school knew.

JOHN'S VOICE (off)

You understand why people find that hard to
believe?

MARION TEESDALE

Of course I understand. But that doesn't alter
the facts. And you need to remember she was a day
girl. There wasn't the same degree of proximity
that there was with the boarders.

Clip of hockey match (actual footage).

VOICEOVER - JOHN PENROSE

But it's hard to comprehend, all the same. And
you only need to look at this clip to see why.
This footage shows the 1997 UK national under-18s
hockey championships. After three days of
play-offs, during which the teams have all shared
changing facilities and dorm rooms, Burghley
Abbey are in the closing moments of a hard-fought
semi-final against Cheltenham Ladies College.
Camilla has already been instrumental in creating
one goal, and is about to score the clincher.
Watch.

*Camilla scores, her team and coaches gather round her,
hugging her and celebrating. Freeze frame and gradual
close-up.*

VOICEOVER - JOHN PENROSE

They called her a chameleon girl, little knowing
how horribly apt that nickname would prove to be.
Camilla Rowan turned out to be more of a chameleon
than anyone around her could have possibly
suspected. Because the girl at the centre of this
picture is nine months pregnant. She has had no
scans, seen no midwife, not even visited her own
GP. But in less than 48 hours she will go into
labour and present herself at the maternity suite
of Birmingham and Solihull General Hospital, where
she will have a healthy baby boy in the early
hours of the following morning.

Later that same day, at around three o'clock in the afternoon, and without the knowledge of medical staff, she will leave the hospital, driving the car her parents bought her for her 17th birthday, and return home to Shiphampton, where she will arrive, alone, at just gone six o'clock, in plenty of time to attend a Christmas party at the local Rotary Club that evening. Indeed, it seems likely that her early departure from the hospital was dictated by the need to make sure she was at that party, so as to avoid raising suspicions with her parents.

MONTAGE: shots of Camilla at the party, dancing with her friends, smiling, drinking champagne, standing next to her father and his friends. She's wearing a close-fitting sleeveless pale-blue dress draped with tinsel and a paper hat out of a cracker. There is nothing about her appearance that suggests she has just given birth.

She looks completely carefree, doesn't she? And yet at some point that afternoon, Camilla Rowan did something to her newborn baby. If you believe the police, she killed that child and disposed of its body; if you believe Camilla, she handed it over to its biological father, a man no one has ever been able to identify with any degree of certainty.

What we *do* know, is that whatever happened to that baby happened very quickly. The drive from Birmingham to Shiphampton would have taken at least an hour and a half, leaving barely half an hour for the handover – or murder – to take place.

So did Camilla Rowan really give the baby to its father? Most young men would run a mile at the prospect of raising a baby single-handed. So it's hard to believe, but not – of course – impossible. But if that's really what happened, why has he not come forward? Why has he not produced the child and saved Camilla from a life sentence?

Or did Camilla kill her baby that day, as the police and Crown Prosecution Service still contend? It might be worth noting in this context that a week after these pictures were taken Camilla Rowan had a tattoo done on her left shoulder. It said 'Dolce liberta', which is Italian for 'Sweet freedom'. Is that a clue? Did she decide that, at 17, she just wasn't ready to be a mother? Anyone could understand that, and most people would sympathise. Or was she terrified of having to tell her parents? Again, no one would blame her for that, especially given what we know of the family dynamic. But if that's what happened, why didn't she just give the child up

```
    for adoption? After all, she must have realised
    that was an option. Indeed, we know for a fact
    that she knew all about it.

    Because she'd already done it once before.

                - freeze frame -
```

*   *   *

I've just been watching Infamous – can't believe I never saw it when it first came out. Is it true they still haven't found the body?

submitted 8 days ago by HickoryDickory77

9 comments share hide report

> Yeah great series isn't it? And no – the baby's never been found. At least it hadn't the last time I looked at any of the boards and in any case something like that would deffo have made the papers
>
> submitted 6 days ago by Danny929292
>
> share hide report

> The Rowans were lucky there was no Twitter back then. I mean, the bloody shit they'd have got
>
> submitted 5 days ago by santaclaws77
>
> share hide report

>> They get enough now – try searching #MillyLiar and see what spews out. Just disgusting. Not that I imagine the family look at that garbage. I certainly wouldn't. It's all just trolls churning out abuse when they know sod all about any of it. Let's face it, *all* families have secrets, and *everybody* lies.
>>
>> submitted 4 days ago by Ifyouvenothingnicetosayzipit
>>
>> share hide report

>>> You think the parents were in on it? They helped her cover it up?
>>>
>>> submitted 3 days ago by cabaretrenee008
>>>
>>> share hide report

87

No, all I meant was that if the press crawled over *anyone's*
life they'd find some dirty washing somewhere, that's all.
I don't think the Rowans had the first clue

↪ submitted 3 days ago by Ifyouvenothingnicetosayzipit

share hide report

Wasn't there some vandalism too, back in the day? I seem to
remember pics in the press of graffiti on their house

↪ submitted 4 hours ago by cabaretrenee008

share hide report

AND some sick shits who pretended to have the baby and
demanded £££. How low can u get

↪ submitted 4 hours ago by cabaretrenee008

share hide report

I don't think the parents knew anything about it. What
happened to that baby was down to Camilla and Camilla alone.
Don't be fooled by her little girl lost act. That's all it is – an act.
She deserved everything she got and right now, she's exactly
where she needs to be.

↪ submitted 2 hours ago by AllieCatz76

share hide report

*　*　*

Adam Fawley
23 October
10.35

'So what do you want us to do?' says Gis. 'Start calling
some of the papers?'

It's the obvious thing to do, but in this case 'obvious'
doesn't mean 'simple'. The mere mention of Camilla Rowan's name will be like stirring up a swarm. The Rowans will
be kissing goodbye to their hard-won anonymity for a start,
and it'll just get worse from there. But what choice do I have?

88

'My other half has a mate at the *Express*,' begins Hansen tentatively. 'I could get him to ask if she's picked up anything on the grapevine.'

I didn't realize Hansen was gay, but it figures somehow. 'You've met her – the mate? Would you trust her?'

He thinks before he answers; I've noticed him doing it before; it's a good sign. 'Yes,' he says eventually, 'I think I would.'

'OK, in that case go ahead. And can you also do a trawl for any recent online interest in Camilla Rowan, especially on places like Reddit – hacks often put out feelers in true-crime chat rooms if they're on this sort of story.' Hansen nods and starts making notes.

'And in the meantime, I'll chase Challow on the DNA.'

Hansen looks up and frowns. 'That's a bit of a long shot, though, isn't it, sir? I mean, I doubt he's in the National Database, not if he's just some journo.'

I start dialling. 'I'm not disagreeing. But we don't know that's what he is yet, do we? Not for sure. And I'm afraid there were plenty of other people who hounded the Rowans. People even further down the food chain than the press.'

Gis nods towards Hansen. 'And trust me, some of those bastards will *definitely* be in the system.'

* * *

'Won't it look a bit odd, me ringing her up out of the blue and asking about this stuff?'

Jack's at college, Hansen can hear voices in the background. Laughter, some sort of tinny music.

'I was thinking about that – could you tell her you want to use it as a case study in a course you're teaching? I don't know, something about how the media report crimes against children?'

Jack laughs drily. 'Or the female psychopath in popular culture, that's always a slam-dunk crowd-pleaser.'

'There you are, I knew you'd think of something.'

There's a pause, then, 'So did you mention me? To the great god Fawley?'

'I did, actually.'

A quick laugh. 'Yeah, but I bet it was just as your "other half" or something equally coy.'

'Well, he knows you're male, if that's what you're asking. And he didn't bat an eyelid.'

Another laugh, warmer this time. 'Ha, told you you've been worrying about nothing.'

Hansen smiles to himself; he wasn't worrying at all, despite what Jack kept on saying. He knew Fawley wouldn't give a toss.

'So you'll do it? Call Zoe?'

A theatrical sigh, but Jack's milking it now, and they both know it. 'OK, if it'll get you some brownie points with the boss. When do you need it by?'

'Like, yesterday. There's a lot of pressure on this one.'

'Yeah, right. Tell me something I didn't know.'

*   *   *

Voicemail

Alan Challow

Mobile

Transcription

Just had the DNA back on the Gantry Manor vic. Without wishing to sound unduly dramatic, this is going to blow the bloody doors off. Can you drop by ASAP?

❚❚ 0.25 ——————————|——————————— -0.09

Speaker   Call back   Delete

* * *

DNA-17 Familial Match Report

Report Generated on:	23/10/2018		Doc Ref:	CAK/231164
Report Generated by:	Cleo Field		Issue:	v1.0

The DNA-17 profile obtained from the deceased (Sample 1) was searched on the DNA Database with a negative result. An amendment to the search parameters generated a close familial match with a different sample held on the DNA Database (Sample 2).

Locus	Index	Sample 1 — Sample ID: EG2508/18J Genotype		Sample 2 — Sample ID: A1667GHD Genotype	
vWA	2.565	15	**17**	16	**17**
TH01	6.389	9	**9.3**	8	**9.3**
D8S1179	35.984	**13**	16	**13**	
FGA	3.951	23	**24**	**24**	25
D21S11	9.236	**29**	32.2	27.2	**29**

D18S51	1.002	**12**	14	11	**12**
D2S1338	13.419	17	**19**	19	
D16S539	1.244	**14**		14	15
D19S433	7.807	14	**15**	11	**15**
D3S1358	1.785	**14**	16	13	**14**
D1S1656	3.873	11	**18.3**	15	**18.3**
D2S441	1.996	8	**12**	12	16
D10S1248	3.971	15		14	**15**
D12S391	2.550	**18**	23	18	
D22S1045	2.141	11	**14**	14	17
SE33	3.792	28.2	**29.2**	26.2	**29.2**
Amelogenin	N/A	X	Y	X	

Interpretation

Combined Index: 3,187,200,590

Having applied an established statistical methodology to the above STR loci, the Probability of Maternity is calculated to be 99.99999999%.

I certify that these results are an accurate and true interpretation of the raw data obtained from the samples stated above. The results contained in this report have been obtained in accordance with the Forensic Science Regulator's Codes of Practice following an approved and validated scientific method as documented in our ISO/IEC 17025:2017 Schedule of Accreditation.

Lead Scientist: *Dr James England*

*   *   *

Adam Fawley
23 October
15.56

'What am I looking at?'

I glance up at Challow. He's frowning, tapping his pen

against the desk. I've known him a long time, and his standard operating procedure is email. He doesn't call, and he certainly doesn't invite you round – in fact, I'm not even sure I can remember the last time I was in here. Or the last time he didn't greet me with a snippy remark.

'I mean, I know it's the DNA report, I just don't know what it's telling me.'

'It's telling you there's a match in the system. A text-book parental match.'

'Well, that's a result, isn't it? Means we know who he is.'

Challow's frown deepens. 'It's not as simple as that. Not by a long way.'

I point to the reference number in the second column. 'So this is the father? SampleA1667GHD?'

He takes a breath. 'Keep reading. It's not the father. It's the mother. Your mystery victim is Camilla Rowan's son.'

*   *   *

```
Channel:              Netflix
Programme:            Infamous, season 4
Number of episodes:   4
First shown:          09/03/2016


[THEME SONG -'KARMA CHAMELEON' [CULTURE CLUB]]
TITLE OVER:
                        INFAMOUS
FADE IN
                    THE CHAMELEON GIRL

MONTAGE: shots of Camilla Rowan at the Old Bailey trial,
interspersed with newspaper headlines - 'Milly Liar: "I did
not kill my baby"', 'What really happened to baby Rowan?',
'Child-killer to serve life'.

                VOICEOVER - JOHN PENROSE

    In the last episode, we looked at Camilla Rowan's
    childhood. At her privileged upbringing, her
    attentive parents, her expensive school. We spoke
```

to her friends, her teachers, people who knew
her, all in a quest for clues as to how this
golden girl with a fabulous life ahead of her
ended up in the dock of the Old Bailey, her only
future the four walls of a prison cell.

But there was nothing – nothing in her
surroundings, her relationships or her experiences –
that could possibly explain the mystery of the
chameleon girl. But perhaps we were simply looking
in the wrong place. Perhaps the answer lies much
closer to home. In Camilla Rowan herself.

TITLE APPEARS OVER, TYPEWRITER STYLE:

Part two

"If I listened to your lies"

*Shot of Birmingham and Solihull General Hospital, entrance to
the maternity suite. Nurses going in and out, mothers
carrying babies, etc.*

VOICEOVER

As we discovered in the previous episode, this is
where Camilla Rowan gave birth to a full-term
baby boy on 23rd December 1997. A baby no one
knew she was carrying, who would leave in her
arms later that same day, never to be seen again.

*RECONSTRUCTION of young woman with baby in hospital bed.
Baby's face not visible.*

But this wasn't the first time Camilla had visited
a maternity unit. She'd already given birth in
another Birmingham hospital not much more than a
year before. She'd already had another child.

VOICEOVER – JOHN PENROSE

The Senior Investigating Officer on the Camilla
Rowan case was DI Howard Lucas, who died in 2013.
His second-in-command was Detective Sergeant
Lawrence Kearney, now a DCI, who gave some of the
most powerful testimony in the Old Bailey trial.

*Cut to: close-up of LK sitting at desk with large sign behind
saying 'South Mercia Police: Protecting People Through
Professional Policing'.*

*TITLE OVER: DCI Lawrence Kearney, investigator on the
Camilla Rowan case, 2002-2003*

LAWRENCE KEARNEY

On Saturday 9th November 1996 Camilla Rowan
presented herself at the front desk of West

Bromwich Women's Hospital. She gave her address
as 13 Warnock Road, Cambridge, and said she had
unexpectedly gone into labour two weeks before
her due date, while visiting friends in Dudley.
However, nurses noted that she had none of those
friends with her. A few hours later she gave
birth to a healthy baby boy.

<u>VOICEOVER</u>

Adrian Morrison was overseeing the unit that
night, and subsequently testified at Rowan's
trial.

Cut to: doctor's office, desk, window behind.

*TITLE OVER: Adrian Morrison, Senior Obstetric Registrar, West
Bromwich Women's Hospital, Birmingham NHS Foundation Trust,
1992-2015*

<u>ADRIAN MORRISON</u>

It was in every respect a normal, straightforward
delivery. The mother was obviously very young,
but clearly fit and well and the baby was likewise
completely healthy. We weren't able to access
other Trusts' computer records at that time, and
it being a weekend I wouldn't have been able to
contact her GP very easily either. But in any
case there was no immediate need. The baby was
doing well, and she said she was returning to her
partner in Cambridge and would pick up with her
GP and midwife as soon as she got home. I had no
reason to doubt the truth of what she said, so I
was quite happy to discharge them both on the
Monday morning.

<u>JOHN'S VOICE</u> (off)

Did you hear from her again?

<u>ADRIAN MORRISON</u>

No.

<u>JOHN'S VOICE</u> (off)

What about the GP she listed on her admissions
form?

<u>ADRIAN MORRISON</u>

I only discovered some months later that that
practice did not exist.

Was there anything else about the baby that, in the light of subsequent events, you now consider could be significant?

ADRIAN MORRISON

(*hesitates*)

Possibly. The child was clearly mixed race.

Cut to: RECONSTRUCTION of young woman in hospital bed. Baby's face now visible and clearly of mixed-race parentage.

VOICEOVER - JOHN PENROSE

So much has changed since the turn of the century that it's hard to remember that having a baby outside wedlock was social suicide in some circles, or that a mixed-race child could be something to be ashamed of. Times have changed, and decidedly for the better. But back in the nineties, attitudes weren't always so enlightened, and especially not in wealthy middle-class rural communities like Shiphampton, which were almost exclusively white.

Cut to: sitting room

TITLE OVER: Marion Teesdale, Housemistress, Burghley Abbey School, 1986-2014

MARION TEESDALE

I don't remember any girls leaving the school because they were pregnant. Some left at sixteen, of course, so I can't vouch for what happened to them thereafter, but we ensured every pupil received comprehensive sex education lessons in the fourth form, so all our girls were fully informed about both pregnancy and birth control.

Cut to: kitchen

TITLE OVER: Leonora Staniforth, Camilla's school friend

LEONORA STANIFORTH

I don't know about 'comprehensive' - it was all a bit sketchy from what I remember. It didn't help that the teacher doing the class was Miss Thorpe, who was about a hundred and five and didn't look like she'd ever actually done the deed. We were all just excruciatingly embarrassed throughout the entire thing - more for her, probably, than for ourselves. I definitely remember her showing us how to use a condom by sticking it on a test tube. Someone at the back fainted. Actually *fainted*. I mean, imagine that happening now.

Cut to: City office

TITLE OVER: Melissa Rutherford, Camilla's school friend

<u>MELISSA RUTHERFORD</u>

I learned more from other girls than I did from school – I imagine most kids do. But if you're asking about attitudes to teenage pregnancy in a place like Shiphampton back then, then yes, there was a definite social stigma attached to anything like that. Girls who 'slept around' were looked down on as 'cheap' and 'common'. As for getting pregnant, that was the ultimate no-no – I think my parents would have literally thrown me out of the house. I can only imagine what Camilla's mother would have done if she'd known.

<u>JOHN'S VOICE</u> (off)

And if the baby turned out to be mixed race?

<u>MELISSA RUTHERFORD</u>

Oh my God, it doesn't bear thinking about. The sky would have fallen in.

Cut to: panoramic drone shot over Shiphampton.

<u>VOICEOVER – JOHN PENROSE</u>

With this in mind, it's not hard to see why Camilla chose to conceal her first pregnancy, even – or perhaps especially – from her own mother. But she was intelligent and well-informed, she had means and more independence than most young people her age. So why didn't she take steps to prevent the pregnancy in the first place? Or arrange for a termination as soon as she realised what had happened, if not with her own GP, then at one of the many clinics offering confidential abortion services? Camilla Rowan has been asked those questions many times, both before and after her conviction, but no one – as far as I know – has got an answer. None that make sense, anyway.

Cut to: shot of West Bromwich Women's Hospital, entrance to the maternity suite.

<u>VOICEOVER – JOHN PENROSE</u>

All we do know for sure is that Camilla Rowan did none of those things. Instead she carried that first baby to term and, as we've heard, gave birth here in early November 1996. But contrary to what she told Dr Morrison, she did not return to Cambridge with her son. She didn't even live in Cambridge, and there is no such address as 13 Warnock Road in that town. No, what she actually did was go straight to an adoption agency only a few hundred yards from the hospital.

Cut to: reception area, water cooler, sofas, posters of children, etc.

TITLE OVER: Yasmin Njoku, CEO, Central Midlands Adoption and Fostering, 1995-2002

YASMIN NJOKU

It's fair to say that's not the usual way we received children.

JOHN'S VOICE (off)

She just turned up with the baby?

YASMIN NJOKU

We had to arrange emergency fostering that day. It was clear she was in no position to look after the child.

JOHN'S VOICE (off)

Do you mean practically, or some other way?

YASMIN NJOKU

Primarily emotionally. When my member of staff tried to say that it would be very difficult to receive the baby there and then she became almost hysterical.

JOHN'S VOICE (off)

So if you hadn't taken the baby - or if there hadn't been an agency like you so close to hand - do you think the child might have been at risk of harm?

YASMIN NJOKU

(*pause*)

Let's just say it wasn't a chance we were prepared to take.

Perhaps Camilla herself feared what she might do
to the child. Perhaps that's why she decided that
adoption was the only way. Because, whatever her
motives, on this occasion Camilla Rowan 'did the
right thing'. Even if the way she went about it
was bizarre in the extreme.

*MONTAGE: sequence of images of Camilla Rowan's adoption
paperwork; as John mentions specific elements these are
underlined on screen and annotated one at a time with
'False', 'Lie', 'Does not exist'.*

Because as the prosecution case later made
abundantly clear, the paperwork Rowan filled out
for the adoption agency - both that day and
later - was a litany of lies. She gave her real
name, but pretty much everything else was a
fabrication. She said again that she lived at the
Warnock Road address, which we already know was a
lie: in fact 'Warnock' - as a sharp-eyed police
officer later spotted - is just an anagram of
'C. K. Rowan'. She gave the same GP details she'd
given the hospital - another lie. The email
address she supplied didn't exist. There were
almost a dozen lies in all. And a mobile number
that always went straight to voicemail. Hardly
surprising, then, that the adoption service
struggled to contact her in the weeks that
followed.

Cut to: reception area interior

YASMIN NJOKU

We tried again and again by phone and in writing,
but only ever managed to contact her once. That
was when the baby was six weeks old and she had
to come in to sign the final papers.

JOHN'S VOICE (off)

Did you see her that day?

YASMIN NJOKU

No, I wasn't in the office, but the colleague
who did said she was in and out in five minutes.
Apparently she said she 'just wanted to get it
over with'.

JOHN'S VOICE (off)

Did he ask her about the false information she'd
given?

YASMIN NJOKU

I think he tried but she kept saying she had
somewhere else she needed to be. And it was
during lunch-hour and quite busy, and there
weren't many staff available. It's possible
she came in then deliberately - to reduce
the likelihood of being asked too many
questions.

JOHN'S VOICE (off)

And what happened to the baby?

YASMIN NJOKU

He was successfully placed in a loving family.

JOHN'S VOICE (off)

His identity was protected during the court case,
but are you aware whether he knows who his
biological mother is?

YASMIN NJOKU

Like all adopted children he would have had the
right to see his records when he reached the age
of eighteen. I don't know if he has done so, and
I wouldn't be able to disclose that information
even if I did.

Cut to: montage of shots of Camilla - playing hockey, with
Leonora and Melissa, at a fireworks party.

VOICEOVER - JOHN PENROSE

When these pictures were taken, Camilla Rowan was
pregnant with that baby boy. Four months, seven
months, eight and a half months. And yet no one
apparently noticed a thing.

TITLE OVER: Leonora Staniforth

LEONORA STANIFORTH

(looking at the pictures)

Well that last one is in the winter, right? So
we'd all have been in jumpers and coats and it
wouldn't have been so obvious. But yes, I know
what you're getting at. I think we were all a bit
naïve at that age, but I can't believe her mother
or the teachers didn't notice anything.

JOHN'S VOICE (off)

Did you know she had a boyfriend?

LEONORA STANIFORTH

No. And I think she'd have told us. Mel, anyway,
even if not me. Those two were always really
really tight, especially around then.

JOHN'S VOICE (off)

So you have no idea who the father was?

LEONORA STANIFORTH

(*shakes her head*)

None at all. I don't think there was a single
black family in Shiphampton back then. I guess
she could have met him in Birmingham or
something, but I've been racking my brains and I
just can't remember her ever going there
without either me or Mel. It's just a complete
mystery.

Cut to: *montage of shots of Camilla Rowan during the trial –
leaving the court, head down, with her mother, with her legal
team.*

VOICEOVER – JOHN PENROSE

And it's just one of the many mysteries that
still haunt this case. One thing we *do* know is
that – for whatever reason – the father of that
baby has never come forward. His identity remains
shrouded in secrecy, just like that of the man
who fathered Rowan's second child, scarcely a
year later. But that second baby was *not* taken in
by a loving family. He was last seen alive at
only a few hours old, in his mother's arms, in a
hospital car park.

Another mystery, more deceit, more chameleon
camouflage. Because as we all now know, when it
came to telling lies, Camilla Rowan had barely
even got started . . .

– *freeze frame* –

*   *   *

'Holy fuck.'

Classic Quinn. But he has a point.

Gis is still looking at me blankly. 'Camilla's *kid*? What the –'

Quinn turns to me. 'How old does Challow reckon the vic was?'

Good question.

'Probably no more than twenty-one. And certainly no younger than fifteen. Something to do with the pubic bone.'

Quinn's obviously doing the calculations. 'So whoever the fuck he is, he had to have been born between 1997 and 2003?'

Gis glances across at him. 'Well, Rowan was either under investigation, on trial or in the slammer from the summer of 2002 onwards, so that narrows it down a bit.'

Quinn looks at me. 'Wasn't there another kid – aside from the mixed-race one? Isn't that how the police got involved in the first place?'

I nod. 'I'm having the full case file sent over, but yes, there was another baby, but that was a girl. Born in 2002.'

Quinn grabs a bit of paper and starts doing the math. 'So that leaves us about three and a half years between her killing that kid in 1997 and getting pregnant with the daughter in 2001.' He looks up. 'Could she really have had yet *another* brat in that time – yet another pregnancy no one noticed, and the original investigation never found?'

There's a silence.

'There is another possibility,' says Gis quietly. He knows it, Quinn knows it, I know it.

Quinn lets out a low whistle and starts shaking his head. 'Jesus.'

Gis nods. 'Looks like that kid didn't die in 1997, after all. He died last weekend, at Wytham. When his grandaddy shot him.'

*　　*　　*

Adam Fawley
24 October
08.27

'Jesus, Adam, you're only just back from paternity leave. You're supposed to be taking it easy. Not having another run-up at the crime of the century. And another force's crime, at that.'

I think he's trying to be funny. 'Trying' being the word – in every sense.

'I know, sir, but there's not much I can do about that. We hardly went looking for it.'

Superintendent Harrison sits back and steeples his fingers. 'How confident are you that this really is the child she was convicted of killing? I don't want us digging all this up again on a hunch.'

'I'm not one hundred per cent sure, sir, but it's a very strong possibility. Mainly because I doubt there could have been another child of the right age that the original investigation didn't find.'

'So where does that leave us with the Swanns? Do you think they knew who he was?'

'Well, he must have known who *they* were – what was he doing there otherwise? We don't know how he found them – and clearly we don't know where he's been all these years either – but I find it hard to believe he didn't tell them who he was when he arrived. Surely it'd be the first thing you'd say?'

Harrison is nodding slowly. 'And yet he ends up dead.'

'I know. I'm struggling to join the dots on that one too. All we do know is that for some reason the Swanns never called 999, and by the time we got there the body had been stripped of anything that could identify him.'

He eyes me for a moment. 'Do you think he turned up unannounced? Or did they know he was coming?'

He's asking me if this could have been premeditated.

And the answer is, 'It has to be possible, sir.'

He looks sceptical. 'You really think a couple of pensioners could have planned something like that? Because it strikes me as a spectacularly reckless way to kill someone and expect to get away with it.'

'But take away the witness, sir, and it's a whole different story. That was pure chance – if that photographer hadn't been up at that precise place that night no one would even have known. The Swanns could have got rid of the body, cleaned up the house, carried on as if nothing had happened. But as soon as they got that message saying the police were on their way they only had one option – to do everything they possibly could to make it look like a burglary. Including the rather amateurish attempt to make the door look as if it had been forced.'

He gives me a heavy look. 'But all that assumes they knew your man hadn't told anyone where he was going that night.'

'I agree. But we won't know the truth about that until we find out who he was. One of the few things in our favour is that we now have a DNA sample, which may allow us to identify the father – that was never an option in the original investigation.'

'You're on that?'

'Yes, sir. DC Baxter's picking that up.'

'Nothing useful on the Twitter appeal?'

I shake my head. 'Not yet, sir.'

'A bit odd, isn't it? Don't we usually get a pretty good response to something like that?'

'Yes, but we're usually trying to ID criminals who live locally, and we're pretty sure this man came up from London. Most of our Twitter followers are in the Oxford area.'

'Should we try the press, then? The nationals?'

'I doubt we'd get much up-take. Not as it stands – not without letting on who we think he is.'

Harrison is nodding. 'And that's the *last* thing we want to do at this point.'

'Exactly.'

Harrison sits back, thoughtful now. 'What I'm still struggling with is why the Swanns would want to kill him at all, when he's living proof their daughter isn't a murderer. Don't they want her exonerated?'

'I know, sir. On the face of it, that makes it much more likely the shooting was some sort of accident.'

'What, Swann blew his grandson's head off and only

found out afterwards what he'd done? Sounds like something out of Thomas Hardy.'

I didn't have Harrison down as much of a reader. Just shows you.

I shrug. 'It's no more far-fetched than any of the other scenarios. Rather less so, in fact.'

He leans back, making the chair creak. 'But whichever way you play it, it's going to be a bloody minefield. If he really is Camilla Rowan's missing baby, she's been locked up all these years for a crime that never even happened.'

I smile grimly. 'Hornets' nest, can of worms, dog's breakfast. Take your pick. And that's *before* the press find out.'

He frowns. 'Who else knows?'

'As at now, just my own team. And Alan Challow.'

'Well, let's keep it at that. At least until we're sure. In the meantime, I'll give the Chief Constable the heads-up. And keep me in the loop on an ongoing basis.'

Three bullshit bingo hits in one sentence – that's good going, even for him.

I cover my smile by getting to my feet. 'Thank you, sir. I'll certainly do that.'

* * *

'So you want me to see if we can ID the father through familial DNA?' Nina Mukerjee frowns. 'You know that won't be cheap, right? Is Fawley OK with that?'

Baxter nods. 'Yeah, don't worry, he's signed off.'

'OK, then I'll get started this afternoon. I'll put the dead man's profile into the National DNA Database and see what potential family members come up. Though just so you're prepared, there'll be a huge number of possible matches, all of them very distantly related and most of them dead ends, so don't hold your breath. And the computer stuff is just the start – there'll be a hell of a lot of legwork after that.'

Baxter frowns. 'Can't you use things like Ancestry.com as well, like they did with that bloke in America?'

'The Golden State Killer? That was done through GEDmatch – that's a whole different ball game. Anyone can put their data on there and it's publicly available information, so you can search literally millions of entries. I'm afraid there's nothing like that over here, only the police version. You'll just have to hope your dead man has some dodgy relatives.'

Baxter gives a grim laugh. 'Wouldn't be the first time.'

She starts to gather her things. 'You put his picture up on Twitter, though, didn't you? I'm surprised that didn't come up with anything.'

'Well, it was just the TVP feed, and we're pretty sure he didn't live round here, so I guess it was always a long shot.'

'Fair enough.'

'Though everything will change, of course, the minute the news about Rowan gets out.'

She gives him a wry look. 'God, yes. I'm glad I'm not in Fawley's shoes.'

* * *

As far as most of the team were concerned it was just another case meeting, but they twig pretty quickly that things have gone up a gear, because Harrison's let me have a couple of extra DCs. With the budget cuts we've had that's like hoisting a neon sign saying 'Something's Up and it's Big'. And when the man himself strides in there's a flurry of adjustment: Harrison at a morning meeting is as rare as hen's teeth. People quickly stand up a little straighter, discreetly rid themselves of gum.

'Right,' he says, taking up his place next to me. 'A little quiet, please.' He clears his throat. 'As you've no doubt guessed, this is about the shooting incident at Wytham last Sunday. Thanks to some good solid policework by DC Hansen –'

Hansen looks up and goes bright red; Ev grins and gives him a pat on the back.

'– we now know that the couple we've been calling Richard and Margaret Swann have only been using that name since 2004, when they changed it by deed poll, shortly before moving here. Before that, they lived in Gloucestershire, and their surname was Rowan. Which, for those in kindergarten at the time, is Rowan as in Camilla Rowan. Otherwise known as "Milly Liar".'

The tension in the room has suddenly jump-started.

'DS Gislingham will be emailing you a link to the case files. There's also a documentary series on Netflix –'

Eye-rolls now, a couple of sneers. Like I've said before,

coppers aren't great watchers of TV crime, and especially not of the idiot-plods-fucked-it-up-again kind.

'I know, I know,' he continues, 'and normally I'd be equally sceptical. But it is relevant, in this case, because the producers claimed to have unearthed new evidence suggesting South Mercia Police failed to pursue all potential lines of enquiry. Which, as you may remember, provoked the usual storm of press chest-beating about this terrible "miscarriage of justice".'

Someone raises a hand. Bradley Carter. A couple of people near him exchange weary glances.

'Wasn't there a CCRC review, sir?'

Harrison looks over at him. 'Yes, Carter, there was. Which, after assessing all this so-called "new evidence", concluded that there was nothing to justify referring the case to the Court of Appeal. So as at now, Camilla Rowan remains in HMP Heathside, with no prospect of parole until 2020.'

He takes a breath. '*However*, DNA tests done on blood found at the crime scene have thrown the entire case into question. There is now a very real possibility that Camilla Rowan did not, in fact, kill her baby. For the simple reason that he could very well be the man we currently have in the morgue.'

Silence.

Harrison clears his throat again. I can't be the only one who finds this irritating.

'Given the vast can of worms we will now be reopening, the Chief Constable wished to consult the CPS, the MoJ and his opposite number at South Mercia before any of this was put into the public domain.'

Someone raises a hand. Bradley Carter. Again.

'What about Camilla Rowan, sir – will she be released?'

'That's up to the Secretary of State. And certainly not before we've conclusively identified the man in the morgue, and established exactly where he's been for the last twenty years. DI Fawley has already arranged to interview her at Heathside later this afternoon – it's clearly vital we speak to her before she hears the news from another source. And to anticipate what I imagine may be the next question, her parents will also be interviewed again as a matter of urgency, with the aim of establishing whether they were aware of the dead man's identity, and if so, when – i.e. before or *after* he ended up dead. Any other questions at this stage?'

No one moves. Teacher's pet isn't a good look. Not that Carter seems to care.

My turn. 'As the Super said, we'll be talking to both Camilla Rowan and her parents. I'll also be seeing the DS on the original South Mercia investigation as soon as we can get that arranged. Once that's done we'll start re-interviewing the key witnesses. Some we can do by phone, but the more crucial ones need to be done in person – DS Gislingham will be sending round an initial list, so if you're down to conduct an interview, make sure you prioritize reviewing the material on that witness.'

Harrison nods to me. 'I'll leave you to it, Adam. And could you pop by my office when you've finished.'

* * *

27 January 2017

Criminal Cases Review Commission Non-Referral of Conviction of Camilla Rowan

The Criminal Cases Review Commission (CCRC) has concluded it cannot refer for appeal the murder conviction of Camilla Rowan. Rowan was tried at the Central Criminal Court of England and Wales (the Old Bailey), on the charge of murdering her newborn baby in 1997. On 6 November 2003, she was convicted by a unanimous verdict and sentenced to life imprisonment, with a recommendation that she serve at least seventeen years.

Ms Rowan has tried to appeal against sentence and conviction but was unsuccessful. After the broadcast of the television series *Infamous* in March 2016, South Mercia Police decided to reopen the case, with particular reference to specific allegations made in that programme. The most significant of these concerned a possible suspect who, it was alleged, had not been properly investigated at the time of the original investigation. South Mercia Police conducted a full inquiry into the claims made in the programme, the results of which were submitted to the Commission. Following a detailed review of this material, the CCRC does not consider that this so-called new suspect took any part in the crime, nor that there is any other new evidence or legal argument capable of raising a real possibility that the Court of Appeal might quash the original conviction. For that reason, the conviction cannot be referred for appeal.

The Commission's analysis of the case and its reasons for the decision are set out in detail in a 64-page document called a Statement of Reasons, which has been sent to Ms Rowan's representatives. Statutory restrictions on disclosure mean that the Commission cannot make its Statement of Reasons public. There are no such restrictions on Ms Rowan or her representatives. Indeed, the CCRC invites them to consider publishing the document, or making it available on request, in order that anyone following the case can understand the CCRC's review and the reasons for the decision not to refer this conviction for appeal. A number of issues relating to the case have already been discussed in public and in the media.

The Commission's role in relation to alleged miscarriages of justice involves applying the 'real possibility test' set out in Section 13 of the Criminal Appeal Act 1995. It says the Commission can only refer a case to the relevant appeal court if the Commission considers that there is a real possibility that the conviction, verdict or sentence would not be upheld were the reference to be made.

– ends –

*   *   *

As the room starts to clear, Hansen takes the opportunity to catch Gislingham.

'I know things have moved on a bit, Sarge, but for the record that contact of mine at the *Express* didn't have anything useful. Doesn't sound like there's been anyone poking about in the Rowan case, which I guess bolsters our theory that the vic wasn't a journo after all.'

Gis gives him a quick smile and a light tap on the shoulder. 'But useful to know all the same. Good work.'

Gis turns to Baxter, who's pinning stills from the

Oxford station footage to the whiteboard. 'Where are we with CCTV on the train?'

Baxter shakes his head. 'Nothing useful. We eventually ID'd him on the train but all he did the whole way was look at his phone. BTP also managed to track him down at Marylebone buying a ticket, but he paid cash, unfortunately. Other than that, all we know for sure right now is that he didn't come from the Tube. Which is a pain as it would've been by far the easiest to track. So now we're stuck with needle-in-a-haystack stuff with buses and taxis. But Hansen's on it, aren't you, Hansen?'

Hansen nods. 'I'm liaising with the Met. But it's going to be slow-going.'

'There was something else too,' says Baxter. 'Apparently there was a problem with the train the vic was on and it was over an hour late. So he'd clearly intended to get here a lot earlier.'

Gis considers. 'Not sure how significant that is – apart from the fact that it meant it was much darker by the time he turned up at Wytham.'

'And the Swanns would have been a lot more spooked,' says Ev, looking up from her desk, 'assuming, of course, that they weren't expecting him.'

'You said he didn't come from the Tube,' says Bradley Carter, 'but what about adjacent streets – couldn't he have arrived on foot?'

Gis glances across at him. 'It's a pretty pricey area round there. He didn't look that well-heeled to me.'

'He might not have lived there,' says Carter, 'there are loads of hotels around the station. And some of those are pretty basic.'

Gis nods. 'OK. Good point. Why don't you pick up on that?'

Carter looks like all his Christmases have come at once; Gis, on the other hand, may be secretly rather relieved to pack him off to London for a while.

'What about the backpack and the other stuff?' he says now, looking round the rest of the team. 'I'm finding it hard to believe we can't find *any* of it.'

'Me too,' says Ev. 'But Barnetson's a good copper. If he says they did a thorough search, then they did a thorough search.'

Baxter makes a grim face. 'Maybe the Swanns have a nuclear bunker in their garden.' People start laughing and he glances round. 'Hey, it's not that outlandish – stranger things have happened.'

'Talking of the Swanns,' says Ev , holding up her phone and nodding to Gis, 'Mrs S has arrived downstairs.'

* * *

Adam Fawley
24 October
10.35

Harrison is on the phone when I get there. But he isn't alone. Ruth Gallagher is with him. My first reaction is suspicion, which my brain tells me is a) ridiculous, but b) natural, given that the last time I was in a room with her it was Interview One and I was on the wrong side of the table. But she didn't have any choice, faced with the evidence against me, and when Gis came up with something that threw all that in doubt she put her heart into proving him right. You can't ask for more than that.

She smiles when she sees me, a little more broadly than strictly necessary; evidently we're both going to bend over backwards to Act Like Nothing Happened. She looks well – a crisp biscuit-coloured suit and a recent haircut. She also has a slight tan, as if she's just got back from somewhere a lot sunnier than here.

'Nice to see you, Ruth.'

'Likewise.'

'Right,' says Harrison, putting down his phone, 'I asked you to drop by, Adam, because you may not be aware that Ruth used to work at South Mercia.'

I turn to her. 'No, I didn't know that. Were you on the Rowan case?'

She shakes her head. 'No, it was before my time. I mean, it was in the ether, of course – everyone knew about it. It was the biggest case South Mercia'd ever had.'

'I thought it might be helpful,' interjects Harrison, 'for you to touch base with Ruth, Adam. Get a heads-up on the lie of the land.'

She glances down at her hands, a tiny smile escaping from the corners of her mouth. I'm obviously not the only bullshit bingo player round here.

'You knew them? The investigating team?'

She nods. 'Larry Kearney was my DS for a while. I didn't know Howard Lucas very well, but he had a good reputation. I'd be surprised if there were any serious problems with the way it was handled.'

'And Kearney?'

She hesitates, only for a moment, but long enough. 'He

was one of the hardest-working people I've ever worked with. Always the first in the office and the last to leave.'

If I was going to damn a fellow officer with faint praise, that's how I'd do it too. She'll be saying he had nice handwriting next.

I turn to Harrison. 'You must have a lot more important things to do, sir – why don't Ruth and I take this one offline?'

Sorry – I just couldn't resist. Though I do make sure not to catch Ruth's eye.

Harrison nods. 'Absolutely. I'll leave you both to it.'

'So what did you really think about Lawrence Kearney?' I press the button for Americano and turn to face Ruth. 'I'm seeing him tomorrow so it actually would be quite useful.'

She leans against the machine. 'Well, let's just say I don't see Harrison calling him a blue-sky-thinking game changer any time soon.'

We exchange a smile.

'On the other hand, one thing he definitely *is*, is goals-driven. It was always about getting a result.' Her turn at the machine. 'But don't get me wrong, he wouldn't cut corners to get there. Or ignore evidence. He's basically one of the good guys. A bit dunderheaded on occasion, but if he's got to DCI it'll have been by putting in all the hours God sends. Talking of which, he always was a stickler for rank, so a bit of brown-nosing wouldn't come amiss. *Three-bags-full, sir.* You know the drill.'

I laugh. 'Thanks for the warning – especially as I'm taking Quinn. The only person he deigns to call "sir" is the bloody Chief Constable.'

She makes a face. 'Gawd, yes. Good idea.' She picks up her cup. 'Well you know where I am if you need anything else. And do tell Larry I said hello. Like I said, under all that bluster, he really is one of the good guys.'

* * *

Interview with Richard Swann, conducted at
St Aldate's Police Station, Oxford
24 October 2018, 12.25 p.m.
In attendance, DS C. Gislingham, DC V. Everett,
Mr T. Unwin (solicitor)

VE: Just to remind you, Mr Swann, this interview
    is being recorded, and you are still under
    caution for murder. Has your solicitor
    explained what this means?

TU: I have. Several times.

VE: [*passes across sheet of paper*]
    For the tape, I am passing Mr Swann a copy of
    his statement dated 21st October. Having had
    time to reflect, is there anything you would
    like to add or amend?

RS: No.

CG: Now would be the time.

RS: No, I'm quite happy with it as it is.

CG: So you continue to maintain that the shooting
    at your house three days ago was undertaken in
    self-defence, and the victim was completely
    unknown to you?

RS: I do indeed. I'd never seen him before in my life.

CG: Yes, I remember you used exactly that form of words when you were interviewed before. The same phrase also appears in your statement.

RS: And your point is?

CG: My point is that never having seen him before is not necessarily the same as not knowing who he was. I think you're very well aware of that, and chose your words very carefully.

TU: I'm not sure what you're getting at, Sergeant.

CG: I suspect your client does. Mr Swann? Or would you prefer I called you Mr Rowan?

RS: [*silence*]

TU: Richard? What's he talking about?

RS: I see precious little point in you asking me questions to which you already know the answer.

CG: You said nothing about this in your first interview.

RS: My change of name has nothing to do with it. Nor, frankly, is it any of your business.

CG: I'm sorry but I'm afraid I disagree. I think it has everything to do with it. I think you know very well who the man in your kitchen was. My question is when exactly you found that out.

RS: I didn't know then, and I don't know now.

CG: Even though you disposed of anything that might have identified him?

RS: I did no such thing. And I resent your
    implication.
VE: There was a witness. Someone saw you do it.
RS: Don't be ridiculous. How could anyone possibly
    have seen anything? There was no one else for
    miles, and in any case, it was completely
    dark.
CG: True. It would have been far too dark to see
    anything with the naked eye. But fortunately
    for us, our witness was carrying night-vision
    equipment.
RS: Please don't insult my intelligence – no one
    carts that sort of thing about with them on
    the off-chance.
CG: It wasn't 'on the off-chance'. He was up on
    the hill above your house. Photographing the
    stars.
RS: [*silence*]
    So what did he say, this 'witness' of yours?
CG: He heard gunfire. A single shot, just as you
    said.
RS: [*silence*]
CG: He was concerned, of course, so he immediately
    called 999 and then waited a while, keeping an
    eye on the house.
RS: [*silence*]
CG: And then he saw something – something that led
    him to believe the shot must have hit nothing
    more significant than a rodent.
RS: [*silence*]

CG: You went out to the garden, Mr Swann. You were
    carrying something in a refuse bag –

TU: I need to confer with my client –

CG: What was in that bag, Mr Swann?

TU: My client will be answering 'No comment' to
    all further questions.

CG: It was the man's wallet and backpack,
    wasn't it?

RS: No comment.

CG: You knew you had to conceal his identity
    because if we'd realized who he was we'd never
    have believed it was just a burglary gone
    wrong.

RS: I have no idea what you're talking about.

TU: Richard –

CG: Did you really think we wouldn't find out?

RS: Find out what?

CG: Are you asking me to believe that you don't
    know?

TU: [*restraining Swann*]
    My client has no comment to make.

VE: Did he tell you how he found you – where he's
    been? Anything at all?

RS: How many more times, I have absolutely *no idea*
    what you're talking about –

CG: You must have known we'd run DNA –

RS: DNA? What the devil is that going to prove?

CG: [*quietly*]
    What DNA always proves, Mr Swann. You and
    that young man – you were related.

RS: [*gapes*]

```
      What on earth -
CG:   He was your grandson, Mr Swann. He was
      Camilla's child.
RS:   [silence]
TU:   [intervening]
      I absolutely insist on conferring with my
      client.
VE:   Interview terminated at 12.48.
```

*   *   *

'I don't think he knew,' says Ev. She and Gis are in an adjacent room now, watching Unwin and Swann on one of the video feeds.

'No,' says Gis. 'I don't think he did either.'

On the screen, they can see Timothy Unwin speaking urgently. There's no sound and Swann has his back to them, but he's holding up his hands, as if in bewilderment. In the other interview room, Margaret Swann is being shown to a chair by a female PC. She's in a heavy tweed coat and clutching a large handbag. She looks cold.

'What are you going to do about the old boy?' says Ev. 'Quite aside from the fact that he looks bloody awful, the clock's ticking – we'll have to decide sometime today.'

Gis sighs. 'I'll check with the boss, but I don't think we have much choice. We'll have to release him under investigation and hope to God we find something.'

Ev nods, then turns to the screen again. 'You ready?'

Gis takes a deep breath. 'As I'll ever be.'

*   *   *

Margaret Swann has her own lawyer now, a slightly flustered young woman who introduces herself as Julia Merrick and says she's one of Timothy Unwin's colleagues. Swann is looking at her with the sort of contempt she evidently reserves for members of her own sex in positions of supposed authority. Everett is getting her fair share of it too, though if Gis were a gambling man, his money'd be on Ev in a straight head-to-head. Swann still has her coat on, and the message is loud and clear. But they're the ones who'll be deciding when she leaves. Not her.

'Mrs Swann,' he says, taking his seat, 'as you know, I'm DS Chris Gislingham, and you already know DC Everett. You should be aware that this is a formal police interview and is being recorded. I also need to advise you that new evidence has come to light which means we now have no choice but to arrest you on suspicion of conspiracy to murder. You do not have to say anything, but it may harm your defence if you do not mention when questioned something which you later rely on in court. Anything you do say may be given in evidence. There may also be further charges at a later date, depending on what comes to light in the course of our investigation. Do you understand?'

Merrick is staring at Gis like a rabbit in headlights: she's obviously never handled anything remotely like this before.

'And precisely what,' says Swann, 'am I supposed to have done?'

'Well, we can start with the fact that you washed your husband's nightclothes, even though you knew they would be important items of evidence –'

'Oh, for heaven's sake –'

'But it's not just that. We now believe that you and your husband colluded in concealing or destroying certain other items, in an attempt to suppress the identity of the man your husband shot.'

'Don't be ridiculous,' she snaps.

Gislingham smiles. 'That's funny. Your husband used exactly the same phrase.'

She gives him a withering look. 'That's because it *is* ridiculous. Why on earth would we do such a thing?'

She doesn't, Ev notes, ask what they're supposed to have got rid of.

Merrick, though, is just about to. 'Can I ask which "items" you mean?'

'A wallet,' says Everett, 'a mobile phone and a backpack.'

Margaret Swann raises an eyebrow. 'And how, pray, do you know he even *had* such things?'

'It's a reasonable assumption, Mrs Swann, as I'm sure –'

'That's not proof,' says the lawyer quickly. She clearly thinks this is a big win.

'True,' says Ev. 'But, luckily for us, there is also a witness.'

'Witness?' says Margaret Swann. 'What *witness*?'

'A taxi driver,' says Gislingham. 'The taxi driver who dropped the man off at your house and saw him walk up the drive to the door. Hardly the behaviour of a random housebreaker, wouldn't you agree?'

She sniffs and looks away.

Merrick is poised, pen at the ready. 'Could you give me the details of this witness, please?'

Ev pushes a piece of paper across to her. 'He works at the station cab rank and picked the man up at just after nine that night. He gave Gantry Manor as his destination, spent most of the journey looking at his mobile phone and paid with cash from a leather wallet. He also had a backpack with him.'

Merrick looks up. 'You only have the driver's word for that.'

Gis smiles. 'Actually, no. We've been able to secure CCTV footage from the station, and that completely corroborates the driver's story. The man can be seen quite clearly coming through the ticket barriers. He also had a return ticket.'

He lets the implications of that settle for a moment.

'And would you believe,' he continues, 'we're fortunate enough to have a *second* witness. Someone who saw Mr Swann outside the house that night, with a black plastic bag.'

Margaret Swann laughs. 'And taking out the rubbish is a crime now, is it?'

Gis pauses. 'No. But I do start to wonder when I'm told this occurred only a few minutes after the sound of gunfire. Gunfire which – as we now know – left a man lying dead in your kitchen with his brains blown out. I don't know about you, Mrs Swann, but "taking out the rubbish" isn't the first task that would come to my mind in circumstances like that.'

The lawyer flushes slightly; she's getting out of her depth and she knows it. 'All the same, you can't prove that wasn't what he was doing –'

'He was walking in the opposite direction of the bins, so yes, Miss Merrick, I think it's a fair assumption.'

Swann stares at Gislingham. 'And have you actually *found* the things you allege we "destroyed"?'

'Not as yet, no. But it's only a matter of time. I hope you know that.' Gis sits back in his chair. 'Your husband says he'd never seen the man before. You're aware of that?'

'Yes.'

'Do *you* know who he was?'

She frowns. 'I told you, I never saw him.'

'That's not what I asked.'

'No, of course I didn't know who he was. He was a *burglar*. We don't know those sort of people.'

'He was nothing of the kind, Mrs Swann, as you well know.'

Swann gives him a poisonous look but says nothing.

'So, for the record,' says Everett, 'you're denying all and any prior knowledge of this man?'

Merrick may be a rookie, but even she knows this is heading in a dangerous direction. As for Swann, she's gripping her handbag so hard her knuckles are white.

Ev fixes her with a cool stare. 'I'm afraid I don't believe you, Mrs Swann.'

Swann lifts her chin. 'I'm not a liar, Constable, or whatever it is you are. And neither is my husband.'

Gislingham nods to Ev, who passes across a second piece of paper.

'This,' she says, 'is a DNA report from our forensics lab on blood samples found at the scene, comparing them with a sample already stored in the National DNA Database.'

Swann pushes the paper away. 'This is all just gobbledygook.'

'It shows a match, Mrs Swann. A parental match between the dead man and a prisoner currently serving a life sentence for murder at HMP Heathside. The prisoner's name is Camilla Rowan. The daughter you never told us you had.'

The silence is so long Gis has time to feel sorry for Merrick, who's staring at them, open-mouthed. She had no idea what a hospital pass this would turn out to be. Swann, on the other hand, isn't meeting anyone's eye. She's opened her handbag and is ferreting about for a tissue. But her hands are shaking.

'You knew, didn't you,' says Ev softly. 'You knew he was Camilla's child –'

Her head snaps up. 'I did not!'

'– in fact, I think you knew exactly who he was long before he turned up at your door. What did he do? Call you? Send you a letter? You didn't tell your husband, though, did you? You kept him in the dark, hoping it would all just go away –'

'This is insane – *you're* insane – the very idea is preposterous –'

'Preposterous? Maybe. But not impossible.'

Their eyes lock and the moment tenses like elastic. But it's Swann who blinks first. She turns to Merrick. 'I utterly refute these deranged accusations. And beyond that I have nothing to add.'

Ev gives her a dry look. 'OK, if that's how you want to play it. Interview terminated at 13.18.'

* * *

I get Quinn to drive, mainly because he likes it so much and, broadly speaking, I don't. I've never got the whole bloke thing about wheels, which is probably why I have a Mondeo and Quinn has an Audi A4. Red. As if you had to ask. It's not a bad journey, on the whole. The weather is dreary but there isn't too much traffic, at least until we hit the M25. Quinn asks if I want music and I'm surprised to find the last thing he was listening to was Radio 4.

'Maisie,' he says, glancing across. 'She likes that sort of thing.'

I haven't met her yet, but the word round the station is that it's serious. And what little I've picked up sounds surprisingly encouraging – surprising because Quinn's track record with women usually has me heaving a very loud sigh. But Ev says she's exactly what he needs – she met them out shopping in Summertown a few weeks back (that alone is headline-worthy – OK, Quinn's always been able to shop for Europe, but with a *woman*?). According to Ev, Maisie came over as bright, confident and extremely unlikely to take any of Quinn's shit. She didn't put it precisely that way, of course, but I got the message. I also happen to know Maisie's parents are very well off, which no doubt adds to the attraction.

'Going well, is it? With Maisie?' I say, trying not to sound like his dad.

He looks a little flustered. 'Yeah.' A pause. 'Actually, she's moving in.'

I try not to look flabbergasted but I suspect I'm not managing it.

'Sounds great. Congratulations.'

He gives a little sideways smile. Now he's got the words out he looks not just relieved but happy. Genuinely happy. I wonder for a moment how many other people he's told. Not many, I'm guessing. Maybe I'm a dry run.

Someone in a Porsche cuts in front of us and he swears under his breath and changes lanes.

'I was talking to her last night, actually – we were watching that Netflix thing about Rowan. Maisie went to the same school as her. Years later, obviously. She said no one at the school ever talked about it.'

I bet they didn't. Rowan may well be their most recognizable old girl, but that's one picture you definitely won't find in their fancy prospectus.

'The woman they interviewed,' he says, 'Marion Teesdale. She was Maise's housemistress too. She said she was all right. A bit of a battleaxe but basically OK. And she really liked Maise.'

So if we decide we want to speak to her, that might help. I get the message. My phone starts to ring: Gis.

'Thought you'd like to know what we got from the old folks, boss, before you see Rowan.'

'Go on.'

'Well, if you ask me, I don't think either of the Swanns knew the vic was coming that night.'

'Interesting – what makes you so sure?'

'The clothes, really. The old girl wouldn't have been in her nightie if she was expecting visitors. Not that generation. Not if my gran was anything to go by.'

'Of course – I should have thought of that myself.'

'As for whether they worked out who he was,' continues Gis, 'either before or after the gun went off – now that's more of a toughie. I don't think *Mr* Swann did – I just don't think he's that good an actor. As for *Mrs* S, well, Ev's convinced she knew exactly who he was but there's no way she's going to admit it.'

Quinn looks across and makes a face. 'Talking of battleaxes . . .'

'And you agree with Ev – you think the old lady knew who the victim was?'

'Yup,' says Gis. 'I reckon she did.'

'OK. Thanks for letting me know.'

'No worries, boss, see you later.'

A sign is looming ahead of us now. Junction Nine, two miles. Quinn checks his mirror and moves over to the inside lane.

* * *

'Watch yourself there, Mrs Swann,' says the PC. 'Don't want you hurting yourself, now do we.'

He waits for her to settle in the back seat, then closes the car door carefully and walks round towards the front. Margaret pulls her coat around herself. It's been a bad morning. The questioning, the form-filling, that irritating lawyer who clearly didn't have a clue what she was doing. Margaret makes a mental note to insist she has a partner with her the next time. Because it looks like there will be a 'next time', much as she was hoping otherwise. She turns, a little stiffly, to check on her husband, but he's staring resolutely out of the far window. Round the front of the car, the young PC who's offered to drive them has now been waylaid by a colleague.

She hears Richard stir beside her, clear his throat. 'They told me who he was. That – young man.' A long pause. 'I assume they told you the same.'

She hesitates; nods.

'They made it pretty clear they thought I already knew.'

She flaps her hand. 'That doesn't mean anything. They were just trying to trap you.'

Her husband is eyeing her. 'Trap me into what, exactly? I was telling the truth. I had no idea.'

She shrugs and looks away, but Richard isn't giving up. 'Did *you* know who he was?'

There's a silence. 'Peggy?'

'Don't be ridiculous. Why on earth would you think that?'

He frowns. 'You did, didn't you – if not before, then after. *That's* why you –'

She raises her hand: the PC is on his way back round to the driver's side.

'Not here, Dick,' she says in a low voice as the car door swings open. 'We'll talk about this when we get home.'

* * *

CRIMINAL CASES REVIEW COMMISSION CASE FILE
R v Camilla Kathleen Rowan (2003)
Case number: 772498525/CR
Document number: 451.1
Document type: Interview transcript, South Mercia Police

Interview with Camilla Rowan, conducted at Calcot
Row Police Station, Gloucester
2 August 2002, 11.55 a.m.
In attendance, DI H. Lucas, DS L. Kearney,
Mrs J. McCrae (Appropriate Adult)

LK: We've asked you here, Miss Rowan, because we
    want to try to clear up what happened to the
    baby you gave birth to at Birmingham and
    Solihull General Hospital in the early hours
    of 23rd December 1997.

CR: Good, I want to clear that up too.

LK: As you know, officers from the Child Protection
    team at Gloucester County Council have been
    attempting to ascertain the whereabouts of the
    baby, after the case was referred to them by
    Mr Steve McIlvanney, of the county adoption
    and fostering service.

CR: I don't know why they had to drag you in. I've
    already told them what happened.

LK: You said you handed the baby to its father, is
    that right?

CR: Exactly.

LK: A Mr Timothy Baker.

CR: Yes.

LK: And this was after you left the hospital at
    3 p.m. on December 23rd.

CR: Right.

LK: So where did this exchange take place?

CR: At a lay-by on the A417.

LK: [*passes across a map*]

Can you indicate which one?

CR: I have no idea – it was years ago and it was getting dark. Somewhere the other side of Gloucester.

LK: Mr Baker must have given you more precise directions than that – you'd never have found each other.

CR: I'm not saying he didn't, I'm saying I don't remember.

LK: That's quite a rural stretch of road.

CR: Yeah, so?

LK: No street lighting, nothing like that. And not that many buildings, so it's pretty unlikely any of the lay-bys would have security cameras nearby.

CR: I have no idea. I doubt it.

LK: So there'd be no proof the exchange had taken place. Or not.

CR: I don't know what you're getting at.

LK: Were there any other cars at the lay-by at the time?

CR: I don't remember any.

LK: No one on foot? Walking their dog?

CR: How should I know?

LK: So no one saw you?

CR: Like I said, I don't remember anyone, but I wasn't really looking.

LK: And this man's name is Timothy Baker.

CR: Right. I told you that.

LK: Was he alone?

CR: Yup.

LK: He didn't bring his mother or a sister? A
    female friend? To look after the baby?

CR: I don't even know if he had a sister. Like I
    told those other people, we only saw each
    other a couple of times.

LK: Was he married? In a relationship?

CR: Not that he told me.

HL: It didn't strike you as odd that a young
    man like that would want to take on the
    responsibility of bringing up a baby on
    his own?

CR: He was its father. I told him I couldn't care
    for it so he said he would.

LK: And when did that conversation take place?

CR: A few weeks before. I don't know exactly.

LK: And how did you arrange the meeting on the
    A417?

CR: I rang him from the hospital that morning.

LK: From a hospital payphone?

CR: Right.

LK: You didn't have a mobile?

CR: Not then, no. Most people didn't.

HL: What type of car was Mr Baker driving?

CR: A white one.

LK: Make? Registration number?

CR: Don't ask me, I'm useless about cars.

LK: And where did you first meet Mr Baker?

CR: At a pub. The King's Head in Stroud.

LK: And did intimacy take place that night?

CR: Yeah, we had sex.

LK: Did you use protection?

CR: No, I was on the pill.

LK: And yet you still fell pregnant.

CR: Yeah, well, it happens.

HL: And where did the intercourse take place?

CR: At his flat.

LK: And that was where?

CR: A block about ten minutes away. Council, I think.

LK: [*passes over a photograph*]
This block, correct? Adelaide Court?

CR: If you say so. It was dark, and he didn't tell me the name.

LK: What number was the flat?

CR: I've already told you all this. I don't know the number, just that it was on the top floor.

LK: Did you go there again?

CR: No. The only other time we did it was in the park.

LK: I should tell you that we have obtained occupancy records for Adelaide Court for the period in question and there was no one called Baker living there. Either on the top floor or anywhere else.

CR: So? Loads of people sub-let.

LK: Officers have also questioned tenants who were living there at the time and no one remembers seeing you.

CR: I'm not bloody surprised. I went there *once* at, like, *midnight*.

JM: [*intervening*]

Camilla, if this man forced you – if there was
any sort of assault –

CR: He didn't *rape* me, if that's what you're
getting at.

JM: I can arrange for you to see a trained counsellor –

CR: Jesus, it was just sex, OK? I liked him, he
liked me. It didn't *mean* anything.

LK: Not until you got pregnant, anyway.

CR: Yeah, well, that wasn't the plan, was it.

LK: And you say that this Mr Baker was going to
register the child's birth?

CR: Right.

LK: Do you know if he did that?

CR: I assume he did. I haven't spoken to him
about it.

LK: Have you spoken to him at all?

CR: No.

LK: Not at all? You gave a virtual stranger your
baby and just left it at that?

CR: Look, I just wanted to move on, OK? The kid
was with its father, he was safe, I just
wanted to forget about the whole thing.

LK: We've accessed UK Records Office data for all
baby boys registered under the surname 'Baker'
on the day your child was born, and for the
six-week period after that date. None of them
is your child.

CR: [*silence*]

LK: We've also reviewed all baby boys listed as
born at Birmingham and Solihull General

Hospital for the same period under any
surname. Again, none is your child.

CR: Look, if Tim's fucked up, then you should be
talking to him, not me.

HL: We'd very much like to. He's proving rather
difficult to find.

CR: I don't see what you expect me to do about that.

LK: If something happened to the baby, if there was
some sort of accident, now's the time to tell us.

CR: [*silence*]

Duration of silence confirmed as 51 seconds

LK: Is there something you want to tell us?

CR: No.

LK: Did you do something to the baby?

CR: No!

LK: Did you kill the baby?

CR: Of course I didn't! I would never *ever* harm my
baby.

HL: We can't find the child, we can't find the father –

CR: Look, can we turn off the tape?

LK: No, I'm afraid that's not possible.

CR: [*becoming distressed*]
You're going to tell my parents, aren't you?

HL: We have to conduct a thorough investigation –

CR: [*wailing*]
And it's all going to come out and everyone
will know – you're going to *destroy* my *life* –

JM: I think we should take a break now, Inspector.

LK: Interview suspended at 12.17.

* * *

They'd barely got through the door before he started; Margaret hasn't even had a chance to take off her coat. She fumbles wearily for a chair. The kitchen is cold; there's condensation on the windows.

'They said he was Camilla's baby – *our grandson*.' She's not looking at him and he takes a step closer. 'Did you know? *Did you know?*'

She says nothing.

'Peggy – I want an answer.'

She starts to pull off her gloves. 'Of course I *didn't know*. How could I *know*?'

He starts to pace the kitchen. 'I went along with what you said – I've stuck to the story –'

'It isn't a *story* – it's the truth – he broke in and threatened you – threatened *us* –'

He turns to her, exasperated. 'For heaven's sake, you know that's not what happened – he was angry, yes, but he wasn't trying to rob us, he wasn't asking for *money*. I've been thinking about it – I think he was trying to tell me something –'

'He was *shouting* – I *heard him* –'

He stops, looks at her, his face suddenly white. 'He called me Grandad. I thought it was just an insult, but –'

'You're talking nonsense and you know it.'

But he doesn't seem to be listening. 'You know what this means, don't you? If he really was Camilla's baby – *that* baby – it means she's been telling the truth, this whole time. Just like she always claimed. She wasn't lying –'

Margaret makes a contemptuous noise and turns away. 'Perhaps not about *that* –'

He takes a step towards her. 'But "that" was the most

important thing, wasn't it? All those other lies wouldn't have mattered two hoots otherwise. No one would even have known –'

She glances up at him. 'So where's he been all these years, then? If she's been "telling the truth" all this time, where was *he*?'

He looks exasperated. 'I don't know that, any more than you do. And as for all that nonsense about "Tim Baker", I never believed a word of it and neither did you. But when she said she didn't harm that child – we should have believed her. And when I think of the way we've treated her –'

Margaret turns away again, and he moves closer.

'Peggy?'

No response. She's fiddling with her gloves.

'Are you absolutely sure,' he says softly, 'that you didn't know?'

She flings him a furious look. 'He turns up here out of the blue – in the middle of the night – how on earth could I have known who he was?'

'And what about afterwards?' He swallows. 'After he – when I went up to change and you were down here on your own, what about then?'

She looks away again. 'I don't know what you mean.'

'You know perfectly well what I mean – you found something, didn't you, in that backpack thing? That's why you suddenly decided we had to get rid of it – that's why you were panicking – when I came back down –'

'Now you really are being ridiculous.'

He stands his ground. 'What was it, Peggy? A passport? Something that gave away who he was?'

She gets up, goes over to the sink and starts filling the kettle. 'I didn't know who he was, not till those horrible police people told me, and I didn't know what was in the backpack because I never looked. Happy now? I just thought we were best getting rid, that's all.' She throws him a fierce look. '*Why won't you believe me?*'

Her hands are shaking so much the water is going everywhere. She drops the kettle in the sink with a clang and leans heavily against the counter. Her breath is coming in raw shallow gasps and a moment later she feels her husband's hands on her shoulders.

He turns her round and pulls her towards him. 'I'm sorry, love, I didn't mean to upset you. This whole thing, it's got us both on edge.' He sighs. 'Who knows, perhaps that's what they want – setting us at each other's throats.' He leads her back to the chair and sits her down, patting her gently on the shoulder. 'You stay there while I make you some tea. We don't want you getting unwell, do we? Not like last time.'

* * *

Adam Fawley
24 October
15.20

Heathside is exactly what its name suggests: right on the edge of Surrey Heath. Though as we emerge from the trees that separate it from the main road, the first thing that comes to mind is that quip about anyone who's been to public school feeling right at home in prison. I can't remember who said it. A con man, probably. Or a spy.

Either way, despite the gates and the high wire fences and the concrete, there's a distinct girls'-school feel to the solid brick block with its sloping roof and ranks of dormer windows. It's not Burghley Abbey, that's for sure, but Camilla Rowan may be better prepared to cope with it than most.

The gate personnel are expecting us, and after the usual sign-in and security faff we're shown into the governor's office by her eager – male – assistant. I can't be the first person to wonder whether that particular recruitment choice was designed to make a point. The room is rather plusher than I would have expected, and the governor is rather younger, with a sleek blonde bob and a linen dress in an aggressive splashy floral. She's obviously quite happy standing out in a crowd.

'DI Fawley,' she says, rising to her feet and extending a well-manicured hand. 'Victoria Winfield. Pleased to meet you.'

She gestures us to sit and folds her fingers carefully together. 'So you're here to see Camilla.'

I'm assuming she knows why, though it's the MoJ who've been liaising with her, so I can't be sure.

'Does she get a lot of visitors?'

Winfield smiles drily. 'Well, certainly not from police officers.'

'Her family?'

A shake of the head.

'Lawyers?'

'Not since the CCRC review.'

She leans forward and flips open a file, but given what she says next I can't believe she actually needed to check.

'In fact, the Duchess hasn't had a single person on her visiting list for more than nine months.'

It takes me a second, Quinn a couple more, then I hear him suppress a snort.

Winfield raises an eyebrow. 'It was rather inevitable. Camilla is hardly a common name among the prison population. And given the way she behaves –' She doesn't need to say any more. 'To be honest, I live in dread of the "other" Camilla deciding she'd like to visit. It would be a riot. Or a rout.' She sits back. 'But I doubt very much that you're here to talk about the royal appointments diary, so what exactly do you want?'

'Has Rowan ever spoken about what happened to her baby?'

A shake of the head. 'Not to me. From what I hear, she's always maintained exactly the same story: she gave the child to its father.' She sits back and looks squarely at me. 'So is that what's prompted your sudden interest? Some sort of development?'

'There was an incident at her parents' house on Sunday. A man was killed. Subsequent DNA testing has proved he was Camilla's son. Almost certainly the son she's supposed to have murdered. Unless there's yet another child we know nothing about.'

She leans forward again and looks at her file, and this time she's reading it for real.

'But there were other adoptions, weren't there? Or am I imagining that?'

'Two. They've been ruled out.'

She finds the relevant place, then nods. 'Ah yes, I see.'

There's a silence.

'So what now?'

'We talk to her. See what she has to say, and go from there. What happens after that will be down to the CPS. And what we do – or don't – find.'

'So there's a chance she'll be released?'

Quinn shrugs. 'We thought someone died. Looks like they didn't.'

Winfield frowns. 'There's been nothing on the news –'

'No,' I say. 'We wanted to speak to Rowan first. Assess her reaction. Based on your observations of her in the last few days, do you think there's any chance she knew her child had been found?'

Winfield shakes her head slowly. 'I'm not aware of anything. She's had no contact with her parents for months, and there's certainly been no change in her behaviour. And surely the first thing she'd have done is get in touch with her legal team?'

'There's no evidence she has?'

'No, not to my knowledge. Letters like that have to be clearly marked, to ensure they're not opened for monitoring. We would know.'

'What about other correspondence?'

She raises an eyebrow. 'Ah, well, she may not get any visitors, but she certainly gets mail. She has quite the little fan club. She gets half-a-dozen letters a week, I think – sometimes more.'

Quinn gapes at her. 'Seriously?'

She makes a dismissive gesture. 'You know what it's like these days – some people find any sort of celebrity irresistible. When she first went to Holloway they were absolutely inundated – "baby-killer", "Hope you burn in hell", that sort of thing. But the vast majority we've had here have been from armchair campaigners and amateur Miss Marples, all buying the Netflix line and thinking they're the ones who will crack the case. Along with the usual slew of sad loner misfits asking her to marry them.'

Quinn snorts. 'Fuck me, they must be desperate.'

She raises an immaculate eyebrow. 'Evidently.'

I sit forward. 'What about more personal communications – from people she actually knows?'

'I'm not aware of anything. These days we try to avoid reading much prisoner correspondence, unless there's a very good reason. "Light touch" and all that. But given Rowan's public profile we do open rather more of hers. Especially anything that looks like a possible candidate for abuse or death threats.' She gives a dry smile. 'After a while, you get a long nose for spotting that sort of thing. But as I said, letters like that have tailed off of late. And as far as "official" policy goes, all incoming or outgoing letters can be opened and read at any time, and prisoners are fully aware of that. We do always check mail that includes enclosures, but I don't recall anything untoward in that respect in relation to Rowan. I would have been informed if there was.'

'All the same, could we speak to the officer who handles the mail?'

'Prison officers don't handle incoming mail. Post-room staff have no contact with prisoners, and there's no one individual who does it – it's a team.'

'Has she written to anyone herself?'

'Not as far as I'm aware, though again, I'd be happy to check for you.'

'If you could.'

She looks at me, then at Quinn. 'So, are you ready for your audience?'

* * *

CRIMINAL CASES REVIEW COMMISSION CASE FILE
R v Camilla Kathleen Rowan (2003)
Case number: 772498525/CR
Document number: 54.2.1
Document type: Pre-trial psychiatric assessment, CPS

CONFIDENTIAL

5th March 2003

Marcus Townsend QC
Beauchamp Chambers
Grandison Court
Temple
London WC2J 9GB

Dear Mr Townsend,

I have, as requested, carried out a full psychiatric assessment of Camilla Rowan. It was, I have to say, one of the most difficult assignments I have ever undertaken – I have never encountered a subject who resists normal psychological classification methodology to such an extraordinary extent. I enclose my conclusions, such as they are; frankly, I do not envy you your task.

Should you have any questions, please do not hesitate
to get in touch and I will do my best to assist.

Yours sincerely,
Diana Whittingham

Dr Diana Whittingham
MBBS FRCPsych
Consultant Forensic Psychiatrist

Encl:

PSYCHIATRIC REPORT

Name: *Camilla Kathleen Rowan*
Gender: *Female*
Ethnicity: *Caucasian*
Date of birth: *30th September 1980*
Date of report: *4th March 2003*

The subject is a 22-year-old woman who has been charged
with the murder of her newborn child in 1997. She has no
previous criminal convictions. This report has been prepared
as part of the pre-trial assessment process. I conducted three
interviews, two at my office, and one at her parents' address,
where I was able to observe the home environment and family
dynamic. I also administered an MMPI-2 test (Minnesota
Multiphasic Personality Inventory 2), the full results of which
are given in the annexe. This is a standard psychological
diagnostic test.

Executive summary

The subject comes from a stable and socially advantaged background, and has had a private education. She is an only child, with attentive and supportive parents. She has no history of mental illness, nor any other significant health issues beyond minor childhood ailments, nor is there any family history of psychiatric issues. She was well presented at interview, well groomed and neatly dressed in slightly formal clothes. When questioned about this, she said her mother had chosen them. She was polite and co-operative, exhibiting neither aggression nor impatience with the process. Throughout the interview she was calm and self-possessed, apart from on certain specific occasions as detailed below. Her affect was normal and congruent.

MMPI-2

This test assesses a subject's mental health on ten scales, including depression, paranoia, and schizophrenia. In this case the data gave no indication of any of the above, and found no evidence that the subject is experiencing psychopathology. However, it is important to note that the subject scored extremely highly on both the 'L' and 'K' scales. In twenty-two years of practice, I have rarely seen scores of this magnitude. High answers on the L scale (commonly referred to as the 'Lie' scale) indicate that the subject is hyper-sensitive to their public image, to the extent of refusing to acknowledge traits or responses that might paint them in a poor light. In respect to the subject, these scores were amply borne out by the observations made in interview. The K scale questions are designed to measure defensiveness, and again, in this case, indicate the subject has an abnormally strong need to be seen positively.

146

Interview

Based on my observations at the parental home, the subject's family milieu has clearly been problematic: the mother masks profound social insecurities under an assertive, almost brusque outward demeanour, and has clearly fetishised social standing almost to the point of mania (a trivial but telling example: on my arrival at the house she made a rather lame joke about being relieved I wasn't wearing a white coat 'so the nosey parkers won't find out'). Numerous items in the house attested to the value attached to the family's position in the local community: photographs of the subject's father with dignitaries such as the Mayor and MP, a cabinet of the subject's sporting medals and trophies, framed cuttings from the local press featuring the family business and charitable events organised by the subject's mother. The immediate community context also served to inculcate a habit of secrecy: the subject described her small rural town as 'the sort of place where everyone wants to poke their noses in – you learn pretty quick how to mind your own business'. The fact that she used this particular phrase was instructive: I note from police transcripts that when the subject's mother was asked by a teacher from another school whether her daughter might be pregnant she replied 'it's none of your business' (I note also that the mother denies this incident ever occurred).

The subject would thus have grown up in an environment in which it would be not only unacceptable but unthinkable to bring shame or embarrassment on the family. This was clearly a major factor in the subject's decision to hide the pregnancies, not just from her parents but from the world in general. However, I believe the issue is more complex than that;

I believe there was, in fact, no real 'decision' or thought process at all. Becoming pregnant out of wedlock (and especially, in the case of the first pregnancy, with a mixed-race child) was <u>literally</u> 'unthinkable': she was unable to think about it, or, therefore, do anything about it. The subject herself described the pregnancies as feeling 'unreal' and 'like it was happening to someone else'. Likewise, when asked why she did not arrange to have terminations, especially after the first live birth, she could not give a coherent answer.

However, it must be noted that while she did not see either a doctor or midwife during any of the pregnancies, and behaved in ways which she must have known would put the unborn children at risk (regular and fairly heavy drinking, playing contact sports), she did appear perfectly capable of thinking rationally about her situation and acting accordingly as soon as labour began. In the case of the missing child, she travelled immediately to a maternity unit, and presented herself in plenty of time – indeed, her behaviour at this point was so prompt and decisive one can only conclude she had researched which hospital she intended to attend some time before, though the subject herself would not be drawn on this. By contrast, women suffering genuine 'pregnancy denial' often fail/refuse to recognise the onset of labour and as a result give birth in traumatic circumstances, such as in bathrooms or lavatories. Likewise, unlike most such women, the subject appears to have had no problem establishing a basic bond with all the children immediately after the birth (both the two she had adopted and the one she is alleged to have killed), with nursing staff attesting to the fact that she held them and breastfed them in the normal way.

I was particularly intrigued to learn that the subject and her two closest friends were known at school as the 'chameleon girls'. Even though this was clearly the result of nothing more than an accidental combination of Christian names, the subject does indeed appear to have developed a form of psychological 'cryptic colouration', adapting her self-presentation to what she believes other people want of her: the Dutiful Daughter, the Good Sport, the Fun Friend, or, in the context of my interaction with her, the Compliant Interviewee. I also noted her adopting some of my own mannerisms as the interview progressed, possibly in a subconscious attempt to 'please' me. Though it should be noted that there is also research suggesting that people are more likely to use mimicry of this kind – again, usually unconsciously – when telling complex untruths.

The only time the subject became distressed was when questioned about the events leading to the disappearance of her second child. She vehemently denied harming the baby in any way, and insisted that as far as she is concerned the child is safe and happy with its biological father. When pressed on the subject of the lies she told the police, and entered on a series of official documents (some 36 in all) she became evasive, looking around the room and failing to maintain eye contact. I was interested, but not surprised, that she also lied at least five times to my knowledge during the course of the three interviews; when challenged on some of these she merely changed the subject. I also raised the issue of the false address she gave at the time of the first birth, suggesting that choosing an anagram of her own name and the number 13 gave the message – whether consciously or not – that she was 'mixed-up' and 'unlucky'. She replied merely that 'it hadn't occurred to her' and she was 'no good at crosswords or stuff like that', a comment which is likewise patently untrue.

Summary

The subject proved extremely hard to assess. She is not mentally ill (within the meaning of the Mental Health Act 1983), she is not a psychopath, she is not a narcissist, and she is not delusional; and while she lies repeatedly, and is clearly comfortable doing so, I am not convinced she is a 'pathological' liar. I believe there may be a degree of psychological 'segmentation' at play, but certainly not to the extent of schizophrenia or Dissociative Identity Disorder (previously known as Multiple Personality Disorder). Many normally functioning people compartmentalise their lives, whether out of fear, self-interest, convenience, or in the interests of privacy; the subject merely does so to an unusually high degree.

I was unable to come to a conclusive opinion as to whether the subject is, or was, capable of intentionally killing her baby. I do, however, believe she is capable of lying about any harm that might have come to the child (whether as the result of an accident or deliberate intent), and doing so convincingly and consistently. It is also perfectly possible that the child is indeed alive and well, as she maintains. That said, I did discern a profound psychological equivocation in relation to the missing child. The version of events the subject gives does not ring true, and while the child must – of course – have had a father, I am unconvinced that the person she describes as 'Tim Baker' is that man. It is worth noting in this context that she continues to assert – as she did in police interviews – that there was no sexual assault, and no element of coercion involved in any of her pregnancies. When pressed on the events of the day the child disappeared, both her words and body language became vague and evasive. I was unable to elicit any more information on this than the police have already ascertained.

Appendix: MMPI-2 analysis

* * *

Adam Fawley
24 October
15.45

We have the visiting area to ourselves. Walls a dull sage green, industrial tiling, a tired-looking children's play area in the far corner. It smells of disinfectant and bad food. We cool our heels for a good five minutes (literally – it's bloody freezing in here) before the door clangs open at the far end and two warders appear. The woman following them is so different from the image in my head that I have to look twice to be sure it's her. She must be two stone overweight on starchy prison food, her hair undyed and dark now, hanging in a greasy ponytail, and a blurry tattoo visible on her neck. But the arrogance is the same: the lift of the chin, the head held high. No wonder they call her the Duchess. As she comes towards us the look on her face is hardened, wary, even cruel; the dark shadow of the Shiphampton princess. But whatever she looks like now, this woman is still that girl – the girl they called the chameleon. Perhaps this is just another, even more necessary, change of camouflage.

She drags out the chair opposite us and bangs it down as far back as the space will permit. One of the warders rolls her eyes. I gesture to Quinn and he takes out a small voice recorder and puts it on the table between us.

'Who are you and what do you want?'

The voice has hardened too. And rasped with years of cigarettes; I can smell smoke on her, even from here.

I flip out my warrant card. 'DI Adam Fawley, Thames Valley. This is DS Quinn.'

She looks him up and down, openly scornful. 'Fuck me, look at the state of that. Are you gay, or what?'

Quinn gapes, opens his mouth to reply, but she's too quick for him. She turns to me; I can see the warder with the spiky hair laughing.

'Thames Valley? You're a long way from home.'

'Not so far from your parents' home.'

She shrugs. 'I wouldn't know. I've never been.'

'Have you heard from them lately?'

She looks sardonic. 'I'm sure the Jailhouse Frock has filled you in on my recent communications, such as they are.'

The Governor, evidently. So the Duchess gives nicknames, as well as takes them. I smile a little. 'Not bad. Did you come up with that?'

She raises an eyebrow by way of answer.

'So you're unaware why we're here?'

'Unaware and, frankly, indifferent.'

I let the pause lengthen. Most people will fill a silence eventually, but not this woman. Then again, all these years, she's had a lot of practice. Quinn shifts beside me. I can hear gates clanging somewhere. The sound of a van engine.

'Food delivery,' she says, watching my face. 'Tuesday

chilled, Wednesday ambient, Friday fresh. Not that it usually merits the term. I used to work in the kitchen.'

Another silence.

'There was an incident at your parents' house. Involving your father.'

She leans back, crosses one ankle over the other leg, man-style. 'If you'd been in prison as long as I have, *DI* Adam Fawley, you'd know that "incident" can cover anything from a bowel movement to a disembowelment, and pretty much anything in between. So what – did the old boy shit himself?'

'No,' says Quinn sarcastically. 'He fucking *shot* someone.'

A smile ripples across her mouth, but it's impossible to tell if it's Quinn or her father who's amusing her so much.

'Well, well, well. Who'd have thought the old man had so much spunk in him.'

She's swaggering now, referencing *Macbeth*, flaunting her intellectual superiority over a pair of clodhopping cops. But two can play at that game, and I'm going to do it on my own terms.

'It doesn't surprise you? I'd be staggered if someone told me that about my father.'

'Your father's probably an accountant. My dear old dad is an arsey old bugger with a hair-trigger temper and a shotgun.'

She sits back and starts drumming her fingers against the base of the chair. She's desperate for a fag; trust me, I know the signs.

'And in any case, what's any of this got to do with me? I haven't seen either of them for months. In fact, it might well be years. If I could be fucked to work it out.'

'The man who was shot was in his late teens or early twenties. According to your parents, he was a random intruder – a burglar.'

She shrugs. 'Yeah, and?'

'And, at first, we thought so too. Until, that is, we ran DNA tests on the victim.'

I pause again, scanning her face. Nothing. Her eyes are blank.

'They were related. This man and your father.'

She swallows, frowns. 'Related? How?'

'He's your son, Ms Rowan.'

Her eyelids flutter and she looks away, drawing a deep breath. Oxygen without benefit of nicotine.

All I can hear now is breathing. Hers and mine.

She swallows. 'Is he OK?'

Because – as you might have noticed – I've made sure not to say. And if she wants to know, she's going to have to work for it.

'Who? Your father?'

A flicker of anger, but only a flicker. She's on the defensive now. 'No – the other –'

I leave a long pause. 'No, Ms Rowan. I'm afraid he's dead. He died at the scene.'

'Tends to happen,' snipes Quinn, 'when you've had your fucking head blown off.'

She's clearly getting under Quinn's skin. I wouldn't have said what he did, but now it's out there I'm intrigued to see how she reacts. Shock, surely. Then what? Anger, sorrow, disbelief? But whatever she's feeling, her face gives nothing away. She lifts one hand and starts gnawing at the skin around her thumb.

154

'Is there anything you'd like to say?'

Her voice is stronger now. 'When am I getting out?'

'That's not up to me. But we'll need a whole lot more information first. Information I'm sure you'll be able to give us.'

Her eyes narrow. 'Like what, for fuck's sake?'

'Like where your son's been for the last twenty years. You know, small details like that.'

'Ha fucking ha,' she says. 'Think yourself quite the fucking comedian, don't you.'

The sudden rash of expletives is telling.

I smile. 'Not at all. I'm just doing my job: asking questions.'

'I've answered a million fucking questions already. I told those goons at South Mercia I gave the kid to its father. I don't know what the fuck happened to either of them after that, and I don't know where the fuck the kid's been since. Satisfied?'

'Not by a long way. You still claim the father was Tim Baker? Despite what came out in that TV series?'

Her eyes narrow. 'Yeah, well, none of that came from me, did it.'

'You're dissociating yourself from it? You never made any of those allegations?'

She smiles; the balance of power has evidently been restored. 'No comment.'

But I'm not playing that game, not with her. Time to take back the initiative. 'Do you know how we can contact Tim Baker?'

She gives me a withering look. 'Don't you think I'd have mentioned it before now if I did? Like fifteen fucking years ago? And in any case, you must know his name, right? You know, from a credit card or something.'

I play dumb. 'I thought his name was Tim Baker?'

There's colour in her cheeks now.

'Not *him*. You know. My – son.'

I shake my head. 'I'm afraid there was nothing to identify him. No cards, no wallet, no phone. Nothing.'

She frowns. 'That's crap. It doesn't make any sense.'

'I agree. Especially when we know for a fact that he had all those things with him when he arrived.'

It's trick-bait, but she doesn't take it. She doesn't ask how I know that, she doesn't ask anything at all. She just sits there, gnawing. The skin around her thumbnail is starting to bleed.

'But you can rest assured we'll get to the bottom of it, Ms Rowan. It may take a while, but we'll work it out. We'll find out what really happened to your baby all those years ago.'

She looks up, meets my gaze, and I smile.

'It really is only a matter of time.'

'Christ, she was a hard-faced cow,' says Quinn, slamming the car door shut behind him.

'Prison will do that to you.'

We sit for a moment in silence. It's starting to rain. A fine drizzle misting the windscreen.

'What do you think?' he says after a long pause.

'About what?'

'Do you think she was surprised? That the kid was still alive, I mean.'

I've been asking myself the same question. Asking, and finding it startlingly hard to answer.

'Not enough,' I say eventually. 'News like that, dropping from nowhere after all this time – she should have been reeling. And vindicated. Triumphant, even.'

Quinn laughs. 'Right – she should have been rubbing our faces right in it. I would have, if it was me.'

'Exactly. So it's obviously not that simple. There's something else in there too. Something muddying the waters.'

'Like what?'

I turn to face him. 'I have no idea.'

'You all right, Rowan?'

She turns and looks back at the prison officer standing in the doorway, her hand on the bolt. She's frowning. Behind her, people are moving past across the landing.

'Bad news, was it?'

Rowan turns away. 'You could say that.' Her thumb is still bleeding and she lifts it to her mouth and starts to suck it.

The officer takes a step closer; in the bottom bunk, Rowan's cellmate turns over and settles again.

'Anything I can do?' says the officer in a low voice.

Rowan glances at her and their eyes meet.

'Maybe.'

* * *

CRIMINAL CASES REVIEW COMMISSION CASE FILE
R v Camilla Kathleen Rowan (2003)
Case number: 772498525/CR
Document number: 451.2
Document type: Interview transcript, South Mercia Police

*Interview with Camilla Rowan, conducted at Calcot
Row Police Station, Gloucester
27 August 2002, 11.00 a.m.
In attendance, DI H. Lucas, DS L. Kearney, Mrs
J. McCrae (Appropriate Adult)*

LK: We've asked you back today, Miss Rowan,
because we've still been unable to locate your
missing son.

CR: He's not *missing*, he's with his father.

LK: So you say, but we haven't been able to track
him down either.

CR: [*shrugs*]
It's a common name. Must be hundreds of them.

LK: Fifty-six, to be precise. Fifty-six men called
Timothy Baker, born in the UK, who would have
been between the ages of 17 and 30 at that
time. We've spoken to every single one of them
and none of them has your child, or knows
anything about you.

CR: [*silence*]

LK: Do you have a photograph of this man?

CR: No.

LK: Can you describe him?

CR: Brown hair, brown eyes – he was just *ordinary*.

LK: Are you prepared to sit down with a police
artist and draw up an e-fit of this man?

CR: Yeah, whatever.

LK: Did he have an accent? Birmingham, say?

CR: No, he just sounded ordinary. Like everyone
else.

LK: And you're sure you have the right name?

CR: [*silence*]

Duration of silence confirmed as 27 seconds

It could have been Dacre.

LK: You're saying his name was Dacre?

CR: I'm saying it could have been.

LK: Tim Dacre?

CR: Or Tom. Maybe.

LK: You don't know the first name of the man you were sleeping with?

CR: Slept with *twice*. Five years ago.

HL: I think most women would remember the name of the man who fathered their child, even if they did only have sex with them twice.

CR: [*silence*]

LK: So let me get this straight. It could have been Tim Baker, Tim *Dacre,* *Tom* Baker or Tom *Dacre*. That's what you're now saying? Or are you just deliberately throwing sand in our eyes?

CR: I'm trying to *help* you.

HL: You're not helping yourself, Miss Rowan.

CR: [*silence*]

LK: We can't find the baby, we can't find the baby's father.' You must know how this looks.

CR: I don't care how it looks – I'm telling the truth.

LK: I should tell you we are now conducting a systematic search along the route you say you took from Birmingham and Solihull General Hospital to Shiphampton. Lay-bys, parks,

woodland, disused ground, anywhere you might
have disposed of the body or buried remains.
We're searching it all.

CR: Search all you fucking like, you won't find
anything.

LK: It doesn't concern you that your own child –
your own flesh and blood – has disappeared off
the face of the earth and no one can find him?

CR: Tim told me that he'd get in touch if there
was a problem, and I've never heard anything.

LK: The mobile number you gave us for him – is
that the only way you have of contacting him?

CR: He said he was going to be moving house so
that was the best way.

LK: You're aware that mobile number is out of
service?

CR: [*shrugs*]

LK: In fact, it has never been *in* service. No one
in the UK has ever had that number. If I was
of a suspicious turn of mind I might be
thinking you just made it up.

CR: [*silence*]

LK: Why did you say you lived in Cambridge?

CR: What?

LK: When you gave your first child up for adoption
you gave your address as 13 Warnock Road,
Cambridge.

CR: So what?

LK: That was a lie, wasn't it? You were still
living at your parents' home in Shiphampton.

CR: What difference does it make?

HL: It makes a difference, Miss Rowan, because you
    knowingly gave false information on an official
    document. One can only infer that you did so
    in order to avoid being contacted.
CR: Look, I didn't want my parents finding out, OK?
    I didn't want a letter arriving and my mum or
    dad getting hold of it.
LK: So why Cambridge?
CR: [*shrugs*]
    I'd just been there. It was nice.
LK: 'It was nice'? That's it?
CR: [*shrugs*]
LK: [*turning to file*]
    But that wasn't the only untruth on that form,
    was it? The GP practice you gave, the email
    address – eleven lies in all.
CR: They weren't *lies* –
LK: What would you call them, then?
CR: I told you – I didn't want anyone to find out –
LK: Do you lie a lot, Miss Rowan?
CR: [*indignant*]
    No, I do not!
LK: Doesn't look like it to me. Looks to me like
    you do it all the time. Indeed, I put it to
    you that you lie so often and so readily that
    you don't even know you're doing it any more –
CR: That's not true!
LK: In fact, I'd go so far as to say that I can tell
    when you're lying because your lips are moving –
JM: Detective Sergeant, that's hardly fair –
CR: [*to Mrs McCrae*]

161

He can't talk to me like that, can he? I've
done nothing wrong.

HL: We've yet to establish that, Miss Rowan.

CR: I've told you - I don't know where the baby
is - I don't know where Tim is - but I didn't
do anything to the baby - I didn't, *I didn't* -

HL: We've done our best to help you, Miss Rowan,
but I'm afraid you leave us with no choice -

CR: [*staring from one officer to the other*]
What? *What?*

LK: Camilla Rowan, I am arresting you on suspicion
of murder. You do not have to say anything,
but it may harm your defence if you do not
mention when questioned -

CR: [*puts her head in her hands on the table and
begins to sob*]

LK: - something which you later rely on in court.
Anything you do say may be given in evidence.

CR: [*muffled*]
It's not fair! It's not fair!

LK: Interview terminated at 11.25.

* * *

Adam Fawley
24 October
17.28

There's a jam on the M25 just south of Byfleet. Ten minutes later we're still sitting there, edging painfully forward,
uncomfortably close to the trapped humans either side. A
kid in the back of the SUV next to us is chewing and

making faces through the window, his parents arguing in the front. The bloke in the van on the other side is smoking, looking at his mobile. It always feels doubly uncomfortable – not just the physical proximity, but the fact that the one thing these metal boxes are supposed to give us is the freedom to distance. I remember being stuck on the A40 once, back in the nineties, heading into London. Nose to tail for half an hour. And the person in the car next to me was Princess Diana. No – I didn't believe it either. Not at first. But it was her. On her own, driving herself. Desperate for privacy but forced instead into an uneasy unforeseen intimacy with a nobody like me.

The truck in front inches forward, then the brake lights come on. Quinn mutters something under his breath. But now the lorry's moved I can see the sign ahead. We're less than a mile from the A3 turn-off. Cobham one way, Wisley the other.

I point. 'Let's come off there.'

Quinn frowns. 'Are you sure? It'll be a crap route across country from there.'

'That's not why I'm suggesting it. Melissa Rutherford lives in Cobham.'

* * *

'You don't recognize him?'

The woman sighs and takes the picture again. 'It's not very clear, is it?'

Bradley Carter gives her a weary look. 'I'm afraid it's all we've got.'

The hotel's called the Park View, but unlike Heathside,

163

it's not living up to its name. The only vista on offer is the kebab house and bookmaker's on the other side of the street, which is solid now with rush-hour traffic. Park View is a four-storey Victorian building and must once have been quite an impressive family house, but hard times have fallen and it has a down-in-the-mouth feel; grimy, peeling, faded, cracked.

The receptionist hands him back the picture. 'I don't think he was here, but I can't be a hundred per cent sure. Sorry.'

'Did any of your guests leave at the weekend without letting you know?'

She gives him an arch look. 'I don't keep tabs on 'em, love. It's not the bleeding Ritz. They pay up front and I don't ask questions. If they want to leave early then that's fine by me.'

'Is there anywhere else round here you can suggest I try?'

She shrugs. 'Your guess is as good as mine. There must be fifty places like this within shouting distance – you're going to be at it all night.' He looks dejected now, exactly the same face he must have had as a chocolate-deprived twelve-year-old. She smiles briefly. 'We have a vacancy, if you need a place to crash. I can do you it for thirty quid – special discount.'

Carter slides the picture back into his jacket. 'Thanks,' he says. 'I'll check with the office and get back to you.'

* * *

I knew Melissa Rutherford had money – that corner office on the documentary was a bit of a giveaway – but the house still manages to be impressive. Big windows, lots of glass and timber and light. It looks like it should be on *Grand Designs*. Perhaps it was; because something tells me she didn't just buy this, she had it built.

She doesn't answer the door, though. It's another woman, wearing a black crew neck and dark trousers. She's barefoot, so I guess the swanky spec included under-floor heating.

'Yes?'

I haul out my warrant card. 'DI Adam Fawley, DS Quinn. Is Ms Rutherford in by any chance?'

A frown flickers across her face, but she doesn't say anything, just steps back. Only a little. Just enough to call back into the house, not enough to let us in. 'Mel? There are some police people here for you.'

Her voice is soft Scots. There's music playing some-where in the house. Jazz. If they have kids they must be in bed, but I suspect they don't. It's all too pristine. Then there's a soft creak of footsteps on the wooden floor and I see Rutherford emerge from what must be the kitchen end of the house, holding a tea towel. She looked impec-cably professional in the documentary – tailored suit, cream blouse, wire-rimmed glasses. But now she's in pale-grey sweats with her hair in a loose topknot. She's the same age as Camilla, but she looks ten years younger.

'Yes, what is it?'

'We're from Thames Valley Police. Could we come in for a moment?'

The other woman makes herself scarce, leaving us in their double-height sitting room with its reconditioned timber ceiling and view down the garden in the thickening dusk. A scatter of golden lights among the borders picks out a water feature, topiary and a pale owl, its wings reared to land, which for half a second I think is actually real.

Rutherford drops on to one of the black leather sofas and gestures us to do the same.

'So what's this about?'

'Camilla Rowan.'

Her face freezes and she sits up, reaching to grip the edge of the sofa. I feel suddenly and overwhelmingly sorry for her – she must have hoped all that had finally gone away.

'Has something happened?'

Quinn suppresses a sardonic snort. Rutherford looks at him and then at me.

'We're awaiting final confirmation, but we believe Camilla's son has turned up.'

Her eyes widen. 'You found the body? After all this time?'

I shake my head. 'No. I'm sorry – I should have been clearer. Camilla didn't kill her baby.'

She's staring at me. 'He's *alive*?'

This is getting complicated. Too bloody complicated.

'He was. There was an incident at the weekend, just outside Oxford. I'm afraid he was killed.'

I can see her rearranging her mental apparatus,

retrofitting all this to what she's always assumed. But she's bright, she's a lawyer; it won't take her long. And it doesn't.

'So where's he been all these years?'

I manage a wry smile. 'That's what we're trying to find out. He was identified only by his DNA – there weren't any documents or other ID on him. We don't even know what name he's been using.'

She frowns; she knows as well as I do that there's something odd going on here, but like I said, she's a lawyer.

'So what do you want from me?'

'Anything you have. Anything you didn't tell the first investigation. Anything you've remembered since.' I pause. 'Anything this news might have triggered.'

She raises her eyebrows, then looks away.

'Do her parents know?' she says, after a moment.

'Yes, they have been told.'

There's a silence.

'Why did you ask about her parents? I must admit, it's not the first question I thought you'd have.'

She shrugs. 'I was just wondering how they'd reacted. I felt so incredibly sorry for them at the trial – the press, the abuse, people crawling all over their lives. Peggy was a wreck.'

I must look surprised because she continues quickly, 'I mean, yes, I didn't like her much when I was younger – she was a terrible snob, always going on about keeping up appearances and what other people would think. But for someone like that – having your daughter accused of infanticide and having to admit you didn't have a clue what was going on in your own house – it doesn't get any worse than that.'

Quinn looks sceptical. 'You really think her mother didn't know? Or did she just not *want* to know?'

But the answer is immediate. 'I *know* she didn't know. If she had, she'd never have let it happen a second time.'

'But she had a lot of opportunities to observe her daughter, didn't she?' I ask. 'And not just at home. She helped with the hockey team, went on day trips with the school. It's hard to believe a mother wouldn't notice.'

She makes a face. 'Well, I don't disagree with you, but it does happen.'

'They asked you on the documentary whether you knew about the pregnancies. I was interested in your reply – you said "she never told me". You didn't say "I didn't know". That strikes me as a lawyer's answer.'

She gives me a quick, dry look. 'Well, maybe they shouldn't have filmed me in the office.' It's half a joke, but only half.

'So did you actually know?'

She sighs. 'Let's just say I suspected.'

'Enough to say anything?'

She hesitates, then nods. 'Yes, I said something.'

Silence.

'Who to? Your mother? A teacher?'

She swallows. 'I spoke to Cam.'

* * *

CRIMINAL CASES REVIEW COMMISSION CASE FILE
R v Camilla Kathleen Rowan (2003)
Case number: 772498525/CR
Document number: 322.2.1
Document type: Witness statement, South Mercia Police

Interview with Peggy Rowan, conducted at Calcot
Row Police Station, Gloucester
13 September 2002, 9.05 a.m.
In attendance, DI H. Lucas, DS L. Kearney,
W. Gilmour (solicitor)

LK: Thank you for coming in today, Mrs Rowan. As I
    explained to you outside, this interview is
    being taped, to assist us with our enquiries,
    but you are not under arrest and can leave at
    any time. You have also elected to bring a
    legal representative with you, which is, of
    course, your right. So, can we start by
    talking about your daughter's first pregnancy,
    in 1996.

PR: I've already told you, I didn't know anything
    about any of it.

LK: She was sixteen, and living under your roof –
    you didn't see her getting out of the bath, in
    her nightclothes?

PR: We're not that sort of family.

LK: Did you know she had a boyfriend?

PR: As far as we were concerned she didn't. She
    was always home by eleven. And she never
    brought anyone home, I can tell you that.

LK: So you don't know who the father might have
    been?

PR: I have absolutely no idea. I didn't even know
    she knew any boys like that.

LK: Black boys?

PR: Exactly.

LK: How would you and your husband have reacted if she'd brought home a black boyfriend?

PR: [*pause*]
I think we'd have been surprised.

HL: You wouldn't have had a problem with it?

PR: [*shrugs*]

LK: [*passes across a photo of Camilla Rowan and two friends*]
She's pregnant with that baby in this picture. Eight months pregnant.

PR: [*pushing the picture away*]
Well, exactly. That's my point. She doesn't *look* pregnant. Any more than those other girls.

LK: Why do you think she didn't tell you?

PR: How am I supposed to know?

LK: She didn't usually confide in you? As her mother?

PR: Like I said, we're not that sort of family. Those women who try to be their daughters' 'best friends', it's never a good idea. In my opinion.

LK: What about the second pregnancy, the baby that was born in December 1997?

PR: I didn't know about that either. Not a thing.

LK: How does that make you feel now – all this going on under your nose and you didn't notice?

PR: She was obviously very good at hiding it, wasn't she?

LK: Did she do that a lot – keep secrets from you?

PR: Not as far as I knew. Seems I was wrong, doesn't it.

170

LK: Have you spoken to her about it since we arrested her?

PR: Briefly.

LK: What did she say?

PR: [*shrugs*]
That she didn't say anything at the time because she wanted to protect us.

HL: Protect you from what?

PR: [*silence*]

HL: Embarrassment? Shame? Loss of face? What?

PR: [*shrugs*]

LK: Do you know who the father of the second baby was?

PR: Not a clue.

LK: Did she ever mention a Tim or a Tom?

PR: Not that I recall. It's five years ago.

LK: Does the surname Baker mean anything to you?

PR: No.

LK: I believe you were quite active with Camilla's school – helping out with events and so on?

PR: I wasn't the only one.

LK: No, I understand that. But we've been told you were particularly active with the hockey team? That in fact you travelled with the Burghley Abbey team to the 1997 UK national under-18s hockey championships?

PR: Yes, so?

LK: It was the night of the final that Camilla went into labour. She drove herself, alone, to Birmingham and checked into hospital.

PR: Well, I didn't know that.

LK: You were with her for three days, watching her
     play hockey – a vigorous and occasionally
     aggressive game, might I add – and you didn't
     suspect she might be pregnant?

PR: I told you –

HL: My officers have also spoken to someone else
     who was at that tournament. A teacher from
     Lady Elspeth Haskell's School in Shropshire.

PR: So?

LK: She said it was perfectly obvious to everyone
     that Camilla was pregnant. That both her
     colleagues and the girls on the Lady Elspeth
     team had mentioned it. Girls who had shared
     changing rooms with her.

PR: [*silence*]

LK: She also said she spoke to someone from
     Burghley Abbey – she was worried about
     Camilla's well-being, and extremely concerned
     that a young girl in such an advanced stage of
     pregnancy should be playing at all.

PR: [*silence*]

LK: She said she approached someone she saw
     watching on the touchline. She thought it was
     a teacher. But it wasn't. It was you.

PR: I don't remember that.

LK: She said she pointed Camilla out – not knowing
     she was your daughter – and asked if there was
     any possibility she could be pregnant.

PR: [*silence*]

LK: You don't remember what you said?

PR: [*silence*]

172

LK: You said it was 'none of her business'.

PR: [*silence*]

LK: So you did know.

PR: No, I told you.

LK: Someone points out your daughter and says she
looks pregnant and it doesn't give you pause?

PR: [*silence*]

LK: Did you speak to Camilla?

PR: No.

LK: Why not?

PR: [*to Mr Gilmour*]
Do I really have to answer all these questions?

WG: No, you don't. And I think that's enough for
today, officers. My client has made it
perfectly clear that she knows nothing about
the baby, or what happened to it –

LK: Her own *grandchild* –

WG: Should you have any further questions, please
contact me to make an appointment.

LK: Interview terminated at 9.40.

* * *

Adam Fawley
24 October
18.25

'You spoke to her? What did you say?'

'I asked about her weight gain. I mean, I didn't put it
quite that way, but that was the gist of it. God, it was
embarrassing. It's a massive no-no, talking to another girl
about her weight.'

'How did she react?'

'She laughed. Said something about having eaten too much Häagen-Dazs.'

'Was she just fobbing you off?'

She spreads her hands, at a loss. 'I genuinely don't know. It's possible she really didn't know she was pregnant.'

'Was this the first time or the second?'

A pause, a frown. 'The second.'

'Then how could she *not* have known? Surely she'd have recognized the signs the second time.'

She shrugs. 'You'd think so, wouldn't you.'

'Did you ever have any suspicions about who the father of that baby was? I know you said you didn't in your original statement, but if there's anything you might have thought of since, however vague, it might really help.'

She gives a lopsided smile. ''Fraid not. Your guess is as good as mine. Better, probably.'

There's a silence.

Quinn clears his throat. 'Sorry to have to ask this, Ms Rutherford, but were you and Camilla ever sexually involved?'

Her mouth drops open. Only a little, but enough.

She swallows. 'How did you know?'

He spreads his hands. 'I didn't. Not till now – what I mean is, you're obviously in a same-sex relationship now, aren't you? And then it struck me that Leonora Staniforth said something in the documentary about you and Camilla having been particularly tight around then.'

She sighs. 'Well, since you're asking, then, yes. We did have a thing. Briefly. No one knew – not even Leo. I think it was just experimenting – for Cam, I mean. It was different for me.'

'Different in that you already knew you were gay?'

'Partly. Cam certainly didn't take it very seriously. It was just a bit of fun. For her. A sideshow to the real event.'

I sit forward. 'And it wasn't for you? It was serious?'

She sighs. 'I thought so. For a time. She has that effect on people.'

'You never mentioned this during the original investigation.'

She flushes a little. 'I was just a junior in the firm then. And people weren't as "open-minded" fifteen years ago, especially not in Magic Circle law firms. And like I said, I didn't know who the father of the baby was. Letting the whole world poke about in my private life wasn't going to change that. My relationship with Cam – such as it was – was entirely irrelevant.'

I leave a pause. 'Not "entirely" irrelevant, surely?'

She frowns. 'I don't follow.'

'If you were having a physical relationship with Camilla you'd have been better placed than anyone to know that she was pregnant. In fact, it's hard to see how you *couldn't* have known.'

She flushes and looks away.

'Ms Rutherford?'

She turns back to face me. 'OK. What I said before – about asking her about her weight – that did happen. The only thing I left out was that it was in bed. On a memorable Sunday afternoon when her parents were lunching with friends.' She stares at me. 'Happy now?'

'And even in those circumstances – those *intimate*

circumstances – she still managed to convince you she was telling the truth?'

She laughs grimly. 'Well, I'm not the only one she fooled that way, now am I?'

* * *

When Quinn finally gets home he's feeling pretty pleased with himself. Tired, but pleased. The lights are on in his top-floor flat and as he walks across the piazza and looks up he can see Maisie moving about. It's the first time he's seen her like that – at home, in his place – and he's side-swiped by a little surprise of joy. He spent weeks persuading himself that asking her to move in was the right thing to do, and was then completely wrong-footed that she didn't say yes straight away and he had to put even more effort into persuading *her*. He'd worried there'd be loads of girly crap about the place, and he'd be nagged, and not be able to just veg in his joggers, but apart from some make-up stuff on her side of the bed and a few more toiletries in the bath-room (some of which he's actually tempted to try), things haven't changed much. Visible things anyway. As for the rest of it, that's fine too. Pretty good, actually.

He opens the door to music and a waft of cooking. Maisie is on the other side of the big open-plan living space, setting the table.

'Hi,' she says, looking up with a smile. 'You OK?'

He throws his scarf and tablet on the side table and drops into the settee. 'Yeah, fine. Pretty good, actually.'

'What was she like – Rowan?'

He grimaces. 'Right hard-faced cow.'

Maisie shrugs. 'Well, fifteen years in prison and all that.'

'Yeah, that's what Fawley said too.'

'So did she say anything?'

He shakes his head. 'Nah. Nothing she hasn't said before, that's for sure. Now Melissa Rutherford, that was a *whole* different ball game.'

She pauses for a moment in what she's doing. 'You spoke to her as well?'

He starts easing off his shoes. 'Yeah, well, it was almost on the way, so Fawley decided to go there on the way back. And I suspect he's rather glad he did.'

He smiles at her, dangling the bait.

She makes a face at him. 'Come on – spill.'

'Well, let's just say you were right. She's shacked up with a woman.'

Maisie's eyes widen. 'I *knew* it – I told you – what that woman Leonora said about those two – I *knew* there'd been something going on –'

He's grinning now. 'Yeah, mega brownie points to you. Fawley didn't make the connection at all, not until I asked her – even though we both knew by then she was gay. I think he was pretty impressed, actually.'

She drops her gaze to hide her smile – it doesn't surprise her that Quinn's taken the credit for what was actually her insight, but she really doesn't care. She doesn't give a toss about impressing Fawley, but she knows Quinn does. Far more than he'd ever admit, even to himself.

He loosens his tie. 'So what's for dinner?'

*   *   *

177

When Bradley Carter woke up the following morning it had taken him a few seconds to realize where he was. The light was coming from the wrong direction, the sheets felt strange. Not his own bed at his parents' place in Marston (though he's been careful not to let on to anyone at work that he still lives at home), but a pokey top-floor room in the just-as-bad-as-he-thought-it-would-be Park View hotel. It turned out the thirty-quid overnight stay was actually cheaper than the train up and back twice, so he washed his grots in the sink and had a night on a lumpy bed with a TV bolted to the wall and no Wi-Fi. It's a demoralizing start to what will no doubt be another demoralizing day. He gives the instant coffee sachet and UHT milk a definite swerve and heads down the stairs, passing a couple of Chinese tourists at reception asking for directions to Buckingham Palace. He stops on the front step, assessing the various coffee options – at this time of the morning it's going to be a trade-off between quality and speed, but when you factor in the weather, proximity is likely to win: there's a thin, mean-spirited drizzle just starting, the kind that doesn't seem to be that wet until you've been out in it an hour and realize you're soaked. He checks his mobile for messages, then turns up his coat collar and heads down the street to the main road.

* * *

Upstairs at St Aldate's, the office is surprisingly empty. Carter's in London, Ev and Hansen are en route to interview Leonora Staniforth at her Cotswold stone pile, and Fawley and Quinn are halfway to South Mercia Police HQ for what's likely to be an uncomfortable encounter. Which leaves Baxter in charge and Chloe Sargent on the coffee runs. And he's going to need all the caffeine he can get: it took South Mercia six months to pull together the database he has in front of him, and he'll be lucky if he gets that many days to go through it all. 'Herculean' isn't in it.

He drags his chair a bit closer to the desk and opens the first file.

GENERAL RECORDS OFFICE, REGISTER OF BIRTHS

ENGLAND & WALES

1997

* * *

Even though she knew they were coming, Leonora still looks alarmed when she opens the door.

'It's about Cam, isn't it – you found her son.'

Melissa has clearly phoned her. She was asked not to speak to anyone but she's obviously made an exception for her old schoolmate. Ev puts on her 'no need to panic' face, first developed when she was a bobby on the beat and an invaluable part of her standard police kit ever since. Along with spare tissues, a packet of mints and a great deal of patience.

'Good morning, Mrs Neville. DC Verity Everett, DC Thomas Hansen, Thames Valley Police. May we come in?'

She looks flustered now. 'Yes, yes, of course, sorry. It's all just been overwhelming, coming out of the blue like that.'

'Don't worry, I totally understand. It was bound to be a bit of a shock.'

They follow her down the hall into the same kitchen

Ev remembers from the Netflix show, though it's had a coat of paint since, and the clutter is rather less artfully arranged than it was on TV.

Leonora fusses about with coffee for a while, but they're happy to bide their time: let the stress settle and they'll get more out of her.

'So, Mrs Neville,' says Ev, when they're finally seated at the table. 'You're obviously aware why we're here. So is there anything you can tell us that may not have occurred to you before?'

She wraps her hands around her mug. 'I've been thinking and thinking, ever since Mel called, and I just can't remember anything.' She lifts her hands. 'I'm sorry.'

'Just take your time, Mrs Neville –'

'You can call me Leonora. "Mrs Neville" makes me sound like my mother-in-law.'

'OK, Leonora, like I said, there's no rush, you may know more than you realize.'

There's a silence, just the ticking of the old grandfather clock in the corner. It's so tall they've had to dig out part of the ceiling to fit it in.

'As I'm sure you'll understand, our first priority is finding out where Ms Rowan's son has been all these years, and unfortunately we don't have any ID –'

'Yes,' she says quickly. 'Mel said.'

'So we're starting on the basis that Ms Rowan was telling the truth and did, in fact, hand the child to its father. Have you had any contact with her since she's been in prison?'

She shakes her head. 'No. No way.'

Hansen's turn. 'Is there anything you can tell us about the boys she was seeing back then?'

She gives him a hopeless look. 'I went through all this years ago – when she was arrested. I told those other police everything I knew. I didn't know anything about that Tim or Tom whatever his name was. She never mentioned him to me.'

Hansen flips open his notebook. 'She did have a boyfriend though, around that time?'

She fiddles with her mug again; she still hasn't drunk any of it.

'There was Peter Anderson, but it wasn't him.'

Everett nods. 'I gather they only started seeing each other some weeks after she must have become pregnant.'

'And he definitely didn't take the baby. He was on holiday with his family. They proved that in court.'

'Are you still in touch?'

She makes a face. 'On and off. Christmas cards, you know.'

'Could you let DC Hansen have his address before we go?'

She looks anxious for a moment. 'It's in Dumfries somewhere. Look, it really wasn't him. Honestly – I'd know. He has two daughters –'

'He's not under any suspicion,' says Ev quickly. 'We just need to eliminate him. No one could be ruled out when the baby first disappeared because we didn't have its DNA, but now we do. It'd be in Mr Anderson's interests, really. It'd let him draw a line under the whole thing once and for all.'

She drops her gaze. 'OK. It's just, you know – I don't want him thinking I dropped him in it.'

'That's understandable. But we'd really rather prefer you didn't talk to him about this until we have a chance to speak to him ourselves.'

She's still staring into her coffee.

'OK,' she says eventually. 'OK.'

'So,' says Hansen, 'other than Peter Anderson, were there other boyfriends you can remember?'

'I said all this the first time. There were a few boys she liked, but no one I'd call a "boyfriend".'

Hansen consults his notes. 'Marcus Crowther and Jamie Fox?'

'Yes, she knew both of them.'

'Do you think it's possible,' says Ev, 'that one of them could have fathered the second baby?'

She shrugs. 'You tell me. Camilla's mother kept her on a pretty tight rein – she always had to be back home by eleven. There wasn't exactly a lot of opportunity.'

'That must have made it hard to get away – when she went into labour.'

Her eyes narrow; she knows what Ev's getting at.

'The second time was when we were at that hockey thing. It was the last night – it was just before Christmas – everyone went out – it would've been easy to slip away.'

'Where did her mother think she was?'

She shrugs. 'You'd have to ask her. She probably thought it was a sleepover with the team or something.'

'And the first baby – what about when she went into labour then?'

She sighs. 'Yes, well, I lied for her that time, didn't I – told her mother she was staying at mine. You *know* that. Look, I was just a kid – I thought she wanted to bunk off down the pub – I had no idea what was really going on –'

'It's OK, Mrs Nev – Leonora – I'm not accusing you of anything.'

182

'I'm sorry, I know you're not. But it was bloody awful – being interrogated over and over again, and then that horrible prosecutor trying to get me to admit I knew something about that baby when I didn't, and then being in the bloody papers –'

Her voice is getting shrill.

'Like I said,' says Ev quickly, 'we're just trying to find out what happened. That's all.'

Leonora raises her mug to her lips. She's trembling slightly, and pulls her cardigan closer round her shoulders.

Hansen takes the still from the CCTV footage from his pocket and places it on the table between them.

'This is the man,' he says. 'The one we believe is Camilla's son.'

She hesitates, then reaches out and pulls the photo closer. 'It's not very clear.'

'I'm afraid it's all we've got.'

There's silence; she's staring at the picture.

'We were hoping he might look like someone you knew back then?'

She slowly shakes her head. 'No, I'm afraid he doesn't. He doesn't even look like Cam.'

* * *

Adam Fawley
25 October
10.30

Turns out I've never actually been to South Mercia Police HQ. I'd definitely remember it if I had. It looks like a football stadium, all swooping rooflines and glass walls. And blue – a *lot* of upbeat, positive, here-to-serve blue.

We park up in the visitors' area and make our way over to reception. It's more like a hotel or a private hospital than a plod shop. There are even sofas. With cushions.

We're on time, we're expected, but they still make us wait. Quinn sits there messing about with his phone, grumbling every few minutes and checking his watch. But if that's how Kearney wants to play it, fine by me. I've had a twenty-year-old case rise from the dead and bite me in the arse; I know how it feels.

A chipper young female PC arrives about ten minutes later and takes us upstairs, collecting coffee orders on the way. Judging by the list of options, their machine is way flashier than ours. Kearney has a big office on the third floor, with a picture window and a decent computer and his own set of armchairs round a small table. I find myself wondering idly about whether they might be recruiting.

'Adam Fawley?' he says, rising from his chair and coming towards me. 'Lawrence Kearney.'

He's older than me – fiftyish, with a bristle of thick grey hair, a rather darker moustache and a pair of intense blue eyes.

'Take a seat.'

I let him choose his preferred chair, then take my own. I notice he pulls up his trouser knees before he sits down. Old school, then.

'So,' he says, 'I gather the Camilla Rowan case has reared its ugly head again.'

'I'm afraid so, sir. I suspect it's the last thing any of us needs.'

'You're telling me.'

'I'm hoping we can make this as painless as possible, but –'

He waves a hand. 'I know how it works.' He doesn't actually call me 'laddie', but it's definitely a possibility. 'You'll go poking about looking under stones, seeing if you can catch us out, causing a whole lot of stress to decent hard-working officers, and end up with bugger all.'

'That's not our intention, sir.'

The door opens and the young PC comes in with a tray.

There's a useful pause, fiddling about with cups, and by the time she disappears Kearney seems to have regained some of his composure.

'So what next?'

'We have the case files already, sir, and we'll be re-interviewing the key witnesses, including the parents. Though that's been complicated by the fact that they're both now under arrest.'

He frowns. 'So I heard. Did they know, do you think – that he was their grandson?'

'They insist not.'

'You believe them?'

'Let's just say the jury's out.' There's a pause. 'Oh, and DI Gallagher asked to be remembered to you.'

He smiles now. 'Ruth's a fine officer. I knew she'd go far.'

'I agree, sir. We're lucky to have her.'

I see Quinn roll his eyes but thankfully he's out of Kearney's line of sight.

'So what do you need from me?'

'If you have time now, I'd like to talk to you about the case, and I'd like DS Quinn to have access to any other officers who had a significant role in the investigation, both serving and retired.'

Kearney turns to him. 'You'll be clocking up the mileage.'

Quinn shrugs. 'It's no bother.'

Kearney bridles slightly and I shoot Quinn a dagger look. He flushes, just a little. 'I don't mind. I like driving. Sir.'

Kearney gets up, rather ponderously, and goes over to his desk. When he returns, he hands Quinn a sheet of paper. He knew exactly what we'd be after and he prepared. Just as I would have done.

'These are the people you need. Start with Mick Havers. Retired now, but he lives local so I asked him to pop in today – thought you might want to talk to him. He's in the meeting room downstairs.'

Blimey, they have meeting rooms too. There's a knock at the door and the PC puts her head round; it's clearly Quinn's signal to leave. He gets up, nods to me and is gone.

The door swings slowly and silently shut and Kearney turns to me. 'OK. Let's cut the bull, shall we?'

* * *

'Two sugars, right?' says Chloe Sargent, sliding the cup on to Baxter's desk. 'And the machine's run out of Twix so I got you a Snickers.' She laughs nervously. 'Hope you're not allergic to nuts.'

'Thanks,' he mutters, barely glancing up. 'I owe you.'

He's staring so intently he doesn't realize that she's still there, five minutes later, looking over his shoulder.

He turns round properly this time. 'Sorry, was there something else?'

She flushes. 'I was just interested – in what you're doing.'

He gives her a heavy look. 'Most people run a mile from stuff like this.'

She tries a smile. 'DC Hansen was talking about digital forensics and I was just wondering what it meant. In a real case.'

He raises his eyebrows. 'Was he now? Well, that's a first round here.'

'So can I see? Is that OK?'

He nods. 'Sure.'

She drags over a chair and sits down.

He points at the screen. 'This is basically what South Mercia did back in 2002 to try and find the baby. It was a bloody awful needle-in-a-haystack job, but they didn't have much choice – murder cases without a body are always an effing nightmare, so the only way to prove the kid was dead was to prove it wasn't alive, if you catch my drift.'

'OK.'

'So they started by looking at all baby boys whose births were registered in the six weeks after Camilla gave birth. She never registered the kid herself, so if it *was* still alive the father would have had to have done it. Only that came up with nothing, so the next thing they looked at was all boys born at Birmingham and Solihull General Hospital on or around the same date. There were thirteen other male babies delivered there that week, but they all checked out, so they widened the search out both by date and geography – to the rest of Brum and the West Midlands, and the two months before and after 23rd December.' He flips to another file. 'See?'

'And they were physically checking out every single baby boy?'

He nods. 'All the ones who fitted the profile, yeah.' He flips through more and more files, each child tracked, traced and eliminated. 'There were over a hundred uniforms on it at one point.'

'Jeez. And there was no DNA?'

'They had hers, obviously, but nothing else, because Rowan left before the hospital could do any blood tests on the baby. So yeah, they did do tests on some of the kids – certainly any of 'em where there was any sort of doubt. But they came up empty every time. And not having the kid's DNA made identifying the father a non-starter.'

'But we have it now, right?'

'Right, and forensics are doing a full familial search.'

She looks thoughtful. 'So what are *you* looking for?' She gestures at the screen. 'I mean, there's so much of it.'

He pulls a face. 'Tell me about it,' he says heavily. 'But yeah, it's a good question. Sometimes you don't know it till you see it. Could be something that pops now, with hindsight, but couldn't have popped then. Or an obvious omission – like data that's logged as being there but actually isn't.'

'Wouldn't that have been spotted at the time?'

'You'd think so, but by all accounts they were still pulling all this stuff together when the trial started. I gather the judge was none too pleased.'

He flips back to the page he was looking at when she arrived and sits back, reaching for the coffee.

She leans forward and reads the first entry: 'Aaron William Dacre, DOB 6 January 1998, Cheltenham General

Hospital, Father – Timothy Dacre, Mother – Phoebe Dacre, née Fenner.'

Baxter makes a face. 'Tim Dacre, Tom Dacre, Tim Baker, Tom Baker, whatever his bloody name was. Though Tom Baker is pretty bloody apt because whoever he is, he must have fucking regenerated –'

She's looking at him blankly, and he realizes he's showing his age. '*Dr Who*,' he says, a little lamely. 'Tom Baker was Dr Who. When I was a kid.'

She's smiling now and he shakes his head. 'Yeah, yeah, don't rub it in – you weren't even born then, right?'

* * *

Hansen puts down his mobile and looks across to Ev. They're on their way back to Oxford.

'That was Peter Anderson. He said he'd go into his local police station this afternoon and give a DNA sample.'

'Great. We'd better call Dumfries and Galloway – let them know he's coming.'

He smiles. 'Next on the list.'

His phone pings and he looks down to scan the message. 'Ah, great – it's an email from Marcus Crowther – he's going to come into St Aldate's tomorrow. Which just leaves us with Jamie Fox. He lives in Stockport, so we'll have to ask Greater Manchester to pick up on that one. But it just so happens my ex works there so I'll give him a call and see if he can get me a contact.'

There's a tiny pause. 'Great,' says Ev. 'Good stuff.'

He wonders if the hesitation was because she was waiting for the lights to change, or because she registered the 'he' and 'him' he slipped in there. He's pretty sure she already knew, but it's high time she did, either way. Though he doubts she'll be fazed, any more than Fawley was. And then she glances across at him with a smile that leaves no room for doubt and he grins back and the smile is still there as she changes up a gear and puts her foot down.

* * *

Kearney pours me a coffee and sits back down. 'So what do you want to know?'

'What did you think happened? At the time?'

He raises his eyebrows. 'To the kid? I thought she killed it. The lies, the evasions, the way she behaved – everything pointed to that. And the jury agreed with me.'

'And now?'

He takes his time. 'How did she react – when you told her?'

'That he'd reappeared? Hard to be sure. Not as surprised as I would have expected.'

'Did she ask about him – where he'd been, that sort of stuff?'

I shake my head. 'No. Nothing.'

'You got kids?'

The minefield question. I had two; I have one. And the present-tense answer is – now and always – the only possible reply.

'A daughter.'

'How old?'

'Three months.'

That clearly surprises him, though he does his best to hide it. He probably thinks I'm one of those second-time-arounders with a shiny new wife half my age.

'And if your daughter turned up out of the blue after being missing for twenty years, wouldn't you want to know where she'd been?'

'Of course. But I wouldn't have given my child to a virtual stranger in the first place.'

He points a finger at me. 'That's the crux of the Rowan case. Right there.'

I leave a pause, clear my throat. 'She didn't ask how he'd tracked her parents down either. Not that I could have told her. All she wanted to know was when she was getting out.'

He gives a quick, grim laugh. 'Right. I bet she did.'

'You still haven't answered my question, sir.'

He sits back. 'You want to know what I think now? I think this case is a bloody minefield. Let's just say I'm glad I'm not in *your* shoes.'

I make a face. 'Join the club.'

That gets a smile. A desert-level dry one, but a smile.

'Is there anything you'd do differently now, sir, with the benefit of hindsight?'

He considers. 'Nope,' he says eventually. 'I think we did pretty much what any competent investigation would do. Then or now.'

'You and your team put in a hell of a lot of hours tracking down baby boys of the right age, and yet you never found him.'

His eyes narrow. 'My lads did a good job. You won't find otherwise.'

'And I'm not suggesting otherwise. But the baby must have been there, all the same.'

He sits back again. 'There'll be an explanation. No bloody clue what, mind you. But there'll be one.'

He picks up his coffee.

'What would you do now, sir, if you were running this inquiry?'

He gives me a dark look. 'Leave the country? No, seriously, I assume you're doing familial DNA on your vic?'

I nod. 'Underway.'

He shrugs. 'Then you're doing what I'd be doing.'

'Did you consider – at the time – whether Rowan might have had the baby adopted? Illegally, that time?'

'She sold the kid, you mean? Yes, we did look at that.'

'I don't remember seeing much about it in the files.'

His eyes narrow. 'That,' he says quickly, 'is because there was sod all to say.'

I wait. Count to twenty. I suspect he may be too.

'As I'm sure you're aware,' he begins, in a voice heavy with irritated patience, 'the illegal adoption trade only really took off after the internet. Back in '97 it was mostly just friends of friends type of stuff – someone who knew someone who knew someone. You know as well as I do that it's near nigh impossible to run that sort of thing down, especially five bloody years later, which is what we were facing. We did have a few leads – West Mids had some contacts and put us on to one or two – but none of 'em came up with diddly.'

'I see.'

'And if Rowan did sell that kid she didn't get much for it – she certainly never came into any significant cash around then; we checked. The only thing she did spend any money on was that bloody tattoo – "Sweet freedom". Now there's an irony.' He's getting into his stride again. 'And remember how narrow the time window was – she left Brum at three and was at home for the Christmas party by five. She had half an hour, max, to get rid of that kid, so if she handed it off to someone she must have made all the arrangements beforehand. And how would a girl like her even *find* an illegal adoption agency? I mean, they could hardly put ads in the bloody paper, now could they? And she lived in Shiphampton, not bloody Sparkhill.'

'But she did give birth in Birmingham, and the psychiatrist who assessed her pre-trial said she almost certainly researched the hospital sometime beforehand. As she probably did with the first baby as well.'

'So?'

'So she could have met someone that way. If she'd been hanging about the hospital she could have met another mother – another girl in her position. They might have given her a contact.'

Kearney shifts in his seat. He's frowning.

I sit forward a little. 'Then after the birth she calls them from a hospital payphone and arranges to meet to hand the child over.'

He raises an eyebrow, sardonic. 'Let me guess – at a lay-by on the A417?'

I shrug. 'Why not? We both know the best way to get away with a lie is to invent as little as possible. What if everything she said about that day was true, apart from the one central, crucial thing? She *did* meet someone at that lay-by, she *did* hand over the child, but the person who took it wasn't its father, it was a backstreet baby broker.'

I wait, again, and eventually he nods.

'Yes, I suppose it's possible.'

'It would also explain why the people who took the baby never came forward. Either the broker or the people who adopted him. They all had too much to lose.'

'But *she* didn't, did she – Rowan? Why didn't *she* come clean? Perhaps not straight away, but at least once she was facing a murder charge? An illegal adoption would've been chicken feed by comparison.'

There's a silence. 'I know. That part doesn't make sense.'

He pulls a wry face. 'Welcome to the warped world of Camilla Rowan. None of it makes any bloody sense – it never did. Apart from her killing it. That *always* made sense. Trouble is, that's the one thing we now know for an absolute fact did not happen.'

* * *

Sent: Thurs 25/10/2018, 12.10   **Importance: High**
From: DCVickyRoom@GMP.police.uk
To: DCThomasHansen@ThamesValley.police.uk

Subject: Jamie Fox

Mr Fox just attended at GMP Fairfax Road. We were in luck – he brought a blood donor card with him. According to what you sent over earlier, your vic is Group A and the mother is Group O. Since Fox is also Group O he can be excluded from paternity. We've taken a blood sample for verification purposes, but I thought you'd like to know straight away.

I'll let you know as soon as we have the results.

Best,
Vicky Room

* * *

Adam Fawley
25 October
12.15

Quinn is waiting for me in the car park, leaning against his car, scrolling on his tablet. He looks up as I approach.

'Did you get much from Havers?'

'Nah,' he says. 'Nothing more than was in the files. He's so far up Kearney's arse all you can see is his shoes.'

Figures.

He unlocks the car with a flashy remote-control thing (as if you couldn't guess) and we get inside.

'I asked Kearney about the illegal adoption theory,' I say, pulling the door shut.

Quinn nods. 'And?'

'He got a bit defensive – said they'd done their best to look at that, but five years after the fact it was an impossible task.'

Quinn starts the engine. 'Well, he's not wrong there.'

I turn and look out of the window. A couple of PCs

walk past the car and up the steps, chatting animatedly. They look scarcely out of training college; even I think the police are looking younger these days.

'I asked him whether they'd spoken to any of the other single mothers who gave birth at the hospital around the same time, in case one of them could have been the link to a backstreet adoption outfit.'

'What did he say?'

'Huffed and puffed a bit. They obviously didn't do it.'

Quinn puts the car in gear and swivels round so he can see to back out. 'Well, that's the only hole in the case we've found so far. But how the hell we're supposed to track any of them down now –'

'There was a social worker, wasn't there – based at the hospital? Isn't she on the witness log?'

'Yeah, but she only saw Rowan once for, like, ten minutes, so it didn't seem that important.'

'Push her up the priority list – if there were other girls thinking of adoption she'd be the one who knew.'

Quinn nods. 'I'll get someone on it.'

He reverses, so fast I'm risking whiplash, and then we move off.

'There was one other thing Kearney said.'

'Oh yeah?' says Quinn.

'He was joking – he said if he was in my position he'd leave the country.'

Quinn laughs.

'But it made me think – if the baby really was adopted illegally, perhaps they took him abroad?'

Quinn glances at me, then back at the road. 'But it'd have to have a passport, wouldn't it? The kid? Or be put on one of the parents'? You can't just rock up at Heathrow with a stroller and they wave you through.'

I'm surprised Quinn even knows what those things are called; perhaps Maisie's softening him up for daddydom. Though the idea of him changing a nappy – well, think *The Scream*. On acid.

He's right, though: no exit without a passport, and no passport without a birth certificate. And South Mercia already checked birth records. Of course, there is such a thing as forgery, and it was a lot easier to get away with back then when passports weren't so high-tech, but it would still have entailed a hell of a lot of time and expense when there were easy and legitimate ways to achieve exactly the same end. Unless there was a reason why you couldn't go the easy and legitimate way. It's not a happy thought.

'You want me to ask Baxter to check the airports? If you're thinking our dead man might have come from overseas?'

I'm about to say yes, but then I start thinking about how many people churn through Heathrow alone on a daily basis and remind myself that all we have is a blurred face and a hunch.

'No, I can't justify the cost. Not without much better grounds. Or a name.'

Quinn nods. 'Yeah, I think you're right.'

'Though it might be an idea to have a word with the Swanns' postie. We know they didn't get any calls from overseas, but maybe our vic wrote to them. I mean, he couldn't exactly track them down on Facebook, now could he.'

Quinn smiles. 'Yeah, good idea. I'll get someone on that too.'

He signals, then pulls out, tyres screeching, on to the main road.

* * *

Channel: Netflix
Programme: Infamous, season 4
Number of episodes: 4
First shown: 09/03/2016

[THEME SONG - 'KARMA CHAMELEON' [CULTURE CLUB]]
TITLE OVER:

INFAMOUS

FADE IN

THE CHAMELEON GIRL

MONTAGE: shots of Camilla Rowan at the Old Bailey trial, interspersed with newspaper headlines -'Milly Liar: "I did not harm my baby"', 'What really happened to baby Rowan?', 'Lawyer says Camilla Rowan "receiving death threats"', 'Child-killer to serve life'.

VOICEOVER - JOHN PENROSE

By March 2002, Camilla Rowan seemed to have put her old life and its troubles behind her. She'd left school with good A levels, done a course in physiotherapy, and then got a job working at a private clinic in Cheltenham. People who knew her back then describe her as 'looking like she didn't have a care in the world'. To those observing from outside, her future certainly looked bright. She had a new flat, a Yorkshire terrier, and a new boyfriend. She was also – unbeknownst to her colleagues, employers, friends or family – once again heavily pregnant.

Intercut: RECONSTRUCTION. Sequence of images: young woman walking small dog, working with patient, arranging flowers, drinking wine with man in restaurant.

Her boyfriend's identity has been protected by the courts, but the investigation subsequently carried out by South Mercia Police quickly established that he was not the father of the child she was then carrying. Indeed this man has always claimed he had no idea that she was pregnant. Moreover, that she deliberately concealed this from him, in part by dictating the sexual positions they adopted in the later months of the pregnancy. It seems hard to believe, and there are many people who don't believe it, even now.

But whatever the truth of it, the fact remains that he was *not* the father of that child, and – since he only met Camilla Rowan in the summer of 2001 – he could not have fathered the baby boy she gave birth to in Birmingham either.

That baby had last been seen on 23rd December 1997, being carried out of hospital in his mother's arms. But it wasn't until March 2002, nearly *five years* later, that anyone realised he was missing.

Indeed, it's one of the most troubling and, frankly, horrifying aspects of this case that it only came to light through a combination of luck, happy accident and the sheer determination of a single council employee.

TITLE APPEARS OVER, TYPEWRITER STYLE:

Part three

"I'm a man who doesn't know"

Interior, sitting room. Urban landscape visible through window. SM walks into shot and sits down, camera team adjust his mic, check he's correctly in shot etc.

TITLE OVER: Steve McIlvanney, Manager, Gloucestershire Adoption & Fostering Service, 1993-2006

<u>VOICEOVER - JOHN PENROSE</u>

This episode is all about Steve. About his perseverance and his commitment, and the sort of professional instinct that 'something isn't right' that only comes with 15 years' experience in child services.

Because without Steve, there would have been no case. Without Steve we may never have known baby Rowan had existed at all.

<u>STEVE McILVANNEY</u>

First time I heard the name Camilla Rowan was when I got passed the case by my line manager in March 2002. All I knew then was that this woman had presented herself at the maternity suite of the Princess Alice Hospital, Gloucester, on 2nd March, and given birth to a baby girl the following day. According to the nurses she'd breastfed the child as normal. Everything seemed absolutely fine. Then later the same day she suddenly told the staff nurse she wanted to have her daughter adopted, and they got in touch with us to handle the case. When my manager gave me

the file she said it was a straightforward
case - 'you'll be in and out in a couple of
days'.

(*laughs*)

Yeah, right.

*Intercut: RECONSTRUCTION: Young woman in hospital bed with
baby in her arms; man in chair at her side filling in form on
a clipboard.*

STEVE McILVANNEY

I went in to see her the first time the day after
the birth and she seemed fine - there were no red
flags at that stage, that's for sure. She seemed
to have thought everything through very clearly.

JOHN'S VOICE (off)

What reason did she give for wanting to have the
baby adopted?

STEVE McILVANNEY

She said she wasn't in any position to look after
a baby. I asked her if she'd been the victim of
abuse or assault but she was very insistent that
that wasn't the case. She said it was just a
one-night stand and she didn't know where the
father was. She said she was in a different
relationship now so there was no question of
keeping the baby, but she wanted to 'do the right
thing' for it. She was very insistent about that
too. So I gave her all the paperwork, and
explained what the process would be.

JOHN'S VOICE (off)

Did she give any indication that she'd been
through the same thing once before?

STEVE McILVANNEY

Absolutely not - in fact, she asked me several
questions that made it sound like she had no idea
at all what was involved.

JOHN'S VOICE (off)

Do you think that was deliberate?

STEVE McILVANNEY

(*shrugs*)

Who knows. Based on what I've learned about her
since, anything is possible. With Camilla Rowan.

*Cut to: MONTAGE: sequence of images of Camilla Rowan's
adoption paperwork for this third child, annotated as
previously, with 'False', 'Untrue', 'Does not exist', etc.*

VOICEOVER - JOHN PENROSE

Camilla went about this second adoption process
exactly as she had with her first baby, filling the
official paperwork with lie after lie. Once again,
she gave her real name, but neither the address
nor email address she provided actually existed.
Once again, the mobile number she supplied always
went straight to voicemail.

But this time, she was dealing with a different
adoption services department. And this time,
there was someone handling her case who wasn't
about to take no for an answer.

STEVE McILVANNEY

We took the baby into foster care the day after
she was born, and Miss Rowan left hospital
later that same afternoon. I told her I'd be in
touch to follow up and she said that was fine, and
she was glad the baby was 'going to a good home'.
It made it sound like it was a puppy or something.

JOHN'S VOICE (off)

Didn't that set off warning signals that
something might be wrong?

STEVE McILVANNEY

No, not then - like I said, I was under the
impression she'd never done this before. I put it
down to nerves.

JOHN'S VOICE (off)

She seemed nervous that day?

STEVE McILVANNEY

To be honest no, not really. She was chatty,
smiling - certainly not distraught. But thinking

about it afterwards, I think she did sense that comment about 'a good home' was a bit crass. She made more of an effort after that. I think she was desperate for me to just tick all the boxes and let her go.

JOHN'S VOICE (off)

What happened next?

STEVE McILVANNEY

She'd put on her forms that she lived in Brighton, and had only been in Gloucester visiting friends. Just like she had with the first baby, though of course I only found out about that a lot later.

Intercut: sequence of images of Brighton. Seafront, Royal Pavilion, etc.

I also had no idea the address she'd given me didn't exist - that'd never happened to me in 15 years. With the benefit of hindsight, I think she deliberately chose Brighton because she knew I wouldn't have either the time or the budget to go all the way down there to see her. Everything was going to have to be done by phone or email and, of course, I got absolutely nowhere with either. Six weeks later, we got to the point where we needed to complete the final paperwork, and I still hadn't managed to speak to her.

JOHN'S VOICE (off)

So what did you do?

STEVE McILVANNEY

It occurred to me she might have given the hospital a different email address - the one she'd given me was one of those Gmail ones with a name followed by a string of numbers, so I thought she could have written it down wrong by mistake. I was kicking myself, actually, that I hadn't thought of contacting the Maternity Unit before.

Cut to: hospital office, charts on wall, computers, cupboards, files, etc.

TITLE OVER: Staff Nurse Penny Curtis, Maternity Unit, Princess Alice Hospital, Gloucester

I'd known Steve for a number of years by then –
we didn't get many babies put up for adoption,
but when it did happen it was usually Steve who
handled the process. He was very good at his
job – always very thorough and conscientious. I
was surprised when he contacted me about the
Rowan baby, though – I thought that had all been
sorted out weeks before. But then he explained
that he kept leaving her voicemails and she never
called him back, so did I have an email address
for her he could try. I asked him to hang on a
moment while I had a look, and while I was doing
that he just happened to mention that she might
be difficult to get hold of because she was finding
the adoption process harder than she'd thought it
would be. After all, she would have had no idea
what to expect.

JOHN'S VOICE (off)

And what did you say to that?

PENNY CURTIS

To be honest, I laughed. I said I didn't know
where he'd got that from but I knew for a fact
she'd had at least one previous child. That's not
the sort of thing you can hide from an
obstetrician. And it wasn't only that either –
just after the baby was born Miss Rowan told me
it had been 'easy, compared to last time', and
when I asked her about the previous child she
said the baby had been adopted. She said that was
why she was so convinced it was the right thing
to do this time as well.

Cut to: Steve McIlvanney

STEVE McILVANNEY

I was gobsmacked when I heard that – there's simply
no other word for it. She'd *explicitly* stated on
her forms that this was her first child. I started
wondering what else she might be lying about, and
whether this was the real reason she wasn't
answering her phone. I alerted my manager, and we
decided to search UK adoption records for the first
child. It took a while because we didn't even know
where to start, but we got there in the end. And
there she was: Camilla Kathleen Rowan, listed as
the biological mother of a baby born at the West
Bromwich Women's Hospital on November 9th 1996.

So I contacted their Maternity Unit and got put
through to a hospital administrator.

*Intercut: RECONSTRUCTION: Woman at computer screen in
hospital office, talking on phone and gesturing at screen, etc.*

> I explained to her who I was and that I was
> looking for information about a Miss Camilla
> Rowan, who was listed as having given birth in
> their maternity unit in 1996. So she starts
> looking back through the Birmingham NHS Trust
> computer records and suddenly says, '1996, don't
> you mean 1997?' So I say no, it was a baby boy
> born in November 1996. And she says, 'What I have
> here is a baby boy born in December *1997*. And it
> wasn't at West Bromwich, it was at Birmingham and
> Solihull General.'

Cut back to Steve McIlvanney

STEVE McILVANNEY

So, to cut a long story short, it turns out there
were *two* previous births – the boy born in 1996
at West Bromwich, who had definitely been adopted,
and another boy born in 1997 at Birmingham and
Solihull who no one seemed to know anything
about. There were no adoption records for that
child that I could find, and I couldn't believe
Camilla Rowan still had it living with her. She'd
mentioned having a dog; she never mentioned
having a four-year-old son. So I did some more
checks on the General Registrar database of
births and couldn't find any baby registered by
Miss Rowan at any time in the six months after
that child was born.

That's when I knew we had a real problem on our
hands. And that's when I called the Child
Protection team.

JOHN'S VOICE (off)

And what did they do?

STEVE McILVANNEY

They called the police.

- freeze frame -

*   *   *

Interview with Keith Phillips, Royal Mail Oxford depot
25 October 2018, 1.35 p.m.
On the call, DC C. Sargent

CS: Hello, Mr Phillips, it's DC Chloe Sargent, Thames Valley Police. I believe you're the person who covers the Wytham area, is that right?

KP: Yes, that's me. The office told me you might call.

CS: Do you know the people at Gantry Manor?

KP: Mr and Mrs Swann – yes, I know them. Very private people. Old-fashioned. They're always very polite, but they don't chat. Not like some on my round.

CS: Do they get much post?

KP: Two or three deliveries a week, I'd say. Bills, the council, official stuff mostly. Apart from the junk mail, of course.

CS: So not much of a personal nature then?

KP: No, definitely not. They don't even go in much for Christmas cards, to be honest.

CS: Do you remember anything that looked personal recently – anything handwritten?

KP: Actually there was something. Must have been four or five weeks ago.

CS: A letter – or a postcard?

KP: A letter. Quite big handwriting. Confident-looking, you know?

CS: Do you by any chance recall if the letter came from abroad – was there an Airmail sticker or anything like that?

KP: Now you mention it, there was. I remember thinking the Swanns had never got foreign post before. Not in my time, anyway.

CS: I don't suppose you remember where it was from?

KP: Sorry, mate – the envelope was a bit of a mess. The postmark was all smudged.

CS: What about the stamp? Do you remember what that looked like?

KP: Now you're asking. That was all messed up too, I think. Could have been a face? That probably doesn't help much, does it. Afraid I only saw it for a minute – Mrs Swann was just coming out of the door with the rubbish so I handed it straight to her.

CS: That's very interesting. How did she react to it?

KP: She frowned, if I remember rightly.

CS: So she didn't look happy to receive it?

KP: No, definitely not. In fact, she tore it up and shoved it in the rubbish bag there and then.

CS: She definitely didn't open it?

KP: No, she just ripped it up.

CS: Do you think she did that because she recognized the writing?

KP: Impossible to tell, to be honest – sorry.

CS: Not at all – you've been an enormous help. If you remember anything else, or if you

recognize that stamp somewhere else, please
get in touch straight away.

* * *

Even if the A417 wasn't the most obvious route back I'd
have asked Quinn to take it: I wanted to go exactly the
same way Camilla Rowan said she went the day her baby
disappeared. I'm sure it's more built-up than it was in
1997, but it's still pretty rural, even now. Every lay-by we
pass, I think, is that it? Is that where she gave her child
away?

The phone goes. Nina Mukerjee. I put her on speaker.

'I just wanted to update you on where we've got with
the familial DNA.'

'Oh yes?'

'Nowhere fast, is the short version. I've found no close
relatives at all. The closest match thus far is three people
who are fourth cousins, but that's pretty distant in terms
of tracking someone down. It basically means the dead
man and the person on the database shared one set of
great-great-great-grandparents.'

'How many fourth cousins would you typically have?'

'Around a thousand.'

'Three doesn't sound a lot, on that basis.'

'This database is a pretty narrow sample, remember,
but you're right – even allowing for that I'd usually
expect to find around thirty matches at this stage. I'll

have a closer look at the three we've found, but like I said, they probably have nothing to do with the man you're after.'

Quinn makes a face and shakes his head. And I get it.

My phone's beeping now. 'OK, thanks, Nina. Can you keep at it? I have another call coming in so just let me know if you get anything.'

I press end and quickly check the number that's now come up on my screen.

This isn't good.

'DI Fawley,' says a woman's voice. A voice I know only too well. 'Could you hold for Superintendent Harrison? He needs to speak to you. Urgently.'

* * *

Mail Online

News Last updated: 13:40 GMT, 25 October 2018

EXCLUSIVE **NOT GUILTY? Shock and disbelief as news emerges that Milly Liar did NOT murder her newborn child. Missing for 20 years, Camilla Rowan's son has now been identified – as a DEAD MAN. Does this mean that after 15 years in prison Britain's most notorious 'baby-killer' will now be freed?**

BY LINDA LOMBARD FOR MAILONLINE

More than twenty years since he was last seen leaving hospital in his mother's arms, Camilla Rowan's infant son has finally been found, the Mail has learned. Rowan, now 38, was sentenced to life for murdering the baby at a sensational Old Bailey trial in 2003, but evidence has now come to light that casts doubt on the validity of that conviction. The baby's remains were never found, and despite several appeals and a Criminal Cases Review Commission review, Rowan has remained in HMP Heathside. But that may be about to change.

Earlier this week Thames Valley Police posted a picture on their Twitter feed, asking for the public's help in identifying a young man (shown below) arriving at Oxford station last Sunday. No further details were given, but it was widely rumoured that the man had been shot and killed at a large country house on the outskirts of the city a short time later that evening. Local residents have identified the property as owned by an elderly couple who've lived there for at least ten years but 'always kept themselves to themselves'. The Mail can now reveal that **DNA tests have proved conclusively that the dead man is Camilla Rowan's missing baby.**

Rowan always insisted that she never harmed the child, saying that she gave it to its biological father, whom she named as 'Tim Baker'. However, no Tim Baker ever came forward, nor, despite exhaustive searches by South Mercia police, has he ever been conclusively identified. Speculation is now rife that Rowan may have been telling the truth all along, and there are bound to be calls for an inquiry into the way the original investigation was conducted. Nothing is known about the identity the dead man has been using, or where he's been living for the last twenty years.

Thames Valley Police have not yet issued a comment, nor has there been a statement from Rowan's legal team. But surely it's only a matter of time before they make an official request for her immediate release.

1,687 comments

Rob__8991
Remind me – exactly how many kids did that woman have? 4? 5? And no-one knew about ANY of them. So how do we know this isn't yet another kid no-one knew about and she palmed off to someone else? Doesn't mean she didn't kill that other baby, just like they said. I hope the police are onto this though that's probably too much to ask. Thickos, the lot of them. She's just going to run rings round them. AGAIN

DawnG667788
I don't trust that woman further than I could spit – there's something fishy about this whole thing

AnaGram5__1984
So is she getting out then?

99AnnieBL99
If you ask me I never thought she did it – its unnatural a mother killing her child. Quite apart from the fact that there wasn't enough time to get rid of the body – not without the police being able to find it

2002SpottheBall
She's going to make MEGA bucks out of this #justsaying

GayZeeBo88
Holy shit this is going to put the cat among the pigeons

LineofDutyfan665
So who are these old people in Wytham anyway – has no-one asked what the hell this bloke was doing there?

TickedBoxforNoPublicity44
I know someone who used to work at Heathside – do you know what they call her there? Only the effing DUCHESS. You couldn't make it up LMFAO

AllieCatz76
I don't believe Camilla Rowan is innocent. I never have. It'll be more complicated than it looks, just you wait. And whatever it is that woman is in it up to her neck

*   *   *

Gislingham knocks at Fawley's door and waits for the muffled 'Come' from inside. The DI is on his feet, coat still on, and clearly only just back. He's flicking through screens on his phone, frowning, and muttering under his breath.

'Sorry, boss, do you want me to come back?'

Fawley glances up. 'No – actually, I need you to fill me in on the Swanns before I go and see Harrison.'

'Yeah, I saw – it's all over the news.'

And Harrison must be crapping himself. Not that either of them say so; they don't need to.

'The hacks haven't worked out who the Swanns really are yet but it's only a matter of time – they can look up the

Land Registry just like we did and as soon as they get Swann's first name and date of birth, bingo.'

Fawley looks grim. 'And where the press goes, the sofa Sherlocks will soon follow. Can you warn the Swanns? Suggest they might want to stay somewhere else for a few days?'

'I can't believe they don't know already, but yeah, we can do that. I'll send Ev.' He gives a wry smile. 'One way or another she's had a lot of experience managing cantankerous pensioners.'

Fawley looks up, his face suddenly concerned. 'How is her dad?'

Gis shrugs. 'Much the same, as far as I know. It won't be getting any easier, that's for sure.'

Fawley nods, and they stand in silence a moment. Then, 'So what else have you got?'

'Well, your hunch about the snail mail was spot on: Chloe Sargent spoke to the postie and it turns out the Swanns got a letter about a month ago which was handwritten *and* had an overseas stamp. Trouble is, a) Mrs S tore it up and threw it away without reading it so we can't prove she knew who sent it, and b) the postie doesn't know which country it came from. We put in a call to her solicitor to ask about it, but all we got back was that she "has no recollection" of getting anything like that. Well, there's a surprise.'

Fawley's looking at him. 'I don't know about you, but there are two reasons why I rip up post without bothering to open it. One – it's junk; or two – I know who it's from and I'm not interested.'

Gis nods. 'Right.' He takes a step closer. 'Do you think

the same thing could have happened to Rowan? The kid wrote to her as well? The timings would fit.'

'But there's still a problem, isn't there? He could find Rowan through Wikipedia, but how the hell did he find out where the parents lived?'

'Quite. They've changed their name, they're not in the phone book and they're not on the public electoral roll either, we checked. And as Hansen found out, it's really bloody hard to find someone who's changed their name by deed poll.'

Fawley looks thoughtful. 'I've been wondering about that – whether it would be as hard the other way round?'

Gis is frowning. 'Not sure what you're getting at.'

'I mean, the only name we had to start with was Swann, and we had no reason to go looking for anything else. But if you were looking for Dick Rowan and you already had a suspicion he might have changed his name, how hard would it be to make the connection back to Swann?'

Gis nods. 'I see what you mean – I'll get Hansen on it. I doubt he'll mind that much – he's halfway to being Baxter's mini-me. Minus the chocolate habit, obvs.'

Fawley smiles. 'Cadburys will be gutted.'

His phone beeps.

'Harrison,' he says, looking at the screen, his smile evaporating. 'Asking where I am.' He drags off his coat and straightens his tie. 'Wish me luck.'

* * *

Interview with Alison Toms
25 October 2018, 2.15 p.m.
On the call, DC T. Hansen

TH: Thanks for agreeing to talk to me, Ms Toms. I
    know it's a long time ago now, but it's about
    the Camilla Rowan case.

AT: Well, I'll do all I can to help but I'm not
    sure what use I can be – as you say, it's a
    very long time ago and I only spoke to her
    once.

TH: Yes, I have the notes here, it says you saw
    her with the baby, that they seemed to be
    'bonding well', and she 'expressed no interest
    in having the baby adopted'. So you left it at
    that?

AT: I had enough on my plate with other cases, as
    I'm sure you can imagine. All her health
    indicators were normal, the baby was healthy.
    I had no reason to think there was any sort of
    problem. And the medical staff agreed with me.

TH: Of course, no one's questioning that. It's
    something else we wanted to ask you about. You
    just said you had a lot of other cases on at
    the time – were those all potential adoptions?

AT: Ah, no – I didn't mean to confuse you. My job
    covered much more than that – basically any
    issue that arose at the hospital. Women with
    injuries that could have been the result of
    domestic abuse, for example, or children who
    might have been mistreated.

TH: I see. So do you happen to remember if you
    were handling many other adoptions at that
    time? Sorry – I should explain: one angle that
    might not have been fully investigated at the
    time was the possibility that Camilla had her
    baby adopted informally. Without the internet
    she'd have found that quite difficult, but we
    were wondering whether she might have met
    someone at the hospital?

AT: A baby-broker, you mean? That seems unlikely –
    people like that don't tend to hang round
    maternity wards.

TH: And you weren't aware of much activity like
    that at the time – in general, I mean?

AT: No, not at all. To be honest, it was barely on
    the radar.

TH: Yes, that's what we thought. But that being
    the case, is it possible that another mother
    in the same position could have given Rowan a
    contact? Another young girl, say, who didn't
    feel able to bring up a child on her own?

AT: Ah, I see. Yes, that would make more sense,
    but I don't recall I was talking to anyone
    else about adoption at that time. And Camilla
    Rowan was only in the hospital for a few
    hours, remember – that's not long to make that
    sort of connection.

TH: We think that she researched the hospital
    during the pregnancy – she went straight there
    when she went into labour as if she'd already
    planned where she was going to go. So she might

have been hanging around in the weeks leading
up to the birth and met someone that way?

AT: Right, OK. Well, I can look back over my notes
for that period, if it would help? See if
there were any other adoptions under
discussion at the time?

TH: That would be great, thank you. You have my
number?

AT: Yes, it's come up on my phone.

TH: Thank you very much, Ms Toms, you've been
really helpful.

*　*　*

Carter gets back to St Aldate's wet, cold, tired and pissed off. He had to stand most of the way back because the train only had two carriages, so the sight of Chloe Sargent, dry, warm and sitting comfortably, does nothing to improve his mood.

She looks up at him and smiles. The mouth-closed smile of someone who wants to appear friendly but definitely doesn't want to be too encouraging. 'Any luck?'

'No, just a load of bloody CCTV I'll now go square-eyed staring at.'

'Don't knock it – there might be something there. We just got a lead that the vic may have been living abroad.'

His eyes widen. 'So I could have been right about him being at a hotel?'

And now she's wishing she hadn't said anything.

Carter dumps his coat and starts to unwind his scarf, which (as Sargent isn't alone in noticing) he's taken to wearing in the same loop knot as Quinn. 'How about you?' he says.

She turns back to her screen. 'Oh, not much. I spent some time with DC Baxter earlier looking at the birth records South Mercia put together back in 2002.'

Carter grimaces. 'I bet that was fun. Not exactly the life and soul, is he.'

'He's OK,' she says, perhaps a little too firmly. 'He knows what he's doing.'

Carter shrugs. 'If you say so.'

He watches her for a moment then wanders over. 'What are you on now?'

She looks up and flushes, quickly changing her screen. 'Nothing, just arranging that interview with the doctor who delivered the first baby, Adrian Morrison.'

'He's not likely to know much about the second kid, though, is he?'

She flashes him an irritated look. 'It still has to be done. Who knows, he might have remembered something since then that could be relevant.'

Carter gives her a 'Yeah, right' look. 'I'm calling Penny Curtis this afternoon. The midwife who helped blow the lid on the whole thing.'

This time, she doesn't look up. 'Good for you, Carter.'

'I might ask DS Gislingham if I can sit in on the Steve McIlvanney one too. Bet that'll be interesting –'

He stops; there's a phone ringing. Sargent reaches quickly to answer it; anything to shut Carter up.

'Hello, CID?' A pause. 'OK, I'll come down straight away.'

She gets to her feet. 'What is it?' says Carter.

'Someone in reception. One of Rowan's old boyfriends we want to eliminate as the baby's father.'

Carter rolls his eyes. 'Whoop whoop.'

She gives him a heavy look, then turns, rather pointedly, and heads out towards the stairs.

Carter watches her go, his face thoughtful.

* * *

Adam Fawley
25 October
14.10

'Ah, there you are, Adam.'

The other person in the office is Elaine Challoner from the press office, and judging by her empty coffee cup, she's been here quite a while.

'So,' says Harrison, as I take my seat. 'Media. And dealing therewith.'

'I read the draft holding statement on the way back, sir. I think it pretty much covered the key points –'

'Yes, well,' he says quickly, 'we've been doing some brainstorming in your absence. Seeing if we can't think outside the box a bit on this one.'

Shit. This doesn't bode well.

'As in?'

'As in getting on the front foot. Being proactive.' He shifts a little in his seat. 'Elaine has suggested – and I agree with her – that on this occasion there would be value in us agreeing to an interview.'

'An interview?' I stare at him and then at Elaine. 'Do you really think that's a good idea?'

'This story isn't going away any time soon,' she says. 'One of the Sundays is planning a major feature, rehashing the whole case. And it won't be very long before someone works out who the Swanns really are – all they need is a quick look at Companies House –'

'I know,' I say, 'I have an officer on the way to warn them they could be in for a tough few days with the press.'

'Exactly,' she says, drilling in the point. 'And *so could we*. So whatever we can do to pre-empt it –'

'All the same –'

But Harrison isn't listening. 'I agree with Elaine. An interview would also allow us to put the whole story in context. Fend off any suggestion that the original inquiry was in any way slipshod or deficient.'

'With respect, sir, we don't know that. Not until we find out what happened to the child. If South Mercia want to defend their own investigation, that's one thing – but you don't want to be seen doing that, not at this stage –'

'I've spoken to the Chief Constable,' he says heavily, 'and we're agreed. While we wouldn't normally comment on an active case, this is an exception. After all, the circumstances are fairly unique.'

I can see Alex rolling her eyes, saying, 'How many more times – something's either unique or it isn't – you can't shove on a bloody qualifier.'

But, on the other hand, I know what the Super's like when he's in this mood and if he's going to force this through regardless, far better to make a virtue of necessity than an obstreperous arse of myself.

'Actually, sir, we've just received some new information that may be relevant here.'

'Oh yes?'

'We've spoken to the postman who covers Wytham and apparently the Swanns had a handwritten letter about a month ago. A letter with a foreign postmark. Unfortunately, we don't know which country it came from. But if we do an interview –'

'Exactly,' says Harrison quickly, his face lighting up. 'We can show the still from Oxford station – increase the chance of someone recognizing him.'

If you ask me, the press are doing a pretty good job on that already without needing any help from us. But he's not asking me. And like I said, if you can't beat 'em . . .

'Yes, sir. Absolutely.'

Elaine sits forward. 'I'm proposing we give one journalist exclusive access – someone who we know will do a balanced and objective job.'

'Who do you have in mind?'

She hesitates. 'John Penrose.'

I stare at her. 'The Netflix bloke?'

She nods. 'He's already been in touch, asking for comment. No surprises there, of course. He's working for the BBC now –'

'But he's the one who got the case reopened – he's just going to bang on about how he was right all along –'

'I agree he has an axe to grind, but no one knows the case better than he does. He's also an old-school pro who'll feel duty-bound to give both sides. And, of course, giving it to him will guarantee maximum impact. Especially internationally. And given what you just said –' She's watching my face, trying to read my thoughts. 'So you'll do it?'

'*Me?*' I stare at her, then turn to Harrison. 'I thought it was you we were talking about, sir.'

'No, no, Adam,' he says briskly. 'You're running this investigation. You're the person the public will want to see.'

* * *

The man reading a copy of *The Times* in reception is well-dressed, dark hair greying at the temples, white shirt, royal-blue suit. He has the physique of someone who used to take his sport quite seriously but no longer has the time: he's thickened round his gut and the waistband of his trousers is showing the strain.

'Mr Crowther?' says Chloe Sargent, walking up to him. 'I believe you're here for a DNA swab?'

The man looks up from his paper, does a quick double-take and then smiles. 'Yes, that's right. I spoke to a DC Hansen?'

She nods. 'He's a colleague of mine. We work as a team.'

'I had to drop off something in Kidlington so I thought I may as well come straight here, DC –?'

'Sargent.'

He flushes. 'Oh, I'm sorry, I didn't realize. God, how embarrassing –'

'No, no,' she says, 'it happens all the time. Sargent – it's my name. And you were right first time: I am a DC.'

He looks ridiculously relieved. 'Phew, thank God for that. So what's the drill – what do you need me to do?'

'If you can follow me, we'll go into an interview room

and I'll take a swab from the inside of your cheek. It'll only take a minute.'

'Just like on the telly, eh?' He smiles.

'Right,' she says, returning the smile almost despite herself. 'Just like on the telly.'

* * *

Ev breathes a sigh of relief as she pulls up outside Gantry Manor. She's in time: no sign of the press yet. No sign of anyone at all, unless you count the fox crossing the lane in front of the car who stops and gives her a long stare before evidently deciding she's of no particular interest and continuing on his way. Ev drags her jacket from the passenger seat and gets out of the car. The cloud is too low to see the top of Wytham Hill – no star-gazing tonight, that's for sure. She locks the car and starts up the drive, feeling the first drops of rain in the cold air.

It's Richard Swann who answers the door. He's in a check flannel shirt and a cardigan with pockets that have bagged with age. He frowns.

'What do you want?'

'I'm sure you've seen the papers, Mr Swann. DI Fawley is concerned the press may turn up here.'

'Why should they? They don't know who we are –'

'Not yet, no, but it won't take long. They can easily find out who owns this house, and from there it's just a couple of checks online and they'll know your name is Richard and you were born on exactly the same day as Camilla's father. And as the boss always says, there's no such thing as coincidence.'

He'd been pale before but he's paler now. 'I see. I suppose you'd better come in.'

* * *

Adam Fawley
25 October
14.55

Elaine Challoner catches up with me at the coffee machine.

'I hope you don't think I dumped you in it.'

I press the button for hot water and turn to face her. 'Don't worry – I know what he's like when he's got a bee in his bonnet.'

We exchange a smile.

'Let me know if I can help, won't you? And obviously I'll come with you to the studio.'

'I've been doing this job twenty years – you really think I need someone to hold my hand?'

She flushes a little. 'I didn't mean it like that –'

And now I feel like a shit, because she's a nice woman and I'm taking my irritation with Harrison out on her. 'Sorry – it's been a bit of a crappy day. I've done media training – I'll be fine.'

She picks up a cup and presses for coffee.

'I'm assuming you did watch that Netflix thing?'

I give her a weary glance. 'Well, I was in the room when it was on – does that count?'

She smiles. 'Fair enough. But you may want to watch it again before you see Penrose. Especially the last episode.'

'You're probably right.'

I fish my teabag out of the cup and drop it in the bin.

'But there's something else I need to do first.'

* * *

```
Channel:              Netflix
Programme:            Infamous, season 4
Number of episodes:   4
First shown:          09/03/2016


[THEME SONG - 'KARMA CHAMELEON' [CULTURE CLUB]]
TITLE OVER:
                        INFAMOUS

FADE IN

                    THE CHAMELEON GIRL

MONTAGE: clips relating to the trial - newspaper headlines,
people holding banners and shouting outside the court,
Camilla trying to escape the cameras, interspersed with vox
pops/news broadcasts/clips.


             VOICEOVER - JOHN PENROSE

    On 6th November 2003, after a six-week trial and
    more than four days in the witness box, Camilla
    Rowan received the verdict of her peers. And that
    verdict was unanimous: Guilty.

    There was uproar in the court. Some people in the
    public gallery cheered, others screamed abuse and
    had to be removed by security personnel.
    Camilla's mother collapsed and had to be given
    medical attention. And over it all, Camilla could
    be heard wailing, again and again, 'I didn't do
    it, I didn't do it'.

Cut to: John's study. Wall of photos and news clippings about
the case, piles of files, computer with Post-its on the
screen, etc.


                  JOHN PENROSE

    The announcement of the verdict may have been
    dramatic, but few observers can have been
    surprised. Anyone who covered the case for the
    press certainly wasn't. Those four days on the
    stand were damning. Some people had questioned
    her defence team's decision to allow her to give
    evidence, but objectively speaking they had
    little choice. The jury was always going to want
    to hear Camilla's story from Camilla herself.
```

Intercut: RECONSTRUCTION: Girl sitting at a table talking to two men, one in barrister costume, referring to papers, etc.

I can only imagine the hours of preparation the lawyers must have put her through. But the prosecuting barrister, Ian Burns QC, was ruthless. He began his cross-examination by taking her through every lie she had told in relation to her pregnancies, forcing her to admit that she had not been telling the truth. It took over three hours. By the time he got to her version of events on the day of her child's disappearance, her credibility was in tatters. No one believed her bizarre story about handing over a newborn baby in a lay-by on the A417. Most people still don't. But are they wrong?

I've taken a long hard look at the Camilla Rowan case in this series, and much of the evidence has been damning. But is it the whole story? Or could there be something – or someone – out there who could throw new light on this baffling and unsettling case?

TITLE APPEARS OVER, TYPEWRITER STYLE:

Part four

"Every day is like survival"

JOHN'S VOICE

Six months ago, I got a call from a woman. I'm going to call her Mandy, though that's not her real name. She said she'd heard I was looking again at the Camilla Rowan case, and had some information for me. And so we arranged to meet.

Woman shown walking into shot and taking a seat with her back to camera, facing John. She's wearing jeans and a T-shirt, revealing tattoos on her arms and the back of her neck. Her face is out of shot.

'MANDY'

My name is Mandy, and I shared a cell with Camilla Rowan in Holloway prison, from 2007 to 2010.

RECONSTRUCTION of two women in cell. Bunk beds, etc.

I was in for soliciting. It was my first stretch and I was shit-scared but Cam really looked after me. I guess you could say we became mates. Twenty-three hours a day cooped up with someone – you get to know them pretty well.

JOHN PENROSE

What did she tell you about the baby?

'MANDY'

She said she never hurt it - that people had it
all wrong. She wasn't that sort of person.

JOHN PENROSE

So she still maintained that she handed the child
to its father?

'MANDY'

Yeah, she did. But I reckon it wasn't as simple
as she made out. There were things she told
me - things she let drop - that made me wonder.

JOHN PENROSE

What sort of things?

'MANDY'

She was abused. When she was a kid, by a family
friend. She said she called him Uncle but he
wasn't a real one. He raped her for the first
time when she was eleven, and it carried on the
whole of the rest of the time she was living at
home.

JOHN PENROSE

So he could have been the father of the missing
baby boy? Is that what you're saying?

'MANDY'

She never said that - not in so many words. But
if you ask me, that's exactly what happened. It'd
explain why she never said anything. Especially
to her parents.

JOHN PENROSE

But we presumably know this man wasn't the father
of the first baby, given that that child was mixed
race.

No, obviously she must've had other boyfriends
as well. But the way she behaved – like the
pregnancies didn't exist – being in denial like
that, it's what happens if you've been abused for
years. I should know. You get a weird relationship
with your own body. Like it's happening to someone
else. It's a survival mechanism – a way of getting
through it. That's what my therapist said.

JOHN PENROSE

She never mentioned anything about this alleged
abuse during the trial, or – as far as I know –
at any other time. In fact, the police
specifically asked her if there'd been any kind of
abuse and she was absolutely categorical that
there hadn't. How do you explain that?

'MANDY'

I think she was ashamed. He made her swear not to
tell anyone. And it can take years for abuse
survivors to speak out – you know that as well as
I do.

JOHN PENROSE

So she gave the baby to *this* man? You think
that's what really happened?

'MANDY'

It's the only thing that makes sense. And even that
lay-by thing makes sense if this bloke lived local.

JOHN PENROSE

It would be difficult for him to hide a baby,
though, wouldn't it? A middle-aged man,
presumably with a wife and family already,
suddenly has a baby in the house? Someone was
bound to have noticed.

'MANDY'

I reckon he got rid of it.

JOHN PENROSE

You think *he* killed the child?

'MANDY'

Why not? He had a lot to lose – he wouldn't want
it all coming out about him being a child
molester, now would he?

JOHN PENROSE

But why didn't Camilla tell the police all this?
Especially when they asked her about possible
coercion? Why come up with that wild story about
Tim Baker or whatever his name was? If she'd been
abused, the police would have been sympathetic.
And they could have taken action against this
man. As it is, he got off scot-free – assuming
what you're saying is true.

'MANDY'

I think she was terrified of him. I think he had
some sort of hold over her.

JOHN PENROSE

Did she ever tell you this man's name?

'MANDY'

No. Just that he was a friend of the family. That
her father played golf with him. But with people
like that, that probably doesn't narrow it down
very much, does it.

*Cut to: panoramic drone shot over Shiphampton. Church, High
Street, park, etc.*

VOICEOVER – JOHN PENROSE

She's not wrong. My own research has turned up
several men in the Shiphampton area who played
golf with Dick Rowan when Camilla was a child.
Two are now dead, and my attempts to speak to
some of the others have met with flat refusals,
and in one case, a solicitor's letter.

Cut to: exterior view of South Mercia Police HQ

I also contacted South Mercia CID, who likewise
refused to speak to me, but did issue a statement
saying that they had adhered scrupulously to the
appropriate procedure when dealing with cases
that might involve sexual abuse, that Ms Rowan
had 'never made any allegations of this kind'
even when explicitly questioned on the subject,
and they would have investigated thoroughly had

227

she done so. They also said they 'had, and still have, no reason to believe this alleged abuser – or indeed any other third party – was involved in the disappearance and presumed death of Ms Rowan's baby', concluding, 'should Ms Rowan make these allegations herself, we would, of course, take appropriate action'.

There was one person, however, we were able to talk to, and that was Sheila Ward. Remember her from episode one? She was Dick Rowan's secretary for over two decades, and knew the family well when Camilla was growing up. We asked her about these allegations as part of our first and – as it turned out – only interview with her.

Cut to: Ward family sitting room, gas fire, Border terrier on sofa, potted plants, etc.

TITLE OVER: Sheila Ward, Dick Rowan's secretary, 1971–1996

JOHN'S VOICE (off)

You knew the family back then – do you think it's possible Camilla suffered abuse as a child? Abuse that may have affected her behaviour when she discovered she was pregnant?

SHEILA WARD

I don't believe a word of it. It's just another one of her lies. If that sort of thing was going on, she'd definitely have said something. She was that sort of girl.

JOHN'S VOICE (off)

But you said yourself she was good at keeping secrets.

SHEILA WARD

When it was in her own interests, yes. That's a very different kettle of fish. If someone was doing something to her she didn't like she wouldn't have suffered in silence. She wouldn't have let them get away with it.

JOHN'S VOICE (off)

Many abuse victims take years to get to the point where they feel able to speak out. Especially in cases where the abuser is a member of the family or a family friend.

SHEILA WARD

That's as may be. I'm just telling you that I
knew her back then and I simply don't believe
she'd have kept something like that to herself.
She's only coming out with it now because she
thinks it will get her off the hook. The minute
anyone gets arrested these days the first thing
they say is that they've been abused - you see it
all the time.

(puts on whiny voice)

It's not my fault - I was a victim - poor little me -

You see it all the time.

JOHN'S VOICE (off)

Perhaps you see it all the time because so many
people who find themselves in the criminal justice
system have indeed been abused.

SHEILA WARD

I'm not in a position to judge those people. But
I *am* in a position to judge Camilla Rowan, and I'm
telling you, she's a born liar. A pathological
liar.

JOHN'S VOICE (off)

The psychiatrist who assessed her says not.

SHEILA WARD

Yes, and Camilla didn't say anything to them
about this so-called abuse either, did she?
Doesn't that tell you something?

JOHN'S VOICE (off)

Let's assume for a moment that it did actually
happen - that she was indeed abused as a
child. Do you have any idea who it could have
been?

SHEILA WARD

Of course not. The whole idea is ridiculous.

You were friends of the family yourself, weren't
you? You and Nigel, your husband?

SHEILA WARD

I was Dick's *secretary*.

JOHN'S VOICE (off)

But you socialised with them as well, didn't you?

*Intercut: montage of images showing the Wards at social events
with the Rowans - Rotary Club, dinner dances, Christmas
parties. Camilla Rowan is clearly in view in the last image,
standing with Nigel Ward. He has his hand on her shoulder.
She's about eleven.*

SHEILA WARD

We met up occasionally.

JOHN'S VOICE (off)

I think it was rather more than that, wàsn't it?
And didn't your husband play golf with Dick
Rowan too?

*Intercut: picture taken at Shiphampton golf club,
showing Nigel Ward and Dick Rowan with their bags of
clubs. Two other men standing with them have their faces
blurred out.*

SHEILA WARD

(*becoming agitated*)

They played together *once or twice*. Hardly
at all.

(*Producer hands her the same picture*)

JOHN'S VOICE (off)

This was taken in 1996. They played in the same
four-ball all that year. Indeed, they came second
in the club league.

SHEILA WARD

I hope you're not suggesting –

<u>JOHN'S VOICE</u> (off)

What did Camilla call your husband, Mrs Ward?

<u>SHEILA WARD</u>

I don't know what you mean –

<u>JOHN'S VOICE</u> (off)

It was 'Uncle', wasn't it? She called him 'Uncle
Nigel'.

Can we speak to him, Mrs Ward? Can we speak to
your husband about this?

<u>SHEILA WARD</u>

(*gets up and puts her hand against the camera
lens*)

That's enough – turn that thing off right now –

Cut to: John, at desk

<u>JOHN PENROSE</u>

We never were able to talk to Nigel Ward, and
Sheila Ward refused to speak to us any further
after that last exchange. And in a way you can't
blame her – no one likes having questions of this
gravity raised about their loved ones. But there
are questions, all the same.

*Cut to: over the shoulder PoV, looking at what John has on
his desk*

Remember this picture? It's the Shiphampton
Rotary Club Christmas party 1997. The same party
Camilla went to the day she left hospital with
her baby son.

And this man, standing just behind Camilla and
her father –

(*pointing*)

– is Nigel Ward.

But you're probably thinking – hang on, if he was
at that party, he couldn't possibly have anything
to do with the disappearance of the baby. There
simply wouldn't have been enough time. And it's a
good point. But I've tracked down a number of
people who were at the event that night, and no

one can remember him being there before nine thirty. And if that's correct, it would *definitely* have given him enough time. But as far as I'm aware, he has never been questioned about his whereabouts that night, either then, or since.

Cut to: image of Camilla, her parents and the Wards at the Christmas party. Gradual close-up to focus on Camilla and Ward.

So was Camilla Rowan really abused as a child? She herself has never said so, not even to the court-appointed psychiatrist. And it would clearly have been in her interests to divulge something like that, if it were true: it could have been a significant mitigating factor. But as of now, we only have 'Mandy's' word that it ever happened.

And even if it *was* true, we have no way of knowing who the man was, unless Camilla herself chooses to tell us. Some things appear to point to Nigel Ward, but in the absence of any sort of police investigation he is, of course, innocent until proven guilty in a court of law. And as I said, there are a number of other potential candidates as well, and to my knowledge none of them has been questioned either.

Which leads me on to the one thing I think we *do* know about this case.

It's unfinished business.

Camilla Rowan has been proved, again and again, to be a liar. A brazen, persistent and accomplished liar. But has she been proved to be a murderer? Because, frankly, I'm not convinced. In fact, the more I learn about the actions – or rather *inactions* – of South Mercia Police, the less convinced I am. And let's not forget, the baby has never been found. The police and the CPS say he's dead, and the jury believed them. But is there cast-iron proof of that? No. No body has ever been located, despite what appears to have been an extensive and exhaustive search.

Though there are some places that I know for a fact were *not* searched. Like the Ward family garden, which backs on to a nature reserve. Or the Shiphampton golf club – nearly 200 acres, including several areas of woodland and a small lake.

Intercut: drone footage of Shiphampton golf club

And why wasn't Nigel Ward questioned at the time? Why did he arrive at the Christmas party so late? Where had he been? Was he the man who abused Camilla? Was *he* the father of her missing baby?

Intercut: series of shots of Nigel Ward – in local paper, at other golf events, ending with one with his father when he was a teenager. His father is in police uniform.

    And was the reason why he was not questioned at the time down to the fact that he had a number of friends within the ranks of South Mercia Police? Men in the Rotary Club, men he played golf with . . .

    We just don't know. All we have is questions. And right now neither Ward, nor Camilla herself, are saying anything.

    What we need now is a proper investigation by the one body who can insist on answers: the police.

Cut to: MONTAGE of headlines from the trial, finishing with a picture of Camilla in tears outside the court.

– freeze frame –

    Why? Because I no longer think Camilla Rowan's conviction is sound. So much so, that I believe we could be looking at a miscarriage of justice. A significant and serious miscarriage of justice.

    Throughout the trial there were headlines screaming 'Milly Liar' on an almost daily basis. Has the time now come for another slogan?

    Has the time come for 'Free Milly'?

TEXT OVER: South Mercia Police were contacted during the making of this programme, but declined to comment.

FADE OUT

FADE IN: Do you have any information about the disappearance of Camilla Rowan's baby? Call Crimestoppers on 0800 555 111 or email Infamous@Netflix.tv.com

– ends –

*   *   *

'I think you could do it, Sarge.'

Hansen has a printout in his hand and that 'got it' look Gis has started to recognize.

'Show me.'

Hansen spreads the printout down on the desk. 'This

233

is from Companies House. Rowan's main company was Rowan Holdings, which he wound up in 2005, but there were a lot of subsidiary companies, which he appears to have used to manage specific projects.' He points. 'Pine Developments, Oak Properties, Poplar Homes –'

'*That's enough trees, Ed*,' says Gis with a sigh.

Hansen grins. 'Right. Most of them were wound up with the parent company. All except one. Beech Management Ltd. That still exists, though it's been all but dormant for at least two years. But because it's still technically trading it has to list its directors and give a current contact address for them.' He points again. 'And there he is: Richard Swann, Gantry Manor, Wytham.'

Gis looks up at him. 'So the boss was right – you *could* track the Swanns down. As long as you knew where to start.'

'Exactly, Sarge. If the dead man suspected Camilla Rowan was his mother, he could have worked it out from there. Though, to be fair, it's fiddly and he might not have known about Companies House if he's been living overseas.'

'But he could do it.'

Hansen nods. 'He could do it.'

* * *

Yup, sure is. I still can't believe the police didn't pursue that bloke Ward at the time

↪ submitted 6 days ago by Danny929292

share hide report

> Wasn't his dear old Dad in the police? That wd explain a lot
>
> ↪ submitted 5 days ago by sweetrubette55
>
> share hide report

This whole abuse angle – I mean, OK, if she was abused it could have been this Nigel Ward bloke, but aren't these things always really close to home? Like *really* close to home? Does anyone know if the police ever had the father down as a suspect?

↪ submitted 5 days ago by timeforcrime1998

share hide report

> I'm not sure I buy the abuse thing – it's all too easy to come out with this stuff years later when you're accused of something. She never said a word about it before, did she? And not every single person who commits a crime has been abused. Just saying
>
> ↪ submitted 4 days ago by digginforthetruth
>
> share hide report

> > You shd try working in victim services. People just bury an experience like that. It happens all the time. Believe me.
> >
> > ↪ submitted 4 days ago by MakeanewplanStan44
> >
> > share hide report

> > And she was really young wasn't she. And completely under the parents' thumb as far as I can tell
> >
> > ↪ submitted 3 days ago by SusieClarke1818
> >
> > share hide report

> > Camilla Rowan is a pathological liar. I don't think Nigel Ward had anything to do with it. Or her father. Just because the baby hasn't been found doesn't mean she wasn't responsible. It just means she's clever. Very very clever.
> >
> > ↪ submitted 3 days ago by AllieCatz76
> >
> > share hide report

Re Dick Rowan, no, as far as I can find out no-one ever said anything about him. Certainly not the police. Maybe they missed a trick? Has anyone ever bothered asking what time HE got to that Xmas party?

submitted 3 days ago by ProofofLife

share hide report

> Well South Mercia ballsed up the rest of the investigation so why not that? Bloody idiots cdnt find their arses with both hands and a map
>
> submitted 3 days ago by LongJohnSilver
>
> share hide report

*   *   *

Adam Fawley
25 October
16.15

I was half expecting a scrum of hacks at the gate, but she's moved since 2016 and they probably haven't been able to trace her. Yet.

She's expecting me, though, to judge by the look on her face when she opens the door. Or if not me, someone like me – someone with a warrant card.

'What do you want?'

'DI Adam Fawley, Thames Valley, Mrs Ward. Could I come in for a few minutes?'

Her face hardens. 'He's *dead* –'

'I know, and I'm very sorry –'

'He had a *heart attack* – it was the stress – the newspapers. It killed him. *She* killed him. And now it's all starting up all over again –'

'That's what I'd like to talk to you about.'

She hesitates, her hand gripping the door.

'I know what the press put you through, Mrs Ward. I'm

trying to avoid that happening again, not make it worse. You have my word on that.'

She sighs heavily, then stands back and waves me in.

It's not the sitting room I remember from Netflix, though the furniture and knick-knacks are no doubt the same. The garden visible from the back window is different too. Thirty feet of tired autumn grass ending in a wooden fence topped with trellis, not the sweep down to trees and a stream they had before. I know, I've seen the pictures. But not on Netflix; in the South Mercia Police file.

* * *

Milly Rowan: Police excavating 'Uncle's' garden for missing baby

By Bruno Stokes

Case re-opened after shock Netflix allegations

Thirteen years after the notorious 'Milly Liar' case in which 23-year-old Camilla Rowan was convicted of killing her new-born baby, Scene of Crime officers from South Mercia Police began a detailed forensic search of the home of friends of the Rowan family, Nigel Ward, 64, and his wife Sheila, 62. Mrs Ward worked as Dick Rowan's secretary for a number of years and Mr Ward was a fellow member of the local Shiphampton Rotary

Late last night reports began to circulate that bones had been identified in a secluded area of the garden, and white-suited officers were seen removing a quantity of material in black evidence bags.

South Mercia Police refused to comment on the alleged find, saying that a statement would be issued in due course. Neighbours report that Ward left the house early yesterday in the company of two plain-clothes officers.

will be referred to the Court of Appeal. Rowan's baby son was last seen leaving hospital with his mother in December 1997 only hours after his birth, Five years later Rowan received a life sentence at the Old Bailey. The alleged abuse only came to light as a result of the Netflix documentary series Infamous, which aired earlier this year, and which led to a Criminal Cases Review Commission review

Daily Telegraph, 14 August 2016

* * *

She fiddles with a cushion on the armchair then sits down, gesturing me to do the same. The TV is on, muted, but she doesn't turn it off. A shopping channel. A woman with too much smile demonstrating a food mixer that looks like it could run the National Grid.

Ward folds her hands. 'I gather you found him. Her child.'

I sit down opposite her. 'Yes, we believe we have.'

'So what's this about?'

'My superintendent thinks there's something to be gained by getting the facts out there, insofar as we know them. He's proposing an exclusive interview with one journalist.' I take a breath, wondering if she's got there already. 'John Penrose.'

A sneer passes across her face and doesn't go away. 'That ghastly man? I am never speaking to him again and that's final –'

'No, no, Mrs Ward, he wouldn't be talking to you. That's not what I meant. The interview would be with us. The police.'

She makes a contemptuous *pffting* noise.

'My superintendent thinks it's a good idea, and I agree with him –'

'No, you don't,' she says quickly. 'It's written all over your face.'

'Either way, Mrs Ward, the interview's going to happen.'

'So you came all this way just to tell me that?'

'In part. Obviously we wanted to warn you in advance, as a courtesy. But it's not just that. Before the interview happens there are things we need to do. Things we need to be able to say. To put this story to bed once and for all.'

Another scornful snort. 'Good luck with that.'

'I understand where you're coming from, but it's different now. There are things we can do we couldn't do before.

Like a DNA test. If your husband was not the father of the child, we're now in a position to *prove* that. Categorically. And then we can say so.'

Her eyes widen. 'And how precisely are you proposing to –' She stops, takes a breath. 'You mean take something from his *body*? You want to *dig him up*? After all they did to us?'

* * *

Rowan case: Police condemn 'criminal damage'

By Alison Poynter

Officers were called to the home of Nigel and Sheila Ward last night after vandals apparently threw bricks through the front windows of their three-

neighbours said they heard the sound of breaking glass, and saw a number of masked men running away from the scene. It is believed that abusive messages were attached

"No-one here believes he was involved in the disappearance of that baby. He's just not that kind of man. Obviously we knew they were friends with

Intruder arrested at Ward home

comes after a number of similar incidents since the premiere of the Netflix show *Infamous*, in which Mr Ward was named as a possible

of South Mercia Police said, "This is clearly a case of criminal damage, and will be prosecuted as such. We need to send a clear message that we will not

Bones in suspect's garden 'family pet'

By Lance Andrews

Forensic investigators have identified bones found at the home of Nigel and Sheila Ward as those of the couple's dead dog, police have revealed. In a statement yesterday, South Mercia Police apologised for any distress caused to Mr and Mrs Ward. Nigel Ward, 64, was named in the hit Netflix true-crime television series *Infamous*

Police apologise for 'distress caused'

searches at the property have been completed, but it is understood that enquiries are continuing.

Lawyers for Camilla Rowan have refused to comment on whether she has formally accused Mr Ward of having abused her as a child. Sheila

Guardian, Metro, Daily Express, 21, 25, 27 August 2016

* * *

'I'm sorry, Mrs Ward. I know how painful this must be. And, believe me, an exhumation would be absolutely the last resort. We all hope it won't have to come to that –'

'It won't come to that because I'm *not going to let you* – you hear me?' Her fury is coming at me like a hail of needles. 'Not after everything we've been through. Do you know why we moved here? Because they made our lives a living hell, that's why. All those busybodies who said there's no smoke without fire –'

'I know there was some vandalism –'

'Vandalism? *Vandalism?* You call having "child molester" painted on your garage door *vandalism*? You call having a brick through your window in the middle of the night *vandalism*? We loved that house – Nigel put twenty years into that garden and you people, you just *trashed* it – it was like the bloody Somme – you dug up our *dog* –'

'I'm sorry, that must have been –'

'We were hounded out of our *own home.* And it wasn't just the abuse – we got letters, phone calls, week after week for months on end. People saying Nigel had been seen burying the baby and we had to pay up or they'd go to the police. The same thing happened to Dick and Peggy after the trial – people claiming to know where the baby was and asking for money – trying to cash in on other people's misery. It was all too much for Peggy in the end. No wonder she ended up in hospital. And all of it – *all of it* – was down to that little bitch Camilla and her vicious lies. She doesn't care how much damage she does – how many lives she wrecks –'

'Mrs Ward –'

She's spitting now, a line of drool hanging from one side of her mouth. 'She didn't even have the courage to say those vile things herself – she got that nasty little cow with the tattoos to do it for her –'

'Like I said –'

But she won't stop – can't stop – all these years of simmering in silence suddenly unleashed. She leans forward, pointing, drilling her anger home. 'And that night – the night of the party – do you know where Nigel was? I'll tell you where he was – he was *visiting his mother* – just like he did every Tuesday. She had a funny turn and that's why he was late back – he was looking after his *eighty-four-year-old* mother, not *murdering a baby –*'

I know that. And not only because it's clear now that no one was murdering that baby. Not Camilla Rowan, not Nigel Ward, not anyone. His mother was long dead by the time *Infamous* came out, but when all that shit hit the fan and South Mercia were forced to try to eliminate Ward as a suspect, they went looking for the old lady's carer. And she backed Ward up: she said he did indeed go and see his mother in Banbury every Tuesday and would administer her evening medication before he left. He never missed a week – the carer would have remembered, and all the more in the week before Christmas. So there was no way he could have met up with Camilla that night, either on the A417 or anywhere else – the distances involved were simply too great.

'I'm not trying to open it all up again, Mrs Ward,' I say gently. 'The opposite, in fact. That's why we'd like to do the DNA test. So you can draw a line under all this.'

Her face is flushed, her breath coming in ragged gasps.

'I was hoping you still had something of your husband's that might give us a usable sample. A hairbrush perhaps.'

She gapes at me. 'He died *two years* ago –'

She sits back in the chair. All the irritation, all the affront, suddenly drained away; she just looks exhausted. Exhausted and lost and old. And I feel like a shit. For the second time today.

'I'm sorry,' she says eventually, reaching into her sleeve for a tissue and dabbing at her mouth. 'I can't help you.'

'What about his family – I believe he had a brother?'

When she speaks again her voice is paper-dry. 'Jeremy. We're not in touch. We fell out after that wretched programme. The press were harassing him – not as bad as they did to us, but bad enough. He blamed Nigel.' She swallows. 'He didn't even come to Nigel's funeral. His own brother. No one did. His friends, the golfers, his old colleagues – nobody. He'd turned into a leper.'

I have a brief mental picture of a bleak winter churchyard with only her and the vicar by an open grave. The Wards never had any children. I wonder now if that was choice, or chance.

'Do you know how we could contact Jeremy?'

She sighs. 'I have his address somewhere. Assuming he hasn't moved. I doubt he'd have bothered telling me if he had.'

She gets up, slowly and heavily, and goes over to a bureau on the far wall.

'Here,' she says a few moments later, handing me a slip of paper. 'This is all I have.'

An address in Burford. The sort that doesn't need a number. I look up at her. 'Thank you.'

She folds her arms. 'And now, I'd like you to leave.'

* * *

'I'm not leaving and that's flat.'

Margaret Swann is perched on the edge of the sofa, her hands gripped in her lap.

242

Ev looks at her and then at her husband, who's skulking behind the furniture where Margaret can't see him.

'I appreciate this is inconvenient – annoying, even – but it really would make sense. As Mr Swann himself pointed out, you're a long way from the nearest police station, and if a lot of press suddenly turn up and start causing you difficulties it's going to be a little while before we can get to you –'

Margaret gives her a dark look. 'We've been through all this once before, young lady, in case it's slipped your mind. There is *nothing*, believe me, that the likes of *you* can tell us about the depths to which the media will sink – doorstepping, telephoto lenses, lights trained on the house all night – we were prisoners in our own home –'

'All the more reason, surely, to go somewhere else for a few days? Just until things die down?'

Ev turns to the old man, hoping he'll be more amenable to reason, but he's refusing to meet her gaze.

'It wasn't just the press,' he says eventually, 'last time. There was graffiti, paint on the car, that sort of thing. Excrement, once. Through the letterbox. The police advised us to move out, just like you are, and we did, but with the place left empty, there was a lot of damage.'

Ev nods. She knows; she's seen the file, read the police reports.

'Not that we were living in this house then, of course –'

Margaret glances up at him. 'I'm not prepared to go through all that again, Dick – I just can't face it.'

'I can talk to DI Fawley,' says Ev gently, 'see if we can have a uniformed officer stationed here while you're away. To keep an eye on the house.'

Margaret stares down at her hands. She seems on the brink of tears.

Swann sighs and comes round to the front of the sofa and sits down next to her. 'It's not the damn house I'm worried about, Peggy, it's you. You're not as young as you were. Neither of us are.' He takes hold of one of her hands. 'You've been in hospital three times already this year and again this week – you know what the doctor said.'

Ev takes a breath, remembering they never did get permission to see Margaret Swann's medical records. 'What did the doctor say, Mr Swann?'

He looks up at her. 'My wife suffers from panic attacks, Constable, has done ever since the trial. They put a strain on her heart. We do our best to avoid stressful situations.'

'I'm very sorry, that must be very worrying. For both of you.'

'It is.' He bends closer to his wife. 'Which is why I'd like you to do what the officer says and go somewhere else for a few days.'

She looks up at him, tears in her eyes. 'Where would we go?'

He looks at her gently. 'Not we, *you*.' She starts to protest but he shakes his head. 'No arguments, Peggy. Not this time. I'll stay to look after the house – there'll be a policeman here so I won't come to any harm. You won't need to worry about me.'

He squeezes her hand and some wordless communication passes between them. 'All right,' she whispers eventually. 'All right.'

Swann nods and squeezes her hand again, then turns to

Ev. 'There isn't really anyone Peggy can stay with, I'm afraid –'

'It's OK,' she says quickly. 'We can arrange a B&B for you – just for a few days.' She tries a weak smile. 'Not as grand as this, of course, but at least your wife will be able to get some peace.'

Margaret stares at her, all anger spent. 'That's why we came here. To get some peace. But it's always going to find us, isn't it? Wherever we go, however far we run. They're never going to let us forget.'

*   *   *

When Sargent comes back from dealing with Crowther, the office is filling up. Hansen's staring intently at his screen, clearly absorbed in something, Gislingham's standing at Baxter's desk, and Carter's talking to Quinn, no doubt making sure he's fully aware of that terrific insight of his about the hotels. Only Ev is missing. Sargent goes over to her desk and sits down, then immediately realizes something is wrong. Someone's used her chair – the height's been changed.

But who, who would even –?

She looks up, her eyes drawn – almost without thinking – to Carter.

He's talking animatedly, his back to her.

*   *   *

Notwithstanding his run-ins with the fourth estate, Jeremy Ward is still in situ. And I'd be reluctant to move myself, if I lived where he does, even if I did have a press mob on my tail. A double-fronted Georgian house on The Hill is about as desirable as Burford gets. Or anywhere else, for that matter. Newly painted too, at a guess; the rich may get the cream but it's a high-maintenance colour. There's one of those Victorian iron things for scraping your shoes by the front door and topiary box in lead planters either side. Real lead, not that faux stuff. The security cameras are real too.

I didn't phone to warn them I'd be coming, so the woman who opens the door greets me with the standard upper-middle 'now who might you be' look. She's wearing black trousers and a blue-and-orange geometrical print shirt that looks like it's hoping to be a kaftan when it grows up.

'DI Adam Fawley, Thames Valley Police. Could I speak to Mr Ward?'

I suspect she'd like to pretend he isn't at home, but I can actually hear him, somewhere close, talking on the phone. She asks to see my warrant card – not that I can blame her for that, in the circumstances – then gives a heavy sigh.

'Is it that ghastly Camilla again? All that nonsense in the papers?'

'Yes, I'm afraid so.'

She gives me a 'here we go again' look, then ushers me

in and closes the door before calling to her husband, 'Jerry – there's a policeman here for you.'

The hall is black-and-white paved and yellow walled; a staircase bending away on the right with light streaming down from somewhere above; a line of white-painted doors on the left, from one of which her husband now appears.

He must be at least a decade younger than his dead brother. Or perhaps he's just had an easier life. Tank top, plaid shirt, cords. Glasses perched on the top of his head, which immediately gets my goat.

'What can I do for you, officer?'

'I take it you've seen today's news?'

'Hard to avoid it.'

'We believe Camilla Rowan's missing child may have been found, and we'd like to eliminate your brother as the father. All I need from you is a simple mouth swab, for DNA. We can do it right now – it won't take more than a couple of minutes.'

And then I can stop cluttering up your hallway like a hairy-arsed artisan. Though I don't say that.

I'm expecting him to agree at once – he has as much to gain as Sheila if they can put all this behind them – but he looks troubled. Unaccountably troubled.

'As I said, it's purely for elimination purposes – the DNA won't be stored or used for anything else –'

'It's not that,' he says quickly. Then pauses, heaves a breath. 'Look, I think you'd better come through to my study. Fiona – perhaps you could get us some tea?'

From the look on her face, he's going to pay for that later, but what's intriguing me far more is the fact that she clearly has no more idea than I do why he's reacting the way he is.

She turns, distinctly crisply, and I follow Ward back down the hall to where he came from. The study is floor to ceiling with leatherbound books that anywhere else I'd assume were fake, but I wouldn't risk betting on that here. He gestures towards a chair, one of those pompous buttoned things with a hood over the top. Porter's chairs, I think they call them. I've never been less tempted to sit down.

His chair, on the other hand, looks rather comfortable. Unlike him.

'Is there a problem, sir? With the DNA test?'

He shakes his head slowly. 'With the test? No. I have no problem with the police taking my DNA.' He sighs. 'The issue is rather with what you'll find.'

I frown. 'Are you saying what I think you're saying?'

He nods. 'That my brother could have been the father? Yes, that's exactly what I'm saying.' He shakes his head a little and looks away. 'I've been dreading a day like this for years. Someone like you turning up and saying they've found the body.'

I sit forward; to be honest, I'm worried that if I lean too far back in this contraption I may never get up again.

'What makes you so sure it was your brother? Was it something he said?'

'That's the point,' he says quickly. 'I'm *not* sure. If I had been, my conscience would have compelled me to say something long ago.'

But instead of that his so-called 'conscience' managed to find a loophole just about big enough for him to protect his brother and safeguard his own comfortable life into the bargain. Like I always say when they get me to talk to new recruits: when it comes to this job, abandon faith in human nature all ye who enter here.

Ward's cheeks are slightly flushed now, as if he knows what I'm thinking. 'I'm sorry. I know that doesn't paint me in a very good light, but –'

'So if you're not "sure", I'm assuming he never actually spoke to you about it?'

He shakes his head again. 'No.'

'So where did it come from?'

He looks genuinely distressed now. 'It was something I saw.' He stops, clears his throat. 'It was 1994, I think, maybe '95. Nigel and Sheila had a party in their garden for her birthday. Nigel's golf mates, the Rotary Club, the whole shebang.'

'The Rowans?'

He nods. 'Camilla was about fourteen. Peggy always had her dressed very prim whenever she was on show but it wasn't fooling me. Or any of the women there.' He makes a face. 'Including my wife. She referred to her later as a "first-class prick-tease". Anyway, Nigel was doing the barbecue most of the afternoon, but by about four Fiona had got bored making small talk with Tory wives and wanted to leave, so I went looking for him to say goodbye.'

'And where was he?'

'Upstairs. With Camilla.'

'In one of the bedrooms?'

He nods. 'The door was ajar. They were sitting on the bed and he had his arm round her. She seemed to be upset.'

He stops again. I wait.

'I heard him saying something about "sorting it out". That she "wasn't to worry".'

'I see. And what did you think he meant?'

'At the time? I wasn't sure. I mean, it could have been anything, some problem at school, a row with her mother. Some teenage angst or other. Though I was surprised she'd gone to him with it – I didn't think they knew each other that well.'

'Did they see you?'

He hesitates, then shakes his head. 'No. And I didn't mention it. Either to him or to Fiona – it would just have been a red rag to a bull where she was concerned. But later, when it all came out about the baby – when Camilla was arrested – I started to wonder whether she might have been pregnant then too. Whether that's what he'd meant about "sorting it out".'

'And she went to him because he was the father.'

He nods. Looks away.

'Why didn't you say anything to the police?'

He's not meeting my eye.

'Mr Ward, you know as well as I do that it could have been crucial evidence in the trial. If there was any question of child abuse –'

'If you must know, that's precisely *why* I didn't say anything. Because of the whole damn Pandora's box that would have let loose if I had. *And* because, whatever went on between Camilla and my brother, it was not child abuse.' He gives me a steady look. 'You didn't know Camilla back then. I did. And believe me, if they were having sex it's because *she* wanted it just as much as he did.'

'You said yourself, he was a grown man – she was *fourteen* –'

His jaw is set now. 'All the same. She'd have had her reasons. She was very good at using people.'

'And you still said nothing, even after the Netflix show came out and your brother was named?'

He looks away again. I can see a vein pulsing in his neck.

'Why didn't you say anything, Mr Ward?'

He takes a deep breath and turns to face me. 'Because blood is thicker than water, Inspector, that's why. And because that night – the night the baby disappeared – when he was late to the Christmas party and said he'd been at Mum's – he was lying. He was never there.'

'But your mother's drugs were given to her as usual –'

'I know. But he wasn't the one who did it. It was me.'

* * *

Ev pulls up outside the B&B and turns off the engine. It's the rather optimistically named Comfy Inn, a three-storey Victorian terrace just off the Cowley Road. She hasn't been here for more than two years, but it hasn't changed much. Though the general direction of travel is definitely down: a bit less paint on the window frames, a bit more rubbish bulging from the bins. The orange street light isn't doing it many favours either. This was where she brought Sharon Mason and her son in July 2016, the night their house went up in flames. They were escaping an angry mob too. Perhaps that's why the mere sight of this place has her stomach in knots. But this time, she tells herself firmly, things are different. Margaret Swann has a home to go back to, for a start. And even if – as Ev suspects – she was no better as a mother than Sharon Mason, there's no question she's a victim now.

She turns to Margaret, sitting huddled in the back. She's been steeling herself for the old woman's reaction the whole way here, waiting for the cutting remarks about the B&B being a dump and filthy and is this what she pays taxes for, but she's just sitting there in silence, apparently not even aware that they've stopped. All the fight has gone out of her. Ev is reminded, suddenly, of her dad, the day she took him to the care home.

She gets out of the car and goes round to the boot for the bags, her throat tight with tears.

* * *

'It doesn't actually *prove* anything, though, does it?'

I'm on the phone, in the car. I've dropped off the DNA sample with CSI and I'm on my way home, about to hit the ring road, and (if I'm lucky) just in time to see my daughter before she goes to sleep.

'Just because Nigel Ward wasn't with his mum that night,' says Quinn, 'it doesn't mean he had to be with Camilla. He could have been shagging someone else.'

Quinn's always been a dab hand at devil's advocate. But then again, he could pick a fight with the sky just for being blue.

'I agree. But the one thing we do know is that some-one took that child, and Ward was much more likely to know how to arrange an illegal adoption than Camilla. Added to which, South Mercia never found any evidence Ward was playing away with someone else, not as far as I know.'

I hear Quinn laugh. 'Yeah, but by the time they started looking it was ten bloody years later.'

'True, but if he really was with someone else that night he'd have had an alibi. Don't you think he'd have men-tioned that when people started accusing him of getting rid of a baby?'

'But no one ever did accuse him of that, did they? That or anything else. Not officially. South Mercia accepted he'd been at his mum's. End of. OK, maybe if they'd pushed harder Ward might have cracked –'

'Or his brother –'

But even as I'm saying it I doubt it; the only reason Jeremy is talking now is that his brother is safely out of harm's way.

'But it didn't happen, did it. Maybe because Nigel Ward was playing golf with half the South Mercia force. Or in the same bloody Lodge.'

There's a silence. I can hear music in the background, the sound of a woman's voice; Quinn must be at home.

'So,' he says, 'what do you want us to do?'

'Nothing yet. Let's run the DNA and establish once and for all if Ward was the father, then I'll do that damned interview and see what crawls out of the woodwork.'

'And what if the lab says Nigel wasn't the daddy?'

'Doesn't mean he didn't arrange the adoption. If he'd

'sorted it out' for her once before I can easily see Camilla turning to him again, even if he wasn't the father.'

'And she had one over on him too, didn't she,' says Quinn darkly. 'He wouldn't want all *that* coming out, now would he? I mean, a shagger's one thing, a paedo's quite another.'

* * *

When Ev gets back to the station almost everyone's gone for the day. Bradley Carter's still at his desk scanning CCTV footage, but other than that the office is empty. No Fawley, no Quinn, no Gis.

Bugger it, she thinks, *I'm just going to call it quits on time for once.* She dumps her paperwork on her desk and heads for the Ladies, only to half collide with Chloe Sargent coming out. She has trainers on and sports gear under her padded jacket.

'Hi,' she says, smiling, 'I was wondering if you were coming back.'

Ev pulls a face. 'I don't know why I did. But I'm not going to hang around.'

'Off out?' asks Chloe.

'No, just a hot date with Hector. My cat,' she finishes quickly, seeing Chloe raise an eyebrow. 'He's marginally less trouble than a bloke. But only marginally.'

Chloe laughs. 'I bet.'

'What about you – gym?'

'Ah, no,' she says, gesturing at the racquet bag which Ev hadn't spotted till now. 'I'm playing tennis tonight. Better to take out my frustrations hitting a ball than anything – or any*one* – else.'

She slides her eyes in Carter's direction and they exchange a knowing smile.

'So you play indoors? I mean – it's dark already –'

'Have to,' says Chloe, 'with this game.'

She sees Ev looking confused. 'Sorry, I should have said – it's *real* tennis.'

Ev's eyes widen. 'Blimey, I had no idea you could play that here.'

'Yeah, I'm really lucky – there's a court on Merton Street. I've been learning for about a year. It takes some getting used to – like a cross between ordinary tennis and squash.' She hesitates. 'Why don't you come? It's quite fun to watch, and we can walk to it easily from here.'

Ev's turn to hesitate; she'd been wondering whether to go up to the JR to see Somer tonight, but you can hardly call that 'fun'. She's not even sure she's doing any good – or if Somer actually wants people turning up and forcing her to make conversation.

'We could have a drink at the Bear after?' ventures Chloe. 'Or Quod if you want to go fancy.'

Ev laughs. 'Now you're talking.'

* * *

When Ev gets to the office the following morning she's one of the last there. She doesn't usually go out on work nights and she's paying for it now, but she had a bloody good time and she's glad she went. The tennis was like nothing she's ever seen before and, frankly, not for the faint-hearted. Chloe's playing partner was a tall, striking-looking New Zealander with the face of a seraph and the devil of a backhand – the heavy little ball was flying every-where, pinging off every hard surface, and (as Ev found out to her cost) sending it careering straight into the spectators' gallery turned out to be one of the easier ways to rack up points, which made her wish she'd brought her riot shield. She got hopelessly lost trying to work out the rules, and had no idea who won in the end (Sarah, as it happens, though apparently it was close), but it didn't matter, and afterwards the three of them went for fish and chips and a bottle of Prosecco, and all in all it was the best time Ev has had in ages.

Chloe's already at her desk, and gives her a broad smile as Ev dumps her bag and starts to take off her coat. 'OK?'

Ev grins. 'Nothing a black coffee and a couple of para-cetamol couldn't fix.'

'Has Hector forgiven you?'

Ev's grin widens. 'He's reporting me to the RSPCA as we speak, but then again, he does that on a daily basis. In fact, pretty much every time I fail to give him prawns.'

Chloe laughs. 'I'm coming back as a cat – no, correc-tion, I'm coming back as *your* cat.'

Carter looks up and makes a face. 'Christ, you haven't got a cat, have you? I can't stand the bloody things. They just look down their noses at me and scarper if I go any-where near them.'

Ev suppresses a smile and turns to Chloe, dropping her voice so only she can hear. 'Hate to tell you this, Bradley my old mate, but it isn't just the cats.'

* * *

There was a broken-down lorry on Headington Road and tailbacks all the way back to the A40 roundabout, so I'm already in a less than perfect mood by the time I get in, and finding Bradley Carter waiting at my door with his laptop in one hand, looking for all the world like school prefect, doesn't exactly improve my humour. Whatever it is, he should be taking it to Quinn or Gis, not me.

'Oh, sir, there you are –'

'What is it, Carter?'

'I think I've found something, sir – something that could be important –'

'Have you spoken to DS Quinn about it? He's the Receiving DS.'

He hesitates, slides a glance down the corridor. 'Yes, I know, but I'm not sure where he is –'

That's a lie for a start – I just saw Quinn myself, heading towards the Gents.

Carter's gone red now. He might as well have an arrow over his head saying 'Busted'. But I suppose I should be encouraging him if he's taking the initiative. And if he's finding it bumpy getting on with Quinn, I shouldn't be surprised: they're both far too pushy – and too alike – to rub along easily.

I shunt open the door and wave him in. 'OK, let's hear it.'

He must have been holding his breath because it all comes out in a rush.

'Thanks, sir, it won't take long, I promise –'

'That's OK, Carter, just show me what you've got.'

He puts the laptop down and flips it open. There are three images on the screen.

I frown. 'That's the clothes the dead man was wearing, isn't it?'

He nods, slightly flushed again. 'I think we missed something, sir.'

'Oh yes – what exactly?'

He clicks to enlarge the picture of the canvas training shoes, and I bend to look. Purple plastic heels, purple laces, the rest cream and pale brown. Originally, anyway. The leather is smeared with dark dried blood, the canvas black with it.

'These are Nike Air Max Futura 270s.'

The inference is lost on me. My trainers are at least ten years old and I wore the last pair until they fell apart. I don't know, and care even less, what bloody make they are. 'I don't see –'

'This particular colourway – it's only just been launched. You can only get them in the US.'

I'm frowning again. 'So, what are you getting at? He got them on Amazon? Had them shipped over?'

Carter swallows. 'Or bought them there.'

Because that's where he was living.

Occam's razor, my old Inspector's favourite – in fact only – rule of policing. He cited it so often people called it Osbourne's razor. *The simplest explanation is invariably right.*

I look up at Carter. 'Speak to DS Gislingham and tell him we need to get on to the airports – see if we can establish when he entered the country. And find some images of current US postage stamps and show them to that postie at Wytham – see if they ring a bell.'

He's flushed with pleasure now. 'Thank you, sir. I'll get on it right away. And I'll tell DS Quinn too.'

He snaps the laptop shut.

'Well done, Carter. Even after we found out about the Rowans getting that letter I didn't think to look at the clothes, and more to the point, no one else did either. Except you. Good work. I'm impressed.'

'Thank you, sir.'

He has the grace – or the sense – to leave without saying anything more, but judging by the grin on his face as he closes the door he's probably off to ring his mum.

* * *

Voicemail

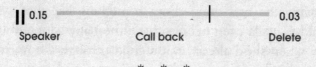

DI Adam Fawley

Mobile

Transcription

Mrs Ward, it's Adam Fawley. I'm sorry to miss you but I wanted to let you know as soon as possible that I was able to get a sample from Jeremy, and the lab have run the DNA test. If you can give me a call back as soon as you get this I can talk you through it. Many thanks.

❚❚ 0.15 ━━━━━━━━━━━━━━━━━━━━━━━━━━ 0.03

Speaker   Call back   Delete

* * *

'Mr Ward? It's Adam Fawley. We've had the results. Your brother wasn't the father.'

I hear him exhale. 'Thank God for that.'

'Yes, I can imagine you're relieved. Let's hope you'll be able to move on now.'

'What do you mean, "hope" – the results are conclusive, aren't they?'

'Oh yes, there's no question about the paternity. But just because he wasn't the father, doesn't mean he wasn't involved in some other way.'

'Like what?'

I can't believe I need to spell it out, but if I have to, I will.

'He could have helped her with the baby.'

I can almost hear him frowning. 'In what way, exactly?'

'He could have arranged an illegal adoption. For example.'

'*Nigel?* You can't be serious.'

There's a pause. I can hear his wife talking to him at the other end. It's not loud enough to hear what she's saying, just a sense of tension, of urgency.

'I'm sorry, Inspector,' he says now, 'but I don't understand. Quite apart from the fact that I can't see Nigel knowing the first thing about something like that, why would Camilla even need to have the baby adopted illegally when she'd already put a child through the normal channels?'

Well, that's one way of putting it.

'I don't have an answer to that question, Mr Ward. All I do know is that a baby boy disappeared and ended up being brought up by someone else. I don't know who, and I don't know where, but somehow, it happened. I'm just trying to connect the dots.'

'Fair enough,' he says, after a moment. 'But, like I said, I just can't see Nigel being any use to her. He had no links to that sort of world, no "dodgy connections" – the very idea is insane –'

'He was a solicitor, though.'

'A *high street* solicitor, not attorney to the Mob.'

'But he did do criminal work, didn't he, as well as the usual property and divorce stuff?'

'Well, yes, but –'

'Then he must have had *some* clients with less than savoury backgrounds – petty thieves, tax evaders –'

He takes a deep breath. 'I have no idea. Probably. *On occasion.* But this sort of thing – it would be on a completely different scale.'

'I've been doing this job a long time, Mr Ward, and in my experience crime is no different from a lot else in life: it's all about contacts. Someone who knows someone who knows someone.'

He sighs. 'Well, yes, I can see that, I suppose. But like I said, why go to all that trouble when the state will do it for you at zero cost?'

'And as *I* said, I don't have a good answer to that. That's why I have to ask these questions. However irritating they might be.'

There's a pause.

'Where was he, that night, Mr Ward? When he wasn't at your mother's and you stood in for him? You never said.'

'I never said because I don't know.'

'You didn't ask?'

'He just told me someone needed his help – that it was important and he couldn't get out of it.' He sighs again. 'And yes, it has occurred to me that that's a pretty good description of what you think he was up to with Camilla.'

'I didn't say I thought that; just that it was possible.'

Another pause.

'Was he having an affair?'

'Not that I knew.'

'Did he have other relationships? Either before that or afterwards?'

'If he did, he kept it to himself. He certainly never told me. Look, Sheila could be a difficult woman to live with but I never saw any suggestion that he had anyone else.'

'So you have no idea who this "someone" was he needed to help?'

'I'm sorry, Inspector, your guess is as good as mine.'

* * *

'If he doesn't stop fucking smirking soon,' mutters Quinn, 'I swear I'm going to nut him.'

Gislingham glances across at Carter, then grins at Quinn. 'Well, I guess you can't blame him. It was pretty impressive.' Quinn's still frowning and Gislingham just can't resist. 'Bit of a surprise, though – him coming up with that. I mean, it's not the sort of thing I'd expect him to know about – shoes and that. Fashion. More your area, I'd say.'

Quinn flashes him a look. 'I'd never spend that much on a pair of sodding trainers.'

'What's this about trainers?' says Chloe Sargent, dumping her bag on her desk. She's just back from lunch and there are splatters of rain on her jacket. 'Have I missed something?'

Baxter looks up. 'Carter just bagged a humungous wodge of brownie points by working out that the vic's shoes must have been bought in America.'

Her face falls. She glances towards Carter. 'Really?'

'Quite the little detective,' says Quinn, raising his voice. 'Aren't you, Carter?'

Carter looks up and flushes. 'Not really –'

'Oh, come on,' begins Quinn, but there's a sharp edge to his sarcasm that Gis knows only too well. People are looking up, trying to work out what's going on. Time to dial it down.

'Ignore him, Carter,' says Gis, deliberately jovial, 'we're all just jealous – me included. Credit where credit's due, but –' turning to the rest of the team now – 'we've got a long way to go yet.'

It's another five minutes before Carter pushes back his chair and goes out towards the coffee machine, by which time everyone's returned to what they were doing. Apart from Ev, who's just got back from lunch herself. Which is why she's the only one who notices Chloe Sargent get up and follow Carter out.

* * *

263

I have to drive into London for the BBC interview so I go via Risinghurst and get a change of clothes. I wouldn't have bothered because I don't particularly care how I look, but Alex does. She would anyway, but as she's already reminded me, this is about more than just making sure I don't have baby sick down my sleeve.

'You need to look like you're at ease with yourself,' she says as I stand staring at my tie rack. 'In control.' And an obvious choice for Thames Valley's next new Chief Inspector. Which, of course, we're both studiously avoiding mentioning.

'I don't feel like I'm in control. I'm not even in control of my bloody tie.'

She smiles. 'All the more reason to look like you are.' She pulls one out and threads it round my collar. It's not the tie I'd have chosen – I'd have gone quieter, more conventional – but that's why she's better at these things than I am.

'What would I do without you?'

She laughs. 'Forget to pay the bills? Run out of clean socks?'

'You know what I mean.'

I pull her into my arms, and her hands slip under my jacket and round my waist.

I put my lips to her hair. 'I should come home at lunchtime more often.'

'Harrison would notice,' she whispers. 'You'd never make it back in the afternoons.'

A laugh now, but not mine, and not hers. I swing round to see Lily staring at us from her cot, her little fists gripped on the bars, her face lit up in a smile.

Alex drops her hands. 'Oh. My. God. Adam – she's pulled herself up.' She stares at me. 'She's never done that before – she's only three months old and she's *pulled herself up.*'

She rushes over to the crib and lifts Lily out, and now Lily's laughing and Alex's laughing and kissing her, and telling her how clever she is, and all I can think is, who gives a stuff about Camilla Rowan, or the bloody BBC, or the promotion, or any of it, because I'm the luckiest bastard in the whole wide world.

* * *

'No, if he was brought up in the US it would make no difference to the familial search results. If the biological father was *born* in the US – or somewhere else overseas – then yes, *that* would definitely give us a significantly different gene pool, but that's not what you're talking about, is it?'

'No,' says Gislingham at the other end of the line. 'Sorry, Nina, my bad. I should have thought.'

Mukerjee smiles to herself; it might have been a waste of time but it was very far from being the dimmest question a police officer has asked her about DNA. And in any case, she likes Gislingham; she's glad to see him making a success of his step up to sergeantship.

'No problem at all – really.'

'I just remember the boss saying you were surprised

you hadn't found as many matches as you usually would and thought this might be the explanation.'

'Well, the first half of that's true, at least.'

Gis laughs. 'Back to the drawing board, eh?'

*   *   *

www.bbc.com/transcripts/Behind_the_Headlines

BEHIND THE HEADLINES aired October 26, 2018 – 18:30 GMT

THIS IS A RUSH TRANSCRIPT. THIS COPY MAY NOT BE IN ITS FINAL FORM AND MAY BE UPDATED.

[18:00:18]

HELEN KERRIDGE, HOST: Good evening, I'm Helen Kerridge and this is BEHIND THE HEADLINES, where we take an in-depth look at a story that's making the news this week. Tonight it's an 'infamous' case from fifteen years ago that's once again making the front pages. Back in 2003, Camilla Rowan, then 23, was accused of killing her newborn son six years earlier. She has always claimed she gave the baby to its natural father, a man called Tim Baker, but this man has never been found. Rowan was convicted of murder at the Old Bailey, and sentenced to life. And that seemed to be the end of it. But then in 2016, investigative journalist John Penrose revisited the case in a now-celebrated series for Netflix, which raised some serious questions about the reliability of the original police investigation. And now, two years on, the case has taken another sensational turn, and we have the man who made that documentary here with us tonight. John –

JOHN PENROSE: Thank you, Helen. Back in 2016, I ended *Infamous: The Chameleon Girl* by asking if the time had come to take another look at Camilla

Rowan's case. Had there, in fact, been a serious miscarriage of justice which led to a victim of child abuse being imprisoned for a crime no one could prove she had committed? A few months later, the Criminal Cases Review Commission did indeed look at that question, but they concluded that the answer, then, was 'No'.

But now we know better. Because earlier this week the news broke that Camilla Rowan's lost baby had been found. Not, sadly, alive and well, but dead; killed in the most bizarre circumstances. Here in the studio tonight we have Detective Inspector Adam Fawley, who is leading the investigation into that death for Thames Valley Police. Inspector Fawley, perhaps you could tell us how you came to identify this man as Camilla Rowan's son.

DETECTIVE INSPECTOR ADAM FAWLEY: Officers were called to a house on the outskirts of Oxford last Sunday night after reports of an intruder. They discovered the body of a man in the kitchen.

PENROSE: He'd been shot. By the owner of the house.

FAWLEY: Yes, I'm afraid so.

PENROSE: The householder thought the man was a burglar?

FAWLEY: It would be a natural assumption to make.

PENROSE: So what led you to connect this incident to the Camilla Rowan case?

FAWLEY: Unfortunately, the dead man did not have any identifying documents on him, so we took DNA samples at the scene, which later proved him to be the biological son of Camilla Rowan.

PENROSE: It seems an awfully big jump from an unidentified corpse in 2018 to a baby last seen in 1997.

FAWLEY: Camilla Rowan is a convicted criminal; her DNA is in the National DNA Database. It was bound to produce a match.

PENROSE: So you're 100% sure this man was her long-lost child?

FAWLEY: We are. Our task now is to establish exactly where he's been for the last twenty years. Without any identifying documents, that's proving a challenge.

PENROSE: Do you have any potential lines of enquiry at all?

FAWLEY: The only lead we have is that the man may have been brought up overseas, possibly in the US. But as you can appreciate, that doesn't narrow the field down very much, so we're hoping that someone who sees this programme may recognise him and come forward.

(SHOW STILL)

PENROSE: This is the man? At Oxford railway station, the evening he died?

FAWLEY: That's right. If any viewers know this man, or can give us any information about who he is, please contact Thames Valley Police on the phone number or email address at the bottom of the screen now. All calls and emails will be treated confidentially.

PENROSE: (GESTURING AT THE PHOTO) He has a backpack with him – surely that must have contained something that would tell you who he was?

FAWLEY: Unfortunately, the backpack has not been found.

PENROSE: That's a bit odd, isn't it?

FAWLEY: An extensive search has been conducted –

PENROSE: It rather argues that the householders got rid of it, doesn't it? Before your officers arrived?

FAWLEY: We don't know what happened to it –

PENROSE: But why would they do that? If he was just a random burglar? Unless, of course, they knew who he was?

FAWLEY: I'm not in a position –

PENROSE: What's the householder been charged with? Murder or manslaughter?

FAWLEY: He's been released on bail. The CPS has not yet made a decision as to charging.

PENROSE: Because it would make a difference, wouldn't it? A big difference. If he's charged with murder there has to be an element of premeditation, and I'm finding it difficult to reconcile that with someone defending themselves against a burglar.

FAWLEY: To repeat, decisions as to charging will be made by the CPS –

PENROSE: But he must have been arrested, if he's on bail, so what was he arrested for – murder or manslaughter?

FAWLEY: As you well know, we don't release that sort of information.

PENROSE: I'm sure you understand why I'm asking: if you're treating what happened here as murder, doesn't that imply that the householder must have known the victim? Known him or even been *related* to him? Have you considered whether the people in the house might, in fact, be Dick and Peggy Rowan, Camilla's parents? Who sold their home in Shiphampton soon after their daughter's trial and severed all ties with their friends, and haven't been seen since. Are *they* the mystery elderly couple at Wytham?

FAWLEY: Given that this is an ongoing investigation, we have not disclosed the names of the people in question.

PENROSE: Have you done DNA tests on them?

FAWLEY: That's not something we would divulge at this stage.

PENROSE: Land Registry records for the house at Wytham show that it's owned by a property company, the main shareholder of which is a Mr Richard Swann, who just so happens to have exactly the same date of birth as Dick Rowan. The same first name, the same date of birth – that can't be a coincidence, surely.

FAWLEY: I think what's important now is to focus on identifying the dead man and establishing exactly what happened back in 1997. We were hoping that Ms Rowan might be able to help us with this but, unfortunately, she has so far declined to do so.

PENROSE: Is she going to be released?

FAWLEY: That's a matter for the Ministry of Justice, not the Police.

PENROSE: It's quite simple, Inspector. She was convicted of murdering someone who we now know wasn't murdered at all. She is, de facto, therefore, completely innocent and should be released immediately.

FAWLEY: We still don't know exactly what happened to the baby, and until we do –

PENROSE: We know she didn't kill it.

FAWLEY: Yes, we do.

PENROSE: So she's not guilty of murder.

FAWLEY: Not of murder, no.

PENROSE: What then? What is she guilty of that justifies a prison sentence of fifteen years? Because that's what she's served, Inspector. *Fifteen years*.

FAWLEY: As I said, those are questions you need to put to someone else.

PENROSE: It was a pretty shoddy inquiry, wasn't it? The original investigation?

FAWLEY: Nothing I've seen suggests that. South Mercia Police handled the case in the same way any other force would have done.

PENROSE: What about Nigel Ward? It was only thanks to me that anyone started looking at him. Me, working on my own, with no access to official documents or the ability to compel witnesses. Whereas South Mercia had dozens of detectives on that investigation, round the clock, for the best part of a year. It beggars belief that they didn't at least think it was worth talking to him.

FAWLEY: I can't speak for South Mercia Police, but in a case like this, it's standard procedure to follow up all potential lines of enquiry. If they'd found any evidence linking Mr Ward to Camilla Rowan there's no reason why they wouldn't have followed it up.

PENROSE: Perhaps they didn't find any evidence because they were looking in the wrong place. Or looking the other way. After all, half of them were his mates. Rotary Club, golf club, who knows, perhaps another sort of 'club' . . .

FAWLEY: I'm not in a position to comment. You'll have to ask South Mercia Police. It was their investigation.

PENROSE: And what about *your* investigation? Have *you* turned up anything, Inspector Fawley? You've got a team of your own, looking at this case. You don't have an axe to grind, you don't know anyone involved – your hands are clean. Have you found anything suggesting Nigel Ward may have been involved in the disappearance of Camilla's baby? Did he help her in some way, either out of the kindness of his heart, or for other, more self-serving reasons, because he needed to keep his own previous 'associ-ation' with her secret?

FAWLEY: As I said before, we never comment on active investigations.

PENROSE: So you are looking into it then?

FAWLEY: What I *can* tell you, is that Nigel Ward was categorically *not* the father of the missing baby. We've run the DNA and there's no question – he was *not* the father of that child.

PENROSE: So who is?

FAWLEY: That's what we're trying to find out. We're running a familial DNA search but that's a long and painstaking process and even then may not yield any results. That's why we hope your viewers will be able to help us. Ms Rowan herself is still insisting that the father was a man called Tim Baker –

PENROSE: Do you really believe that? You're an experienced police offi-cer, you know how much legwork went into trying to find this man – do you really think he's out there after all this time?

FAWLEY: I have no idea. But we have to assume he is. Unless and until someone can prove otherwise.

PENROSE: (TURNING TO CAMERA) Thank you, Detective Inspector Fawley. We'll certainly be keeping in touch with this story as it develops. Back to you, Helen.

HELEN KERRIDGE: Thank you, John. A fascinating story, and one I'm sure we'll be hearing more of in the coming weeks. And now, Brexit – with the UK and EU still unable to reach an agreement over arrangements for the Irish border, will Theresa May ask for an extension to the transition period?

*   *   *

'What did he say when you confronted him?'

Ev and Sargent are in the Ladies. It's about the only place they can avoid being disturbed, but that's not why they're here. They're here because when Ev came in ten minutes ago she found Sargent at the mirror, reapplying her mascara. She'd clearly been crying.

Sargent sniffs a little now. 'He denied it all – said he'd had no idea I'd been looking at the trainers – that we must have just come up with the same idea at the same time.'

Ev doesn't buy that for a minute, but she's trying to stay neutral. 'Did you believe him?'

'Of course I didn't believe him, the lying little shit.'

She heaves a heavy sigh. Her pretty face looks drawn and pale.

'I'm sorry,' says Ev. 'I'm not sure what to suggest.'

Sargent sighs. 'It's fine,' she says, her voice slightly choked. 'I just needed to vent at someone. Sorry.'

'No need to apologize.' There's a pause. 'Do you want me to talk to Gis?'

Sargent shakes her head. 'I have to fight my own battles.'

'I know, but he's a mate – and it'd be less formal coming from me.'

'There's no point, is there? I can't prove anything – I know someone sat on my chair but I can't prove it was him, and I don't see how he could have got into my PC.'

'You definitely had the screen lock on?'

'Of course – I always do. We had it drummed into us by my first sergeant.'

Ev looks hopeless. 'Then I'm not sure what else I can do.'

Sargent tries a weak smile. 'How about buy me a drink? After work?'

Ev checks her watch; it's gone six. 'How about right now?'

* * *

'It was a bloody disaster – he crucified me.'

The phone's on speaker but the line's not good, and the noise on the motorway isn't helping.

'Honestly,' says Alex, 'everyone thinks that when they see themselves on TV – there was nothing wrong with it.'

I can hear her *sshhing* now, making little soothing noises. I'm not sure if they're meant for me or Lily.

'It was a bloody clusterfuck.'

'Adam, it wasn't – really. He's trained to be a tricky bastard in interviews –'

'So am I,' I say with a sigh. 'Allegedly.'

'You gave as good as you got. I mean it.'

'I actually heard myself say "what's important" – for fuck's sake. Who do I think I am, Tony bloody Blair?'

She laughs. 'I didn't even notice! But maybe there were one too many "unfortunatelys" –'

'Gee, thanks, that's all I needed.'

'Stop it! It was fine – more than fine. You got out the message that you wanted to get out and you didn't shoot yourself in the foot. If anyone came off badly it was South Mercia.'

I swipe at the phone screen. ITV, BBC, Sky. 'At least we seem to be getting some decent coverage.'

'There you are then.'

She starts cooing again. I can hear Lily's little gurgly laugh.

'I should only be an hour or so now.'

'It's pouring here so be careful – you know what you always say about most accidents being in the first or last ten minutes of a journey –'

'Thanks, Mum.'

'– and you have a meal in the oven and a glass of wine waiting to be poured.'

'Have I ever told you I love you?'

'Maybe,' she says, with laughter in her voice, 'perhaps once or twice.'

* * *

Sheila Ward goes over to the sideboard and pours herself a brandy. Her hands are trembling and she spills a few drops on to the silver tray. A wedding present from her parents. Nigel always hated it. Said it was just plate, not proper solid silver. Not the 'real thing'. She remembers the tone he used every time he said it. As if it was her he was really talking about. As if she was substandard goods too. Not the woman he thought he was marrying. Not the real thing.

She goes back over to the sofa, feeling the hit of alcohol on her empty stomach. The TV is still on, some politician all hot under the collar about Brexit. As if it matters. As if any of it matters.

She sips again at the drink and tips back her head as the liquid burns down.

Not the father of that child
Not the father of that child
Not the father of that child

The words keep playing in her head. There's something comforting in the rhythm of them. Like a nursery rhyme. 'Three Blind Mice'. Or 'Ring a Ring o' Roses'. So charming and innocent and half nonsensical, until you find out where it came from and realize that the song your child is singing is about plague and death. Not *her* child, of course. No child of hers ever sang anything because she couldn't have one. She wasn't a proper woman, you see. Not the 'real thing'.

Not the father of that child
Not the father of that child

Ring a ring the words go round. When Fawley phoned earlier she could tell he thought he was bearing good news – that she'd be happy and relieved. Vindicated. But there'd never been any doubt about it, not in her mind. She knew Nigel hadn't fathered that baby, for the simple reason that Camilla had dumped him long before. She'd heard him, on his office phone when he thought she was asleep, begging the little tart to take him back and getting the cold shoulder because she was bored with him and had only let him screw her in the first place because it was her way of sticking it to her parents. Not that Nigel realized it, of course. He thought it was all about him. Men – men and their bloody egos.

She takes another shot of brandy, a larger one.

Not the father of that child

True. But very far from being the whole truth and she knows it. What about the other child – the one that came before? The one that wasn't even given the chance to be born – what about *that* child?

She still remembers the look on Nigel's face, the day it came out about Camilla. The day it was all over the news, and there were journalists at the door, and a police investigation, and he sat her down and gave her a brandy. It's the only other time she's ever drunk the stuff. Perhaps that's why it's coming back so vividly now. He gave her a brandy and he told her. What he'd done, and how ashamed he was, and how it had never happened again, before or since, and she had to believe him that he knew nothing – *nothing* – about the missing baby. That bit about other affairs was a lie, for a start, but she'd let him burble on, sitting there gripping her hand in his hot chubby fingers, wallowing in his terror and self-pity, and when he'd finished she told him she already knew. She'd known for years. She knew he'd got the little slut pregnant when she was barely fourteen. She knew he'd used *their* money to pay for her to get rid of it. She knew it all. The look on his face was almost worth the wait. His slack mouth opening and closing like some huge stupid goldfish. A rather tacky and unedifying pleasure, admittedly, but no less sweet for that. All those years, he'd thought he was the one with secrets, but he couldn't have been more wrong.

Because there was something else she knew. Something she never told him. Not that day, not ever.

The message on his office phone, the message he never got. The woman didn't leave her name, but Sheila knew it was Camilla – she'd have known that voice anywhere. Whining on and on, saying she was sorry for how she'd treated him in the past but she needed him now. That there was no one else she could turn to, no one else who could help, no one but him. That there wasn't much time – if she waited any longer it would be too late – too late to 'sort it out' –

She knew what the little tart was going on about, of course. She'd gone and got herself banged up again, hadn't she. Well, Nigel wasn't going to be spending their hard-earned money fixing it – not if she had anything to do with it. Not this time. Not when it wasn't even his kid. So she'd just pressed 'Erase' and walked away. But she hadn't forgotten, and all those years later, when it started to come out, she'd wondered. Because she was pretty sure it had been that summer, the summer of 1997, right about the time the tart must have realized she was pregnant with that baby. The one they said she killed. Sheila didn't feel guilty – oh no, the little cow deserved everything that was coming to her – but she'd wondered all the same. Because if Nigel had actually heard that message, none of this would have happened. Camilla would have had another abortion and that would have been the end of it. No missing child, no scandal, no court case. No press harassment either, and no bloody Netflix.

And no heart attack?

Maybe.
Maybe not.

She settles back against the cushions and closes her eyes.
It doesn't matter. Not really.

None of it does.

Not any more.

* * *

There's a delay on the line. An international delay.

'Inspector Fawley, is it?'

A man's voice. An accent. Which I'm crap at, as Alex
never ceases to tell me. But it's definitely not American.
Southern hemisphere, I think – Kiwi? Australian?

'A friend of mine saw that interview you did – on the
Beeb.'

My interest is ticking up. 'Oh yes?'

'It was the photo, really, and of course when I saw it –
basically, I think they might be right –'

'I'm not following you, Mr –?'

A quick laugh. 'Sorry, mate, it's just that it's the first I
knew about any of this – I'm still trying to get my bloody
head around it, to be honest.'

'Around what, exactly –'

'I think I knew Camilla – back in the day. Sorry – I

should have said. My name's Tinus, but people usually just call me Tin. Tin Boekker.'

*   *   *

Chloe gets in a few minutes after Ev. She looks just as she always does: neat and professional. Only the faint shadows under her eyes give anything away. Ev watches her for a few moments, and sees Carter get up and go over to speak to her, but he gets nowhere. She moves briskly past him and goes to hang up her coat.

Hansen's obviously noticed something too and flashes Ev a questioning glance, but she just gives a tiny shake of her head by way of response: *Leave it be.*

When she goes out to the coffee machine a few minutes later, Gis is already there. He smiles at her, stirring his tea.

'So,' he says evenly, 'are you going to let me in on what's going on?'

*   *   *

Adam Fawley
27 October
10.15

Safe to say it's the first and only police interview I've done by Skype. But then again, I don't have many options, not with my witness being in Cape Town. See, I told you I was crap at accents.

Tin Boekker looks nothing like the e-fit Camilla Rowan gave South Mercia back in 2003, but he does look unnervingly like the man on the Oxford station CCTV. Looking at that footage must have been like seeing his own ghost, back in 1997,

280

when he was bumming across Europe on a gap year which included three months in the UK doing the odd bit of bar work. Which is how he ended up collecting glasses at a pub in Stroud. Though it wasn't the King's Head, like Rowan said, it was the King's Arms. And I bet that wasn't a memory fail on her part, either: yet again it's the same pattern – all her lies steer tantalizingly close to the truth but swerve away at the crucial moment. The pub, 'Baker'; so similar, yet crucially not quite the same. But even if South Mercia had known Tin's real name, I doubt they'd have found him. He left the UK within a month of his two-night stand with Camilla, and by the time the case blew up he was a sous-chef at a crazily expensive spa retreat in the wilds of British Columbia with zero Wi-Fi. He tells me she said she was on the pill, and if he'd known about the baby he'd have done something, helped her somehow, even come back. And I think he's telling the truth. There's a disarming boyish frankness about him – even in his forties, even on a jumpy video call. And when he tells me he always wanted to be a dad and it's never quite happened, and now he's only found out when it's too late, there's a break in his voice I know he couldn't fake.

It takes one to know one.

* * *

'So as at now,' says Quinn, looking round the room, 'we're waiting on the sample arriving from Cape Town, but I don't think there's much doubt we've got our man.' He holds up a sheet of paper. 'Boekker even managed to find a photo of him and Camilla from back then which is basically hashtag shagging.'

He turns and pins the picture to the board. Tin and Camilla are standing with their backs to the bar, he has his arm about her, she's pulling him towards her and trying to bite his ear.

'And Boekker can prove,' continues Quinn, 'that he was in Sydney by the time the kid was born, so that old lay-off in the lay-by story is the load of old crap we always thought it was. Trouble is, we're no closer to finding out exactly what did happen.'

'What does the DI think?' asks Carter. 'I mean, he's not here, so –'

Quinn's eyes narrow, just a little. 'The boss, Carter, is in with Superintendent Harrison, giving him a briefing.'

Ev now. 'So what do we do next? Where does that leave us with the Swanns?'

Quinn nods to Gislingham, who gets up. 'The CPS still want to wait on the old man to see if we can clarify whether or not he knew who the vic was, and whether he gets charged will depend on what they decide. But as at now, they're pretty relaxed – I mean, there's not much risk of the old boy bumping anyone else off in the meantime. We've taken his bloody shotgun for a start.'

'What about Camilla? Does she know?'

'That we've found Tin Boekker? The boss has told her lawyers and asked to see her again, but I gather they're stalling. I'm not holding my breath.'

'And the airports?' asks Hansen.

Baxter looks up. 'On the case. But there are over a dozen possible entry points and half-a-million Yanks coming through them every month, and since we have no idea exactly when he got here –'

'Has to be within the last five weeks, though, doesn't

it?' says Hansen. 'If we're assuming that foreign letter the Swanns got was from him?'

Baxter gives him a heavy look. 'That's still a hell of a lot of people. Like the Sarge said, I'm not holding my breath.'

* * *

Adam Fawley
27 October
10.20

I hit four on the Harrison bullshit bingo card, which is pretty good going. The BBC interview was apparently a 'landmark moment' and a 'game changer' which proved this force is 'leading the way on best practice'; and giving it '110 per cent'. To be fair, the whole thing was his idea, so he's allowed to crow a bit. And at least I left him in a good mood; he practically had the Chief Constable on speed dial. Let's just hope it lasts.

* * *

The Guardian

Opinion
'Milly Liar'?

Sat 27 October 2018
10.30 GMT

f ⬛ ✉
32 242

What does the Camilla Rowan case tell us about the criminal justice system – and ourselves?
Tim Halston

Bungling and bias still play far too large a part in convictions

I can't be the only one who was left profoundly uneasy by the baying mob outside the Old Bailey in November 2003, after Camilla Rowan's conviction for murdering her baby. The torrent of abuse, the cries of 'baby-murderer' and 'kill the whore', were more reminiscent of a Salem witchcraft trial than the workings of a modern, progressive legal system. Admittedly, this was fifteen years ago, but have things really changed so much?

Because it now appears that a conviction that was always based on circumstantial evidence may have been founded almost entirely on a lethal combination of incompetence and prejudice. Incompetence on the part of the investigating police force, who apparently failed to follow up a number of important leads, and prejudice because Camilla Rowan simply didn't 'play the game'. She didn't fit our template of Caring Motherhood. She put her babies at risk while they were still unborn, she gave them away to complete strangers without appearing to be traumatised, and she walked away thereafter and she didn't look back. It was all too easy a jump from this apparent callousness to the assumption that she was capable of a far more brutal cruelty. She may not have been 'too posh to push' but she was certainly 'too posh to gush': she had too much money, too much privilege, and – worst of all – she kept her emotions to herself; she didn't cry. How many times did the media describe her as 'stony-faced', 'hard' or 'cold'? And they hated her for it, oh, how they hated her.

The rejoinder here – inevitably, I've heard it at dinner parties already – is that she 'didn't tell the truth'. That 'if someone else harmed the baby why didn't she say so?' I understand that response, and I imagine more than one member of her jury also stumbled at that, and ended up finding it an insuperable barrier to a vote for 'Not Guilty'.

But as now seems distinctly possible, there could have been valid and deep-seated reasons why she didn't feel able to 'tell the truth'. As case after terrible case has surely taught us by now, some truths are just too dark to tell;

they are literally 'unsayable'. Though as things stand, in Rowan's case, this remains mere speculation. Another police investigation is underway, which we must all hope will do a better job. And at the risk of stating the obvious, whatever else Camilla Rowan is, she is not a murderer. She has served fifteen years for a crime that no one committed, and she should be set free.

• Tim Halston is a Guardian columnist

*   *   *

Adam Fawley
27 October
12.15

'We've found him, boss. Camilla's kid – we've found him.'

It's Gis, at my door, half out of breath, a sheet of paper in his hand.

'Where?'

'Stansted. He flew in from Italy on October the 19th. But Carter was right – he's a Yank.'

He reads from the sheet: 'Noah Randolph Seidler, resident in New York, but *born in the UK*.' He glances up, then stabs a finger at the paper. 'But this is the *real* clincher, the place of birth is listed as *Birmingham and Solihull General Hospital* on 14th September 1997. Here,' he finishes, holding it out. 'Take a look.'

I take the sheet from him. 'But that's more than three months before Camilla's baby was born – it doesn't make any sense.'

He makes a face. 'I know. Just like the bloody rest of it. But it would at least explain why South Mercia didn't find him.'

'Are we contacting the hospital?'

'Yup – Baxter's doing it as we speak. Do you want to come and listen in?'

'Yes,' I say, 'I do.'

I follow him back down the corridor to the main office, and word has clearly got about because people are gathered round Baxter's desk. Hansen, Ev, Carter, Quinn. Right now, there's only one call going on in the entire room.

'So you definitely have a record of him?' Baxter is saying, scribbling on the pad in front of him.

'Right, and the parents' names?'

More scribbling.

'And when was he discharged?'

His face changes, there's a pause and he's writing again, faster now. 'And you're absolutely certain about that?'

A pause.

'OK, I see. Can you email me copies of everything you have? Brilliant, thanks for your help.'

He puts the phone down, takes a long breath and looks up at me.

'Noah Seidler was born at 3.45 a.m. on 14th September 1997. He was seven weeks premature, with severe breathing problems, and was transferred immediately to the neonatal ICU, where he was put on a ventilator.'

I think I know where this is going and I don't like it –

'He stayed there several weeks, and the records show him making good progress and being transferred to a general paediatric ward on December 20th. Then suddenly, out of the blue, the following day, he had a bad relapse – had some sort of seizure and stopped breathing –' Baxter swallows. 'He died at 2.30 that morning. It all happened so fast the parents were still on their way.'

Gis has gone pale; he's had a premature baby. So have I.

'Shit,' Gis says under his breath. 'Those poor bastards.'

'What do we know about the parents?'

Baxter glances down at his notes. 'David and Renee Seidler. Address in Edgbaston at the time, though they're both Americans. He's in the hospital records as "Professor" and she's "Doctor" so one or both could have been academics teaching over here. If so, we should be able to find them easily enough.'

There's a long silence. Everyone's moving the jigsaw pieces about – trying to work out what the picture looks like now.

It's Quinn who speaks first.

'So the Seidlers took Camilla's baby?'

Ev glances across. 'Or bought it,' she says darkly.

But Thomas Hansen is shaking his head. 'It still doesn't make sense – if Camilla gave them the baby, with or without money changing hands, why didn't she say so, right up front, when South Mercia first questioned her? Why come up with that ludicrous story about "Tim Baker"?'

Ev nods. 'You're right. Even if it was a dodgy adoption, it would have been way better to admit to that than being sent down for murder.'

'Perhaps the Seidlers stole it,' says Quinn. 'The woman saw the kid in a cot – she was grieving, maybe suffering from post-natal depression –'

'Still doesn't make sense,' interrupts Baxter, folding his arms. 'If the kid was snatched, why didn't Rowan report it there and then?'

'Maybe she was glad to be rid of it? Maybe she was planning to have it adopted anyway so thought – fuck it, this is a lot less hassle?'

They're talking about a baby like it's a second-hand bike. But it's not because they're insensitive, it's because they're following the logic of the case. If that's how Camilla Rowan behaved, if that's how she thinks, then that's how they have to think. Even if it does ice my heart.

'Yeah, OK,' says Baxter, 'I can see her reacting like that *at the time*, but like Ev says, what about later, when she was arrested? Why didn't she admit what happened then?'

Quinn shrugs. 'Perhaps she thought people wouldn't believe her?'

Baxter scoffs. 'Yeah, right, and all that crap about Tim Baker was such an obviously better option?'

'One thing we do know,' I say quietly, 'is that the more we find out about Camilla's lies, the more truth there is in them. Perhaps there's some link between the Seidlers and Tin Boekker.'

Baxter looks sceptical. 'Boekker never said anything. And he struck me as being pretty on the level.'

'Me too. But maybe even he doesn't know the whole picture. Maybe he introduced Camilla to the Seidlers?'

Quinn frowns. 'He was a South African kid on a gap year working in a pub in Stroud, they were Yank academics living in a posh bit of Birmingham – sounds pretty damn unlikely to me.'

'I agree, but let's just make sure, shall we?'

Ev nods. 'I can email Boekker – ask him if the name rings any bells.'

'Good, and let's get on to the US embassy too – find

out what we can about the Seidlers. But we need to be dip-
lomatic about it, please – and I make absolutely no apology
for the pun. Whether it was a kidnapping or an illegal
adoption, the Seidlers were quite possibly party to a crime,
which means we could be looking at an extradition
request at some point, so let's not piss the authorities off
gratuitously.'

'It's OK, boss,' says Gis. 'I'll pick that one up myself.'

* * *

Interview with Jeanine Castellano, Consular
Officer, US Embassy, Nine Elms, London
27 October 2018, 1.45 p.m.
On the call, DS C. Gislingham

CG: Ms Castellano, this is DS Chris Gislingham of
    Thames Valley Police.

JC: Nice to talk to you, detective, how are you
    today?

CG: I'm very well, thank you. And thanks for making
    time to talk to me, especially at the weekend.

JC: No problem, always happy to help.

CG: I believe you've received a copy of my email
    concerning Noah Seidler?

JC: I have it right here, and I've had one of my
    staff check Immigration records. It seems Mr
    Seidler left the United States on October 16th
    on a flight to Florence, but from what you say
    in your email he can only have stayed in Italy
    two days before catching a flight to London.

CG: Did he travel alone – from the States?

JC: Yes, it appears so.

CG: And is there anything you can tell me about the family?

JC: All I have right now is that the Seidlers moved to Brooklyn ten years ago, and prior to that were in Princeton. David Seidler was on the Political Sciences faculty there. And back before *that* they spent two semesters in the UK, in 1997. But you knew that already.

CG: And Mrs Seidler?

JC: Renee Seidler trained as a teacher after her postgrad and then taught junior high, but I have no record of her working since 2016. But putting it all together, it looks like that must have been around the time David was diagnosed, so I guess she gave it up to look after him.

CG: Diagnosed?

JC: He died last fall. The death certificate cites bowel cancer as the principal cause of death. Not a nice way to go.

CG: Were there other children?

JC: No, just Noah.

CG: And what do you have on him?

JC: Graduated high school with a GPA of 3.6 then got accepted on a liberal arts program at Columbia but deferred for a year, probably because his dad got sick. No criminal record, no trouble with law enforcement. Basically just a nice, bright kid.

CG: I assume you know that he was the victim of a fatal shooting?

JC: I'm aware. Have you spoken to his mom?

CG: We'll be liaising with NYPD on that. But I'm afraid it's not just a question of breaking the bad news: there are questions we need to ask about the circumstances of Noah's birth.

JC: Yes, I have your note here – it says you believe he's not the Seidlers' biological child, as stated on his birth certificate and social security records, but a British baby that went missing in 1997? This 'Milly Liar' case?

CG: That's right.

JC: Sounds like something out of Agatha Christie.

CG: I suspect it won't end as neatly as that. More's the pity.

JC: Please be sure to inform us when you have clarification – there could be consequences here. Possible fraud, conveying false or misleading information – you know the drill.

CG: Of course, we'll certainly do that. Clearly, our first priority is to establish exactly what happened – what degree of involvement the Seidlers had.

JC: What does the birth mother say?

CG: Up till now she's been sticking to her original story. But even she must realize she's turning into King Canute on that one.

JC: [*laughs*]
The guy on the beach, right?

CG: Yeah, sorry.

JC: No worries. Well, if that's everything, I have
    a family event at two o'clock. Let me know if
    I can help with anything else. You got a name
    at NYPD?
CG: No one specific, so if you –
JC: Sure, no problem. I'll email over some details.
CG: Thank you. And thank you again for your time.
JC: You're welcome. Enjoy your day.

* * *

It's a bright cold morning in New York City. Clear skies
but winter's within touching distance and Ritchie Gonzalez and Marie Kimball pull on gloves as they get out of
their car opposite the Seidlers' house in Brooklyn Heights.
It's a brownstone: lower-ground floor, flight of steps up
to an ornate porch, long windows, iron railings, planters.
The sort of house people who don't live there usually
associate with New York, but very few New Yorkers actually get to own. The Seidlers have either made money or
inherited it; perhaps a bit of both.

The two detectives stop on the front step and turn to
face each other.

'So how are we playing this?' says Kimball. She only
made Detective six months ago, so a fair proportion of
what she gets to do each day is for the first time. Though
telling a mother the child-that-isn't-hers-after-all has turned
up dead in a foreign country she might not even know he'd
gone to definitely hasn't cropped up before.

Gonzalez hasn't done precisely this before either, not
even in fifteen years. But he's had a lot worse.

He gives a dry smile. 'Start with the facts, see how she reacts. Take it from there.'

'You think she'll come in?'

'Voluntarily? Let's hope for the Brits' sake she does, because otherwise this is going to get messy pretty damn fast. The minute she lawyers up, they're sunk.'

'Well, *I* wouldn't,' she says, shaking her head, 'not if I was in her shoes. No way.'

'Yeah, but not everyone's as crabby as you, Kimball.'

She grins and he reaches to pull the bell. They hear it ringing somewhere back in the house, but there's no answering noise, no sound of footsteps. Gonzalez rings again, then steps back to stare up at the house. No curtains twitching across, no faces at the window.

'Looks like no one's home.'

Kimball takes a few steps down towards the street and glances up and down. 'Shall we try the neighbours?'

Gonzalez shrugs. 'I guess so.'

Next door is divided into apartments. There's no response to the ground-floor bell, but down the steps the door's answered by a woman in dungarees with a bright print scarf tied round her hair and a paintbrush in one hand.

Gonzalez shows her his badge. 'Gonzalez and Kimball, NYPD. We're looking for Mrs Seidler?'

'Renee? Oh, I'm afraid you missed her – she left this morning.'

'Do you know where she went?'

The woman pushes her hair out of her eyes, leaving a smudge of green paint. 'JFK. She took a cab.'

Kimball is making notes. 'Did she say where she was going?'

'Europe, I think. It was all a bit rushed –'

'So it wasn't a planned trip, then?'

'Oh no, definitely not. She just knocked on my door at seven and said she had to go away and would I feed the cat for a couple of days. I usually do it – not that she goes away that often –'

'How did she seem to you?'

The woman blinks once or twice. 'Now you mention it, she did seem rattled – I mean, it was stupid o'clock and I was half asleep but yeah, she was a bit antsy –'

'Upset? Mad? Worried?'

'Worried,' she says. 'She said something about Noah and it was all a mistake but she had to sort it out. Noah's her son.'

Kimball's scribbling. 'Did she say anything else?'

'No, not really. Just some stuff about the cat food. Like I said, it was all a bit rushed.'

Kimball smiles at her. 'You've been a great help, Ms –?'

'Truchan. El Truchan.'

Kimball hands her a card. 'If Mrs Seidler gets in touch, let us know, OK?'

'I can ask her to call you?'

'No,' says Kimball quickly. 'We'd rather you just reached out to us. We'll take it from there.'

Truchan is staring at the card, her face troubled. 'Sure. She is OK, though? Renee?'

Gonzalez gives her a quick smile. 'She's fine. Don't you worry about it. We just need to talk to her.'

* * *

'So we checked with JFK and she left on Delta 4371, due to land in London at 20.05 your time.'

Gislingham notes down the flight number and checks his watch. Six fifty; plenty of time to arrange a welcoming committee.

'Thanks,' he said. 'I appreciate it.'

'You're lucky,' says Gonzalez, who sounds to Gis like he's straight off the set of *Law & Order*. 'She could have been fleeing the jurisdiction. But instead she's walking straight back into your arms.'

'Saves me the mother of all admin headaches, anyway.'

'You and me both,' says Gonzalez with a dry smoker's laugh. 'You and me both.'

* * *

'Mrs Seidler? Could you come this way, please?'

She's a petite woman, with small wire-framed glasses and auburn hair with a tinge of purple that betrays the dye. Her thick fringed wrap looks almost too heavy for her, and the dark circles under her eyes won't just be down to the long flight. The crowd coming off the plane parts and sweeps past them like river water round a rock. A few curious stares, one little boy who starts pointing and is dragged away by his father. But most people have other things on their minds after eight hours in a thin tin box – they just want to get through as fast as they can and go.

'Who are you?'

'Detective Sergeant Chris Gislingham and Detective Constable Thomas Hansen. We're from Thames Valley Police.'

A flash of irritation, but it's gone almost as quickly, to be replaced by resignation. She must have known there was a high chance of this.

'Is it him? Are you sure it's him?'

'I'm afraid so, Mrs Seidler.'

'Can I see him? I need to see him.'

Gis takes a deep breath. 'Let's talk about that once we're back at the station.'

* * *

The first time I see Renee Seidler is on a video screen. In Interview One. She's sitting calmly, an untouched cup of – admittedly ghastly – office-machine coffee on the table in front of her. She gives a strange impression of being shrunken, of having once been larger. And perhaps that's true; she's spent most of the last two years watching her husband die.

'Did you offer her a lawyer?'

Gis nods. 'Yup. And someone from US consular services to sit in, but she turned us down.'

So she's either conscience-clear or spectacularly stupid. She doesn't strike me as stupid.

'OK. Let's see what she has to say for herself.'

* * *

Interview with Renee Seidler, conducted at
St Aldate's Police Station, Oxford
27 October 2018, 9.55 p.m.
In attendance, DI A. Fawley, DS C. Gislingham

CG: For the purposes of the recording, Mrs
    Seidler, we are interviewing you in connection
    with the disappearance of a baby in December
    1997. We now know that you and your husband
    subsequently raised this child as your own
    son. You have been arrested, pending
    clarification of the circumstances that led
    to these events, and your involvement in them.
    You have been informed of your rights, and
    as you are aware, you can ask for legal
    representation at any time. Is there anything
    you need us to clarify at this stage?

RS: No. Thank you.

CG: So perhaps you could take us back to the
    beginning. To September 1997.

RS: [*pause*]
    You don't know what you're asking, Detective.

AF: [*quietly*]
    We do know what you went through at that time,
    and I'm sorry we have to ask. I know what it's
    like to lose a child.

RS: [*pause*]
    We'd almost given up – I'd had three
    miscarriages, I was almost 40. We'd even
    started talking to people about adopting.
    David had heard of a program to bring children

to the US from Peru – orphans with no hope of a decent life. But then I got pregnant. Just after we arrived in England. I thought to start with it was just the disruption of moving, but when the doctor confirmed it we were beside ourselves. I don't think I've ever been happier – not even when David and I first met.

AF: But the baby was premature.

RS: Thirty-two weeks.
[*becoming tearful*]
He was so tiny – all those machines – I couldn't even hold him –

AF: I'm sorry.

RS: [*wiping her eyes*]
But then he started getting better and we thought – perhaps – just *perhaps* – it will be all right. And then they took him off the ventilator and he was breathing on his own, and we started telling people we thought it was going to be OK – that we'd be able to take him home –
[*crying*]
But then he had a relapse. Out of the blue – in the middle of the night. It was just so quick – we were still on our way to the hospital. I never forgave myself for that. Not being there – not being with him when he died.

CG: You couldn't have known. And you must have been exhausted. All those weeks –

RS: You're right. We were. But it was still no excuse. One of us should have been there.

AF: [*pause*]

And that was 21st December 1997.

RS: [*nods*]

AF: But you didn't tell anyone. Your family, friends –

RS: [*shaking her head*]

It wasn't like it is now. No WhatsApp or
putting a running commentary of your life
online. We hadn't even sent anyone any
pictures – not with him in an incubator with
all those horrible tubes. And then he was dead
and we were going to have to call people and
tell them and we just couldn't face it. Not
straight away. It was too raw.

AF: And two days later? The 23rd?

RS: [*takes a deep breath*]

It was raining. I remember. Just sheeting down
like the whole world was drowning. But it was
suffocating in the house – I couldn't
breathe – all that stuff everywhere you looked
about Christmas and the miracle of birth and
'Away in a Manger' – I just couldn't deal with
it. I had to get out. So I walked. I can't
remember – hours – in the mud and the cold,
feeling the water just running down my face.
Miles and miles till I could barely stand up.
By the time I got home it was dark. And the
lights were on and there was this lovely
smell – tea, and toast, and warm milk, and
there was David and he was holding a baby in
his arms – a tiny baby, making these little
mewling noises, and I thought – I really

299

thought - that I had gone mad. That I was
hallucinating - I wanted this so much and it
had been taken from me and my mind had broken -
[*breaks down*]

AF: [*silence*]

What did your husband say - about the baby?

RS: He wouldn't tell me anything. He said it was
best I didn't know. That I couldn't be blamed
if I didn't know.

AF: Nothing else - nothing at all?

RS: He said that the baby was ours now. That we
were rescuing him. That was his word. Rescuing.

AF: Do you know where your husband had been that
day? Had he been out?

RS: I don't know.

AF: You didn't ask?

RS: No, I didn't ask. I didn't want to know.

CG: And you had already registered the birth of
Noah?

RS: Yes, David had, just after he was born.

CG: And applied for a passport for him? Because
you knew you were going back to the US that
January?

RS: [*nods*]

Every single day before we left I sat at home
waiting for the knock at the door. For someone
like you to come looking for him - to take him
back. But no one ever came. And when we went
to the airport to go home I was so terrified I
thought I was going to pass out but still no
one said anything, and when we arrived back at

JFK no one said anything, and when we got
home everyone simply accepted that he was our
son and they were just happy for us, happy
that he had pulled through. And then more
weeks went by and went by and eventually we
realised that no one was ever going to say
anything, because no one was looking for him.
And I started to believe what David had said.
We *had* rescued him. No one was looking because
nobody cared. Nobody except us. We *loved* him.
And he loved us.

AF: [*silence*]

But then he found out.

* * *

21 August 2017, 7.45 a.m.
175 Toussaint Street, Brooklyn Heights, NY 11201

She never saw it coming. Perhaps she should have. But all those
years of make-believe and disavowal can layer on a cocoon,
erode your watchfulness. So when it did come, she was utterly
unprepared. No speech carefully rehearsed, no easy explanation
ready to hand. Just sharp words breaking into a fitful day-sleep
full of phantoms.

'Mom, can I talk to you?'

When she opens her eyes, he's standing there. Her son. Her
kind, thoughtful, considerate son. But he looks none of those
things now. There's a frown across his dark-blue eyes.

She struggles upright. There's an ache in her neck where
she's lain crookedly. This sofa was never designed for sleep.

Just as her bed was never designed for hours of waking. Her days are all the wrong way round.

'What's the matter?' she says groggily, checking her watch.

'This,' he says, holding out something. 'As in, what the hell is it?'

It's a piece of paper. No – not paper. A photograph. There's a rush of bitterness in her mouth. She knows exactly what it is. Buried, like the memories, all these years, but like those memories, never lost. She wasn't supposed to keep it; she promised David she'd destroyed them all, and he'd held her as she sobbed and said he knew how hard it was but it was the only way, the only safe way, because he'd looked into the future and seen a day like this, seen the abyss it would open up in their lives.

'Where did you get it?' she says. Faux-naif. Buying time.

Noah's frown has deepened. 'In that box of yours. In your underwear drawer. As if you didn't know.'

'What on earth were you doing in there?'

'Just answer the question, Mom.'

He's been talking, lately, about going to law school. On this showing, perhaps he should.

'It's a picture of you, sweetheart. In the hospital.'

The one David took the day the hospital moved their baby to the general ward. The first day they were allowed to hold him properly, after all those dreadful weeks when they thought they'd lose him. Their miracle son. Doing so *well*. Putting on weight, his little cheeks rounding out –

'It can't be,' he says.

'Why not?'

'Because of this.'

A second photograph. And this has no secret history. It's the one they took, After. The one they had no choice but take because they'd promised everyone back home that they would send a photo and there was no excuse any more because he was out of the hospital and home for Christmas – their first Christmas as a family . . .

That tiny sitting room in Edgbaston she always hated, Noah on her lap, David's arm around her. And yes, looking at it now, perhaps his grip is a little tight, perhaps the smiles are a little stiff, but no one back then thought that was odd because everyone knew what they'd been through.

Or thought they did.

'It doesn't add up,' he says, stubborn now, pointing again at the first picture. 'Look.'

She doesn't need to. She knows what he's talking about. That bright strawberry mark on her son's brow. The one they told her would fade over time; the one she never even began to fret about because it was so trivial, so inconsequential, compared to everything else they were dealing with.

She swallows.

He's watching her face. 'I googled them – those birthmark things. It can take *years* for them to fade.' He holds up the other picture. 'But here, two months later, *max*, and it's gone. There's nothing there at all. It's as if it was never there.'

He's still staring at her, waiting for her to deny it – waiting for some sort of explanation. But nothing comes.

'It's not me, is it? The kid in the hospital. It's Noah, but it's not me.'

She looks up at him, expecting anger, fury, incomprehension. But his eyes are full of tears.

'Who am I, Mom?'

* * *

AF: What did you say?

RS: I told him exactly what his father had told me. That we had rescued him. That that was all I'd ever known.

AF: How did he react?

RS: [*sighs*]
He didn't believe me. He wanted to go straight to his father and demand the truth. He said he'd been lied to his whole life – he wanted to know where he came from, who his 'real' parents were.

AF: That must have hurt.

RS: Yes, it did. But I couldn't blame him. He was right: we *had* lied to him. Out of love, and for the best reasons. But right then, all he could see was the lie.

AF: And did he speak to your husband?

RS: No.

AF: You're sure? Noah never spoke to him about it at all?

RS: David was in the hospice by then. He was on so many pain meds he barely knew me. He probably wouldn't even have understood what Noah was saying. And I didn't want him dying with that on his mind. So I made Noah promise not to say anything.

CG: [*hesitantly*]
And I'm guessing you didn't want your husband's last days disturbed by the possibility of prosecution? I mean, you don't just 'rescue' other people's babies. Even if

```
        you didn't know exactly what David had done,
        you knew he'd almost certainly committed a
        crime. You both had.
RS:    [quietly]
        That was a consideration, yes.
AF:    And all this was when, exactly?
RS:    Last August. August 2017.
AF:    And fourteen months later Noah flies to the UK,
        by which time he evidently knows exactly who
        he is and who he's looking for. How did he
        find out?
RS:    I don't know.
```

*   *   *

3 June 2018, 10.15 p.m.
175 Toussaint Street, Brooklyn Heights, NY 11201

He sits back in his chair, staring at the screen. He hadn't expected it to be so easy.

He kept his promise. He never did speak to Dad. He'd thought about it, once or twice, but just the sight of him, in that bed, his skin like yellow paper – he couldn't do it. And then Dad died and it all went to hell for a while, and though he toyed with doing some digging about that baby in the picture, the more he thought about it the more likely it was that the truth – whatever it turned out to be – would end up bringing down a whole load of shit, and he just couldn't do that to his mom. Not then, not in the state she was in. And that's where his head stayed.

For a while.

Then other thoughts came creeping. How could they be so sure his real mother didn't want him? Did she know where he was? What if they didn't 'rescue' him at all – what if they took him? What if he'd been snatched?

And that's why he started looking. Because if that really was what happened, there'd be something to find. If his mother had given him up willingly there'd probably be nothing, nothing he'd be able to track down, anyway. But if he'd been taken – if he'd been lost – there'd be a trace. A search, a story –

A crime.

And there was. He's found it. Only it isn't the one he expected.

Not a kidnap, not a snatching, not a looked-away-for-five-minutes-and-gone.

A murder.

His mother is in prison for murdering him.

Because the woman he's staring at on the computer screen – cowed, harried, abused as a baby-killer – she's his mother. She has to be.

There are just too many coincidences. A baby boy last seen on December 23rd 1997, who's never subsequently been found. A baby boy born at the exact same hospital he was. That birthmark that disappeared so miraculously. It makes sense; it all makes sense. Even the fact that he doesn't look like either of his parents and never did.

And now she's in prison. His mother.

He reaches for the keyboard and does another search. Seems it's quite easy to track down a prisoner in the UK. Pretty easy to write to them too.

The harder part is knowing what to say.

* * *

AF: You're aware that we've identified Noah's
    biological mother?

RS: This woman Camilla Rowan. Yes, I am aware.

AF: Do you know her?

RS: No.

AF: You don't recall ever meeting her? At the
    hospital? You were there at around the same
    time.

RS: We were in the neonatal ICU. She must have
    been in the main ward. It's a big place. And
    in any case, we weren't there to make
    friends - we hardly spoke to anyone.

AF: Could your husband have met her? In the
    cafeteria, say, or at a coffee machine?

RS: [*sighs*]
    I guess he could have. Though she wasn't in
    there very long, as far as I can make out -
    there wouldn't have been much time. David
    certainly never mentioned anyone. Like I said,
    we were just focused on Noah -

CG: But it is possible - that they could have met?

RS: I suppose so - though why -

AF: The day your son died - the 21st - was that
    the last time you were at the hospital?

RS: Yes. I never wanted to go there again.

AF: And your husband?

RS: [*hesitates*]
    Yes. He did go back. A couple of days later,
    I think. There were some papers he had to
    sign? I don't really remember - I wasn't in a
    good place.

CG: So he could have met Camilla Rowan then –
    perhaps even found out that she was thinking
    of having her baby adopted?

RS: [*looking bewildered*]
    But why not tell me?

CG: You said you were in a bad place – perhaps he
    wanted to wait until you were feeling better?

RS: I still don't understand – none of this makes
    any sense.

* * *

JUNE 5 2018
NOAH SEIDLER
PO BOX 5653, NY 11201

I DON'T KNOW WHAT TO CALL YOU. CAMILLA, I GUESS.

I'm NOAH. AT LEAST, MY PARENTS HAD A KID THEY
CALLED NOAH IN 1997.

BUT THAT KID ISN'T ME.

THAT MUCH I KNOW, BUT IT'S AS FAR AS I'VE GOT.
MY MOM CLAIMS SHE DOESN'T KNOW WHAT HAPPENED —
SHE WENT OUT AND CAME BACK AND MY DAD WAS THERE
WITH A BABY. HE SAID HE'D 'RESCUED' IT. RESCUED <u>ME</u>.

BUT THAT'S IT. SHE NEVER ASKED, HE NEVER TOLD.
AND NOW HE'S DEAD AND I'VE NO WAY TO FIND OUT.

SO IS IT YOU? ARE YOU MY MOTHER? DID YOU GIVE
ME AWAY?

AND IF YOU DID, WHY ARE YOU IN JAIL? WHY DID
YOU LET THEM THINK I WAS DEAD? WAS IT LIKE THAT
NETFLIX THING SAID? WAS THAT MAN WARD MY

FATHER? Is that why you LIED — BECAUSE OF WHAT HE DID to you?

SORRY — too MANY QUESTIONS. I KNOW THIS HAS PROBABLY COME AS A SHOCK. It DID to ME — I REMEMBER WHAT it FELT LIKE, FINDING out. AND it's PRETTY SHITTY HAVING to DO STUFF LIKE THIS BY LETTER. MUCH BETTER to TALK to PEOPLE, BUT RIGHT NOW I DON'T HAVE MUCH CHOICE.

AND I COULD BE WAY OFF ABOUT ALL THIS AND it's NOTHING to DO WITH YOU. IN WHICH CASE, I'm SORRY.

But EITHER WAY, CAN you JUST WRITE ME AND LET ME KNOW? I'VE PUT A PO BOX ON THIS — I DON'T WANT A LETTER COMING FROM ENGLAND AND MY MOM SEEING it. SHE DOESN'T KNOW I'm DOING THIS AND I DON'T WANT to HURT HER — NOT IF THIS IS ALL JUST A FALSE TRAIL.

THEY'VE BEEN GOOD to ME, MY PARENTS, BY THE WAY. IN CASE YOU WONDERED.

IN CASE YOU CARE.

NOAH

* * *

AF: Talk me through the days before Noah left for Europe.

RS: He was doing a Renaissance arts program this fall and he talked me into letting him go to Florence.

AF: You had no idea he intended to come to the UK?

RS: None at all. I thought he was still in Italy.

AF: Do you think he'd already been in contact with Camilla Rowan by then?

RS: If he had, he hid it from me. I didn't know.

CG: He'd obviously found out who his mother was.

RS: Like I said, I didn't know that. I didn't know about any of it. Look, I've answered all your questions – I want to see him –

AF: I'm sorry, Mrs Seidler, that's not possible.

RS: He's my son – I have a right to see him –

AF: I know how painful this must be –

RS: Doesn't someone have to identify him? How can you even be sure it's him? It could all just be a terrible mistake –

AF: We've done a DNA comparison with Camilla Rowan, and we've also identified him on CCTV footage at Stansted. There's no mistake.
[*hands across photo from Border Control*]
This is your son, isn't it?

RS: [*begins to weep*]

* * *

Adam Fawley
27 October
22.15

Bryan Gow has been in the adjacent room all this time, watching on the video screen. I suspect he's had more enjoyable Saturday nights; I know I have. When I open the door he looks up and makes a face.

'Grim.'

I nod. 'She looks shattered.'

'Small wonder. Keeping a secret like that all these years – it's like living over an unexploded bomb, never knowing when it might go off.'

I take a step closer. 'You think she was telling the truth?'

'When she said she didn't know where the baby came from? Yes, I do. I suspect that's the defence mechanism she's been clinging to all these years: "I didn't know – it wasn't my fault." The human mind is extraordinarily good at self-exoneration.'

'I wonder how the husband coped.'

Gow shrugs. 'Perhaps he didn't. Didn't you say he died of cancer? There's some truth in those old wives' tales about the dangers of suppressed emotions. Perhaps the guilt got to him in the end.'

'Yet the wife seems to have believed him when he said they were "rescuing" the child.'

Gow raises an eyebrow. 'Well, what else could he say? What would *you* say? "Hi honey, I just snatched this child from a loving home"?'

'Fair enough.'

He gets up and reaches for his notepad.

'Oh, by the way, I had a look at those other tapes you sent me.'

'The Swanns?'

'Right. And I agree with you – I don't think either of them knew Noah was coming that night. They definitely weren't expecting him.'

'And afterwards? Do you think they realized who he was?'

'Ah, now that's more interesting. If you ask me – and you are, of course – the old boy was still in the dark. I don't think he had a clue. As for her – well, there, I'm not so sure. She's very hard to read.'

'Like mother, like daughter.'

He raises an ironic eyebrow. 'Quite. I read Camilla Rowan's pre-trial report. Now there's someone I'd pay good money for a closer look at.'

I smile. 'Funny you should mention that, Bryan. I think I'm about to make your day.'

* * *

'What's that?'

Baxter looks up. It's Chloe Sargent, staring at his screen. He's getting to like her – she takes an interest and she listens properly: he hasn't had to repeat himself once, which is some sort of record.

'Noah Seidler's social media,' he says.

She squints slightly. He's spotted her doing it before. He suspects she needs reading glasses but isn't fond of the look.

'Lots of pictures of Florence,' she says.

'Yup. Even after we know he'd left Italy for the UK. Though he's taken the location tagging off those. And I suspect he didn't take a lot of these later ones himself. Looks suspiciously like a Flickr job to me.'

She glances at him. 'So, what – they were just a smokescreen?'

Baxter gives her a heavy look. 'Probably didn't want anyone knowing where he was. Least of all his mum.'

She nods; makes sense. Baxter reaches for his keyboard and scrolls to the end of the feed. A shot of a plate of spaghetti and a beer; in the background, tourists throng a sunlit square.

♡ ▢ ◁   ◻
50 likes

Having a fantastic time – always loved Italian food, which is just as well eh? 🍝🥂😊

Sargent sighs. 'Look at all the comments. A lot of people liked him.'

'It's not just that, though, is it,' says Baxter. He points at the screen. 'Look at the time. Two hours after this was posted he was dead.'

* * *

Adam Fawley
28 October
11.15

Gow can barely contain his excitement. The last time I saw anyone look that thrilled was when we got Jake a unicorn cake from the shop in the Covered Market for his ninth birthday. And perhaps the analogy isn't actually that far off: Camilla Rowan must be the psychiatric equivalent of a horse with a horn. Gow drives himself because he's going on to something in London afterwards, so DC Carter gets the short straw of working Sunday morning. Not that he seems to mind; he's positively chipper. Like a dog getting an unexpected walk. With added mud. And yes, I know, Carter probably wouldn't have been your first choice of bag-man – he

313

wasn't Gis's either and Quinn made no secret of his scorn.

'Why him? He's just out for himself.'

I was tempted to ask if he was playing the role of pot or kettle on that one, but you don't get anywhere with Quinn when he's in that mood.

'I'm taking Carter because he made a genuine breakthrough identifying those trainers and I want to give him some encouragement.'

Quinn gave me a dark look. 'Just make sure he knows it's you running the show.'

'I have done this before, Quinn. And we have this useful thing called "rank" in the police force, just in case anyone's ever in danger of forgetting who's in charge.'

That last was actually meant for Quinn, but as usual with him, I suspect it didn't land.

That said, and even though I wasn't about to admit it to Quinn, I was more than a bit wary of spending so much time in the car with Carter, but he just seemed intent on impressing me with his driving skills, so there wasn't much by way of conversation. And judging by the way he reacted when we got to Heathside, I'm pretty sure he'd never set foot inside a prison before. He was trying to look like an old hand, but managed to drop his car keys twice before we even got to security. Gow, on the other hand, was taking it like a regular. Which it turns out he is: one of the warders greeted him by his first name.

When they show us into a private meeting room — we've gone up in the world, evidently — Camilla's lawyers are already in situ. A black woman and an Asian man. They introduce themselves ('Madeleine Parrish'; 'Dev Desai') and I do the same. Gow is safely out of the way in an adjacent room. No point frightening the horses.

Parrish turns to me. 'I'm not sure what you expect to achieve with this, Inspector. Ms Rowan is going to be released – all we're waiting for is the paperwork.'

I'm about to reply when the door opens again and they bring in Camilla. She clearly has more perks, now she's on the verge of freedom. Her hair looks washed and she has a can of Coke in one hand.

She makes a point of ignoring us, turning instead to Parrish. 'Any news?'

The lawyer shakes her head. 'It'll be Monday now. But I'll chase them again then.' She glances at me and then back at Rowan. 'Why don't you sit down, Cam.'

Rowan does what she did before, dragging the chair backwards until it's practically against the wall.

'Perhaps you could begin, Inspector,' says Desai, pen in hand, 'by explaining exactly what you hope to achieve from this meeting?'

'As Ms Rowan knows, we've been looking again at the events that preceded the disappearance of her baby. We've made significant progress, and I'd like to update her on that, and ask for her help in confirming certain facts.'

See, I can do police-lingo bullshit with the best of them, when I put my mind to it.

Parrish looks towards her client, but there's no response. No words, no change of expression.

'So I'm going to offer you a deal, Ms Rowan.'

A ripple at that. No more than a blink, but enough.

I sit forward. 'I'll tell you what I know, if you tell me what you know.'

A silence. A longer silence. But two can play at that game, and I'm an old hand.

She lifts her chin. 'OK, I'll bite. What exactly *do* you know?'

I make her wait. And she's better at it than her lawyers, who look respectively unsettled and sardonic.

'I know a number of things. I know, for example, that you did *not*, after all, hand the baby to its father as you've always insisted.'

She raises an eyebrow. 'I see. So you've spoken to him, have you?'

'We have.'

That stumbles her, though again, the flicker across her face is gone as quickly as it came.

'Turns out his name's Tin Boekker, not Tim Baker. He's South African. But, of course, you knew that, didn't you.'

She looks away.

'You don't want to hear what he said?'

She throws me a glance but says nothing.

Parrish clears her throat. 'Well, I for one would like very much to know what he had to say.'

I turn to her. 'Mr Boekker freely admits having had a – very brief – sexual relationship with your client but denies knowing she was pregnant. He can also prove that he wasn't even in the country when the child was born.'

Parrish and Rowan exchange a glance. Rowan gives a minute shrug. *So what?*

'I also know that by the time Ms Rowan was arriving at that Christmas party in 1997, her son was already in the care of an American couple in Edgbaston, who took him back to the US with them a few weeks later.'

Rowan is still unmoving, but there's a rigidity about that stillness now. A tension and a watchfulness.

'What I *don't* yet know is what happened in the two hours between you leaving the hospital and your baby's arrival at that Edgbaston home.'

She fixes me with her slatey stare. 'You should be asking them that. Not me.'

'The wife wasn't there when the baby arrived. When she got back later that evening her husband refused to tell her what had happened. All he would say is that they had "rescued" the child.'

She starts chewing the side of her thumb. Which I know – and I'm sure Gow, sitting next door, has guessed – is the closest thing she ever gets to a 'tell'.

'What's he saying now, this man?'

'Nothing.'

She frowns. Parrish looks at Rowan, then at me. 'But surely you've questioned him –'

'As I said, right now, he's saying nothing. Which gives Ms Rowan the chance to give us her version first. So,' I force her to meet my gaze, 'over to you.'

Silence.

'Now's the time, Ms Rowan. If you handed your baby to this man – if you met him at the hospital and made some sort of arrangement –'

Still nothing.

Carter sits forward. 'Look, we all know you didn't want that child, any more than you wanted the others. There's no way you were going to bring it up on your own. So perhaps those Americans seemed like the perfect solution – perhaps you took pity on them –'

She flashes him a look, then turns away again.

'Is that where you went?' I ask. 'Edgbaston? After you left the hospital? The timing adds up – it would have been barely out of your way –'

Rowan sighs, then takes a deep breath and turns to face me.

'OK,' she says. 'OK.'

'OK what?'

'That's what happened.'

'You went to their house?'

She picks up the can and throws back a slug, then wipes her mouth on her sleeve.

'No. I met him on the way back from the hospital.'

'You definitely didn't go to the house?'

'I never knew where they lived.'

'So why didn't you say all this back in 2003? Why go to prison for something you didn't do?'

She hesitates, then shrugs. 'I don't know – I suppose I wasn't thinking straight.'

I sit back. 'I find that hard to believe.'

She smiles. 'Well, thankfully, that's not my problem.'

OK, I'll run with this. See how far she takes it.

'How did it come about – this arrangement to give them your son? How did you meet?'

'At the hospital, like you said.'

'Where?'

She picks up the can. 'In the café. I met him in the café.'

'He approached you – you approached him – what?'

'He came to me.'

It's like drawing teeth. Desai is already on his second page of notes.

'When was this?'

She gives me a sarcastic look. 'Well, it must have been the 23rd, mustn't it, genius?'

'You only gave birth that morning – you'd really recovered enough to nip downstairs for a coffee?'

She raises an eyebrow. 'I don't tend to let these things cramp my style, Inspector. As I'm sure you know.'

And I can't argue with that. She'd been on her feet within hours of the other births.

'So what did he say?'

Another deep breath, a draw on a fag she doesn't have. 'He said he'd seen me on the ward and I was obviously a single mother –'

'Had he? Seen you on the ward?'

She shrugs. 'Maybe. I don't remember seeing him, but he was pretty nondescript.'

'What did he look like?'

'I just told you – nondescript. Brown hair. *Boring.*'

She said the same thing about 'Tim Baker' to South Mercia, all those years ago.

'Go on.'

'He said he could see I was a single mother – that it would be understandable if I was feeling daunted. That if I was considering giving up my baby, then him and his wife would give it a great life.'

'What did he say about his circumstances?'

'Nothing. He just said they were desperate for a baby.'

I stare at her. 'And that's it. You gave your child to a stranger, based on that?'

Her eyes flash. 'I gave the others to strangers. What's the bloody difference?'

319

'Those were strangers who'd been carefully vetted by the adoption service – this man could have been anyone – a paedophile, a child trafficker –'

She rolls her eyes. 'He didn't look like a paedophile.'

'They rarely do. *As I'm sure you know.*'

She shrugs again. 'If you say so.'

But it's just a diversion and I didn't come down in the last shower of rain.

She empties the can and puts it down on the table. 'He showed me a picture of his wife, OK? She seemed nice.'

'But you never met her.'

'No.'

'What did she look like?'

She frowns. 'What?'

'You saw her picture – what did she look like? I mean, I can't believe you don't remember. This was the woman who was going to bring up your child.'

She starts making circles on the table in the moisture dripping from the can. 'I don't know. Ordinary. She looked ordinary.'

'You'll have to do better than that. If you want us to believe you.'

She looks irritated now. 'Small, probably smaller than me.'

'How do you know that?'

Her lip lifts in a sneer. 'They were both in the picture, weren't they. He was a lot taller than her.'

And it's true – Renee Seidler is relatively short. But it could just as easily be an educated guess.

'Anything else?'

'Her hair was dark. Reddish. She had it in a long plait. And she wore glasses. With wire rims.'

This is different – and way too specific to guess out of nowhere. I see her following my thought, and the tiny curl of triumph in her mouth.

'See? I am telling the truth. Whatever you might have thought.'

'So what happened? How did you arrange the handover?'

'He gave me a phone number and told me to call him when I was leaving the hospital.'

'And you met on the A417?'

Half her mouth smiles and she points at me. 'You're sharp. For a plod.'

'I've been doing this a long time. So you meet him at a lay-by on the A417, then what?'

'I gave him the kid. Like I said.'

'So why did you say you gave the baby to its father?'

She sits back. 'By the time anyone started asking, he *was* the kid's father.'

'That's sophistry, and you know it.'

And she knows what the word means too, as the expression on her face makes clear.

'I don't believe you, Ms Rowan. Frankly, I don't even think *you* believe you.'

'I don't give a shit what you think. He'd been with them five years by then – he was *their* kid, not mine. I didn't want him taken away from them.'

'You didn't know that would definitely have happened.'

She laughs drily. 'Yeah, right.'

I sit forward. 'It meant that much to you? You were prepared to sacrifice decades of your life – to go to *prison* – rather than incriminate two complete strangers?'

'Complete strangers who were *bringing up my kid*. And in any case, I didn't know I was going to be convicted, now did I?'

'Fair enough. But you could have raised it afterwards – when you filed all those appeals.'

There's a silence. She's drawing circles on the table again.

'It makes no sense,' I say in the end. 'You *know* it makes no sense.'

Rowan looks up. But not at me. She leans forward and whispers to Parrish, who nods and turns to us.

'I think Ms Rowan has given ample evidence that she knew the people who took the child. More importantly, there is now incontrovertible proof that Ms Rowan did not harm her son. If any crime was committed – and I, for one, remain to be convinced – it was at worst an offence under the Adoption Act 1976, which would certainly not have resulted in a custodial sentence of the length Ms Rowan has served. Whichever way you cut it, she should now be released.'

'Not my department, Ms Parrish, sorry.'

That's a bit of a sorry-not-sorry, if I'm honest. But I'm not sorry about that either.

Parrish frowns. 'Are you charging these people – the as-yet-unnamed Americans?'

'As per my previous answer. That's up to the CPS, not me.'

She and Desai confer for a moment, then she turns briskly to me. 'So are we done?'

Desai has already flipped shut his notebook. And like I've said before: when you're at a brick wall, stop pushing.

'We're done.'

* * *

July 2 2018
Noah Seidler
PO Box 5653, NY 11201

YOU HAVEN'T EVEN WRITTEN ME BACK. NOT EVEN TWO FRIGGIN LINES.

IF I'M NOT YOUR KID JUST SAY SO, SO I CAN WRITE THIS ONE OFF AND MOVE ON. BUT THAT'S NOT REALLY IT, IS IT. YOU KNOW I'M YOUR KID AND YOU'RE JUST HOPING THIS ALL GOES AWAY BECAUSE YOU CAN'T FACE DEALING WITH IT. WELL IT WON'T GO AWAY — YOU HEAR ME? AND IN ANY CASE, DON'T YOU THINK I DESERVE THE TRUTH? EVERYONE CLOSE TO ME HAS BEEN LYING TO ME MY WHOLE LIFE. I'M PISSED. YOU KNOW THAT? I. AM. PISSED.

YOU KNOW WHAT ELSE I'M PISSED ABOUT? YOU DON'T EVEN WANT TO KNOW ABOUT ME. WHAT I'M LIKE. WHAT I DO, WHAT I'M INTO. NOTHING. I'M YOUR LONG-LOST KID AND YOU DON'T ASK ME A SINGLE FRIGGIN QUESTION. AREN'T YOU EVEN JUST A LITTLE BIT CURIOUS? DO YOU REALLY NOT CARE?

323

OK RANT OVER. AND THERE'S A BIT OF ME THAT
KEEPS SAYING THAT MAYBE YOU'RE JUST FREAKED OUT BY
THIS WHOLE THING — THAT YOUR LIFE MUST BE SHIT
BECAUSE YOU'RE IN PRISON AND YOU NEVER KNEW THIS
WAS COMING AND IT'S JUST THROWN YOU FOR A LOOP.
SO I'VE DECIDED I'M GONNA GIVE YOU THE BENEFIT OF
THE DOUBT. FOR NOW.

SO I'VE PRINTED YOU OUT A COUPLE OF PICTURES.
EVEN THOUGH YOU DIDN'T ASK FOR ANY. ONE'S OF ME
AND MOM WHEN I WAS LITTLE. CUTE, HUH? I ALWAYS
LOVED THE ZOO. AND ONE FROM A COUPLE OF YEARS
AGO, JUST AFTER DAD WAS DIAGNOSED. IT'S HIM AND
ME AT YOSEMITE. HE ALWAYS PROMISED ME WE WOULD
GO. IT WAS OUR LAST TRIP.

AND I MEANT TO SAY — I'M TRYING TO GET MOM
TO LET ME COME TO EUROPE FOR FALL BREAK. I'M
GONNA DO A MODULE ON THE RENAISSANCE AND I'M
THINKING FLORENCE MIGHT BE GOOD. AND ENGLAND'S
JUST A HOP FROM THERE, RIGHT?

NOAH

* * *

Adam Fawley
28 October
11.55

'What do you think?'

We're in the car park. Parrish and Desai are still inside,
having a con with their client. And I'm out here, trying to
decide whether 'con' is, in fact, the word of the day.

324

Gow takes his time replying. The wind's getting up and I'm starting to wish I'd brought a coat. Carter's looking smug in a waxed Barbour thing that I bet isn't a real one.

'She's a piece of work,' Gow says eventually. 'That's what I think.'

I give a dry smile. 'I didn't need to pay for a profiler to know that.'

But maybe it's a more revealing answer than it seems. When a forensic psychologist is reduced to that sort of reaction, that alone should tell you something.

'Deftly handled, by the way,' says Gow. 'Managing not to let on that Seidler's dead.'

'I think, Dr Gow, that you'll find every word I said was strictly true.'

He smiles. 'Indeed. Dead men aren't terribly talkative as a rule, are they. Like I said, deftly handled.'

'You still haven't told me what you think.'

He draws a breath. 'I think she has an innate capacity for mendacity.'

'She's a pathological liar?'

'It's risky making any diagnosis on the basis of such limited observation, but if she took a polygraph I suspect she'd beat the machine. Lying is as natural to her as breathing. She has none of the moral or socially conditioned qualms that trip up the rest of us.'

I'm frowning now. This wasn't quite the angle I expected him to take. 'You're saying she was lying back there?'

'I'm saying I doubt if even I could tell the difference.'

'But there were things she said that she couldn't have made up – or guessed. Like what Renee Seidler looked like –'

'You're sure about that?' he says. 'Because she doesn't look anything like that now, does she?'

I show him my phone. 'I just texted her. She sent me this.'

A picture of Renee Seidler with her son. A dribble of snow on the ground, a gaggle of kids in woolly hats and mittens, and what looks like a polar bear in the enclosure behind. It must be Central Park zoo; Alex loves that place. On the screen, Noah's laughing and clapping his little hands. He must be around two. And Renee – crouching, smiling, her hand gently steadying him – has a long auburn plait slipping over one shoulder.

'I just don't see how Rowan could have guessed she wore her hair like that.'

Gow's frowning now. 'I see what you mean. And you're absolutely sure, are you, that Noah never contacted her? Because that's the only way I can think of that she could have found out something that specific.'

'The governor wasn't aware of anything. According to her, all her post was just fan mail. Though she did say she'd check.'

'Might be worth chasing up on that. Given that we're here.'

I turn to Carter, but he pre-empts me. 'You want me to go and ask, sir?'

'Thank you, Carter.'

We watch him go, then Gow turns to me. 'So what now?'

I shrug. 'The lawyer was right. There's no reason why Rowan shouldn't be released. I'm sure that's the line the CPS will take.'

His face darkens.

'I know, Bryan – I'm as uneasy about it as you are. But what possible reason can there be to hold her? The murder conviction's void, and she's just come up with a story that tallies with what we now know.'

'As far as it goes, yes. But there are still gaps – huge gaps –'

'I'm with you, but what can I do? With David Seidler dead there's no one to challenge her. Rowan's story is the only game in town. There's nothing I can charge her with. Unlike her poor bloody father, who's almost certainly going down for manslaughter, if not murder.'

He sighs. It's probably the most emotional I've ever seen him, and I've known him upwards of five years.

'You still want a report?'

I nod. 'Please. I need to talk to the CPS, but I suspect they're just going to tell us to close this one down. As I'm sure Superintendent Harrison will agree.'

* * *

July 10 2018
NOAH SEIDLER
PO BOX 5653, NY 11201

I DON'T CARE WHAT YOU SAID ABOUT NOT BEING ALLOWED VISITORS, I'M COMING. WHETHER YOU LIKE IT OR NOT. I'M COMING.

YOU KNOW WHY? I GOT SOMETHING FROM OUR LAWYERS TODAY. A LETTER FOR ME, FROM DAD. HE LEFT IT WITH THEM WHEN HE WAS FIRST DIAGNOSED. SAID HE

DIDN'T WANT IT GIVEN TO ME TILL NOW TO GIVE ME
TIME TO DEAL WITH ALL THE CRAP AFTER HE DIED. AND
HE DIDN'T WANT MY MOM UPSET SO I WASN'T TO TELL
HER, BUT HE THOUGHT I SHOULD KNOW THE TRUTH.
THAT HE WAS THE ONLY ONE WHO COULD TELL ME,
BECAUSE MOM NEVER KNEW WHAT REALLY HAPPENED. BUT
I HAD A RIGHT TO HEAR IT, AND HE DIDN'T WANT ME
EVER BLAMING MOM BECAUSE ALL SHE'D EVER DONE —
ALL EITHER OF THEM HAD EVER DONE — WAS LOVE ME.
IF I WAS GOING TO BLAME ANYONE IT SHOULD BE THE
PERSON WHO DESERVED IT.

   <u>YOU</u>.

YOU'VE BEEN LYING TO ME. DON'T EVEN TRY TO
DENY IT BECAUSE I KNOW. I KNOW THE TRUTH. NOT
ALL OF IT, NOT ALL THE DETAILS, BUT ENOUGH. THE
SMELL AND THE PISS AND THE DIRT. I <u>KNOW</u>. YOU
HEAR THAT?

   I KNOW WHAT YOU DID.

*   *   *

Adam Fawley
29 October
08.35

'So that's where we are. I'm not happy about it and I doubt
any of you are either, but sometimes this job just isn't
black and white.'

It's a grey Monday all round. In here as much as outside, where low cloud has settled into an insistent spitty
drizzle. Some towns manage to wear rain well; trust me,
Oxford isn't one of them.

'I still don't understand why she didn't say any of this years ago,' says Ev.

'Bloody waste of time, the whole sodding thing,' mutters Quinn.

'Yes,' counters Ev, turning to him, 'but most of all, *hers*. All those years inside – and for nothing?'

'She claims,' I say, 'that she didn't want the child taken from its adoptive parents.'

Baxter makes a face. 'Even if you buy that – and she doesn't strike me as that altruistic, in fact quite the bloody opposite – surely she could have said something once the kid got older? He was legally an adult at eighteen, that was over *two years* ago.'

'I know. Yet again, it makes no sense. But what else can we do? Her story tallies with Renee Seidler's, and she knew things about them that she couldn't possibly have found out any other way, including what Renee looked like back then –'

'And we're absolutely sure, are we, that she hadn't been in touch with Noah?' says Quinn. 'Because that makes a damn sight more sense to me –'

'DC Carter checked. When we were at Heathside.'

Not an answer calculated to appease Quinn. He turns to Carter. 'And what did they say – *precisely*?'

Carter starts a little. 'Just what the boss said – that as far as they were aware, Rowan doesn't get letters from people she knows, just sad losers with nothing better to do –'

'Did they remember anything from the States?'

Carter shakes his head. 'I did ask, but there's no one person who handles the post so it's hard to pin down. But she did say no one had mentioned anything.'

' "She" being – ?'

He glances at his notebook. 'Prison Officer Andrea Sullivan.' He looks up. 'She was trying to help, but there wasn't much more she could do – prison letters don't have to have the sender's address on the envelope and they don't read all of them anyway.'

Quinn frowns. 'What about outgoing mail?'

'Same story,' shrugs Carter. 'Not as far as anyone could remember –'

'Did you ask them to search Rowan's cell?'

Carter blinks, glances at me. 'Er –'

Time for me to intervene. 'I'm not sure there'd have been much point, Sergeant. If Noah did write to Rowan, she's hardly likely to have kept it – it'd be far too incriminating.'

Quinn's frown deepens. 'But –'

'And as far as I'm concerned we've done as much as humanly possible to establish whether there was any such letter and come up with nothing. You can only go so far trying to prove a negative.'

Silence.

'So what happens next?' asks Baxter.

'Rowan will be released. Apparently, she could be out of Heathside as early as the end of this week.'

Ev makes a face. 'And straight from there to a TV station.'

But Baxter's shaking his head. 'Nah. Not yet. She'll want to negotiate a big fat fee for that.'

Quinn glances across. 'How do you know she hasn't done that already? She has enough bloody lawyers.'

The exchange is getting tetchy and, more to the point, pointless: whatever Rowan chooses to do – whatever mud she chooses to throw – there's sod all any of us can do about it.

'Let's just concentrate on our jobs, shall we? The next one being to try to close the case on Richard Swann. The CPS still have some questions before they can make a decision on charging, specifically what exactly he did or did not know. So we're going to have another go at getting some answers, now he's had time to consider his position. Uniform are picking him up this morning.' I look round. 'Anyone have anything else? No? In that case, can you wrap up the rest of the paperwork on this one ASAP, please. No point in hanging around.'

* * *

The problem with Wytham is that whichever route you take there's always a risk of the Tractor Factor. A twenty-minute journey can easily take you twice that, and more in a downpour. Which goes most of the way to explaining Ian Barnetson's less than sunny mood as they finally signal to turn into Ock Lane.

'I actually feel quite sorry for him,' says Puttergill, breaking the silence. The rain's coming down so hard they can barely see, even with the wipers on full speed.

'Who? Swann?'

'Right. I mean, poor old sod – must be tough finding out you killed your own grandson by mistake. Even if you did think he was dead already.'

'We don't know it was a mistake,' says Barnetson darkly.

Puttergill glances across at him. 'That's what they told you? CID?'

Barnetson turns to look out of the window. 'Quinn gave me a pretty heavy hint. He reckons the wife definitely knew who he was. After, even if not before.'

Puttergill gives a low whistle. 'Jesus.'

There's a lorry coming towards them now and the lane isn't wide enough for them both. Puttergill pulls over and comes to a halt.

'But why would the old couple want him dead? Makes no sense.'

'Nope,' says Barnetson. 'In that family – nothing ever does.'

The lorry up ahead isn't moving and Barnetson starts cursing. 'Stick the bloody siren on, can't you? Get that bloody thing out of the way.'

Puttergill looks faintly alarmed. 'I assumed we didn't want Swann to know we were coming.'

Barnetson flashes him a look. 'What's he going to do? Make a quick getaway on his Zimmer frame?'

Puttergill suppresses a smile and reaches for the switch. 'You're the boss.'

* * *

BBC News

29 October 2018 Last updated at 10:09

BREAKING: Camilla Rowan could be released 'within days'

According to the lawyers acting on her behalf, Camilla Rowan could be freed 'within a few days'. No official announcement has been made with regard to a release date, but it is understood that her lawyers are in advanced discussions with the Ministry of Justice about ensuring this is done in 'an orderly manner'. For technical reasons, she is likely to be released on licence pending a review of her conviction by the Court of Appeal, but it is understood that will be 'just a formality'. Press speculation about the case has been rife since proof emerged that Rowan's baby son was not in fact murdered in 1997 – proof which came to light as a result of a fatal shooting at a property outside Oxford on October 21st. The property has been widely rumoured to be the home of Rowan's parents, Dick and Peggy, who are believed to have changed their name after their daughter's 2003 trial.

Thames Valley Police are now leading an investigation into the original inquiry. They have made no comment about the timing or circumstances of Rowan's release.

More news on this as we hear it.

* * *

Adam Fawley
29 October
10.11

I'm on my way in to see Harrison when his PA waylays me. 'Ah, DI Fawley, how fortuitous. I just picked up a call from downstairs. There's a woman there to see you. She says it's urgent –'

'I'm afraid I can't –'

She raises her voice a notch, in the way of people

who intend to finish and are not accustomed to being interrupted.

'Her name is Alison Toms. She seems to think you'll know who she is –'

'Well, I don't – and I don't have time –'

But then I stop – because I do, in fact, recognize the name. But why on earth –

'Actually, Maureen, I will see her. Give my apologies to the Super, would you? And ask DC Hansen to meet me at the front desk.'

* * *

Barnetson pushes open the car door, pulls up his collar and strides towards the lorry.

The wind has picked up, throwing squalls of sharp rain against his face. He was already pissed off, and now he finds that the lorry hasn't just stopped, it's parked, and the cab is empty. There's a small pack of journalists behind the tape at the end of the drive who are pointing at him and grinning. It's been thin pickings stuck outside in the rain all morning with no one going in or out, so this counts as cabaret.

'For fuck's sake, you could at least have put your bloody hazards on,' Barnetson mutters, edging his way along the hedge to the back of the truck.

But then he stops.

Stops, hesitates a moment, and then – despite the sudden clatter of camera noise – starts running.

* * *

The woman in reception manages to come off as both tired and anxious all at once. She looks every year of fifty but could well be younger; she's wearing a crumpled linen dress, a cotton cardigan and espadrilles, which were a bad choice in this weather and are now soaked through. She gets to her feet as soon as she sees us, hauling one of those striped hessian bags off the chair next to her.

'DI Fawley, is it?'

I nod. 'And this is DC Hansen. How can we help you?'

'We spoke before,' begins Hansen, but the woman isn't listening.

'I left home as soon as I heard – on the news – has it happened yet? Am I in time?'

'In time for what, Ms Toms?'

She stares at me, her lips trembling, white about the eyes. I've seen that look before. This is someone at the point of no return.

'Ms Toms?'

She takes a breath, then presses her lips together, swallows. 'In time to do what I should have done twenty years ago.'

* * *

By the time Puttergill gets to him, Barnetson is halfway down the garden, running full tilt along the line of plastic piping snaking its way across the grass towards the rear fence. Puttergill can just about see the lorry driver bent double in one of the borders, his back to them, apparently unable to hear Barnetson's increasingly desperate shouts.

'Police! Stop what you're doing!'

* * *

Interview with Alison Toms, conducted at St Aldate's Police Station, Oxford
29 October 2018, 10.55 a.m.
In attendance, DI A. Fawley, DC T. Hansen

AF: This isn't a formal interview, Ms Toms, and you're not under arrest, but it may be necessary for us to do that, depending on what you have to tell us. You can ask for legal representation at any time. Is that clear?

AT: Yes.

AF: So, let's start at the beginning. December 23rd 1997.

AT: I was the social worker at Birmingham and Solihull General at that time. It was my first job.

AF: And you were interviewed by the police in 2002, when the disappearance of the baby first came to light?

AT: Yes, I was.

AF: [*consulting file*]
According to that statement, you said you only spoke to Ms Rowan once during her short time in hospital.

AT: Yes, that's right.

AF: [*reads from file*]

'Miss Rowan bonded well with her baby, and
expressed no interest in having him adopted.'
That's from Ms Rowan's hospital records,
entered and signed by you on the morning after
she discharged herself. Do you remember
writing that?

AT: Yes, I do. But it wasn't true. She didn't bond
with him at all.

AF: Enough to worry you – as a professional?

AT: Yes.

AF: But you didn't raise this with anyone else at
the hospital – you can't have done – there's
nothing in the records.

AT: It was different back then – people weren't so
quick to rush to judgement. And like I said,
it was my first job – I wanted to be sure – to
watch her for a little longer before I did
anything. She'd only given birth a few hours
before she discharged herself – I had no idea
she would leave hospital so quickly.

AF: On the afternoon of 23rd December. When the
baby was only a few hours old.

AT: Yes.

AF: And yet the following morning you made an
entry in her records saying all was well, when
you clearly had significant cause for concern.
Not only that, by *not* raising those concerns,
you could actually put the child at *more* risk.
Why on earth would you do that?

337

AT: [*silence*]

AF: Ms Toms?

* * *

23 December 1997, 2.45 p.m.
Birmingham and Solihull General Hospital

She'd popped down to the shops to buy a sandwich and
stopped off to collect her dry cleaning on the way. There was a
queue – four women ahead of her collecting party dresses they
probably hadn't worn since last Christmas – so she ended up
being ten minutes late getting back. She thought a lot about
that, afterwards. Those ten minutes. Because if she hadn't had
to wait, she'd never have seen. Nothing would have happened.
Not to her, at any rate. It might have been months before the
news broke. Years even. And by then she'd have forgotten – by
then it would have been nothing to do with her.

But it didn't happen that way. Alison was late, and she saw,
and her life was never the same again.

Though it took her a while to realize what exactly it was that
she was seeing.

When she first pulled up in the car park she didn't even
notice her. It was only when she released the seat belt and
turned for the door handle that she realized Camilla Rowan
was walking towards her, a handbag over one shoulder, the
baby held against the other, wrapped in a hospital blanket. She
was confused for a moment, wondering if the girl was heading
in her direction, but then she stopped by a black VW Golf two
cars over. But that didn't make any sense – Rowan couldn't be
actually *leaving* – it was way too soon. OK, Rowan was young

338

and healthy, but as far as Alison knew, the baby hadn't even had its heel-prick test, and Rowan still hadn't managed to breastfeed him, wasn't even holding him properly – you only had to look at her now –

Alison was about to get out of the car, but hesitated – she wasn't exactly sure what authority she had, and perhaps she was being a bit too judgemental. Maybe Rowan was meeting someone – her parents or her boyfriend: none of them had been in yet. Perhaps they'd come to see her and brought some things for the baby.

But when the young woman unlocked the car door and yanked it open it was obvious there was no one else there. She was alone, and she was leaving.

Alison watched as she threw her handbag on to the passenger seat and then opened the back and bent over the rear seat. It was impossible to see exactly what she was doing but it didn't take long – a mere two or three seconds later she straightened up again and swung the door shut. Alison grabbed at her own car door and started to get out of her car – she couldn't possibly have strapped the baby in correctly in that time – was there even a proper car seat in there? But it was too late – the Golf had already started and was beginning to reverse.

She had no choice.

That's what she told herself, afterwards.

She had no choice.

* * *

AF: You followed her.

AT: Yes.

AF: You didn't think to alert someone? Flag her down?

AT: How could I alert anyone? I didn't have a
    mobile phone - no one did, back then. And she
    was driving fast - it was all I could do not
    to lose her.

AF: So you followed her - where to exactly?

AT: She got on to the M5, going south.

AF: And then?

AT: She came off at Brockworth and headed towards
    Cirencester. On the A417.

* * *

As far as Puttergill is concerned, Barnetson should be looking pretty chuffed right now, seeing as it looks like he's cracked it. But he just looks grim.

'I should have thought of this before,' he mutters, staring down into the open manhole. 'It was odds-on they weren't on the mains, not all the way out here.'

'Well, to be fair, this one ain't that easy to find,' says the lorry driver. 'Not if you don't already know. Most of the time I come it's covered in leaves and crap.'

As for Puttergill, he didn't know people even had septic tanks in this day and age, especially this close to a town. He's certainly never seen one before. He wrinkles his nose. 'So is it, you know, actual *shit* down there?'

The driver glances up from the other side of the hole. 'It's a tad more sophisticated than that, son, but yeah, there'll be plenty of faecal sludge at the bottom if you get down far enough.'

Puttergill looks alarmed. He can't seriously be suggesting –

Barnetson gives a hard laugh. 'Don't worry, I'm not looking for a volunteer. I'm sure Mr –'

'Tull,' says the driver. 'Dennis Tull.'

'I'm sure Mr Tull knows exactly what to do.'

But Puttergill doesn't reply. He's staring up towards the house. Barnetson turns to look and sees at once what's distracted him. There's a figure at the upstairs window. A pale face, a hand pressed against the glass.

Richard Swann.

Barnetson's mouth sets in a grim line. 'They must have thought they'd got away with it.'

* * *

23 December 1997, 3.50 p.m.
A417, Gloucestershire

She remembers thinking that Rowan knew where she was going – that she must have been there before. But she didn't realize what that meant. Not then.

At the time, it was all she could do to keep up with the car in front, which barely slows, even after they leave the main road. It's as if there's a task to do and not much time to do it in. That's something else she remembers, later.

Alison had only been to Cirencester once before, and that was the quaintsy tea-shop chocolate-box bit, certainly not this colourless every-town-has-one area of warehouses and industrial buildings. She couldn't think of a single good reason why a woman who'd only just given birth could possibly want to come here. There were bad ones, yes – desperately bad ones – but at the time her mind simply didn't allow those to gather into words. Not yet.

A left turn, a right, another left. They'd passed two cars on the way in, but now, nothing. It was starting to get dark and there was no one around; the day before Christmas Eve, of course there was no one around.

When the car in front finally slowed, turned into a car park and disappeared out of sight, Alison pulled over and switched off her engine. She never could explain why she held back – it must have been pure instinct, nothing more. Because everything would have been different if she'd followed her in there – if there'd been a confrontation, if she'd demanded an explanation, offered help –

But she didn't. She just sat in her cold car, her hands sweating against the steering wheel, until the Golf appeared again, picking up speed, passing her –

Gone.

* * *

AF: Do you know where this place was? Would you remember it again?

AT: It's hard to forget.

AF: All the same, such a long time ago –

AT: That's not what I meant. The road was called Love Lane. *Love Lane*. You don't forget something like that. Not in those circumstances.

TH: So what did you do next?

AT: I got out of the car. I wasn't sure what to think – I just couldn't work out what she was doing there –

TH: And then?

AT: I walked over to the car park.

TH: What did you see?

AT: Nothing. It was completely deserted. Just a
     cat somewhere. Yowling.
     [*silence*]

*   *   *

23 December 1997, 4.05 p.m.
Love Lane industrial estate, Cirencester

It wasn't a cat.

Some part of her knew that. She'd had cats, growing up. None of them sounded like that.

But she still wanted to believe that's what it was, even when she realized where the sound was coming from. The big green dumpster by the wire fence on the far side, half hidden by a pile of old tyres.

Some bastard abandoning kittens – shits like that deserved dumping themselves –

Even now, she still doesn't remember walking over, or struggling to get the lid open, or whether there were sounds from inside as she did.

Just the rush of sour sweet odour – warm and fetid and unmistakable.

*   *   *

AF: The baby.

AT: [*nods*]
     The baby.

343

AF: You could see that - straight away?

AT: [*swallows*]

No. She'd - she'd put rubbish over it. Him. Plywood, broken tiles. Builders' stuff.

TH: She'd put it *on top of* the baby?

AT: [*nods*]

I know - I felt sick, just seeing it. But it wasn't just that. When I dragged it all off and found him - he was in a plastic bag. A bin liner. She must have *brought it with her* - she'd *planned* it - all of it -

[*becoming distressed*]

No one would have realized - the bin men - not after - not once he was -

[*weeping now*]

AF: Take your time, Ms Toms. I know this must be distressing.

AT: I'm sorry - it's just that all this time, I've tried not to think about it.

AF: What did you do next?

AT: I took him back to the car. He still had his blanket and I had some wet wipes so I could clean him up a bit.

AF: But you didn't take him back to the hospital, did you? Or to a police station. Or to the adoption services, who would have found him a loving home.

AT: No, I didn't.

AF: You took him to Edgbaston. To the Seidlers.

AT: I'd sat with them every day for weeks - I'd seen what they'd gone through. I knew they

344

could give him a good life. That they might not get another chance –

AF: [*softly*]

You played God.

AT: If you want to put it that way.

TH: You must have known what you were doing was wrong.

AT: In your book, perhaps. Not in mine.

TH: Why didn't you say something to the police after Camilla was arrested? You perjured yourself at that trial –

AT: I know. But remember how young the child was at that stage – barely five. He'd have been taken from them. My job wasn't the only thing at stake.

AF: All the same –

AT: I would have done, OK? I would have said something. If she'd been acquitted, I'd have said something. But she wasn't, was she? Justice was done. No one knew that better than me.

TH: And since then?

AT: What do you mean, since then?

TH: What have you done since then?

AT: [*apparently at a loss*]

I'm not sure I understand what you're getting at.

TH: Have you stayed in touch with the Seidlers? Kept tabs on the case?

AT: Of course not – that would be far too dangerous, both for them and for me. And in any case, I've done everything I possibly can to forget the whole thing.

TH: [*silence*]
    But that's not strictly true, is it?
AT: I don't know what you mean.
TH: I've been spending a lot of time in true-crime
    chat rooms lately, looking at what people say
    about this case. The theories they have, what
    they think really happened.
AT: So?
TH: So, I think you've been doing the same. There
    was one name that kept coming up – one person
    who's been talking about this case on a
    regular basis ever since that Netflix
    documentary. Always taking the same line,
    always insisting that Camilla Rowan got what
    she deserved. The user's name is
    'AllieCatz76'. It never occurred to me till
    now, but as soon as you make the connection
    it's blindingly obvious. It's you, isn't it?
    AllieCatz – Alison Toms. And you were born
    in 1976.
AF: Is that true, Ms Toms?
AT: [*silence*]
TH: I can only imagine how horrified you were when
    John Penrose started suggesting Camilla could
    be innocent. No wonder you wanted to do what
    little you could to redress the balance. To
    make sure she stayed where she was.
AT: [*silence*]
AF: Alison Toms, I am arresting you on suspicion of
    child abduction. You do not have to say anything –
    [*Door opens and DC Sargent enters*]

346

CS: I'm sorry to interrupt, sir, but we've had a
    call – I think it's important –

AF: Really?

CS: Yes, I think so.

AF: [*getting to his feet*]
    DC Hansen, could you continue, please.

TH: Ms Toms, you do not have to say anything, but
    it may harm your defence if you do not mention
    when questioned something which you later rely
    on in court. Anything you do say may be given
    in evidence.
    [*DI Fawley exits the room*]

TH: Would you like to speak to a lawyer now, Ms Toms?

AT: Yes. I think that's probably a good idea.

TH: Interview terminated at 11.26.

* * *

23rd December 1997, 5.25 p.m.
116 Ruskin Road, Edgbaston, Birmingham

'Allie? What are you doing here?'

The porch lamp above his head throws long shadows down
his face, making him look even more gaunt. He's lost so much
weight in the last few weeks.

She steps forward, into the light, and his face changes. Con-
fusion, apprehension, disbelief –

'What on earth –'

The baby is mewling now. He's cold and hungry and needs
changing, but she didn't dare stop on the way to get him
anything – she couldn't run the risk.

She gathers the child, feels his weight, then steps forward. 'Take him.'

'But –'

'Take him – please – before I change my mind.'

He reaches out and lifts the child gently into his arms. And the tenderness of that gesture, the unconditional acceptance, despite the shock and the filthy blanket and the smell of sick and urine, is enough. She no longer doubts what she has done.

She starts to back away down the path. 'Don't tell Renee. About me.'

He frowns. 'But I have to say something –'

'Just say you rescued him. And you have. Believe me. You've rescued him.'

* * *

Richard Swann watches the two policemen walk up the garden towards the house. They've been down there for what seems like hours. But it was only a matter of time, once they'd found the manhole; he knew the game was up. It was a miracle they didn't find it the first time. The taller officer, the sergeant, is talking on his phone, and the younger one has a large evidence bag – a bag he's holding as far away from himself as he possibly can. As they near the house the sergeant looks up and stares straight at Swann. Their eyes lock, just for a moment, then Swann bows his head and turns away.

* * *

'What the hell is it, Sargent?'

OK, that sounds a bit tetchy. My bad. It's just that 'no interruptions' is Interviewing 101 – a rule you just don't break –

She flushes. 'I'm sorry, sir, it's just that we've had a call from Heathside. Camilla Rowan's release has been brought forward. I thought you'd want to know –'

'When?'

'Later today –'

There'll be time to apologize to Sargent later – time to commend her for taking the initiative – but not right now. Right now I have other priorities.

I drag my phone out of my pocket and fumble to find the Heathside number.

'Victoria Winfield, please. DI Adam Fawley. She'll know who I am.'

I turn to Sargent. 'Get on to Surrey police – tell them to get someone over to the prison – they'll get there quicker than we will.'

She nods. 'Right, sir.'

'And when you've done that, find DS Gislingham and DS Quinn and tell them what you told me.'

There's someone on the other end now.

'Is that the governor's office? I need to speak to her. Yes, it is bloody urgent and no, I don't care if she is in a meeting, just get her. Right now.'

* * *

The object in the evidence bag is coated in thick brown slop. 'Like chocolate sauce,' Puttergill had quipped when Tull finally dragged it out. But it doesn't smell like chocolate sauce, and in here, with the windows closed, it's near-nigh unbearable.

Richard Swann is standing on the other side of the table. He didn't say anything when he came to answer the back door, and he hasn't said anything since. He's just staring down at the bag.

'I assume you know what this is, Mr Swann?'

The old man flickers a look at them but that's all they get.

'It's the backpack your intruder was carrying. When you shot him.'

Still nothing. Barnetson and Puttergill exchange a glance, then the sergeant reaches for the backpack and starts to unfasten it. Not for the first time, he gives thanks for the sturdiness of forensic gloves. The zip sticks once or twice, but – hallelujah – the inside is almost clean.

Passport, wallet, keys. Everything they expected to find.

And something they didn't.

* * *

Cathy Doyle is only three months out of prison officer training, and days like this are making her wonder whether this job is really a keeper, after all. First Sullivan throwing her (frankly, considerable) weight around, and now the bloody police. Two of them. The bloke looks quite nice, but the woman he's got with him just looks bored out of her brain. Perhaps she's regretting her career choices too.

'As I explained,' says the male officer, 'we've had a call from Thames Valley re Camilla Rowan –'

'And as *I* explained,' says Doyle, 'there's nothing I can do –'

'What's going on?'

Even without turning, Doyle knows that voice. What's the governor doing down here? She hardly makes a habit of waving prisoners off at the gates, so why today, of all shitty days? Doyle takes a deep breath and turns round.

'Doyle, isn't it?' says Winfield, with a frown.

Doyle is about to reply, when the police officer steps in. 'PC Hugh Tomlinson, Surrey Police, Governor. As I was explaining to your colleague, we've had a call from Thames Valley –'

'I know,' says the governor quickly. 'I've had one too. That's why I'm here. Apparently we need to put a temporary hold on Camilla Rowan's release – I gather TVP are talking to the MoJ as we speak.'

'I'm sorry, ma'am,' says Doyle, 'but it's too late – Rowan left half an hour ago.'

The governor's frown deepens. '*Left?* What do you mean, *left*?'

Doyle's shit day is clearly about to get a whole lot shittier. She feels herself going red, even though none of this crap has anything to do with her.

'I know the email said noon, ma'am, but Officer Sullivan said she'd handle it before she went off shift.'

And 'handle it' was the operative phrase, thinks Doyle. That full search that even Doyle knows was totally unnecessary. The two of them giving each other furtive looks when they thought Doyle wasn't watching. But they're not fooling anyone – the whole bloody prison must know by now. Except, by the looks of it, the governor.

'I'm sorry, ma'am, but given it was only an hour or so

early I didn't think it would make much difference, and Officer Sullivan kept saying we needed to do it before the press started turning up –'

'Where is Officer Sullivan now?'

'Like I said, ma'am, she went off shift.'

'Can I see the release form, please.'

Doyle hands her the sheet of paper; even the bored policewoman looks interested now. 'Rowan's been given a hostel place in Dorking – she said she was going straight there –'

'Call them, please. Now.'

She can feel the three of them staring at her as she finds the number. As if she's the one who fucked up – frankly, even if she had tried to stop Sullivan she wouldn't have got anywhere, there's never any reasoning with her when she's in that mood –

'Hello – HMP Heathside here – just checking that prisoner Rowan has arrived as scheduled? Ah, I see. Could you call us when she does? No, no cause for alarm.'

Though as she finishes the call it's clear that last bit was rather wide of the mark, judging by the looks she's now getting.

'So we have no idea where she is?' says Tomlinson.

Winfield glances at him, then down at the release form. 'She has an appointment with her probation officer at three fifteen – she'll have to attend for that or she'll be recalled.'

Tomlinson makes a face. 'It's a long time till three fifteen –'

'I am aware of that,' snaps Winfield.

'Actually, ma'am,' begins Doyle, not sure at all if this is a good idea, 'it might be worth trying Officer Sullivan –'

'I thought you said she'd gone off shift?'

Doyle feels herself going red again. Like she's a kid in the playground crapping herself about snitching on the school bully. 'No, I mean, she may know where Rowan is.'

The governor is frowning but Tomlinson's sharp; he's got there already. 'They were an item, those two?'

Doyle nods. 'I think it's been going on a while.'

The governor is the one flushing now, dark-red blotches creeping up her neck. She turns to the officers. 'I suggest you accompany me to my office,' she says briskly, 'and I'll get you Sullivan's home address.'

They head off down the corridor but, just as they reach the stairs, Winfield turns back and nods.

'Well done, Doyle. That was the right call.'

Doyle allows herself a small smile at the governor's retreating back. Seems today is not quite so shit, after all.

* * *

Adam Fawley
29 October
12.30

I really don't want to be standing as near as this to Ian Barnetson. Even the other side of the table is way too close. It's hardly his fault; in fact, he deserves props for quick thinking. We might never have found this stuff otherwise. But, Christ, he smells.

Quinn's actually holding his nose and even Gis is looking a touch bilious, though Nina Mukerjee doesn't seem that bothered. But I guess liquid excrement is all in a day's work for her. And unlike the rest of us, she has a mask.

'It's all in miraculously good condition,' she says, looking up at Barnetson. 'Considering it's been underwater for over a week.'

He nods. 'The backpack was good quality – kept most of the shit out. We've entered the wallet and the rest in evidence, but I thought these were best left to you.'

Mukerjee's eyes give little away behind her mask. She nods and reaches for the evidence bags.

* * *

It's a small 1970s block on the outskirts of Claygate. Red brick, windows a shade too small, balconies that say more than a census about the people inside: an orange space hopper and a tricycle on one, assorted plastic plant pots crowding out a single garden chair on the next, a washing line strung with running gear on the top storey, a tattered pro-EU banner draped across the railings.

'Andrea Sullivan lives at number three,' says PC Tomlinson, 'which by my reckoning should be on the ground floor.'

'You don't say,' mutters his colleague.

'Come on, Malloy,' he says, with just a touch of irritation, 'this is what qualifies as interesting, in this job. This woman, Rowan, she's all over the papers.'

That's as may be, thinks Malloy, as she follows him towards the entrance, *but I reckon the chances of her actually being here are approximately zero. If she's doing a runner, she's long gone.*

They push through the heavy main door, which opens with a wrenching squeal, then go down the corridor to the third door. A brass number, a sign saying NO JUNK MAIL, NO HAWKERS. There's no sound from inside.

Tomlinson raps on the door. 'Surrey Police, Ms Sullivan. Can you come to the door, please.'

They can hear voices from somewhere above their heads, the sound of steps on the concrete stairs. But nothing inside.

Tomlinson tries again, louder now. Still nothing. Malloy has the jaded face of the cynic who's rarely wrong.

'OK,' says Tomlinson. 'You stay here, I'm going to check outside – see if I can find her car.'

*　*　*

Mukerjee opens out the two letters and lays them flat on the table. They're stained, and still a little damp, but they're both legible. One's a thick textured sheet of notepaper with a lawyer's comps slip still clipped to the top: Brockman Fells LLP, and a New York address. The writing on the sheet underneath is shaky and irregular, as if completed at several attempts. One word at the bottom: 'Dad'. The other letter is handwritten too, this one on cheap lined stationery. And even without the standard wording at the top, I know where this one came from. I've seen paper like that before. I bend to read the first, then gesture to Quinn and Gis to do the same. A moment later Quinn looks up.

'So the social worker was telling the truth.'

I nod. 'Not that I ever doubted it. She had no reason to lie.'

Gis takes a deep breath. 'But it's not just that, is it?'

355

Dear Noah,

I've left this with the lawyers to give to you after I've gone. Once you've had time to start to deal with it. This is between us – you and me. Not your mother. There's nothing she can tell you and it will only cause her pain.

I'm going to tell you this because you deserve to know. I can only say how sorry I am that I never told you before it was too late. There's no easy way to do it so I'm just going to come straight out and tell you the truth. You are not our child. You are – you _were_ – the son of a woman who did not want you. But it's not as simple as that may sound. It's possible that one day you will find out exactly who she is (I have good reason to fear this, as you may one day realize), and if I don't speak now you won't know who to believe. I can't risk you blaming your mother – the only mother you've ever had. I swear to you Noah – she knew nothing about it. She just came home to find you there. I watched her – saw her see you and her face change from grief and loss to love and healing – from that moment on you were the center of her world. You still are.

You were our miracle. I didn't go looking for you, I didn't make it happen. I just opened the door and there you were – cold and hungry and covered in dirt and sawdust and smelling of piss and the woman said, take him, and I did. I will not tell you her name – she took such a huge risk for us, for you, I can't let that come back to haunt her now. All I will say is that I never asked her where you came from, and the only thing she said to me was that we'd be rescuing you. The state of you, I believed her. I didn't know who your birth mother was – not then, not for years, all I knew was you'd been abandoned, and in the cruelest possible way. By the time it all came out – when I worked out who your mother was and what must have happened – you were our little boy. Not hers, <u>ours</u>. And when they put her in prison for killing her child I knew right had been done.

Remember that, if she ever comes looking

Remember that

Dad

* * *

'Who are you and what the fuck are you doing?'

Malloy looks up and almost loses her balance. She'd been crouched down trying to look through the letterbox, an undignified posture at best, and even worse when you're caught out doing it.

The woman looking down at her is thickset with dark hair in a spiky short cut, a pair of grubby jogging bottoms and a plastic basket of laundry under one arm. Malloy clears her throat. 'Sorry, Miss –?'

The woman's eyes narrow. '*Ms* Sullivan. Andrea Sullivan. Your turn.'

Malloy straightens up. Where the hell is Tomlinson when you need him?

She pulls out her warrant card. 'PC Julie Malloy, Surrey Police. We're trying to track down Camilla Rowan.'

The woman raises an eyebrow. 'And? What's that got to do with me?'

'You signed her out this morning, so naturally –'

'Naturally,' she says, sarcastic. She leaves a pause. 'Look, as far as I know she's seeing her probation officer later this afternoon. What she does before that is none of my business. Or *yours*. Unless something's come up –'

'Not at all,' says Malloy quickly. 'Just a bureaucratic cock-up. Someone probably forgot to get the right forms done. You know what it's like.'

She rolls her eyes and Sullivan seems to thaw a little. 'I ought to, fifteen years on the job.'

Malloy slides a glance over Sullivan's shoulder. Still no sign of bloody Tomlinson. How long does it take to check a bloody car park?

'Do you know where Rowan was going when she left Heathside?'

Sullivan sighs. 'Look, you'd better come in.' She hitches the basket on to her hip and fiddles in her jogger pockets for her keys. She has three locks so it takes a while but eventually they're inside.

She takes the washing through to the tiny kitchen, then comes back to the sitting room. She obviously hasn't lived here long; there are still pictures wrapped in bubble plastic leaning against one wall and a stack of cardboard boxes labelled in big letters with red felt-pen, LOUNGE, SPARE ROOM, BEDROOM.

She doesn't offer Malloy to sit down, so they stand awkwardly between the furniture, slightly encroaching on each other's personal space.

Malloy gets out her notebook. A useful thing to occupy your hands, as she's discovered in situations like this more than once.

'So Ms Rowan didn't say where she was going, when you were completing the release procedures?'

There's a knock on the front door. Sullivan goes to open it and returns with Tomlinson behind her. He catches Malloy's eye and gives a minute nod.

'This is PC Tomlinson,' says Malloy brightly. 'He was just having a quick fag outside.'

Tomlinson looks momentarily startled but then smiles sheepishly. 'Keep trying to give the bloody things up.'

Sullivan gives a quick dry laugh. 'Yeah, you and me both, mate.'

'Ms Sullivan tells me she has no idea where Camilla Rowan might be,' continues Malloy.

'I see,' says Tomlinson. 'Do you know how she was plan-ning to get to her hostel from Heathside? Bus? Minicab?'

'Like I said, no idea.'

'You didn't by any chance give her a lift? Given you came off shift at exactly the time she left?'

'Not sure how hot your map-reading skills are, mate, but Dorking's hardly on my way. And in any case, it's strictly against the regs, even if I'd wanted to. Which I didn't.'

'Do you know if she has access to any sort of vehicle?'

Sullivan raises her eyebrows. 'I doubt it, she barely had enough cash for a sodding Happy Meal.' She looks from one to the other. 'Is that it? Cos if there's nothing else, I have things to do.'

'Of course,' says Malloy with a smile. 'It's obviously just an admin mix-up. We're sorry to have troubled you.'

As soon as they're outside Malloy turns quickly to Tom-linson and lowers her voice. 'We need to run an urgent vehicle check.'

Tomlinson frowns. 'On what? Her car's still here.'

'You didn't see – when she got back to the flat she was carrying that basket of washing.'

'So?'

'So, I don't think she brought it back home with her from work, do you? She wasn't wearing a coat either *and* I never heard the main door open. I think she was upstairs – I think she brought that washing down to do it for someone else. Looked like old lady stuff to me, as well.'

Tomlinson grins. 'Big knickers, eh? So you're thinking a neighbour, maybe?'

Malloy nods. 'More likely a *relative*. And Sullivan clearly hasn't been living there long – maybe her mum was already in one of the other flats and she's moved here to be closer to her?'

'And in that case,' says Tomlinson slowly, 'it's possible that dear old mum has a car too –'

'Exactly,' says Malloy. '*Exactly.*'

*   *   *

> Just had two plods here asking questions. Surrey not TVP

Shit

What were they asking about?

> You obvs

And?

> Don't think they caught on. Just a couple of uniforms

> Think they checked my car but thats still there isnt it. Doubt they know about Mums

We're way ahead of them, don't worry

> Just stay off the bloody motorways OK?

> Yeah yeah

> And text me when you get there

* * *

'Noah knew about Rowan,' says Gislingham, staring at the letter. 'He knew what she did.'

I nod. 'He knew.'

Quinn gives a low whistle. 'Jesus, all those years she's saying she never harmed the baby –'

'She didn't. That's the point. Strictly speaking, it's the truth. She didn't kill him and she didn't harm him. She just left him.'

'Oh, come on,' begins Gis. 'A kid that was only a few hours old dumped in the middle of winter in a *plastic bag*?'

'Don't get me wrong – I'm not saying I agree, not for a minute. I'm just saying that's how her mind works. How many times have we seen her do that – all those "lies" that turn out in the end to be quarter-truths? This is just another one: "I never harmed my child".'

'I'm not so sure about that.'

It's Barnetson, looking up from the second letter.

'Have a read of that.'

In replying to this letter, please write on the envelope:

Number: A1667GHD   **Name:** CAMILLA ROWAN

Wing: HP HEALHSIDE C25

27/8/18

DEAR NOAH

I KNOW YOU'RE ANGRY — I KNOW YOU THINK I DID SOMETHING TERRIBLE, BUT YOU'RE WRONG. YOU DON'T KNOW, YOU REALLY DON'T. I WANT TO TELL YOU BUT IT'S NOT SOMETHING YOU CAN WRITE DOWN, ESPECIALLY NOT IN HERE. I DON'T THINK YOU HAVE ANY IDEA HOW HARD IT IS FOR ME TO TALK ABOUT THIS STUFF, EVEN THINK ABOUT IT, EVEN ALL THESE YEARS LATER. YOU KEEP ASKING WHY I LIED — HAS IT OCCURRED TO YOU HOW PAINFUL THE TRUTH WAS? HOW FRIGHTENED I MIGHT HAVE BEEN ABOUT TELLING ANYONE? I WAS YOUNGER THAN YOU ARE NOW. I WAS ALONE, I'D BEEN ABUSED BY THE ONE MAN WHO WAS SUPPOSED TO PROTECT ME. THE MAN WHO TOLD ME IT WAS 'OUR SECRET' AND HE WOULD KILL ME IF I EVER SAID ANYTHING. AND I BELIEVED HIM... WHY WOULDN'T I. I'M SORRY IF THAT MAKES YOU ANGRY BUT THAT'S THE PROBLEM WITH TELLING THE TRUTH, SO IF YOU WANT TO KNOW WHAT HAPPENED HE'S THE PERSON YOU NEED TO ASK, NOT ME. THOUGH HE'S NOT THE MAN HE USED TO BE, AND NOT JUST BECAUSE IT'S A LONG TIME AGO. THESE DAYS HE'S JUST SWANNING AROUND IN A MANNER LIKE GENTRY. I FORGOT — YOU DON'T HAVE CRAP LIKE THAT OVER THERE, DO YOU? GUESS YOU'LL JUST HAVE TO LOOK IT UP.

YOU'RE RIGHT NOT TO TELL YOUR MOM
THERE'LL BE A TIME FOR THAT, BUT NOT YET

* * *

363

'Hold on a sec, let me write that down.'

Hugh Tomlinson notes down the registration number and finishes the call, then turns to Malloy. 'You were bang on – a Mrs *Noreen* Sullivan has lived upstairs in that block for the last ten years. She was recently disqualified from driving due to failing eyesight, but she is still, at this precise moment, the registered owner of a grey Vauxhall Nova.'

Malloy feels a little surge of triumph, almost despite herself.

'So I'm going to pop over to the car park and look for that car, which I'd lay a good deal of odds isn't there.'

'What about me?' says Malloy, feeling suddenly useless again.

'You,' says Tomlinson with a grin, 'are going to go straight back in there and stop Sullivan giving her girl-friend a heads-up that we're on to her. And then you're going to phone DI Adam Fawley of Thames Valley Police and tell him what a bloody clever copper you are.'

* * *

Adam Fawley
29 October
12.45

'She set him up,' says Quinn. '"I'm sorry if that makes you angry", my arse. She sent him bowling in all guns blazing to a couple of paranoid old gits who were terrified about intruders. And the kid didn't need sodding Companies House to find them, either. She laid it out on a bloody plate. "*Swanning* around", "a *manner* like *gentry*" – she knew he'd work it out.'

'All guns blazing wasn't just the kid,' says Gis grimly. 'She knew better than anyone about that incident with her dad and the shotgun after the trial. On top of which the train was late, so the Swanns had already gone to bed and would've been even more jumpy. That poor bastard, how unlucky can you get.'

Barnetson shakes his head. 'I still can't believe she did that to her own son.'

I turn to him. 'But what other explanation is there? She deliberately inflamed the situation, then told him how to find her parents, knowing exactly what the consequences might be.'

'All she cared about was herself,' says Gis. 'She thought that baby had been dumped in landfill twenty years ago. And suddenly, out of the blue, he's not just alive but knows what she did and is threatening to talk. She had to shut him up.'

'"Don't tell your mom", yeah, right,' mutters Quinn.

Gis turns to me. 'So what now, boss? I assume we don't believe that crap about her father abusing her?'

'Well, we know from the DNA that he wasn't the father of the baby,' I say. 'But even without that, no, we don't. It's just another one of her lies – what she did was so horrific, the only possible excuse was something even more appalling. Saying her father had raped her was the one thing Noah might just, conceivably, forgive.'

'So where does that leave us? We can try and bring her in but is there any point? It's never going to go anywhere – she's already served fifteen years.'

'That's not up to us. We apprehend people who've committed a crime, regardless of what time they've already served. As far as I'm concerned we now have pretty conclusive evidence of attempted murder, which Rowan never stood trial for. So we find her, and we bring her in, and after that it's up to the CPS.'

'Easier said than done, though,' says Quinn. 'Given the start she's had, she could be bloody anywhere by now.'

'Right, so let's get on with it, shall we? Starting with an All-Ports Warning –'

My phone is ringing, a number I don't recognize.

'Adam Fawley, hello?'

A woman's voice, slightly breathless at first but then she gets into her stride.

'I see – you think they were in a relationship? What's the reg number?' I grab a pen. 'Right, and what does this prison officer look like? Yes, I think I saw her when we were at Heathside. Could you ask her to produce her passport, and if she won't – or *can't* – get a search warrant. Brilliant, thank you. Good work. And keep me posted.'

I put the phone down and turn to the others. 'That was Surrey. Seems Rowan was involved with one of the prison officers at Heathside – a woman called Andrea Sullivan –'

'Using her, more like,' mutters Quinn.

'Either way, this woman just so happened to be on shift when Rowan was released this morning and Surrey are pretty sure she gave her a lift. Not just a lift, in fact, but quite possibly a car as well.' I rip out the sheet and hand it to Gis. 'A grey Vauxhall Nova. Let's get an ANPR alert out on that, straight away, please.'

'Right, boss.'

He's already leaving, but I call him back. 'And that

All-Ports Warning – add Sullivan's name to it.' He gives me a questioning look. 'I think she may have given Rowan more than just a car. I think she may have given her a new identity.'

* * *

She used to love driving. Funny how easily it comes back, even after all these years. It's cold outside, but she winds the window down anyway, just to get the wind in her face. That's something she hasn't had for a while. She glances in the rear mirror but the road behind is clear, at least as far as she can see; no one following. She pushes a hand through her hair – Sullivan actually did a reasonable job, given all she had was kitchen scissors. She might even keep it short. But blonde, obviously. There's no rush though, there'll be plenty of time to decide on stuff like that. She checks the phone again but there's nothing since the last message. All this new techy stuff is going to take a bit of getting used to, but Sullivan showed her how to use WhatsApp ('only use that, nothing else – it's encrypted'), and set her up with an email address. In fact, she's done everything she said she would – tankful of gas, bag of food on the back seat, suitcase of clothes in the boot. Everything she needs for now. Certainly enough to get her where she's going, even if she is being forced to go on fuck-boring routes to stay under the radar. Whatever. She'll still get there with time to spare, and after that there'll be no way the plod can track her down, even if they do catch on. And as she's taken care to ensure, exactly the same applies to Sullivan. She's been great and all that, and she couldn't have done this without her, but there's no way she wants her trailing around after her like a wet weekend; she wasn't that good a shag. In any case, this needs to be a clean break – the chance to ditch Camilla Rowan for good and be someone else. Lose a few pounds, buy a new passport, *get a life*. And no risk of the past catching up with her. Not again, not ever.

She'd thought to start with that he was just another chancer, pretending to be her long-lost kid – she's had more than her fair share of that shit over the years. And let's face it, what were the odds on that baby ending up in bloody New York, for fuck's sake? She'd chucked the letter, guessing – wrongly, as it turned out – that he'd just give up. Only he didn't. He was stubborn, he wouldn't let it go. Yeah, well, she knows now where he got that from. But even in that last letter, with its barely veiled threat, there was nothing that *proved* he was legit. So why not offload him on her fucking parents? Let them sort it out. After the way they've treated her, they deserve all they get. At least, that's what she told herself. And if things wound up getting a little heated, well, that was hardly her fault, was it? She never harmed that kid in the first place, and she hadn't harmed him now.

And now she's free and clear and not looking back. Sullivan said that with fifteen years done they'd have struggled to send her back anyway. Maybe she's right. Maybe she's not. But why the fuck take the risk.

She reaches for the radio and flicks it on. It's one of those 1980s nostalgia stations. She turns it up and sings along happily to the last few verses of 'Sisters are Doin' It for Themselves', until the next song cues up and she's suddenly laughing out loud and turning it up as loud as it will go.

> *There's a loving in your eyes all the way*
> *If I listened to your lies would you say . . .*

* * *

Adam Fawley
29 October
14.15

'What's Sullivan saying?'

There's a crackling on the other end of the line.

'Not a lot, surprise, surprise.'

Surrey have clearly escalated this one: the person I'm talking to now is another DI.

'She can't produce the passport but claims it must have been mislaid in her house move.'

'Did she report it as lost?'

'No,' he says, 'but since she still hasn't unpacked half her boxes it'll be hard to pin her with that one. And before you ask, I have two uniforms going through those boxes right now, as well as a CSI team on-site. Whose task is being made a sight harder by an irritable old lady badgering them every five minutes about her washing.'

'So they haven't found anything?'

'Nope – at least nothing that ties Sullivan to Rowan. If they're communicating by text it's not on her main phone. And if there's another one we haven't found yet, we do at least know she isn't using it where she is right now, i.e. in Elmbridge nick.'

'Are you checking Sullivan's finances? If Rowan's trying to get out of the country –'

'We're on it,' he says, slightly tetchy now. I suppose I can't blame him. 'Look, we may not be the Met but we have done this sort of thing before. And rest assured, if we find something, you'll be the first to know.'

* * *

Sent: Mon 29/10/2018, 16.13   **Importance: High**
From: NickyBrown@CPS.gov.uk
To: DIAdamFawley@ThamesValley.police.uk

Subject: Camilla Rowan – CONFIDENTIAL

We've just had a meeting to review your new evidence, and I agree that there is a prima facie case to answer. The question, of course, is whether a prosecution for attempted murder passes the public interest test, given Rowan has already served fifteen years. However, the judge's original recommendation was for a minimum of <u>seventeen</u> years, which she clearly has not served, and her release on licence was predicated on the reappearance of the child, which invalidated the original murder charge. Should the public come to learn what Rowan actually did to her baby there is likely to be a considerable backlash, accompanied by calls (informed or otherwise) for her to – at the very least – serve out the rest of her recommended minimum sentence. Taking all these factors into account, we believe there should be a second referral to the CCRC, pending which Rowan should be arrested and returned to custody: she has clearly breached her licence conditions by failing to turn up to the meeting with her probation officer.

Please do not hesitate to get in touch if you have any further questions.

Regards,
Nicky

*　*　*

The DI from Surrey calls me at five. What he has to say barely qualifies as 'news', but it's just about enough to force me on to my feet to go and update everyone. Just as well, to be honest, because I've been sitting at this bloody desk for three hours now and my arse has gone to sleep. And, frankly, the atmosphere in the main office isn't much livelier. If you graphed the collective mood since we realized Rowan had slipped through our fingers the line would be straight down.

'OK, everyone,' I say, raising my voice a little, 'I've just had a call from DI O'Neill at Surrey Police. The team that did the search for Sullivan's passport also noticed a few cut hairs on the kitchen floor, so it looks like we could be right that Rowan's altered her appearance to look more like Sullivan.' I look round the room. 'I'm assuming there's still no trace of either Rowan or the Nova?'

Baxter shakes his head. 'Nothing on ANPR, so she's probably avoiding motorways. Doesn't help that we have no idea where she could be going.'

'Channel Tunnel has to be the most likely, surely?' says Carter.

'Also the most obvious,' replies Gis. 'And if we've learned one thing about this woman it's not to underestimate her.'

There's a silence, then Ev sits back in her chair. 'I think we missed her, boss. I think somehow or other she got out of the country.'

I shrug. 'Perhaps. But maybe they anticipated this happening and planned for it – they'd have had long enough, after all, and unlike Rowan, Sullivan's been on the outside and free to do whatever she likes. Maybe she's fixed it for Rowan to go to ground – hole up somewhere until it all dies down.'

Quinn scowls. 'And meanwhile she gets a new ID, a new car –'

'I know. But all that costs money. We'll have to hope Surrey find something in Sullivan's financials.'

'Well, they've not found diddly yet,' says Baxter.

'No, they haven't. But she may have other accounts we know nothing about.'

'Actually,' begins Chloe Sargent, 'I was thinking about that –'

She stops. Everyone is looking at her.

'Go on,' says Hansen.

'If Sullivan's been looking after her mum – doing her washing and that – isn't it possible she manages her money as well? She could even have power of attorney – I mean, when my gran –'

'You could be right. Let's see what we can find in the mother's accounts. And make sure Surrey are in the loop – we don't want to piss them off, not if we don't have to.' She's nodding and flushing and making a note all at once. 'And well done, Sargent. Good for you.'

On my way out I turn at the door; Gis is making a big thing of clapping Sargent on the back in front of everyone. Good for him.

* * *

Transcript out-of-hours 101 call
Essex Police

29.10.2018 18:52:08

Operator:	Essex Police, can I help you?
Caller:	There's a car on fire.
Operator:	Is anyone in danger?
Caller:	No, it's on waste ground – abandoned. I can't see anyone there. But it's the third time this month and our councillor told us to report it.
Operator:	And where are you?
Caller:	Bromness, just off the main road.
Operator:	And it's waste ground, you say?
Caller:	Kids go there to joyride. Place is a bloody eyesore.
Operator:	I'll get someone to attend. Please don't put yourself in any danger, or confront anyone –

Caller:	Confront who? Those tykes'll be long gone by now.
Operator:	If you can hold on I'll get you a reference number for the incident for your records.

*   *   *

Adam Fawley
29 October
19.40

'Did you get the email?' I'm on the phone to DI O'Neill, practising what I preach. 'It's the mother's bank statement.'

'I'm just opening it now.'

Most of it's the usual stuff: outgoings to Tesco, BT, British Gas, Southern Electric; incomings that look like pension payments. The same things, week in, week out. But then you get to a cash deposit three days ago, and an outgoing one of exactly the same size immediately afterwards. An electronic transfer to 'Select Country Cottages Ltd'.

'So, what?' says O'Neill. 'She arranged accommodation for Rowan?'

'A cottage just outside Plymouth. And you're going to like this bit. It's listed as "a recently renovated property on one of Devon's most scenic stretches of coast, the idyllic Bluff Cove".'

I can hear him sigh. 'They're pissing us about.'

'They most certainly are. The cottage is owned by the pub next door. It's called the Wild Goose. My DS thought it was a coincidence.'

But I knew better, because I remember Leonora Staniforth on that Netflix show talking about how Rowan was the one who came up with the 'chameleon girls', and how she was 'always really clever about things like that'. This has the same supercilious little fingerprints all over it.

O'Neill sighs again and then takes me by surprise by starting to laugh. 'You've got to hand it to her. It's pretty fucking funny.'

Only I'm not laughing.

I finish the call and get to my feet. Time for a change of scene. Or, even better, a bloody beer.

* * *

Voicemail

DI Brendan O'Neill

Mobile

Transcription

Sorry I missed you – maybe you've done the sensible thing and gone home. This is just to say I've heard back from Devon and Cornwall. No one's turned up yet but apparently Sullivan emailed them to say she could be a day or so late and not to worry. Local uniform will keep an eye. Cheers.

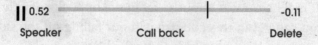

❚❚ 0.52   -0.11

Speaker   Call back   Delete

* * *

It's bad enough getting up for the baby; I'm definitely too old to pull all-nighters. I must have dozed off because I jolt awake when the door opens. It's Gis.

He grins when he sees me. 'Sorry.'

I sit up. 'Don't be. I shouldn't have fallen asleep.' I glance up at the clock. 'Shit, is that the time? Why are you still here?'

I thought he'd gone home; everyone else has. None of them wanted to be the first to throw in the towel, or at least not in front of me. But when I picked up the last voicemail from O'Neill I decided enough was enough and told them to go and get some sleep.

'I was just checking some stuff,' says Gis. He takes a step closer. 'And I found something.'

'Go on – make my day.'

'I found the car. Or rather, Essex Police have. Looks like Rowan dumped it and some local wags took it out for a ride then torched it.'

'*Essex?* What's it doing there? I thought that rental place was in Plymouth?'

'It is. The car was about as far in the opposite direction as you can get in this country without falling off the side. Somewhere I've never heard of called Bromness.'

I sigh; more bloody Rowan mind games.

'And Essex are sure it's the right car?'

Gis nods. 'I just had a chat with one of their uniforms and she said they've been having a spate of joyriding round there. You know what it's like – bit of wasteland off the beaten track, they're on it like wasps on jam. And as we both know, those old Novas are pathetically easy to nick.' He gives a wry smile. 'We should be grateful old Mrs Sullivan had such crap taste in cars.'

I nod. 'First thing to go our way.'

'The second, actually, boss. Seems this particular site has become so much of a problem the locals have a Neighbourhood Watch thing going, to try and put pressure on the Council. So we have a bunch of sharp-eyed old biddies to thank for the fact that Essex got there quickly enough to ID the reg plate on the Nova before it went up like Guy Fawkes.'

'Or that they bothered turning up at all.'

He nods; we both know how low down the list that sort of petty thuggery usually is.

'Still doesn't answer the question, why Essex? Unless of course there's a twee little rental nearby with a name like "Fuck You, Fawley".'

Gis grins. 'I think I can do better than that. Bromness – it's less than half an hour from Harwich.'

I'm having trouble jump-starting my brain, but even I can make the connection on this one.

'Harwich as in bloody massive port?'

His grin widens. 'The very same. And Felixstowe is within striking distance too.'

'Judging by your face, I'm assuming you've got hold of passenger manifests?'

'Essex are on it. Shouldn't take long.'

'How many crossings a day?'

He hands me a sheet of paper. 'Even taking into

account driving time and not using motorways, Rowan could easily have made it in time for the Harwich to Hook of Holland sailing at eleven p.m. There were also three freight crossings to Rotterdam: one from Harwich at ten thirty, one from Felixstowe at eight and another from Felixstowe coming up at two thirty.' He checks his watch. 'In almost exactly an hour, in fact.'

I'm looking at the list. 'You said the Rotterdam crossings are freight only? You think she could be on a lorry?'

'On one or *in* one,' says Gis drily. 'Why risk being in the cab and having that "borrowed" passport checked?'

Fuck, why didn't I think of that.

'You've spoken to Customs?'

He nods. 'They didn't pick up anything at the Border, but apparently outgoing freight isn't routinely searched, not unless there's intelligence and that's pretty much always about contraband or drugs, not people. I mean, it's not the Channel, is it, plus it's going the wrong bloody way.'

'But we can get Dutch Police to pick it up the other end? When do the boats dock?'

'First one gets in at four thirty our time, so don't worry – we're on it.'

'Bloody well done, Gis. That was great work. The whole team's pulled a blinder on this.'

'Thanks, boss.'

He heads for the door, then turns suddenly, his face troubled now. 'But what if all this is just another diversion? Rowan sends us careering off across the North Sea like the Keystone Cops and all the while she's just quietly changed cars and headed off God-knows-where in a pair of sunnies and a pink wig?'

I smile, despite myself. 'They don't call her the chameleon girl for nothing. But she'd need to get that new car from somewhere, wouldn't she, and we haven't found any record of Sullivan getting her one.'

He considers. 'She could have just rolled up and asked for a rental?'

'True, but she'd need documentation, which seriously ups the chances of getting caught. And in any case, remember what my old governor used to say about the simplest possible explanation?'

He smiles. 'Osbourne's Razor.'

'Right, so let's rule these crossings out first before we go looking for any more trouble.'

As soon as the door closes I reach for my phone. It's a bloody antisocial time to call anyone, but I don't have much choice.

'DI O'Neill? Adam Fawley. Sorry if I woke you. I need you to check something for me. Got a pen? Yes, it's about Andrea Sullivan. Can you see if she has any links to the haulage industry? Brother, father, mate, anything.' A pause. 'In one – we think she could be on a lorry.'

* * *

It's pretty basic, as accommodation goes, but after all those years inside, one-star counts as deluxe, and a three-foot divan feels like queen size. She tosses her bags on the floor and flings herself down on the bed, feeling her shoulders start to relax. There's a stain on the ceiling, and a vague smell of diesel, and a throbbing sound from somewhere nearby, but she doesn't care. It's her own space, for as long as she's here. Hers alone. There's even a bathroom en suite, Sullivan made sure of that. She sighs at the thought of a proper bath, all to herself, that she can stay in all night if she chooses. And with that special bath oil Sullivan gave her –

A knock at the door. She sits up, feeling her heart rate go into long-learnt overdrive. *Stop it*, she thinks, *it'll be nothing. Just some routine check or shit like that.*

She slides to the edge of the bed and gets to her feet. Another knock, more insistent. The sound of someone just beyond the door.

She moves as quietly as she can to the door, and slips the chain on. Then she takes a deep breath and opens it a crack.

She's never seen this person before, but she's seen pictures; she knows who they are.

A raised eyebrow, a half-smile.

'I think you're expecting me?'

* * *

Adam Fawley
30 October
02.47

I was going to go in the spare room, but when I get home there's a light on in the nursery. Alex is sitting in the old chair her mother gave her when she was pregnant with Jake, Lily nursing quietly in her arms, the lamp on the table throwing gentle golden shadows.

I stop in the doorway and just stand there, watching. She looks up and beckons me over, but I shake my head; I don't want to break the moment. 'You look like a Vermeer.'

She smiles. 'Wonderful what soft lighting can do,' she whispers.

'How is she?'

'Fine, the health visitor came today and was really pleased with her.' She looks down at her daughter and reaches a hand to touch her cheek. Lily gazes up at her, her eyes huge in the half-dark. I remember reading a description once of what newborn babies can see. Not in one of those childcare manuals, it was a novel. Something about how eyes unfocused and washed with newness see the world only as a kaleidoscope of colour and shape, but can still recognize, from a sense even deeper than sight, the warm glow of their mother's face and the halo of her hair.

And then I remember Noah. The first Noah, who would have been twenty-one now, who barely got to see his mother except through the glass wall of an incubator; and the second, whose last sight of the woman who bore him was as the suffocating black plastic closed over his face.

* * *

'There's a bed, and a telly, though obviously keep that off until we're through. Some people find it claustrophobic in there with the partition shut, but it's never bothered me. Figure you'll probably be the same, eh?'

It's a fair assumption about anyone who's been inside. As Rock evidently has. Rowan didn't need to see the tatts to know that.

They're sitting on the bed at the B&B, eating McDonald's. It was the only place open this early; it'll be at least an hour before it gets light. Rowan has a breakfast flatbread, Rock has a double sausage and egg McMuffin. Twice. Rock has a big appetite. In fact, most things about Rock are big. The hands, the gut, the shoulders under the Iron Maiden T-shirt.

'What time do we need to leave?' Rowan asks, checking her watch. Again.

'Sevenish, I reckon. We've a way to go yet.'

'Doesn't bother me. Sooner the better.'

Rock laughs. 'That figures too.'

'You don't think there'll be a problem?' She tries to make it sound matter-of-fact but if this goes wrong –

Rock watches her face. 'It'll be my fat butt hung out to dry as well as yours if there is.'

Her heart rate is still painfully fast. 'But what if they want to search the cab?'

Rock gives a snort, sending a spray of crumbs over the bedspread. 'They won't. Trust me, they can't be arsed to do that, not without good reason. Coming back, now, that'll be a different matter. Specially with a full load. But that's my problem, not yours.'

'I'll take your word for it.' She pauses. 'And thanks again. I couldn't do this without you.'

Rock shrugs. 'Don't thank me, thank Sullivan. The boss owed her one.'

Rowan finishes her food and starts clearing up. Rock eyes her, then reaches for a napkin. 'Though I guess you're the one who owes her now, right?'

* * *

By the time the rest of the team get in, Gis has already been there an hour. He managed not to wake Janet last night by the simple expedient of sleeping in the spare room, but he still got a bollocking this morning. 'You'll get an ulcer at this rate, haven't you got DCs to do the late ones?' But being up first and doing breakfast (egg and bacon for the two of them and pancakes for Billy, which he loves but Janet hardly ever does because of the time and the mess) means he got off pretty lightly, all things considered.

It's an interesting exercise, watching the team arrive. Bradley Carter at 8.15, always on the alert for brownie points; Ev and Sargent soon after, coffees in hand from the same shop, which leaves Gis wondering if Ev gave her a lift; then Baxter, moaning about traffic, then Hansen, and finally Quinn, in that *Luther*-style greatcoat of his, with a silk scarf and an almond croissant from the posh place in Jericho.

'What time did you get away?' he says, coming up to the front, where Gis is pinning the latest on to the board.

'Must have been two-ish in the end. Boss left just after.'

'Fuck.'

Gis makes a face. 'That's one word for it.' He looks back over Quinn's shoulder. 'Looks like we're all here. Eyes down for a full house.'

Quinn starts to unwind his scarf. 'You're not waiting for Fawley?'

Gis shakes his head. 'He said to carry on if he wasn't here by eight. He's up to speed on most of this, anyway.'

He turns to the rest of the team and raises his voice slightly. 'OK, so here's where we got to overnight. Essex Police have found the Vauxhall Nova – and yes, I did say Essex. Looks like Rowan left it on a side street somewhere and hoped it would go unnoticed, at least for as long as it took for her to get away. Luckily for us,' he continues drily, 'the local joyriding fraternity had other ideas.'

He points to the map. 'This is where it was found – place by the name of Bromness. Obviously we don't know exactly when or where Rowan dumped it, but it's a fair bet it wasn't that far away and, that being the case, we made an educated guess that she could be on a ferry either out of Felixstowe, here –' he points again – 'or Harwich, here. As you can see from the list I just circulated, there were four sailings last night, one from Harwich to the Hook of Holland, one from Harwich to Rotterdam, and two from Felixstowe to Rotterdam.'

'Hang on,' says Ev. 'Those were all passenger ferries?'

'No, only the Hook of Holland one. The rest are just freight.'

Ev stares at him. 'You think she's on a *lorry*?'

Gis shrugs. 'We couldn't rule it out. And one thing we know about this woman is better safe than sorry.'

Baxter's looking openly sceptical. 'What, she breaks into a truck to leave the country – like the Channel Tunnel in reverse? I guess it's possible, but can you really see the Duchess slumming it in the back of a forty-tonner –?'

'Yup,' says Quinn. 'I sure can. You haven't met her. She'd be up for almost anything, frankly, as long as there was enough in it for her. And blagging in is way more likely than breaking in, if you ask me – I'm sure she'd be prepared to "make it worth their while". I mean, look at how she's been using that poor cow Sullivan.'

'But it'd be a huge risk, wouldn't it?' says Ev, turning to him. 'Just turning up on the off-chance, and risking getting either spotted or reported? The way they've planned all this – her and Sullivan – it's way more organized than that.'

Hansen nods. 'I agree. I think she went there because she was meeting someone. Someone who'd agreed to give her a lift, no questions asked.'

Gis is smiling. 'Which is exactly why the boss called Surrey last night – they're checking any links Andrea Sullivan might have to the trucking industry. Anyone who might be prepared to do her a favour.'

Quinn finishes his croissant and wipes his fingers. 'How far have they got?' He's frowning slightly, evidently wondering how to get himself back on the front foot.

Gis makes a face. 'Nowhere, last I heard. Father was a postman, no uncles, no brothers, no obvious family links at all. But they're interviewing her again this morning.'

'And have Dutch Police checked those overnight crossings?' asks Sargent.

'They searched the Hook of Holland one that got in at four thirty and came up empty.' He checks his watch. 'We should be hearing about the eight and eight thirty arrivals any time now.'

'And the passengers?' asks Bradley Carter, not to be outdone. 'We don't *know* she was on a lorry.'

Gis shakes his head. 'No Camilla Rowan or Andrea Sullivan on any of the manifests, and no one answering the description. Apparently it wasn't exactly busy.' He gives a wry smile. 'Not sure I'd fancy the North Sea at this time of year either. Not for eight bloody hours, anyway.'

Quinn is up by the map now. 'I'm assuming we're ruling out airports?'

'The APW should catch that,' says Gis steadily. 'That *is*

why they call it an *All-Ports* Warning. But we can do a follow-up with Stansted and Southend if you think it's worth it. They're the closest.'

Ev looks at the map. 'But both of those are still over an hour away. She'd need transport. Maybe she picked up another car?'

'I talked about that with the boss – he didn't think a rental was much of a runner. Too much documentation.'

'Sullivan could have left another car for her in Felix-stowe?' offers Carter.

Quinn snorts, but Gis is keeping a straight face. 'That's a possibility, of course, but in the scheme of things, pretty unlikely.'

Carter flushes. 'I just meant I couldn't see her wanting to go by train – too much risk of getting spotted.'

'Coach?' suggests Ev. 'Not so much surveillance there.'

Gis nods and turns to Carter. 'OK, why don't you pick up on that? Get on to the coach companies?'

Quinn grins. 'Careful what you wish for, Carter, eh?'

*   *   *

She hears the cab door bang open and then the swing of weight as Rock climbs in. The partition is drawn across, but there's no doubt who it is. The smell's a giveaway, for a start. Coal tar soap. Her father always used that stuff. Brings it all back. And not in a good way.

'You OK in the back there?'

Rowan fights down the nausea; seasickness was one thing she hadn't bargained for.

'Fine, thanks.'

'I've got some mints if you want them. It might get a bit rough later.'

What do you mean, later? she thinks.

'We'll lose mobile signal too, just so you know.'

She didn't, but it makes sense.

'I've been checking the news,' continues Rock. 'Nothing about you. Not that I can find, anyway.' There's a pause, then, 'Have you heard from her?'

'Who, Sullivan? No, not since yesterday.'

'You think the filth are on to her?'

'Maybe. They were asking questions. But she knew it'd probably happen sooner or later. And she'll be OK. She's a tough cookie.'

Rock laughs. 'I bet.'

There's the sound of the glovebox opening and then the partition slides back an inch or so and a packet of Extra Strong Mints drops on to the end of the bed.

'I'd better go. We aren't supposed to be down here when we're at sea. You gonna be OK?'

'It'll be a long day tomorrow, I'm going to try and get some sleep.'

A laugh. 'It'll be worth it. All the cheese you can eat, eh.'

Yeah, well, she thinks, *I need to be losing a few pounds, not putting them on.*

'It'll do,' she says. 'For now.'

* * *

'Sorry, boss. We're coming up empty.'

Looks like our run of luck has run aground.

The whiteboard is covered with red crossings-out: not on the Harwich passenger ferries, not on any of the freight ones, not on any known flight. We're running out of options, and we're running out of time.

'So,' I say, forcing some energy into my voice, 'anyone got any other ideas?'

'I think we should widen the search, sir,' says Sargent. 'To other ports.'

Quinn's smirking but I ignore him. 'Why do you say that?'

She looks a little nervously at Quinn, then back at me. 'I know you said it's unlikely she'd rent a car, and public transport was probably too much of a risk –'

'Go on.'

'Well, if we're right and she's on a truck, then isn't it possible it picked her up at Bromness –'

'We've already ruled that out,' says Carter, with a Quinn-like sigh. Not sure if he's consciously copying or just imprinting. Like baby geese. Come to think of it, with that tufty hair of his, he does look rather like a gosling. 'They've checked – she wasn't on any of the ferries.'

'Not those, no,' says Sargent. 'But that's not what I meant. I meant maybe she picked up the lorry there – a lorry that's now on its way somewhere else. To *another* port.'

Quinn frowns. 'Yeah, OK, *maybe*, but it'd be like looking for a needle in a bloody haystack – where the hell would we even start? She's already got at least twelve hours' head-start on us, we have no idea who this hairy-arsed bloke is she's with, and we can't start searching every bloody lorry leaving the country –'

'Actually,' says Hansen, looking up from his screen, 'I had a thought about that. I checked a couple of websites and apparently commercial driving's a popular job option with ex-cons. As long as they haven't been done for dangerous driving –'

I stare at him; everyone stares at him. And no wonder: it's been right under our noses this whole time.

'Call Heathside – we need the names of all prisoners released in the last three years and then cross-reference that list with DVLA – and tell them it's urgent. I've got a contact there if you hit a jobsworth.'

He opens his mouth to ask why but I get my answer in before the question. 'You can't drive an HGV without an advanced driving cert, Hansen, con or no con.'

I look round the room. 'Seems we may not be looking for a hairy-arsed bloke after all. We're looking for a woman.'

* * *

Voicemail

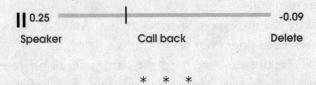

DI Brendan O'Neill

Mobile

Transcription

Just to say still nothing useful from Sullivan. We've asked her about any contacts in haulage but she just smirked and said No Comment. Again. Though one thing I did notice was that she kept checking the time. I think you may be right about a ferry.

| | 0.25 ————————————|————————————— -0.09

Speaker   Call back   Delete

* * *

Adam Fawley
30 October
14.15

'Sir – do you want to join us? I think you'll want to see this.'

It's Hansen, at my door.

I get to my feet. 'I'm coming through.'

The office is crowded now, and buzzing. People on phones, someone from the press office. Harrison, of course; talking to Quinn, of course.

I nod to him. 'Sir.'

'Good work, here, Fawley. Very impressive.'

'She's not in custody yet, sir. But thank you. The team have done very well.'

I turn to Hansen, just to emphasize the point. 'So where are we?'

'We've identified a driver she could be travelling with.' He turns to his screen and brings up the DVLA record. 'Woman by the name of Teresa Grant. She was at Heathside for eighteen months for social security fraud, released late last year.'

'Did she ever share a cell with Rowan?'

He shakes his head. 'No, not as far as we can tell. But she would have known Sullivan, that's for sure.'

'Who does Grant work for now?'

'Company called Ronnie Harmsworth Freight Ltd – it's an all-female outfit and makes a big thing about giving opportunities to ex-offenders.'

'You've spoken to them?'

He nods. 'Grant was booked on this morning's ferry from Newhaven to Dieppe –'

'*Was?*'

'It left at ten and it's a four-hour crossing.'

I check my watch. 'Shit, it's gone two already –'

Gis looks up from his desk and indicates his phone. 'I'm on to them now, boss. We were lucky – the weather on the Channel was shite this morning so it's only just docked.'

'We're in time?'

He makes a face. 'Still waiting to confirm – I'm not making much headway – this bloke's pretending he doesn't understand me –'

'Want me to try, Sarge?' says Sargent. 'My French isn't too bad.'

'Be my guest,' says Gis heavily, handing her the phone.

* * *

They've been docked at least fifteen minutes now, and the nausea is finally starting to ease down. The last couple of hours were grim. She'd promised herself she wouldn't throw up – that those paper bags Rock left in the pocket by the bed were just for wusses – but in the end she had no choice. Jesus, it was bad. She doesn't know how Rock does this, week in, week out. She's clearly even tougher than she looks.

There's a clanging now, a groaning of metal against metal, and then a draught of cold diesel air as the cab door swings open. Rock says nothing, but there are probably other drivers about. Rowan pulls the duvet over her head, more from instinct than anything else – it's hardly going to stop anyone spotting her, if they decide to search the cab. But Rock says they won't, Rock says they won't . . .

* * *

Adam Fawley
30 October
14.22

Sargent's been talking to the port official for a full five minutes and I can tell you one thing: her French is a hell of a lot better than 'not bad'. Trouble is, you don't need much grasp of the language to realize it's bad news.

'*Vous en êtes sûr? Il n'y a aucune possibilité d'erreur? Je vois. Merci beaucoup. Je vous rappellerai dès que possible.*'

She puts the phone down and turns to me. 'I'm sorry, sir, nothing doing. They pulled over Grant's truck as it disembarked and carried out a full search. There was no one there. And Grant's claiming complete ignorance.

392

French police are holding her just in case but it's looking like a dead end to me.'

Gis shakes his head and walks off up to the whiteboard.

'I'm sorry,' begins Sargent, but I hold up my hand to stop her. One thing this isn't is her fault.

'What a fucking disaster,' mutters Quinn, turning away. 'She's run bloody rings round us.'

Maybe. Maybe not. Because something's nagging at me.

I join Gis at the board. Because if there really is a 'something', it's here. Somewhere.

I scan the accumulated ten days of work. Maps, photos, lists, theories, question marks. Trying to see it all for the first time, waiting for something to snag. A good half of me is wondering if I should get someone like Ruth Gallagher in here, purely for the sake of a fresh pair of eyes –

But I don't need to. Because there it is. On a bloody Post-it.

I yank it off and hold it out to Gis.

'This trucking company – what's that about?'

He frowns. 'I don't get you.'

'You said it was an all-female outfit, right?'

'Right.'

'So why's it called Ronnie Harmsworth Freight?'

Gis nods. 'Good point – certainly worth a look.'

We turn to Baxter but he's heard us; he's already on it. 'I'm checking Companies House,' he says. 'Give me a sec.'

He taps his keyboard for a moment then scrolls down. 'According to this, the MD and majority shareholder of Ronnie Harmsworth Freight is a *Veronica* Harmsworth, DOB 14 March 1974.'

'Am I right in thinking you can still be a company director if you've been inside?'

The energy in the room jolts up a notch; they know where I'm going with this.

Baxter taps again, then nods. 'Yup, you can. As long as it wasn't for something like fraud.'

Hansen's at his screen now too. 'Veronica Christine Harmsworth,' he says, glancing up. 'Did three years in Holloway for ABH from 2009 to 2011. Went for her husband with a hammer – claimed he'd been beating her up.'

'Did Sullivan ever work at Holloway?'

He does another check, then looks up and nods. 'Eight years – 2008 until it closed in 2016.'

It's as if the whole room is holding its breath.

'Who spoke to Harmsworth Freight before?'

'Ev,' says Gis. 'We thought it would be better coming from a woman –'

I turn to her but she's already picked up her phone. 'Get a list of all the drivers they have scheduled on ferry crossings, both last night and today. But keep it low-key – I don't want a message getting through to Rowan.'

Quinn comes up to me. 'You think Sullivan fixed it with this bird Ronnie?'

'It has to be a possibility. And right now, it's all we have.'

* * *

Rock warned her it might take a while. That it isn't as simple as rolling off a car ferry, so not to rush to panic. So that's what she's telling herself. *Don't panic. These places are huge, there's a ton of lorries to process, you know what the bloody French are like.* Being stuck in this stuffy cab under the duvet isn't help-ing. Nor is the smell. She's going to have to get Rock to stop as soon as they're through so she can dump the sick bag. *As soon as they're through, as soon as they're through . . .*

Voices now, close by; that hasn't happened before. Someone outside talking to Rock. She tries to gauge Rock's tone from the dribs and drabs she can hear. It doesn't sound like she's concerned. Some admin crap? There must be a ton of that to do. She's just being paranoid.

Of course she is – because suddenly there's the sound of the ignition. A rumble of engine noise, then the hiss of air brakes and – hallelujah – the truck shudders into life.

* * *

Adam Fawley
30 October
14.25

'I spoke to the fleet manager's secretary and she's emailing me the list,' says Ev, putting down her phone. 'She said she'd do it straight away, but I can't promise – I couldn't afford to sound too keen.'

There must be a dozen of us round her machine now, watching for a bloody email like it's a new Pope. The machine pings, but the way my luck's going it'll be HR banging on about changes to pension entitlements. But no – that secretary is as good as her word.

It's one of those Gantt charts that give me a headache just looking at them. But Ev's good at this sort of thing – she leans forward, scanning down the tiny type. 'Looks to me like there's three possibilities. There's an A. Cameron on a boat that left Immingham at five this morning going to Brevik – don't know where that is –'

She looks round quickly but no one else does either.

She turns to the screen again. 'Well, wherever it is, it takes *thirty-six* hours –'

'Scandi somewhere,' says Baxter. 'Taking that bloody long.'

'Then there's a J. Ford going out of Tilbury at ten this morning, due in at Zeebrugge at six tonight our time. And finally –'

She takes an in-breath. 'B. Hudson on the Newhaven to Caen this morning, which left at eight fifteen.'

'When does it get in?'

She glances at her watch. 'Ten minutes ago.'

* * *

The truck's picking up speed now, changing gear. Rock is singing along to the radio, tapping the steering wheel, slightly out of time. But who cares.

They're moving.

She hears the *clang clang clang* as they go down the ramp, and then the dull rumble of concrete under the wheels.

Dry land.

Freedom –

* * *

'*Si, c'est très très urgent. Oui, oui, je tiendrai – merci –*'

Sargent puts her hand over the receiver and looks up at me.

'The boat's just unloading now, sir – like the sarge said, the weather was bad on the Channel last night so it was twenty minutes late getting in. They're checking to see if Hudson's load has already left.'

My blood pressure can't stand much more of this. I turn to Gis. 'What do we know about this woman Hudson?'

'She did time at HMP Foston Hall for knifing someone she said tried to rape her. Judge must have believed her, though, because she only got five years even though the bloke nearly died.' He gives a dry smile. 'Apparently she was known as Rock. Mainly because of the surname, but I gather she's not exactly a gazelle, either.'

'If it was Foston Hall I assume there's no direct connection to either Rowan or Sullivan?'

He shakes his head. 'No, the only link's through Ronnie Harmsworth.'

'What about the other two drivers?'

Baxter looks up. 'Still checking, sir.'

* * *

Something's wrong – they're slowing down –

Stop bloody catastrophizing – it'll be traffic lights or a round-about or some completely bloody ordinary thing –

But then the radio goes off and they're shuddering to a complete halt.

The hiss of brakes, then a voice outside – barking something –

She can't hear – she can't *hear* – there's too much noise –

But now the engine's thudded to silence and Rock's yelling, 'OK, OK, it's off, all right?'

And the doors are opening and they're telling Rock to get out and she can hear noises at the back of the truck and the rear doors banging open and her heart is beating so hard her chest hurts –

And the voices are closer now and louder and the duvet is pulling away and there are rough hands gripping her by the arms and dragging her up and she knows – she knows –

It's over.

* * *

BBC News

30 October 2018 Last updated at 16:34

BREAKING: Camilla Rowan 'could stand trial again'

The BBC has learned that an arrest warrant for Camilla Rowan has been issued by Thames Valley Police. Rowan, who served fifteen years for the supposed murder of her newborn son, was released from HMP Heathside early yesterday morning, but apparently did not report to her probation officer as required by the terms of her licence. Her current whereabouts are not known. Thames Valley

Police have not confirmed the exact nature of the new allegations, but it is understood that new evidence has come to light which would potentially justify a new trial.

More news on this as we hear it.

*   *   *

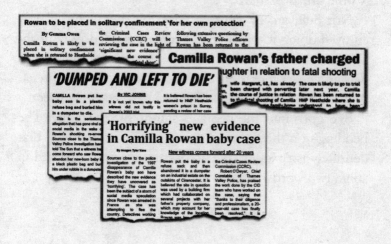

*   *   *

'Home sweet home,' says the prison officer, thudding the cell door open with a smile. A smile that could curdle milk.

They took her to Oxford to start with, after another stomach-emptying ferry and three hours in the back of a security van. The cell there wasn't too bad. Only it came at a price. As in endless interviews with that smug bastard Fawley and the other one who clearly thinks he's God's

399

gift. And the two of them laid it all out about Renee Seidler and that bloody social worker poking her nose in and
she just kept on saying 'No Comment' and all the while
she could sense that stuck-up lawyer of hers sitting on the
next chair, rigid with disapproval, just going through the
motions, desperate to drop her like a hot turd.

The prison officer jerks her head towards the cell door.
'Come on, look sharp.'

Not Sullivan, of course. They told her – and clearly
enjoyed doing it – that she's been suspended. Will probably lose her job. Either way, she won't be coming back.
Rowan's never met these arse-faced cows on the Segrega-
tion wing but they don't look like a very good prospect.

She goes into the cell and stands there, staring. The
bedding's on the floor, lying in a pool of something that
definitely isn't water, and across the far wall, smeared in
stink, two words.

BABY KILLER

*   *   *

Adam Fawley
12 November
14.00

There are only two of us at the service. Aside from the
minister. A hired-by-the-hour suit who clearly knows
nothing about Noah and will do three more of these
things before the day is out.

Renee is sitting in the second row. She's wearing the
same wrap she wore on the plane. Probably because it's
the warmest thing she has. It's icy in here.

When I told Alex where I was going she was surprised Renee wanted to have the cremation here, until I pointed out how expensive it is to ship a body internationally. An urn is a lot more portable, but it makes for a grim and lonely funeral that's barely a notch up from industrial. No music and no reading, just a single white rose on a plain wooden box. When the curtains close finally across the coffin I get to my feet, but Renee remains absolutely still, staring somewhere I can't see.

Outside, the wind is getting up, but the sky is clear. High white clouds gusting across the bleached blue. I fish out my keys and walk down towards the car. It's only then that I realize there's someone here. Someone else as well as me.

On the far side, beyond the banks of flowers from an earlier service, a tall figure in a long dark coat, keeping his distance.

But he's not a stranger.

He's family.

Richard Swann.

* * *

Broadcast Industry News ONLINE
15 November 2018

Netflix commissions second series of *Infamous: The Chameleon Girl*

New episodes will explore the shocking revelations that led to Camilla Rowan's re-arrest

Netflix have announced that there will be a second series of the global hit *Infamous: The Chameleon Girl*. Journalist John

Penrose, who wrote and presented the original show, has been recommissioned to front and produce the six-part follow-up. The new episodes will re-examine the original 'Milly Liar' investigation in the light of recent revelations, and provide 'fascinating insights into how Thames Valley Police finally solved the 20-year-old case'. It is understood the series will also explore the circumstances that led to the tragic death of Rowan's son last month, including the discovery of his true identity, as well as a dramatic reconstruction of what really happened to him after he was last seen leaving hospital with Rowan, when he was only a few hours old.

Mac McQueen, Netflix's Head of Factual, said, 'There is overwhelming interest in this case from across the world, and we are delighted John has agreed to return to it. His 2016 investigation played a crucial role in finally getting to the bottom of what really happened to Camilla Rowan's baby, and I can promise viewers an extraordinary and compelling show.'

Thames Valley Police told Broadcast Industry News they do not comment on media activity of this kind, and would not confirm whether serving officers would be taking part in filming.

* * *

'My round?' says Gis.

'No, it's my turn. I'll just wait till the queue dies down a bit.'

Sunday lunch at the Vicky Arms. We're at a table by the window; there's a fire in the hearth and a smell of woodsmoke, and two pints, nearly finished, in front of us. Outside, it's bright but cold, and down by the river, Janet and Alex are braving the wind with the children to feed the ducks. Janet took a lot of persuading, and I don't blame her – she wasn't really dressed for it – but Alex has been on my case to talk to Gis about the christening and gave me a look that said *OK now's your chance* as they got up to leave.

I'm fiddling with my glass, the way blokes do when they're about to Have A Conversation. Though Gis, being another bloke, doesn't seem to have noticed.

'Won't be as cold as this where you're going, eh, boss? Where was it again?'

'Caribbean. Leaving December 20th.'

Two weeks in the Grenadines. After the year we've had, I want Alex to have a proper holiday. Something special for our first Christmas as a family.

'Look, Gis, there's something I've been meaning to mention.'

He smiles. 'Don't worry, boss, I already know.'

'You already *know*?'

The smile looks a little sad now. 'A little bird told me. You're going for Chief Inspector, right?'

Well, I definitely didn't see that coming.

'Look,' he says quickly, 'it's OK, really. I'd do the same if I was you. We'll just be sorry to lose you. All of us.'

I swallow. 'Well, it might not mean a transfer – not necessarily –'

He picks up his glass. 'It usually does, though, doesn't it. Deputy Area Commander, something like that.'

Now there's a thought. 'Look, it's months off. If it happens at all. And I might not get it.'

He grins and finishes his beer. 'With a spanking new personal commendation from the Chief Constable on your file? I'd put money on it.'

There's an awkward pause. 'Does everyone know – I mean the whole team?'

He shakes his head. 'Just me, I reckon. If Quinn had got wind of it he'd be beating a path to the Super's door.'

I laugh and turn to look down towards the water. Alex is rocking Lily against her, the wind catching her hair, and Billy's down by the water with Janet, flinging bread at the flotilla of ducks, scattering and plashing as the pieces hit the surface.

I nod towards them. 'Reckon you're raising a cricketer there, Gis, not a footie player.'

He grins. 'Nah, Chelsea all the way, my Billy.'

I reach for the glasses. 'Do you want to join them for a bit while I get the drinks in? Give Billy a hand with his bowling technique?'

He starts a little. 'Well –'

I get to my feet. 'It'll be a chance to get to know your new god-daughter.'

He gapes at me, and then, as realization dawns, his face spreads into a huge grin.

When I look back from the bar a few minutes later he's still sitting there, shaking his head a little, smiling to himself.

Epilogue

21 October 2018, 9.35 p.m.
Gantry Manor, Wytham

The TV is on loud. Louder than his wife would prefer, but she knows he doesn't hear as well as he used to, and it's not as if they'd be disturbing the neighbours. One reason – among many – they like living this far out of town.

'That was the doorbell,' she says.

Swann grunts something non-committal; he didn't hear anything.

A moment later she tries again. 'Dick, that was the doorbell.'

He looks across at her. 'I didn't hear anything.' He turns back to the television. 'And in any case, it won't be anyone. Just some religious nut. Or the Liberal Democrats.'

She gets up and goes to the window and squints down. 'I can't see anyone.'

The bell rings again. Insistently. Even he hears it this time.

She turns towards him, her hand still gripping the curtain. Her face has gone pale. 'It's a man. He's going round the back.'

Now that he is absolutely not going to tolerate. It's bloody trespassing, for a start. He reaches for his dressing gown and starts to shuffle on his slippers. 'I'll go. You stay here. No need to be alarmed. He's probably just seen the light on and assumed there's someone in.'

He knots his gown and goes out on to the landing, flipping the light on as he goes. The bulb hums and plinks into life, throwing a pallid glow down the stairs. When he gets to the bottom and pushes open the kitchen door he can see through the window that there's someone outside. A young man, all in black, some sort of backpack over one shoulder. He looks for all the world like a burglar; only burglars don't ring the doorbell. Probably one of those ex-cons trying to sell dishcloths. It would account for the persistence. He goes over to the glass. The man is mouthing something. He makes a 'Go away' gesture, but the man – boy – takes no notice.

He hesitates. A tiny moment, upon which – as he will later bitterly reflect – a whole life will hinge. And not just his own. There's no chain on the back door, but the lad doesn't look threatening. A little impatient, maybe, but not actually dangerous. He just needs to be told, firmly, to sling his hook.

He unlocks the door. 'I don't care what it is you're selling, we don't want it.'

'I'm not selling anything.'

An American accent. Now that does throw him for a loop. His grip on the door loosens a little.

'Look, it's late and I don't know who you are –'

'I'm sorry about the time – the train was late. And you do know who I am – well, in a way –'

This isn't making any sense. Swann starts to close the door, but the man sticks his foot in it. 'Please, just hear me out. You owe me that at least. Both of you do. But especially you.'

'What on earth –'

But it's too late, the man's pushed past, he's in the kitchen, rounded on him, his eyes flashing now. This is all going horribly, frighteningly wrong.

'Look, lad, I don't know what it is you want –'

'I want an *explanation* – I want the *truth* –'

Swann's starting to wonder if this chap's all there – if he might be Care in the Community or whatever the bleeding hearts call it now –

'Don't you think you owe me that?'

'I don't think I owe you anything at all, sonny. You're trespassing and I'd like you to leave. And if you don't, I'll call the police.'

The young man laughs. '*Sonny?* Is that what you Brits call irony? And, frankly, I reckon the cops are the *last* people you're gonna want pitching up right now. You will *not* wanna let them hear what I've got to say. Because *I know* – you hear me, *Grandad*? I know what you did to her – your own *daughter* – you sick fuck –'

The old man is gaping at him. 'I haven't the faintest idea what you're talking about –'

There's a movement, suddenly, in the shadows behind the young man, and Swann feels his heart jolt. His wife. At the kitchen door. *Holding his gun.* Her hands are trembling and she can barely keep it straight, but he taught her, years ago. She knows how to shoot.

'Peggy, put that down, love – I'm sure we can sort this out –'

The lad's swung round, he's staring at the old woman as if he can't quite believe it. 'Whoa – no need for that –'

Peggy comes slowly towards him. Her face is gaunt in the yellowish light, two spots of high colour in her cheeks and that frantic look in her eyes that Swann had hoped he'd never see again.

'Peggy,' he says, stepping forward, so close to the young man now that their shoulders are almost touching. 'There's no need to be alarmed, love – the young man is just leaving –'

'No, I'm not,' he says, 'I've come a long way and I'm not leaving until –'

'Until we pay you?' she retorts, too shrill. 'You think you can get money out of us – like all those other crooks? Showing up here, making threats –'

'Peggy,' says her husband quickly, inching round to her side, his hand outstretched, 'just let me have that thing before someone gets hurt –'

But she's pushing forward, forcing the young man back towards the wall.

'I'm not making *threats*,' he says, glancing at the old man and then back at her. 'I don't want your damn *money* –'

'*Yes you do*,' she spits, edging closer, the heavy gun slipping in her hands. 'You all do – you vicious little *shits* –'

'Now hang on,' he says, facing up to her now, standing his ground, his anger kindling. 'Don't you call me that – I just came here to talk –'

But there are no more words, not ever. Everything speeds up and slows down and collides as Swann reaches for the barrel and the old woman tries to jerk it away and in a detonation of noise and heat and shock and impossibility and blood –

the gun

goes

off

Acknowledgements

Several of the Fawley books have taken a real-life crime as their springboard (for example, the Josef Fritzl case for *In the Dark*), and the same is true of *Hope to Die*. The case in question this time is that of Keli Lane, an Australian woman who was jailed for the murder of her newborn daughter Tegan, whose body has never been found. She had concealed the pregnancy from everyone around her, and the existence – and disappearance – of Tegan only emerged by accident some years later. More bafflingly still, it was neither the first nor last time she had a baby in secret: two further children were given up for adoption, one before and one after Tegan. Lane continues to assert her innocence, insisting that she handed Tegan over to her biological father, a man who has never come forward. There's a fascinating series about the case called *Exposed: The Case of Keli Lane*, available on Amazon Prime, and it was also covered by the programme *60 Minutes Australia*. If you watch either of them you will see why I was so drawn to the case. That said, Camilla Rowan is, of course, a fictional character, and not a portrait of the real Keli Lane, and clearly there are many elements of Camilla's life that are entirely different from Keli's.

So the first person I want to thank this time is Andy Chilcott, who shares my love for true-crime TV and suggested I try the *60 Minutes* series. The same goes for my marvellous team of professional advisers, DI Andy

Thompson, Joey Giddings, Nicholas Syfret QC and Dr Paul Zollinger-Read. I had one new specialist helping me this time round whose help has been invaluable – Sue Weedon (with thanks also to Jane Corry for the introduction). I'd also like to thank George Allan for helping me understand a bit more about the haulage industry! As ever, any mistakes or inaccuracies that remain are mine alone.

Hope to Die is the sixth in the Fawley series, and for various reasons it's a good time to take a moment to give special and deep-felt thanks to the whole Penguin team, past and present, who have built the series from an unknown debut through two Richard and Judy picks, a Nielsen Gold bestseller award, and more than a million book sales. You have been amazing, every one of you, and I will be forever grateful: Katy Loftus, Olivia Mead, Chloe Davies, Ellie Hudson, Georgia Taylor, Sam Fanaken, Rosanna Forte, Victoria Moynes, Poppy North, Jane Gentle, Rose Poole, Lindsay Terrell and, most recently, Harriet Bourton. Also the wonderful production team headed by Emma Brown, my copy-editor, Karen Whitlock, Jessica Barnfield and the whole team at Penguin audiobooks, and everyone at Dead Good. Likewise to my fabulous audio narrators, Lee Ingleby and Emma Cunniffe.

Anna Power, Hélène Butler and Claire Morris at Johnson & Alcock have once again been exceptional – I seriously don't know what I'd do without Anna. Thank you also to my early reader panel – Sarah Wall, Sally Rogers, Stephen Gill, Andy Weltch, Deborah Woudhuysen, Richard Croker, Elizabeth Price, Neera Gajjar, Stuart Fletcher and Trish Fletcher.

Last, but most definitely not least, I'd like to mention

Chloe Sargent, who has given her name to a new member of the Fawley family. She's named after a real person, after I donated a character name to the NSPCC for one of their charity auctions. Chloe's mum Lynda won, and asked me to name the character after her daughter, who's been fighting a long battle with cancer. She's been immensely brave, coping not only with the treatment process but with lockdown, and all the extra stress and isolation the pandemic has created for all of us. She's a very special and very brave person, and I hope she likes the character who bears her name.

All the Rage

**THE FIRST GIRL CAME BACK...
THE NEXT MIGHT NOT BE SO LUCKY.**

A girl is taken from the streets of Oxford.
But it's unlike any abduction DI Fawley's seen before . . .

Faith Appleford was attacked, a plastic bag tied over
her head, taken to an isolated location . . . and then, by
some miracle, she escaped. What's more, when DC Erica
Somer interviews Faith, she quickly becomes convinced
that Faith knows who her abductor is.

Yet Faith refuses to press charges.

Without more evidence, it's looking like the police
may have to drop the case.

Faith's attacker is still out there. Will they strike again?

'Fantastic . . . my favourite series ever!
Shari Lapena

'A mass of cork-screwing twists'
Sarah Vaughan

'One of our most exciting crime writers'
John Marrs

OUT NOW IN PAPERBACK, EBOOK AND AUDIO

Close to Home

HOW CAN A CHILD GO MISSING WITHOUT A TRACE?

Last night, eight-year-old Daisy Mason disappeared from a family party. No one in the quiet suburban street saw anything – or at least that's what they're saying.

DI Adam Fawley is trying to keep an open mind. But he knows the nine times out of ten, it's someone the victim knew.

**That means someone is lying . . .
And that Daisy's time is running out.**

'The last twist was a genuine stroke of genius'
John Marrs

'A mazey, gripping read'
Ian Rankin

**'Compulsive, with an ending you
will not see coming'**
Emma Kavanagh

OUT NOW IN PAPERBACK, EBOOK AND AUDIO

In the Dark

**DO YOU KNOW WHAT'S HIDING
IN THE HOUSE NEXT DOOR?**

A woman and child are found locked in
a basement room, barely alive.

No one knows who they are – the woman can't speak,
and there are no missing persons reports that match
their profile. The elderly man who owns the house
claims he has never seen them before.

The inhabitants of the quiet Oxford street are in
shock. How could this happen right under their noses?
But DI Adam Fawley knows that nothing is impossible.

No one is as inncocent as they seem . . .

'Agile, fresh, unpredictable'
Nicci French

**'You're not going anywhere
until you finish reading'**
Emily Koch

'Your next riveting, twisty read!'
Shari Lapena

OUT NOW IN PAPERBACK, EBOOK AND AUDIO

No Way Out

WHAT IF SOMEONE WANTED YOUR FAMILY DEAD?

It's one of the most disturbing cases
DI Fawley has ever worked.

The Christmas holidays, and two children have just been
pulled from the wreckage of their burning home in
North Oxford. The toddler is dead, and his brother
is soon fighting for his life.

Why were they left in the house alone? Where is their
mother, and why is their father not answering his phone?

Then new evidence is discovered, and DI Fawley's
worst nightmare comes true.

Because this fire wasn't an accident. It was murder.

And the killer is still out there . . .

'I was hooked from beginning to end'
Clare Douglas

'A cracking detective novel'
Michelle Francis

'Kept me guessing to the bitter end'
Fiona Barton

OUT NOW IN PAPERBACK, EBOOK AND AUDIO

THE
WHOLE
TRUTH

AN ATTRACTIVE STUDENT. AN OLDER PROFFESSOR. THINK YOU KNOW THIS STORY? THINK AGAIN.

She has everything at stake; he has everything to lose. But one of them is lying, all the same.

When an Oxford student accuses one of the university's professors of sexual assault, DI Adam Fawley's team think they've heard it all before. But they couldn't be more wrong.

Because this time, the predator is a woman and the shining star of the department, and the student a six-foot male rugby player.

Soon DI Fawley and his team are up against the clock to figure out the truth. What they don't realise is that someone is watching.

Someone with a plan to put Fawley out of action for good.

'So twisty, so timely, so terrific'
Nicci French

'A masterclass in twists'
Jo Spain

'My new favourite crime series'
Louise Candlish

OUT NOW IN PAPERBACK, EBOOK AND AUDIO